SKYDIVER

♦

To Schatz

My beautiful, Asian

rose.

Love Robert

SKYDIVER

◆

R. D. Fresh

iUniverse, Inc.
New York Lincoln Shanghai

Skydiver

Copyright © 2006 by Robert D. Rice

All rights reserved. No part of this book may be used or reproduced by any means, graphic, electronic, or mechanical, including photocopying, recording, taping or by any information storage retrieval system without the written permission of the publisher except in the case of brief quotations embodied in critical articles and reviews.

iUniverse books may be ordered through booksellers or by contacting:

iUniverse
2021 Pine Lake Road, Suite 100
Lincoln, NE 68512
www.iuniverse.com
1-800-Authors (1-800-288-4677)

This is a work of fiction. All of the characters, names, incidents, organizations and dialogue in this novel are either the products of the author's imagination or are used fictitiously.

ISBN-13: 978-0-595-40838-2 (pbk)
ISBN-13: 978-0-595-85201-7 (ebk)
ISBN-10: 0-595-40838-9 (pbk)
ISBN-10: 0-595-85201-7 (ebk)

Printed in the United States of America

To my nearly saintly mother, who has been a great source of inspiration.

A special thank you to the beautiful and dynamic Yaakova.

Her tireless editing made the transition from thought to the finished product unique.

PROLOGUE

What is it about the thrill of the chase that makes it so inviting? Is getting caught solely for those who don't have the brains to figure out how to remain invisible?

THE PROBLEM

◆

"Somebody's chasin' us! And they're gainin' fast!" the panicked pilot yelled, through an awkwardly aligned clown's mask, finally ripping it away, tossing it over his shoulder, leaving strands of shiny tinsel clinging to his neck.

It was MAYDAY in September. Crisis time had arrived, with the moment for living declining faster than the fuel that was pouring from a widening hole in one of the chopper's modified, extended range, tanks. The LED gas gauge flickered, screaming to be refueled, louder than an infant having waited too long to be breast fed.

He desperately tried to reposition the underpowered Sikorsky that was treacherously twisting to the point of nearly flipping over. It was a losing battle against lethal crosswinds that threatened its ability to remain aloft. With tranquility long ago forgotten, there was nothing that he could do to make it reappear.

Frantically, he wiped cascading sweat that poured from his wrinkled forehead into rapidly blinking, baby-blues; constricted pupils that hadn't seen true rest in more nights than he was able to bring to a mind that was in and out of vertigo.

He tried to make sense of the multi-directional gale that had come out of nowhere. Its intensity was strengthening with each unsteady split second. He was in the center of contradictory weather systems that had come together to form the worst case weather scenario. Meteorologists called it the cruelest storm to hit the southwest United States since they started keeping track of such un-heavenly events.

He freed his line of unclear vision from salty sweat with a stroke from the back of a hand that had hard to locate veins; that reflected too many years of high value heroin use with infinitely inferior results.

He saw the sky around him as a sea of swirling blackness, overwhelmed by impulses that detonated at each of his frayed nerve endings.

With that he selfishly thought, God, help me. His mile-a-minute prayers were met with, "All lines are currently busy. I'll have to put you on hold."

"He ain't listenin'," the lone passenger said, spitting gooey saliva through a spacious gap between his rarely brushed front teeth.

That man was Bubba Thorne. And he knew damn well that if there was an Almighty, he'd hardly be in the mood to help an escaped murderer who was fleeing a prison sentence; that was imposed by a judge who intended what was left of his gutted soul to rot away four floors underground in one of the nation's supermax prisons. Rehabilitation was a word that never applied to Bubba. He was a convict who had long ago had lost all sight of right and wrong.

Bubba put the 'S' in strange. To know him was to dislike him. Few could accurately explain his erratic negativity. It affected everyone with whom he came near. It was very much akin to electricity spraying from a dancing high-voltage wire that he recently snapped in half; the way it twisted and wiggled, searching for someone to permanently stun. A decent person's skin would crawl whenever he came near.

His threatening presence was something that everyone felt, even if they only read the many explanative weeks of horrid newspaper accounts from his trial, and the litany of things that witness after weeping witness said he had done to them.

He took great pride in being sadistic—down to the most infinitesimal detail—with killing being his only real hobby. If there was supposed good in all men, this monster surely violated that rule.

The pilot's concerns were glued to flip-flopping electronic gauges that could no longer be relied on, leaving him at a loss about what to do next.

Bubba tried to ascertain if what he heard was true. He had great difficulty turning his stiff neck around to see. Besides, he didn't want to understand anything past his crooked ambitions.

"I don't see nothin'," Bubba countered with the vernacular of a man baptized in any sewer.

The pilot couldn't determine which was more stupid: Bubba's remark, or springing him from maximum security in the first place. It really didn't matter.

There it was. A faint flickering from a light source that was at their aeronautical six o'clock. Rapid-fire shots from behind them sent flashes zipping past the chopper. He ducked, hoping that whoever was in the rear would hit Bubba.

"The fucker back there's got his gun up our ass."

"Can't you fly this thing any faster!?" Bubba injected, wrenching his thick neck, straining to pierce the solidly drenched sky, to ascertain what the dazzling darts were about; if his sights were confusing him with slight of 20/20 eye tricks.

His view was marred by the incessant spears of ultra-bright lightening that came within a few scary feet of the battered craft. The harder he tried to make sense of anything that might be out there, the more he could not.

The on-n-off partial glimmer flying in their wake convinced Bubba that whoever it was certainly was unwelcome. It had become apparent that their low altitude flight path had drawn the unwanted ire from the cops.

"Do something, damnit!" Bubba shouted above the sputtering, overhead, engine of the S-92 deluxe.

The helicopter sputtered, plunging, taking both of their stomachs with it. The front of the aircraft skittered up and down. The drone of the engine made the pilot think that it couldn't hold out much longer. The interior air temperature was dropping just as fast.

"What do-ya want me to do?" was the shivering, panic filled, response; as the man behind the failing controls scanned lowering pressure readings on all of the remaining working gauges on the instrument cluster in front of him. "The engine's at half power!"

In an attack of everybody does it, slow motion, nostalgia on the way it all could have been, he reflected upon the temptations that came to own him. How could he have allowed Bubba to talk him into such misdeeds? During his pre-bad guy years he had made-out profitably as an instructor pilot, making legally scheduled deposits at every bank across the state. So how did it come to this?

The pilot's greed wanted a faster socio-economic climb; that had corralled what would have been normal goals, hogtying his common sense, subjugating his used-to-be morality; to the enticing proposition that only a hard cash existence can offer. He was knee-deep in the abyss of indefensible vice, a quagmire from which he was never able to extricate himself. As much as he wanted to be good, it wasn't sustainable. A man can fool others about who he is, but never himself.

Pounding thunder rocked the already splintered craft, making the tail rotor into an unmanageable spiral before miraculously straightening.

"I'm having trouble steering it. She won't hold steady." He continued fighting with both arms flexing.

For once, the pilot was telling the truth.

"Do it!"

"You gotta be kiddin'," the pilot said.

That was when the he caught the unmistakable look of Bubba's fully loaded nine millimeter semi-automatic pointed inches from his temple.

"Does this look like I'm jokin'?"

Mentally gone, and unable to meet Bubba's undoable stipulation, he was far behind the timeline to think of something that would keep his brain from being splintered at Bubba's hand.

"Do me, and we crash for sure," he verbally battled back to Bubba.

Unwillingly, Bubba took an argumentative back seat, changing his tact to let someone else do the thinking as to how they were going to get out of this alive; especially since he was hardly good at anything beyond violence. He un-cocked the gun, reluctantly pointing it away.

Full time malfeasants had become this duo's chosen behavior, threatening to end what they loosely called their lives. Just as well. They were hundreds of feet above rocky ground that was more than willing to accept both of them face down dead. Nobody of consequence would have cared if today was their last day.

They had often resigned themselves to the impossible possibility that their appointment with destiny would finish badly. The criminally minded, un-dynamic, duo had reached the dreaded meeting point where fatality was waiting with an anticipated embrace. Silently, both of them wondered why this had to be that day. Bubba had countless times broached the intersection where life met death, each time feeling that his second chance lives hadn't exceeded the envied number of nine.

"I sure as hell didn't breakout to die up here, like every other hangin' dick. Land this fucker!"

The pilot looked out into the all consuming darkness. Windshield wipers slopped and sloshed back and forth slightly out of sync against the curved cockpit glass, struggling to sweep away the water, making it very difficult to see anything beyond the rain.

In a flash, the state of the art instrument panel went completely out.

The pilot gasped, "How'm I gonna do that? Got no instruments to go by." His mind whirled in a vicious degree of constantly fluctuating figure-eight curves.

Fear controlled him—like a puppeteer holding his favorite manikin—with ever-changing thoughts that were split between the charcoal sky ahead, and the unreasonable lunatic in the passenger seat to his right.

Tapped out, the savagery and horror that was their daily manner had left them no emotions from which to draw. Heartless, their gutted feelings about the future had dwindled to measly afterthoughts of what could have been.

Bubba was completely unwrapped. "You're the pilot, think of something!"

They had no safety net. There were no more slick transgressional resources of evasion to get them out of this tightening noose. The pursuit of a safe place to land was nothing more than a dwindling possibility.

The glorious, spendthrift, years of excess money, fast women and hard drugs had reached the prime vantage point from which the devil stood to gaze at his protégées, to see their final curtain ingloriously dropping.

Chasing that which was forbidden had never allowed them to understand the steepness of the downside, the flipside of the freedom card. The countdown had begun on their future breathing privileges. Five. Four. Three. Two. One.

Bullets from the chase aircraft pierced the rear of the helicopter, passing straight through it, shattering the windshield.

"Ahhh!" the pilot screamed when jagged glass fragments flew into his face, sending blood everywhere. The pain forced him to release the controls. The helicopter fiercely dove, loosening his Little Ferry Cubs baseball cap on his head.

Hacking crosswinds toyed with the structurally weakened chopper like dandelion seed head having been shaken by a child, sending it in roller-coaster fashion at hundreds of feet per second.

Suddenly, the aircraft lurched upward, creating intolerable stress, causing its bolts to pop loose. The cabin was filling with damaging rain. Evening out the aircraft was a failing endeavor.

Bubba reached over, grabbing him with an iron right fist, trying to shake him to awareness.

"Wake up, you bastard!" he bellowed, with hopes to learn something from the pilot about how to fly a helicopter. It was of no use. The bloodied man was either unconscious or dead. And there wasn't any time to figure out which.

The aircraft nearly flopped, thrusting Bubba hard against the side, jamming his elbow. His questions went out into the night with no answer coming back. Fighting with his pain, he rose to make his way within the topsy-turvy fuselage to get out through the rear side door. The unpredictable combination of dizziness and turbulence compromised his balance, bouncing him from one wall to the other. Bullets from the pursuit aircraft continued ricocheting, clipping his elbow. Pure hate for the trigger happy chasers held in that scream.

When he kicked open the door instant suction snatched up the pilot's cap. It floated through the interior toward the open door. Bubba made an all-pro, shortstop-like, attempt to snare the cap but failed as it zipped past ten spread fingers. Out into the puzzling, rain-soaked night sky it was lost.

The revulsion of what awaited him below—when he un-assed the impossible to stabilize helicopter—was something that Bubba was unwilling to entertain. He rushed to strap on one of two parachutes that were clumped together on the flooded floor.

It was then that he pulled from the recesses of his sinister mind how he had tampered with one of them so it wouldn't open properly. He figured, if anything happened to go against his escape plan, he wasn't about to allow the pilot to live to tell about it. In the confusion Bubba couldn't be sure which one worked.

His decision to jump out was made coldly and with no imagination. When he did, the baseball cap inexplicably flew back inside the aircraft. The pilot was startled to semi consciousness when the cap's bill hit his face.

It was a night that everyone would remember.

THE MARRIAGE

◆

Interior stormy weather.

The neighborhood was usually quiet; with morale in the Luckett home having taken a backwards U-turn in both spirit and hate driven intent.

The final delivery on Stagger-Lee's list of evening stops was at one of a growing number of gated living communities in the city of Albuquerque.

When he climbed off the front bucket seat, he left behind the latest issue of Sights & Sounds Illustrated. Beside it was the Albuquerque Tribune. The newspaper's cover page shouted an attention-getting headline: **Second Jewelry Store Hit. No Suspects.**

The interior of the home was tastefully appointed. Heather had the ability to mix and match what she liked with what furnishings remained. There were agreeable two-tone walls that matched well with furniture items in each room, to coordinate with the overall interior decorative scheme. Here were the basic appurtenants that a family of three needed. Although, it was apparent to anyone visiting that items were missing. Perhaps, it was the many indentations in the carpet where furniture once was.

In contrast to the sparse decorative pleasantries, harsh bickering from inside the home rose in intensity, and could easily be heard by Stagger-Lee as he approached.

Not many feet from the delivery boy came arguments that had malicious conclusions.

"I'm tired of being trapped living here with you!" Heather shouted. "Your gambling debts have me losing my mind. One by one, the Collector's been coming in here to take everything we used to own. The furniture. My jewelry. Our car." She hammered home that point. "Our car, Jack! How am I supposed to get to work without a car?"

Being a church going woman, it bothered her to scold him, but out it came anyway.

She was crumbling in a feminine pile of endless tears. "My depressing life is all I have left. And I don't want that anymore."

"Keep your voice down. Do you want Rikki to hear you?"

"In case you haven't been paying attention, the Captain switched her work hours, and she won't be home till morning."

Heather's explanation was breaking down. Her emotional surface was fading, much like a tsunami having gone back out to sea. On hands and knees, she slapped her palms until they were red.

"I can't live like this anymore. I'd rather die than stay with you."

Jack jumped at that. "That's your choice!" he venomously agreed.

He was further angered when her wedding ring—a microcosm of her suffering—was hurled from the shadowy recess of her side of the room into his pitiful direction. Missing him, it pinged against the nearest baseboard.

"I went to Sparkles last week to have my ring cleaned."

Jack knew what was coming. He was boxed-in, and she was rattling his cage with a verbal crowbar.

"Want to know what he told me?"

Hearing her continue wasn't high on Jack's wish list.

"He said someone had removed the diamond, and a cubic was put in its place."

Having been caught, he pretended to be shocked by the accusation.

She controlled the sobs long enough to continue, "I said that can't be. Obviously he had me mixed up with someone else. That was when he said that you were there last week, selling off my diamond. It didn't take me long to figure out why you did it…You didn't even have the balls, the common decency, to tell me before I went there to be humiliated."

Jack's crippled emotions were too tangled to unravel. She was force-feeding him truisms too quickly for him to digest.

He had convinced himself that he was still committed to her. Suddenly, there was an unveiled falseness to their once steady union, cracks that ran to their marital foundation. It would be very difficult, if not impossible, for their differences to ever even out.

"I want a divorce." And she meant every syllable of it.

That dashed away his idea of bliss ever returning to them.

Hers was an unveiled frustration, brought on by the provocation of being with an out of control addict. Addict, or not, Jack wasn't going away quietly.

"We'll meet in fiery hell before I see you in divorce court!"

He was viciously certain of himself with that potent remark, misguidedly feeling he had indulged her whims for too long. Alas, he was mistaken again.

With energy that was nonexistent, she stood, pivoted, turning back to the bedroom, slamming the door to keep him at bay. An impacting clunk sounded when an indoor potted plant was launched at her, tearing a wide gash in the door.

Through the hole she saw him staring at her. His once sensitive, brown, eyes had lost that invitation of curious masculinity. They had become portholes to a soul that had gone away long before this argument ever hit full stride. She had never seen that look on him before. She feared what would happen next.

Minutes later, the door opened. Heather came out wearing a startling, powder-blue, dress that he used to love seeing her in. With it wrapped around her, it was more a part of her than a hole was to a doughnut. In spite of her ill will toward him, she came across as nothing less than sexy.

He blocked her path.

"Where do you think you're going?" asked the supreme commander, demanding an answer. He didn't have long to wait.

Hers was a deep dislike from a woman fed-up, filled to her brim. "I'm going out. Alone."

"Like hell, you are!"

She stepped left, and he to his right.

"You should see yourself."

Her melancholy manner went right through him to the exit—the path out to the driveway and street beyond—away from all that bothered her.

"All I see is failure."

With that, his legs turned to rubber, unable to move him. She waltzed around him. She was the one with the unfinished passages of pent-up frustration yet to be expounded.

"Don't preach how I'll be nothing without you. I'm nothing with you."

Jack's rage was strangely silent, with thoughts that were made unmanageable, when he imagined where she might be going. No doubt, to give the pussy to someone else. Someone who she thought was more deserving of its feel and taste.

Stagger-Lee had just stepped from the last patch of smooth, bland-white, stones in the driveway. He was at the highest of three steps that led to the door. In his hands was a square, red and white, pizza box. The pungent Italian aroma seeped from its sides, making for biting taste bud stimulation.

He had been privy to all of the interior verbal thrashing, listening to Jack's threats, and was uneasy about knocking. In the background was a cricket chirping; adding a non-infectious, futile attempt to calm an otherwise hostile indoor flavor. The hour grew late. Having waited long enough holding the hot box, he rang the bell.

Then there came sounds from numerous locks being unlatched; which suggested that the door wasn't going to open as fast as he wanted it to.

Thoughts about how much he hated his job crept into his head, accelerating ideas of how to turn this negative situation into a positive one. He felt motivated to read those High-tech magazines more deeply—to learn more about making believable films and CD's. Perhaps then he'd be able to find a better job. Until such time, he found himself in the line of husband and wife fire.

Suddenly Jack was standing there wearing a transfixed, hypnotic, stare. Finally, he snapped out of it to speak through his shell shocked haze.

"Sorry bout so many locks," Jack apologized. "A person can't be too careful. Especially when a burglar's been working the neighborhood…The people down the street were robbed, and we don't want to be next."

Stagger-Lee knew more about that incident than he would ever let on. But since he wasn't asked about that crime, volunteering anything about it was well ahead of any level of helpfulness that he was prepared to offer.

Jack saw what Stagger-Lee held in his possession. "I didn't order pizza," he rejected.

Stagger-Lee's concentration became crisper, observing meanness in Jack that he was trying to disguise. The older man's unsettled demeanor confirmed augmented self doubt about his wife who had since retreated to the bedroom.

The younger man figured to give the details as to why he was there, then walk back to the Jeep.

"My boss at the pizza parlor said somebody called-in the order. I only deliver."

Jack loosened, when it dawned on him that the item in question was hot and spicy.

"Come in," Jack said.

Stagger-Lee did so, allowing Jack to close the door and not latch it. Stagger-Lee didn't care. All he wanted was the tip, carefully observing the interior, settling in with the standard "You got a nice place" comment.

Seated on the edge of the bed, Heather rolled her eyes—at the very idea that her personal hell was referred to as nice.

Stagger-Lee walked into the living room/dining room combination, bothered by an untied shoelace, bending to retie it.

Jack had hoped that Heather would ride out the duration of her volatility in the other room; so as not to continue the prize fight—with Stagger-Lee as the uninvited referee.

Jack called to her, "Honey, did you order pizza?" How he managed to say 'honey' in that atmosphere was anyone's supposition.

Her return shout said it all. "<u>Drop dead, numb nuts</u>!"

Jack reacted as if hers were remarks made as part of some type of lover's jesting, a pet name of sorts. Then he thought, how else can numb nuts be interpreted? Instead, his outwardness plummeted along with his bottomless shame.

A foreign feeling of calm overcame Jack when it hit him that their marriage pretense was just that. Strangely, he was in complete acceptance of the inevitable. Love had its consequences. Rivers of their friendliness that once happily flowed, had been filtered through reality's difficulties, leaving a runoff into pessimism's bleak backwater. When the shouting settled there would be their daughter, Rikki, to clash over. The constant infighting had to cease.

Stagger-Lee was in the middle of it all, wanting out. "I came at a bad time."

From behind the door, Heather watched the way in which the boy moved. He was lean and tight, causing her carnal fantasies to expand. Strangely, he had invoked in her boundless sexual imagination. There it was, all that she wasn't supposed to think about.

In her vision she had him trapped. The pure want for his member to pound in her was by itself uplifting. Her skin would be touching his in a devoted demonstration of what heated, unrestricted, fun would come down to. It was pent-up, unfulfilled, passion that demanded of her what she sexually wanted—all to spite Jack.

In her fantasy he was giving-in to her thoughts, her extremes, with Jack scratched from consideration for as long as she insisted and further; in a valiant effort to make up for time that she had set aside so long ago.

After focusing on the word Johannesburg that was written on the delivery boy's shirt, she wanted them to be swept up by easterly winds and carried there. Far away from all that troubled her, from everything that Jack was and represented. Quietly, she widened the door to be better seen by the youth. She slowly lifted her dress, invitingly bending over to reveal her bare buttocks.

Stagger-Lee saw Heather, imagining what it would be like to have her. The idea was effortless to levitate by. Carnal anguish over his inability to capture her had him wiping his craving face as though he had just seen a mirage. He had all he could do to contain himself from overpowering Jack to physically seize that opportunity.

After setting the box on a nearby end table, he maneuvered Jack a few feet to one side, keeping his back to Heather's performance. He had to keep Jack unaware of her motives and delicious offering.

"If you don't want it, somebody else will," Stagger-Lee optioned.

The boy's mental return to actuality rivaled a sizzling comet roaring to earth, afire with the endless possibilities of what he desperately wanted to happen.

"How much will it cost me?" Jack compromised.

His eyebrow jumpty-jumped, watching Jack rummaging for pocket money. "I want to play you."

"You want to play me?" giving closer attention.

"Get your ears cleaned, kid. I want to pay you for the pizza."

While moving about Jack walked on an empty beer can's pop-top. Its aluminum sharpness pierced the sole of his bare foot, causing him to fall. The thud rattled the room.

"The bill comes to eight o-nine," Stagger-Lee said, wanting to leave this den of insatiable temptation.

Jack was on his stomach, looking directly at an alarm clock. "That's strange. The time is eight o-nine." He was frozen by the oddity of the similarity.

With the bedroom door having drifted nearly closed, Stagger-Lee tried to catch a repeat look through the hole in it. His eager eyes were locked to where Heather was no more, leaving him yearning for more of the tantalizing sight of her that he savored earlier. In his thoughts, Heather should be in there ready for nothing but sex, wearing the newest S & M getup, complete with latex everything—ready to be tamed.

"How's the job?" Jack interrupted.

"The pay's bad, but the hours are worse." In a choppy language style he tried to make the truth sound droll.

After Jack got up, he looked at the pizza, remembering how the end table was a present from Rikki. And he dared not pawn it, given that she still lived there.

Jack moved to his lounge chair. The other one had long since made a midday exit from the property—while Heather was at her job unaware—thanks to the Collector.

Next to Jack was a static filled police scanner. After additional meaningless time periods, he referred to the scanner.

"On its best day, the thing's as clear as mud…I paid good money for it. Now all I get is stinko reception."

"When I was a kid."

"You're still a kid." Jack interrupted, hinting of his superiority above any commonality with a delivery boy.

Stagger-Lee scowled then chose not to release his emotions. Heck, he only had a little while longer to remain in their home, hopefully get a tip, then be the hell out of there.

"I used to work for a company that made scanners. Maybe I can do something with yours."

Heather continued her wide-awake dream, gently tracing her index and middle fingers down from her throat, between both craving breasts, stopping to place her palm over her navel.

"What've you got to lose?" Stagger-Lee touched upon.

Jack grabbed a slice of pizza, swallowing huge, ill-mannered, chunks with a hungry man's chomp. A second slice was then downed with equal savagery. He finally emptied his mouth enough to speak. "Feels like forever since I last ate."

Through the hole, Stagger-Lee saw Heather stroking between her attractive legs. "I'd gladly take a mouth full."

She slid from the edge of the bed, lowering to a furry rug, rolling over it to silently indulge herself amidst tickly animal hairs.

Stagger-Lee turned away from the hole in the door, doubting that she would reappear, making his concentration to whatever Jack was saying arduous.

Over the scanner came, "Be on the lookout for the burglar who—" the broadcaster's alert was absorbed by the rising static. The device's reception faded as fast it attempted to distinguish the announcer's words. When the broadcaster came back on, he spoke of a local string of home break-ins that had become a concern for police.

"That's the criminal I was talking about," Jack said. "He's probably the same thief who stole some of our furniture." Jack's lies journeyed to explain why the room was so sparsely appointed. Then he looked at the young man in front of him, seeing a drift in Stagger-Lee's demeanor. "I know what's happening here."

He was afraid that Jack had somehow seen him looking in on Heather.

"Come Judgment Day, the guilty will pay." Jack impressed himself with a derivative of biblical speculation.

Unable to fully take his mind from the man's wife, he mumbled inaudibly, before continuing to turn the scanner's dial, until a meteorological prognosticator spoke of how the unsettled weather that had been battering the region would continue.

Stagger-Lee's thoughts swelled back to dreamy aspirations of being with Heather who was so very near.

Not many feet away, she remained bare, stripped to her basic, overwhelming, beauty. She pressed her hands along the sleek, feminine muscles along her long thighs, admiring the strength to stand up to Jack. She wanted to mellow, and the only way she felt that would happen would be to ease into an old fashioned, porcelain bathtub. She wrapped herself in a terrycloth robe and headed for the bathroom.

There, bathtub water gushed from a stainless steel spout, releasing clean, liquid, goodness. When it reached its brim, she twisted the release knobs to tightness. She answered the comforting enticement by carefully stepping over the side, lowering into that which her every day was absent of. Pleasure.

She squeezed a washcloth's soapy liquid atop her head, letting the suds run. She closed her eyes, allowing wishes to dominate over hopelessness.

If it weren't for feelings of eternal captivity, she could be off somewhere exciting, with someone who could give her all of the extras that she needed. Normally, she would have dismissed such fantasy, reasoning that it wasn't suitable for a married woman to consider such things. But that was before her sexual entombment with Jack began.

Along with the 'till death do us part' commitment to Jack, her marital beliefs had withered—along with the rest of the town's brittle vegetation—to wilt and tumble away. She was left to wish with feelings of lighter than air romance, with all of its endlessly positive possibilities, with an eternity having glided past her. She still subscribed to the strict code of honor; her only fault being that she no longer had confidence in Jack. She wanted love, if only for its own sake. Marriage was nothing like it read in wedding brochures.

Her bent, glistening, legs parted, spanning both knees to opposite sides of the tub's cool porcelain, allowing a stream of water to seep between them. Her fatigued mind shutdown before her head sank below the surface. Upon surfacing, the water ran down her daydreaming head. Slender fingers rummaged, penetrating her loosened vagina with deepened sexual curiosity.

"Want some?"

She heard Jack shifting topics, disturbing the bathroom's soothing atmosphere with his negative verbal flow.

From the other room…

"Huh?" Stagger-Lee asked, somehow snapping out of it, forced to pay closer attention to Jack.

"A beer?" Jack strained to muster a fake smile, adding with a disgruntled husband's bitterness. "Do you indulge?" When he pulled back the pop-top on the tall can it squirted.

Heather's hand pumped wildly, splashing the bath water—that trickled over the edge, out onto a miniature Bible that she had left on the floor. She quivered while releasing volcanic spurts from within. Unfortunately, she was again feeling it alone.

Jack gulped what remained of his second Budweiser, whispering, "I like beer. It helps living here."

"God'll get you for that!" they heard Heather shout.

Needing to be higher, Jack began rolling a marijuana joint. The pungent smell of the leaves had him quickly lighting a match. Then he rotated back to Stagger-Lee.

"How much do I owe you?"

"Eight-o-nine." Stagger-Lee repeated.

Jack gazed in frozen fashion at the match's flame. It wavered and grew as it got closer to his fingers. A quick burn caused him to drop it.

"Did you already say that?" he reached to pick up the joint.

Then he went into his front pants pocket to take out a wrinkled fifty dollar bill.

Stagger-Lee grasped the money. "This bill's too large. I have to go outside to get your change."

Jack crudely burped the beer, forgetting where the joint was, thinking that downing another can would help his memory. "I'll be waiting," he called to Stagger-Lee.

Jack being here is the problem, Heather thought. She stood in the tub, looking through the partially open window, watching Stagger-Lee walking back to the Jeep.

Heather thought of the difficulty closing her eyes at night, wanting the next day to bring a better life; instead awakening with sadness that her days were mere depressing extensions of the ones that had passed before.

She moved from the sill having seen enough. In front of her was a full-length mirror. She looked into her eyes, disliking what she had come to realize. She dried herself, walking back to the bedroom. She bent to pull out a cartable travel bag. She unzipped it, having to fill it before Jack came in. First to go inside of it was a wide beam flashlight and a one-way Greyhound ticket.

She was a wife going through used-to-be matrimony. "I'll see you in hell before I see you in divorce court." His words rang in her head like the round starting bell from any timekeeper sitting ringside. She was deathly afraid of what he would do if he knew that she was leaving him forever.

Out in the still night air Stagger-Lee parted with what he wanted. What he needed was time to think, and that was never an easy chore. Strangely, the crickets had ceased. Perhaps, they too had sensed that something unholy was in the making. Nothing registered that allowed Stagger-Lee to understand the wayward vibrations that had overcame him.

Heather was as tempting as vanilla ice cream. And he wanted to get all of the mouth-watering licks that he could before she slipped away unattended.

Desirous suggestions had told him that he could do nothing about her marital predicament, but he wanted to try.

With anger building, he turned to see through their front window. Jack's head wavered before falling into unconsciousness, dropping the can of beer, snoring with an out-of-it heaviness.

Stagger-Lee cupped the sides of his head with his hands that were trying to silence indescribable manly pressures. Why was this happening? He'd done nothing wrong, yet.

"God'll get you for that. God'll get you for that…God'll get you." Heather's earlier declaration rang continuously inside his teenage brain. The more he tried to siphon it away, the more her rooted words reverberated. He had to choose between the hormonal pleasure, and the civilized societal standards of social correctness which punished such impulses.

His obsession with Heather was the barrier that blocked any hope for common sense to take control. And he wasn't about to leave without a souvenir.

THE NEWS
◆

Being a cop has its drawbacks.

Nothing worthwhile ever comes easy. The rules were changing. So when Rikki's mother went missing, her problems seemed to have peaked. Or so she thought.

Gold's Gym was where Rikki Luckett did her best to concentrate on a workout routine that wasn't going very well. One thing about barbells, a person's mind has to be on them, or calamity quickly comes calling. In the middle of the first set of reps, she finally figured out who was sending her those threatening letters.

It was a sickening stream of cryptic notes that had been anonymously delivered to her mailbox. It took some doing before she was able to decode that they emanated from McAlester, Oklahoma.

"It's hard to get the energy to come in here," said her next door neighbor, Thelma Hawkins, who had grown mightily fatigued after a series of sit-ups that should've been done before she went on vacation—instead of after a too short two week absence.

Thelma grunted, "Shucks, child. When I was your age I could do it all night, and come back for more the next morning." She bent-over at the waist, chuckling, "The only problem was, there was nobody there the next morning to give it to me."

Rikki got up from the bench press machine and prepared to leave. "Talk to-ya later."

Thelma merely waived her ethnic version of good-bye.

Rikki got home earlier than would've normally been the case. With so much weighing heavily on her mind, physical fitness was not very high on her list of important matters.

In search of a distraction, she grasped the TV remote, pressing buttons to find CNN.

This just in to the newsroom. Sometime yesterday, there was a prisoner escape at the maximum security facility at McAlester—

The remote fell to the floor, switching the channel. By the time she got back to the original broadcast, the original news station was on something else.

Her dry mouth fell open, thinking how jailbreaks from big-time places like that don't happen anymore; forcing her to realize that it had in fact occurred.

What were once feral rants from a convict who was guaranteed to remain behind impenetrable reinforced steel walls had instantly changed; Rikki could all but feel his homicidal breath beating down on her, removing any hint of a promising professional future that she'd hoped to have.

Within minutes after listening to the chilling details, she flipped open her cell and dialed. The rings totaled a mere few before someone answered on the other end of the phone line.

"McAlester Penitentiary," said the receptionist, with a monotone that foreshadowed a wish for an end to a work day that had become chaotic, and under great scrutiny from higher-ups, after the escape was discovered.

No longer seated in the waiting area was a man with a bushy beard, who had walked away when the telephone rang.

"Gimme the Warden," Rikki blurted in her usual cop's—I don't want to be kept waiting—tendency.

"Whom should I say is calling?" the employee asked, looking at her—I'm way past my going home time—desk clock, needing the overtime on her next paycheck, but not wanting it this bad.

"Rikki Luckett."

"Please, wait."

The receptionist put the call through to an adjoining office, to a secretary who typed beside a gold leaf desk plaque that read: Barton L. Blunt.

While still typing a letter to the Bureau of Prisons, she answered the call with her opposite hand. There was a hesitation, a type of quasi familiarity, with the woman's reaction—as though Rikki's name rang with some meaning.

"I'll see if he can speak with you."

Rikki was jolted when a man came on the line so quickly.

"Blunt, here," he tersely introduced himself, as was customary for a man in his unenviable position.

He was busy taking notes of some kind, wanting to keep his line free in case someone important called. Just then the door opened, and in walked the man with the bushy beard. The Warden turned, revealing a balding patch on his crown.

"Hi—" The Warden said with obvious familiarity.

"Call me Sonny."

The man sneezed.

"Mahafkan," the Warden said.

The Warden covered the phone, motioning with the pen that he was holding, for him to take a seat and wait while he ceased with who-the-hell-ever-it-was on the other end of the phone.

"Morning, Sir." Rikki did her best to control her angst, figuring that he would detect it from the unsteadiness in her voice, and might be less inclined to be helpful—if he thought she was some whimpering woman.

"Ma'am," he politely greeted her.

He was weary from another day of working underground, supervising savage men all day, only to have one of them come up missing by the final head count. In spite of that, he managed a shred of nice.

"What can I do for-ya?"

"I calling about one of your inmates."

"Which one?"

"Bubba Thorne."

He snapped the freshly sharpened pen between two strong, yet jittery fingers. The man with the bushy beard looked at him, feeling alarm growing in the tight air.

"I heard about the escape at your facility."

Her troubled voice began to hark an in-depth reason for this call—beyond the curious 'I saw it on TV, and had nothing better to do.

"Was he the one who got out?"

She gathered strength for the possible affirmation to verbally come back at her. If there is a word every warden can't stand to hear, it's 'escaped'.

The Warden was leery of this being another media trick, an interview designed to make him look incompetent.

He understood the need to sell newspapers. The problem that he had was whenever the press spoke with him they twisted his answers, intent upon trapping him into an admission that would again get him in trouble with the governor.

After this conversation was finished, his secretary and he would have a loud sit-down—on the subject of her better screening all calls before she summoned him to accept the incoming call.

Rikki had more to burst, "Was he the one they said was helicoptered over the wall?"

His edginess was sharply on the rise. "Are you with that-there newspaper?"

"I'm a detective with the Albuquerque police department. The last thing I'm going to do is pick a fight with you, Sir."

"What's the reason for your call?"

"Threatening letters have been coming to me out of H-Unit."

"Convicts are stupid. That's why they end up here. But who is dumb enough to sign a letter, only to have it traced back to their cell to get'm in more trouble?"

He wanted certainty that Rikki had the correct threatening author. "Yeah," he flatly admitted, "Bubba's the one who bolted out of here."

Her heart sank. The only time her palms got moist was when she was nervous, and that time was upon her.

She cleared her mind of personal clutter, shifting to straightforwardness. She swallowed.

"You're sure, he's the one's been sendin'm?"

"I was the one who put Bubba in H-Unit. Can't be nobody but him."

The Warden's thinking shifted from the idea that the woman on the phone was a jilted ex-lover, a lonely pen-pal cast adrift, or a wife who was afraid that homosexual, inmate sex had gotten the best of her husband while behind bars. Unfortunately for the Warden, this Rikki character sounded like the real thing. Crap.

The Warden opened-up to project. "Yesterday, some clown in a chopper swooped down and sprung-em d-hell out of here. That's all I can tell you."

She fought to get the words past the watermelon size lump in her throat. "Has he been caught?" Whew, she said it, with stifled hope about the answer that she wanted to hear.

"Not yet."

Damn. For Rikki, there was no resolution on the horizon. Not one that she could see or feel.

Her torment brought out the parent in him. He reached to adjust a framed photo of his twin daughters to better face him, warmly gracing their faces with his scratchy finger tips, needing to be protective.

"Hell, I didn't say he ain't gonna be caught." He switched the telephone to his opposite ear, nestling it. "What's in those letters he sent-ya?"

"Your employees must read prisoner's mail."

"That's a fact," he freely admitted.

"Why do you let inmates send out written threats?" The cloak was coming off her nervousness, turning her side of it into out-n-out anger.

"Basically, we check mail for contraband."

Then came more of what she didn't want to hear.

"It's against the law to read the outbound mail, and try to do anything about what was read."

Here was another example of a legal system gone haywire because of procedures that fellow cops had been at odds with for so long.

His tone turned mordant toward that same set of legislative guidelines by which he was forced to abide. "Unfortunately, detective, convicts have rights. So said the courts."

He took out his favorite pipe—which was easy because he only had one—stuffing it with a cherry blend tobacco that the Captain of the guards bought—days before any of this disturbing escape commotion started.

The secretary got a whiff of the imported blend, promising to bite her tongue on the unpopular subject of a smoke free workplace.

The Warden continued with Rikki, "All I can tell-ya' is, Bubba ain't here."

The cold manner in which he said that, had her frame of mind sinking faster than the last penny tossed into the wishing fountain at any church bazaar.

She was in her own world, sick of legality, rules of right and wrong, that kept getting in the way of her tormented wishfulness to shoot bad guys—those dynamic methods that her superiors disapproved of. The lack of information she was getting from this call was akin to wanting the impossible. Useful answers.

Careful with the way he concealed it, the Warden was hiding something. Her watermelon had changed into a hand grenade that exploded, bursting her hopes from within when she said, "I'm dead."

"Don't talk like that." Anything further that he wanted to add was clipped when she hung up.

She knew then that Bubba was coming after her.

THE GOODBYE

◆

Michael Tellata popped another Viagra, wanting his erection to last. When his member touched the cool glass of the Pyramid Hotel's window, he was forced to stand back. He was uncaring about much beyond the shapely body who was preparing to leave. He held in his sexual frustration, because the short-stay room was paid for another ninety minutes.

"It's bigger," said his latest mistress, Lorna Loon.

She sat on the edge of the unmade, queen-size bed, straining to reach behind herself to latch her double-D cup. On the bed beside her was the morning paper, which had as its lead the follow-up story about the jewelry robberies.

He looked out from the highest floor onto the spacious field. There an assemblage of hot air balloon enthusiasts prepared to inflate their sacks for the day's ascent.

One balloon owner's son adjusted the gondola's flame hastily, causing it to rise exceptionally fast.

"Careful, son. You don't want to set the balloon on fire." The warning was obvious. As was the stupidity in the son's reaction.

"I'm not a child anymore. I'm fifteen years old," the upstart replied, hating someone looking over his shoulder, monitoring his every move. "All bases are covered," the boy explained with a know-it-all sincerity.

Dad, however, continued keeping tabs on the situation, wanting to make certain that everything went just so. "My kid," he said under his breath. "One day I'm gonna knock'm on his ass."

His son had increased difficulty manipulating the pulsating flame, because he was too proud to ask for help. "We'll be liftin'-off any minute."

The ground level atmosphere was tight and wishful. Not that the father could pinpoint what that uneasiness was. Something just didn't feel right. And it had nothing to do with the weather.

Just then, a blind man wandered the area looking for his seeing eye dog. Stopping for a brief respite, he knocked over a leaking propane tank. It exploded.

"Help me!" that sightless man wailed, before collapsing in a writhing pile of flaming pain.

Rikki ran into the raging area to get closer to the mayhem, frantically motioning, "Get an ambulance!"

There were guttural screams from people scrambling in all directions. The chaos was spreading.

Rikki watched fellow police and medical personnel trying to revive the blind man. Within seconds that lasted forever, she turned for the exit, self-absorbed in her problems.

Distant emergency sirens signaled the rush to leave for the highway to take the burned man away. Meanwhile, she searched for reasons to care about what was happening around her but could not.

Rikki liked being liked. She hated jealous coworkers who shared collective, negative, opinions of her. They were the conspirators, who were constantly plotting against her. When she made detective—ahead of self-absorbed others who impatiently waited in the labor queue—her popularity within the force wasn't enhanced.

The struggle wasn't between the law and the law breakers. The adversarial disadvantage rested uncomfortably between her ambitions—to be the best cop that she could be, against rooted resentment towards her that many of her co-workers harbored.

A few months back, she was transferred from a small precinct upstate—a hole in the ground town that had dead car batteries in the middle of winter as the biggest crisis.

In the beginning, policing in Albuquerque was exciting. The eminent possibly of one day not returning home safely made it more so. Her zeal wasn't where it should've been—so said her once a week therapist.

Lately, she'd been written-up for skirting the rules, short-changing proper police procedures. Something about her day to day was growing old faster than she had been warned it would, by the few whom she felt comfortable confiding in; those who used to be sincere cops.

She was changing to another side of her inner self, one that she refused to allow anyone to see. She knew that the solution to what troubled her would come from pure evil.

When the fiery skirmish from the ballooning had finally been quelled, she sat on the ground beside her car to reread Heather's farewell note. It sketched how she had left Rikki and Jack forever.

THE MAKEOUT

◆

When the best got better.

Lens was a tall, lanky, string-bean of a guy who probably didn't weigh more than the expensive digital camera that he had strapped around his pencil neck.

He reached to secure the camera with both hands, and still he wasn't holding it all that steadily. The six glasses of beer that he had gulped since arriving earlier that cloudy afternoon weren't helping him focus that camera on his subjects. He raised the camera, aligning the eyepiece to one bloodshot pupil, doing his best to steady it, appearing anything but relaxed.

"Aren't you gonna tell us to say cheese?" Chief (Fat Tony) Fatino asked, hiccupping from his internal accumulation of beer suds.

"What if I ask-yall to shut up?"

"You'd be wastin' time," Erik Smooth added.

"Hoooow-so?" Lens lowered the camera from his narrow, pockmarked, face.

"I've been holding in an A-bomb fart for the past ten minutes," Tony answered. "When I let-loose, there won't be anybody left standing to photograph."

Fat Tony was a man of his word. And that forced Rikki and her co-workers to dissolved their tight formation by many wide yards. It was time to protect the nostrils at all cost.

"Just testing your emergency preparedness," Tony laughed, waiving them to again stand closer for Lens's attempt.

Getting the group shot over with was high on everyone's we're tired and want to go home—mind.

"Thought you said the camera has auto focus," someone called out to Lens.

"We need an auto photographer," Rikki said, glancing around at the others for the laugh she didn't get. The jealousy factor even extended to laugh values.

"What about an improved grade of models?" Lens insulted, orchestrating the shorter members of the group to stand in the front, ultimately for them to bunch-up so he could capture them all.

Behind them was Conchas Lake, which made for a nice backdrop. It was a place where Lens wouldn't mind pushing the limited assemblage. Then he started his countdown.

"One." He made the necessary distance adjustments to camera. "Two."

He backed up on an uneven mound, bracing himself against a thick trunk tree, to stand uncomfortably with his feet at different heights. Suddenly, he snapped the picture.

"What happened to three?" Rikki asked, having smiled into the camera's perspective a second too late.

"I wanted to catch everyone off-guard," Lens answered.

"You little shit," Fat Tony said.

"Spell my name right," Lens grinned.

Dusk's twilight marked the end of the great police outdoor get-together for Albuquerque's Finest until next year.

In the manner in which they arrived, they began to disperse. The attendees gathered what remained from their food and party favor offerings. Then they began the task of cleaning up. Each of them had both hands filled with assorted items. There was no way that they would leave the place a trashed mess, for members of the Parks Department to have to come by later to restore the park to its pre happening look. If that were to happen, they would surely bitterly complain to the police officer's union to foot the bill for their work efforts and the associated overtime costs.

After nearly an hour of making certain that nothing of trash value was left behind, Rikki and Erik watched Lens's Chevy Suburban dipping and diving along the bumpy path that led back out to the highway.

"It's just you and me left," Erik said.

Her tapered eyebrows traveled up then down, before relaxing in agreement. She smirked, not expectant of anything to follow beyond frivolous small talk between them. The alcohol induced loud back and forth all afternoon had died down. All that remained was the way in which he looked at Rikki.

Protocol always ranked a distant second to a person's earthy needs, those sensory essentials that guide all of us—even during sleep; when we're not paying close enough attention to notice their influence to ward-off lust's advancing determination.

Mellow breezes, coupled with the solitude of them being out there with no one around to see, was getting to both of them. Sexual urges had sought them out, to show that they were no different. Here, they too couldn't resist those needs.

He looked at her with carefully aimed, visual inspection. His was an optical penetration. She wanted desperately to stand firm to show that she wasn't one of his flock—other women who could not withstand his charms.

With equal consideration was her wish to have the foresight nice girls all seem to possess—to have hitched a ride home with the others.

Rikki's thoughts were shifting in her head about Erik, the dominant one, and how she fantasized what it would be like to lie with him. Minute after unobstructed breezy minute, her resistance was weakening, leaving her unable to muster the energy to rebel against his carnal carnivore hints.

"It's all over but the shouting," he said, trying to add a theatrical gesture to that suggestive verbal flavor.

She had no immediate reaction when he touched her chin. When her eyes closed the wonderment was rekindled more strongly.

Looking at the muscles on his chest flexing beneath a gentle cotton shirt, the feeling hit her harder. Rikki couldn't be certain how much she wanted from him. But she knew that she had to have it immediately.

She had never thought of herself as sexy. But he made her hot and bothered in all ways that were worth pursuing. Perhaps, it was his scent. Or, the way that his stroke brought out the beast in her that had been trapped for too long with no opportunity to vent. There was no place suitable for hiding. She was out into the brilliant light of erotic obviousness. She was of high basic morality. But with him she wanted to be good at only one thing—being bad.

Darkness had fallen like the final curtain at the last Sunday night performance on Broadway.

Beneath a partially covered moon that was too timid to peek out, Rikki and Erik had relocated to occupy the back seat of his steel gray Crown Victoria. Initially, the scheduling was to simply drop her back at his apartment. Suddenly, the two of them alone together had changed all that.

She stroked the sides of his face. He closed his eyes, afraid to keep them that way, for fear of missing out on this up-close examination of beauty. His hands rubbed her thighs, traveling to their inner side, sliding her plaid skirt up, removing her panties without any hint of resistance. Instead, there were muted, exploding, moans that urged him on.

In a single motion, she slithered from beneath him to be on top. Turning around, she submissively reacted as he snarled, ravaging her treasure with his mouth, as could only a wolf having waited long enough. After a series of rippling orgasms that were seamlessly connected, he repositioned her, unlatching the final button on her blouse to take in each long, sensitive nipple.

Damning morality, she wanted pleasure for its own sake. The variety of which she knew only he could give to her.

"If anyone sees us, our jobs are down the drain," she muttered from behind the moisture covered glass, wishing to heaven that he would release her—hoping like hell that he wouldn't.

"We're supposed to set an example," she added, suddenly no longer caring what others thought, ahead of the immediacy of her submissive openness. "If Tony ever finds out about the portable satellite navigation that you bought me, he'll track me to a departmental dismissal."

To indicate that the GPS tracking device was safely inside her tube of lipstick, she placed that tube back inside her purse.

They looked at each other without speaking, with panting breaths that made the windows steamy, filmy from inside, making it difficult to see what was about to happen.

His experienced manner, and the raw heat of the moment, thwarted her attempts to resist. Her memory of how long she'd thought about being with him, coupled with Erik having had those same ideas about her, made everything overwhelming. There was something about him that washed away everything from all other lovers.

"Don't stop," was the surrender phrase in her failed protest.

His hot breath against her tingly flesh made her pulse race with sexual unreasonableness, with a relentless cadence, giving him an uncontrollable motivation to restrain her. He held her hands behind her exposed back, allowing him full and unrestricted right to use all of her that he needed.

He allowed her to reach lower, grabbing hold of his hardness. She needed to keep it, hoping to feel him inside her drenched opening long after their encounter was over. In her churning mind she knew that this time together would never be over. He was every fantasy that she ever prayed for, and it was all coming together right then.

"It's ok if you hurt me," she purred.

With her fully restrained, using wrestling moves he incorporated from his police academy training, he placed her legs in line with his. With all of his enhanced strength, he raised her torso, sliding his throbbing deeper inside of her—aided by her sticky liquidity—wanting more than anything to touch her electrified heart.

She moaned like a woman who had been waiting for the chance to be set free from personal and emotional turmoil. Parting her knees ever wider, she allowed him a slippery access to her bubbling, workable, center.

Gyrating back and forth, she again exploded, repeatedly assuring her that peaking had arrived.

Many yards away, a distinct splash distracted them.

"What was that?" she gasped, mentally releasing herself in that panicked period, turning to see outside.

Suddenly, there was her climax after-shock that sent her arms tightly around him, scratching paths across his spine, love lines into his flesh, holding him steady in her thankful clutches. In the war of conscience, victory was more than a stone's throw away—too far for any of her leftover energy.

She rubbed her forearm against the smudged glass to see. Wearily, they began throwing on their clothes, fumbling to find which articles belonged to whom.

She whispered, absorbed by enveloping fear, "Somebody's out there."

THE BODY
◆

By 6:30 the following morning, it was obvious that the sky had opened to deposit someone into hell. Little did Rikki foresee at that time, but her voyage into darkness had only begun.

Marble size hail had fallen on the usually placid face of Conchas Lake. Millions of speckled pitter-patter craters of various sizes appeared on the water's choppy surface, speedier than a drummer's hands during halftime of a Grambling University football game.

Not too many miles away, a steel-gray Crown Victoria raced toward the shoreline. The flashing, spinning lights atop its numbered roof whirled silently, sirens calling out with an ear-piercing announcement, as it bounced toward the suddenly forbidden lake. It continued speeding along a road that should've been the test course for Midas shock absorbers.

"I'm on my way. Detective Luckett out," Rikki said into a microphone that didn't promote voices as well as it had years earlier.

She didn't wait to hear back from Dispatcher Jamison, especially since she was within visual range of another squad car that was parked on the dirt road up ahead, not too close to the mud that extended to the water's poorly defined edge. Its driver's side door was swung wide, with no one inside.

Why pester me on my vacation when there's a unit already here?

She always saw Dispatcher Jamison as a tight-ass who would jump at the chance to do it. After their little spat back in the summer, he was sure to send her out on the problem calls that came into the 911 center that none of the other officers wanted to take.

She reasserted her concentration to the problem a few hundred feet ahead. How quickly all had changed from the night before; when she and Erik were aware of little past each other's hot-n-sweaty bodies. Suddenly, that seemed like such a long time ago.

She stopped the Crown Vic two car lengths from where roped-off onlookers stood bundled together, whispering in a gossipy effort, struggling to see what they weren't supposed to.

Rikki stepped out from behind the wheel into inviting mud.

"Shit," she exclaimed, wishing that she'd worn a pair of who gives a damn work boots, instead of the reasonably nice pair she'd been saving for a reasonably nice holiday away from work.

What-da-heck, it's only money wasted.

Erik had finished stretching yellow police tape that connected several trees to each other, nearly a quarter of the way around the northeast section of the lake. It was routine to keep a crime scene free from outside influences. His official capacity—which was a far cry from thirteen hours before—was prompt and efficient. Upon seeing Rikki approaching, though, his mind wandered back to the preceding evening's edible festivities.

"Glad you could make it," he said in a rugged—John Wayne warding-off the approaching Indians—voice.

"Did I have a choice?" she complained, one heel up, arching to scrape away caked on mud from her sole.

"What happened, you got lost and accidentally returned to the scene of our crime?" He reminded her of the romantic hotness about which she was hardly able to forget. So much for his official police posture.

"I was dumb enough to answer Jamison's call, telling me to come out here on the double." She scanned the immediate area. "Fill me in…And don't talk about us."

"See the lake?"

Her sights were highlighted to one thing in particular. "What's that?" She pointed to a wrinkled, dark-yellow and blue item of relative distinction that was floating atop the gently shifting water.

"It's a parachute."

She wondered how he could be so certain of that, given she couldn't make it out from that distance.

His voice lowered. "That's what we heard splash last night."

"So?"

With countless directions that her policing instincts wanted to travel, she instead went down the single investigating lane that Erik was leading her. And there was one thing left to add.

"I haven't been in homicide as long as you, but usually where there's a parachute there's a parachutist attached to it…One way or the other, we'll be certain after the scuba guys get here."

Unconvinced, Rikki thought about more enjoyable things that she could've been doing with her well earned time off, other than looking down at her non waterproof boots that were probably ruined. And that was without the department financially compensating her for them.

"When'r those bozos due to arrive?" Then she realized about whom she was referring. "Probably, after they learn how to scuba."

Her sights returned to the water. The twisted parachute was slowly being pushed by a weakened breeze—the byproduct of strong winds that had since died-down. The chute was basically in one place, restrained by the heavy, nylon cords that disappeared beneath the surface of the fresh, rippling, water.

By then, more than half of her soap opera watching time had passed. Annoyed, she eyed the hour. "When'r they showing-up to make the dive?"

He motioned to the lake. "You wanna jump in?…There could be an Outstanding Service medal in it for you, if you don't drown."

"We'll wait forever."

Out of view—on account of the bystanders being in the way—a third city owned vehicle arrived. Much to Rikki's relief there stood Jonathan and Larry, looking like they just fell off of a vegetable truck that sputtered in from Mexico.

They advanced toward Rikki and Erik, wearing wet suits, flip-flopping. They were less concerned about finding whatever they were told might be at the bottom of the lake, than they were to dry off as quickly as possible to get back to the three drink minimum titty bar that they had just left—not fifteen minutes in the opposite direction.

"You guys finally made it," Erik congratulated.

"Without your seeing eye dog," Rikki insulted, having minimal faith in their ability, as the result of her last encounter with them on a different case.

"For the record, I'm here under duress," Larry retorted, looking over at Jonathan—the bachelor no more.

"Get here on time," she scolded. "As your superior officer, I could put yours in a sling for holding up an investigation while you two chasse the desires of your dicks."

When Larry came within arms reach, Rikki slapped his butt. Oddly, the jealous Erik saw the pat and didn't react.

The divers continued toward the water. Rikki and Erik watched them wade into it. Ankles, knees, then waist high, the chilly water gradually overcame them as they submerged. Bubbles from their oxygen tanks popped to the surface, assuring that each breathing apparatus was working properly.

The nine o'clock hour was minutes away when the divers surfaced, having salvaged the parachute and the soul to whom the strong cords were coupled. Normally, that combined weight wouldn't have been a problem for Jonathan, the avid weight lifter. But he had a sore elbow. And Larry, who was as lazy as a cat, was in no mood to add any of his strength to the retrieval.

They dragged, then dropped, the body on the ground at Rikki's feet. The person was covered from head to toe with a black parachutist's suit, making it immediately impossible to determine the person's gender.

"Are we done here?" the divers asked in near unison.

"Looks like it," Rikki said, wanting to get on with the examination of the find. Afterwards, shoe had planned to do something that didn't comprise police work. And that may, or may not have, included Erik.

The divers sloshed back to the truck. Against the sound of that third car leaving, Rikki went to work writing on a notepad, looking at the dead someone on the ground in front of her.

She leaned to remove the jumper's rubber head covering.

"We have one male, Caucasian, deceased," he said.

Around the base of the man's neck were small amounts of costume tinsel. After prying the parachutist's hand from a metal hook, she removed the man's gloves, dropping the man's limp arm. His lifeless hand splashed the shallow mud on her.

"There goes the other boot," she bitterly complained. Widening water stains rolled from the body, forming a more pronounced outline on the used to be dry, yet still stony, ground.

"He's definitely deceased. But from what?" she furthered, unable to take her sights from the body's ten disfigured fingertips. "Obviously, he wanted his identity a mystery. Look at his fingers."

He popped a stick of gum in his mouth, chewing comfortably. He offered her a stick of spearmint, but she declined.

"Wonder how he bought it."

Erik tried his best not to be sarcastic. "I assume he died from the fall, Detective."

Why can't anyone state my rank without being snide about it?

She turned back to Erik. "Anybody see the human comet crash land?"

He wished that he could answer in the affirmative. "If anyone did, they haven't come forward."

He stopped chewing long enough to add, "Not many of Santa Rosa's residents are awake in the middle of the night to hear much of anything, let alone a muted splash in its most bountiful lake."

She glanced at the onlookers whose curiosity had them watching in earnest. She thought that perhaps one of them might lend some helpful information as to what happened. Quickly, she gave up thinking that they would be willing to talk to the police about it. As a rule, people need the cops, but hate talking to them.

"Who discovered the chute?"

"Just before dawn, an old man was out here walking his dog. Claims, he saw the chute floating and called it in…Jamison said the witness sounded very upset. Too grossed-out to talk much about it."

"Or—" she added with the suspicion that only a trained cop would have, "that's what the caller wanted us to think."

"You're losing me."

Her curious eyes panned the peacefulness around them. "Look around and listen," she commented. "What about this area would have anybody feeling sick to their stomach, to such an extent that they couldn't talk about what they saw? Seeing a harmless parachute floating on that water is enough to have a person lose their lunch? How could that sight bother anybody that much?"

"Maybe the caller figured as I did, that somebody was under the water tied to the chute," he defended. "And that's what freaked him out."

"Where's our good Samaritan now?" she pushed.

"The caller didn't stay on the line long enough for the precinct's computer tracking device to get a read on his location."

Preparing for a closer inspection of the body, Rikki took out a pair of latex gloves, tossing a pair to Erik.

"Help me roll-em."

They turned the corpse over, careful not to get any of the man's soiled mess on themselves.

"Other than the bits of glass stuck in his face, there'r no intense bruises to indicate that he died from the fall."

She saw a slight swelling around one of the neck vertebrae.

"Except this," she felt a twinge of distortion about her original point as to the probable cause of death.

"What'r you getting at?" he asked.

One of her knees was on the soaked ground, sending a chilled feeling up her leg, and that bothered her. By that time the whole getting wet dilemma threatened to distract her sufficiently.

"Things aren't always as they appear." She continued, switching back to the corpse, sharpened to doubt that the man on the ground died accidentally. "Other than a bruise on his jaw, where's the ton of blood that should've accompanied a fall like this?"

Erik pointed to the pattern of smears inside the pliable headgear that hadn't completely washed away.

"Sure, there's got to be some blood," Rikki agreed, "That probably came from the glass."

Her mind danced with a detective's intrigue. "I'm not an expert on falldowns, but this guy doesn't look like a man who dropped in from outer space. The body's in too gooda shape."

"He landed in water."

"Falling from that high up makes water feel like concrete. Does this guy reflect somebody who landed on concrete?"

A squeaking, weighted-down, Chevy Suburban rolled in. A minute later, Lens was standing next to them. This time he was serious. Not the jokester that he was at the picnic.

From over his shoulder, he gripped, then aimed his camera. He bent to click away at the lifeless body from as many different positions as possible, allowing for the accurate truth to be told later in 8X10 glossies.

Within a few seconds, he looked at Erik. "Got another sticka gum? My mouth's pretty dry."

"Like your jokes," Rikki said.

"When it gets out how truly funny I really am, nothing'll hold me back," Lens clarified. "Comedy Central here I come."

Erik peeled away the wrapper, sliding a flavored sliver to him.

"Thanks," Lens said, before turning to walk back to the truck, carefully avoiding loose sections of earth that Rikki didn't.

"When do I get to see the shots?" she asked matter-of-factly.

Lens was feeling rather defensive. "Did they rush Picasso?"

"If they didn't, they should have," she said.

"Kinda-sorta, possibly you'll get a private screening later today." He hedged, "But don't hold me to it." He got back into the Suburban, slammed the door, cranked the steering wheel, and four-wheeled it through the quagmire that was once an easily drivable road.

Rikki regained her focus on the deceased. "That continues to bother me."

Erik mentally lagged behind.

"He was still holding the ripcord handle to the main parachute."

His head shook within the confines of millimeters, his fingers partially opened in a 'so what' fashion.

"Why didn't the chute open?" she wondered aloud.

He suggested that her attention be more closely paid to the parachute in front of them. "What do you call this?"

"Look how small it is."

He did, unable to distinguish it from any other kind.

"This is the backup chute. He never pulled the main one, as was evident by him still holding onto the main chute release." Recognizing what was obvious, she wasn't about to let it rest. "A knowledgeable jumper doesn't pull his own chute—to get that welcomed relief, feeling the nasty yank when it finally fully opens?"

"Who says he was experienced?"

The man's flight suit captured her sense of how much things cost. She stroked the rubbery material.

"The suit he's wearing. They don't discount this in the coupons at K-Mart. It's the finest quality."

"How's that?"

"I once dated a guy who was into this stuff."

"Was he any good?" Erik felt sexually threatened.

Her head tipped toward him.

Here's another jealous man who thinks that every woman didn't have had a past life before him.

"I can only say he landed better than this guy," she replied.

She got a stymied shrug in return, as both of them watched the morgue boys close in. Strangely, they were glad to be at work; especially since one of them was just coming off a two day suspension for repeated absenteeism.

"It's sad when Frick-n-Frack get to the crime scene ahead of you guys."

One of the boys spoke. "Larry and Dopey weren't buckin' headwind the whole way over here like we wuz."

She plucked a blade of grass, dropping it. It fell straight down, exemplifying how calm the air was.

The second of the boys couldn't hold it in. "It was a lot windier earlier, let me tell you."

She and Erik backed away from the men, who were wrapping the body in a black body bag. When they zipped it closed, the bag made a hard vinyl crunching sound around the dead man. Then they carted it to the open rear door of their waiting city box truck.

"That's our cue," Erik said, directing Rikki to follow him back to his squad car that was parked a dozen yards from where the morgue boys finished loading their truck.

After taking a few items from the trunk, Rikki and Erik were in the back seat looking at those articles of interest.

"Earlier, I found these near the lake," he said. "They must've separated from the jumper on his way down...I put'm in the trunk for safe keeping, so we could inspect them once things died-down."

"Interesting choice of words," she said.

She watched Erik take out a watertight nylon backpack and belt bag. Inside the backpack was a clear plastic bag enclosing a 9mm Beretta, a waterproof wallet, a compass, maps, a pocket knife, a weird looking key, and camouflage painted goggles. From inside the belt bag he took out a wallet.

"The driver's license says he's Sonny Sixkiller...That name mean anything to you?"

While mildly shaking her head, she noticed a silvery-white dust on the inside of the clear, plastic, bag.

Erik opened the belt bag. Its contents were unmistakable, causing their eyes to widen considerably to behold the sparkle, the sheer luster, of polished blue diamonds. She was in awe with an indecipherable feeling that people get from the enormous value of such things.

He asked, "If I give you one of these will you marry me?"

"Like the song says, Maybe Tomorrow."

She reached to change the focus, pointing to the military decorated goggles. "Our guy was in the service?"

"My uncle was in the Navy, and he never mentioned them paying like this."

Inside the bag were enough hundred dollar bills to chock a truck; a large truck at that.

"There must be ten G's here," he said.

Reverting, she couldn't disengage her sights from the diamonds. A few elongated seconds elapsed before she glanced out the side window. At the far edge of the lake was a private residence. There, a teenage girl was dressed in Army fatigues, reaching to take articles from a clothesline. Immediately, she forged a linkage between the style of clothes the girl wore, and the markings on the goggles.

"Who lives in that house?"

"Where," he asked.

She motioned, "Over there."

A big time lawyer named Tellata. Why?"

"Just asking," she quieted.

Erik switched, "I gotta wait for the crime lab people to come and finish going-over the scene. Why don't you take this stuff to the precinct, and log it into evidence."

She watched him replace the items—including the hundred dollar bills—back inside the bag. Before he closed it, she silently inspected the odd looking key, seeing a series of letters inscribed on it.

"What's wrong with you taking it to the station? Technically, I'm still on vacation."

He pulled the final inch on the zipper to close it. "It could easily be forever before they finish processing this scene. In the mean time, you can have all of this stuff logged-in, with plenty of time for you to get back home to finish doing whatever you were doing."

She knew that outranking him left her with the responsibility of removing the items back to headquarters.

"See you later." His thumb and index finger went to the brim of his hat, straightening it. Then he winked at her.

Their doors squeaked open, and out they climbed. Erik headed back to the gradually diminishing crowd that had grown bored, deciding to leave in favor of anything drier. Rikki went to her car, uncertain about a most puzzling morning.

THE CASE
◆

It promised to be a wild ride.

Something big was strangling the city.
From the on-the-take mayor who was always multiple steps ahead of being indicted, down to first graders who couldn't leave the safety of their beds and blankets to attend school; to speculating citizens who, one by one, got word that there were still more jewels sunken at the bottom of Conchas Lake. Everyone was talking about the mysterious man who fell from the sky the night before.

There was a twenty-four hour police guard around the lake, with orders to arrest anyone caught within three hundred feet of the water.

Jonathan and Larry were pulling down more overtime than either of them could spend on half a lifetime of lap dancers, making sure that no one was under the surface with scuba gear, prospecting for riches that weren't rightfully theirs. Free money was the name of the game. And the new city wide pastime was far from over.

This was all novel to Albuquerque. The old timers on the police force had grown accustomed to low level crimes that backlogged their caseloads for years. But a few hours ago vice of noteworthy proportions had descended upon them in a most flamboyant way. That was a ton of trouble for anyone to write home about. This was one crime that screamed for attention. And it got it.

It wasn't an everyday occurrence when transgressions fell right into the arms of the cops, who itched for just one skull to crack; to send a meaningful message throughout the criminal community to cease and desist, in case folks figured to pile-on to make a big crime more profitable for themselves.

Thanks to Erik telephoning ahead, the excitement level in the central precinct had peaked, as everyone in the stationhouse waited for Rikki to arrive with the purported incalculable dollars and questionable gems that were found on the failed parachutist.

Rikki pushed through the entrance doors with continued annoyance over having answered Jamison's call. Her black sole shoes scuffed, dropping mud atop linoleum that was scheduled to be waxed two days ago. But at the last minute, Tony recalled how he wrenched his knee the last time they made the floor too slippery, so the waxing was put on hold. And the night cleaning crew loved not having to do the floor.

Tony was secluded in his office, engrossed in his work when he heard, "She's in the building," from someone whispering through his intercom.

A sigh of relief went up inside his worried brain, while he watched a Best Buy television that rested where the wall met the drop ceiling. It retold the story of the parachutist ad-nauseam. Every TV channel had been preempted with detailed footage that explained the late night episode. It could've easily been addressed in five minutes. Instead it took hour after hour, with newscasters who never ran out of words about the mysterious man in the swanky flight suit who was dredged.

The local press was a pack of hungry wolves, having chased the situation of the carcass that was deposited at the feet of Rikki and Erik hours before; with their editor being the hovering vulture riding the wind currents of conjecture, waiting for the snoops to come back to him with their written copy.

Rikki saw Eric in the hall outside Tony's office. After exchanging visual pleasantries, she saw that Tony's door was strangely ajar. She backed into his office, hitting her shapely buttocks on the point of his desk. Her yelp was silenced, when he looked up to see her standing in front of him. His tolerance had also been stretched, after waiting out the exacerbating minutes.

"I wonder if Bin Laden himself could walk in here without you noticing before it was too late," she said.

"I wish. It's been too long since I last shot somebody." Tony switched, "Bout freakin' time you got here."

He was especially agitated, not knowing what to make of the case he'd been listening to for the past three hours, without the benefit of the evidence seized at the scene—by an overdue detective who took her sweet time bringing said physical confirmation back to him. He was fast losing hope that her items of interest would do anything to cool the gossipy office air.

"Nice to see you cleaned up your office," she snickered about the lack of cleanliness around his antique desk.

He ignored that, rubbing his temples, feeling sabotaged by the jumper.

"Why couldn't the bastard have been blown into another county? Anywhere, other than in my backyard."

Yep, that was policing in the desert southwest. There a cop's aspirin bill was always a drag on their take-home wages.

"I've seen enough," Tony complained, switching off the television.

Seconds later, turning it on.

"I'm sick of it. Then I feel like I'm missing something if I don't keep watching the damn tube." He popped two Tylenol, washing them down with a manly swallow of spring water from a twelve ounce, plastic, squeeze bottle that he refilled countless times at the water cooler down the hall.

"It ain't easy being the boss, kid."

"Where's all the junk?" she asked, referring to the top of his usually cluttered desk.

"I knew you were coming. So I wanted to make everything just so."

He was more sarcastic than truthful. It was during the unending broadcasts when he barricaded himself in his office to make it for the most part tidy.

"I got a present for you," she said.

She reached to unzip the belt bag. He watched her pull out every item that Erik had presented to her a few hours earlier.

"Why'd you bring this to me?"

She removed the last of the items from the bag, pinging and ponging them under his stuffy nose.

"Evidence storage said they're afraid to keep this much in diamonds on the premises. And that it'd be safer with you. That's when I stopped listening to'm."

"I wish I wasn't listening," he sighed, holding his head in both chubby hands. He peeked through his fingers at the glittering geological rocks that were laid out in front of his—why couldn't I have gone into orthodontia like my aunt wanted me to—worried face.

With no place else to turn, he picked up the AT&T, pressing the numbers from memory.

"This is Captain Tony Fatino." He looked at Rikki, listening to someone on the other end. He was the man with whom Tony had less than a stellar verbal exchange when Tony was an on the way up police officer.

"I'm down here in Albuquerque…I got a problem."

Tony listened.

"Yes, sir, I should lose a few pounds."

He scowled at Rikki—as though it was all her fault that he was talking to the man in the first place. She stuck out her tongue at him in defiance.

He continued, "Sir, we got a bunch of diamonds from the fella who fell out of the sky last night."

He listened.

"You heard right, sir. Hellova story…I don't like keeping that much in precious gems here…Do me a favor. Hold'm for me, until I can make heads or tails about what the hell's going on with this case…What's that?"

He palmed the mouthpiece, whispering to Rikki. "Says, he'll do it."

Rikki relaxed at finally being able to hand over the rocks to someone else, and out from her responsibility.

Tony continued to Rikki, "Says, he's short handed and can't come git'm. Says I've got to send somebody to him with the evidence."

She shook her head, defying any suggestion that she be the one to do it.

Tony was back to the man on the line, "Yes, sir. She's on the way…Say hello to your wife for me."

He looked to Rikki, who ceased shaking her head. "The Federal run is yours."

"Mine?" Her alarm was genuine—and genuinely negative—with spirits that were rapidly declining like a worker's attitude on April fourteenth. "How do you expect me to solve the case, and be a five dollar an hour courier wanna-be at the same time?"

"You're the detective. Figure it out." He pushed the contents towards her. "When you hand it to'm, make sure they give you a receipt."

He couldn't help but to notice her resentment. "Look at it this way, your work in this regard will inspire others to keep up with the high standards you set."

"Bullshit," was what she burbled to his non-uplifting words of falsified praise.

Tony shifted, "Well? What's with the case so far? Something I can sink my teeth into? Anything to get it off the goddamn television news and into the closed cases drawer?"

Dejected from having to be the designated delivery girl, she snarled, "I'll hit you up when I get back from the drop-off."

"You haven't forgotten my number."

"Unfortunately, no."

"Leave the cash with me…Then get out." His word was succinct and scolding, his fingers wiggling to escort her out of his office proved that.

The boss's rudeness was his manner, but she would've preferred a touch more of an explanation as to why she had to be the one to go. Hell, the Federal

Building was far enough away that it would take until late in the afternoon before she returned home. By then the day would be a complete wash. Not to mention, her not getting any overtime pay for her efforts. Hers was a vacation that started out as work. What could be sadder?

In the hall were those people who normally would quickly walk past Tony's door, fearing that he would somehow sense they were out there, and summon them inside for an unwanted assignment. But this time—after hearing about the gems—there was a limited assemblage there, with ears peeled to take in all they could—for possible roundtable dinnertime tête-à-tête.

By this time, Rikki was back out in the hall.

"We're all proud of youuuu," Tony called from the other side of the door.

Parallel in time, Fat Tony sat transfixed. His once many thoughts had narrowed to a lone ordeal. Something was bothering him. And unfortunately, he knew exactly what it was.

Rikki thumbed away a droplet from the edge of her mouth, finishing-up at the water fountain, feeling like a child who was just told that she had to finish the spinach on her plate if she wanted post meal ice cream. That was when she saw Erik looking at her, she figured that Mister Budinski had been listening outside Tony's door the whole time, and wanted to verify what he thought he had heard.

"You didn't mention that we were at the lake long after the picnic ended."

"Did I say by the way, Tony, I was out fucking Erik at the scene of the crime?"

He was embarrassed into silence.

The 'be real' face that she made gave him assurances that his name never came up in the meeting with Tony.

"What about tonight?" he hopped right in, with the hope that a farfetched yes from her might be on the plate.

"Can't. After I make this drop," she jiggled the beltbag that had to go to the Feds. "I told you, I take night classes at the college," she rebuffed.

"Tomorrow?" He wasn't through—not with hormones calling the shots.

"Can't. I have a class."

"Why don't we get together when you've got no class?"

She batted her naturally long lashes, and with that she was walking away, refocusing what energy she had left, on getting to the drop-off at the Feds before it got too late. Driving in rush hour traffic never helped her mood.

* * *

Late into that same night she couldn't stop thinking how there was something about the parachutist having two different driver's licenses with the same photograph. It was apparent to everyone that the human falling rock was no honest Abe who happened to be victimized by normal circumstances.

Then there was the way in which the body wasn't that beaten-up; for someone who was supposed to have fallen hundreds of feet before crash landing. Perhaps, he died some other way, and was dropped in the lake to make it look as though he bought-it from the fall. Lastly, she dwelled on the idea of Erik, and what it meant to make love in the back seat of his car.

THE DECISION
---◆---

Where reckless determination met high risk, there was Rikki. She never took the diamonds to the Feds.

THE LAM
◆

Until last Friday, no one had ever escaped from the super-max prison facility at McAlester. The day before that, Bubba used to live there.

It was a miracle that he made the climb from its lowest tier of cubbyhole cells, to reach the rope ladder that hung from that helicopter. If the Guard, Jefferson Tisdale, had been at his assigned work station, the plot would have been foiled before it began.

There was an official inquiry as to why Jefferson wasn't there. The results of that inquest were promptly submitted to his superiors. Less than an hour later, the Correctional Officers Union officially signed-off on his termination. The day after that the state went after his pension.

All things considered, Bubba didn't find his cell-block day life—if one could call that a life—exceptionally bad. Behind bars he got what he needed; sex, drugs and best of all violence. Apart from the fierce ant population that was constantly dining on what little fat there was on his muscularly exaggerated body, he had grown accustomed to the regiment of confinement. In a very odd way, he sort of liked many things about the place. He was also keenly aware that his take-down was a high profile plan that was bound to make the Warden out to be some kind of hero, rather than the tunnel-vision fool that he really was for allowing Bubba to escape in the first place. In the end, Bubba vowed to die rather than be captured.

Bubba's face hadn't seen a smile since three sunrises before the whirly-bird hovered above the mess hall's roof where he had hack-sawed his way out. He knew that there would be only one guard on the roof, with the other man at the local hospital tending to the birth of his first child. Additionally, Jefferson's eyesight wasn't the best, making for a better than ever chance that he would misfire trying to hit the helicopter—if he were to start shooting at all. That tragic intersection of circumstances allowed Bubba to soar into the stormy night air.

For Bubba, it was first things first. He had to kill Rikki.

Once she was within his range, he wanted to get an unimpeded pistol shot at her before she could react to the intrusion. Simply wounding her would be less than the thug thing to do. More than hating her for having him locked up, he was absentmindedly crazed because Rikki never bothered to write back to him.

Riding as a passenger in a late model Plymouth, Bubba withdrew a flask from his sagging breast pocket, taking a hard swig of cheap, watered-down, bourbon before screwing its scratched stainless-steel cap closed.

His youngest brother, C.C., was behind the wheel, twitching with uneasiness, in an effort to scratch his ass. He didn't feel comfortable behind the wheel, having not driven since he got locked up. Even more than his attachment to the foam covered steering wheel, was the connection that he always had with Bubba.

By the age of eleven, C.C. had more than a nodding acquaintance with the juvenile level of the criminal justice system. It wasn't until a major attempt at a felony of noticeable consequence, that had a no nonsense jury issuing him a heavyweight conviction, had him transferred out of the county lockup to McAlester. There, he got his wish and was reunited with Bubba. That was society's pledge to remove from consideration both of their shoeprints on any sidewalk in America for many years after that.

"How'd your jump go?"

"Just shut-up and drive the car," Bubba snarled back at him.

"I was just askin'," C.C. sulked, wishing that he hadn't brought it up.

When the car hit another bump Bubba winced, tough-guy style, from agony in his lower back. He knew that his little brother was concerned, and that eased him. "Since you made it someaya-business, jumpin' should only be for grasshoppers."

"You think Sonny made it?"

"Last time I saw'm, I was bailing from the chopper."

Bubba wanted his flying mate to be alive and well, but optimism isn't the sort of thing a convict carries around in his bag of wishes.

Bubba began rolling a handmade cigarette, spilling precious, flaky, tobacco each time the third-hand sedan rocked sharply. They were on a roadway that was too far gone for anyone to think that a simple paving contractor could ever make a difference. When he finished rolling the cigarette, he lit-up, then exhaled rings of rising, thinning, smoke.

"We'll hear about Sonny soon enough…If he ain't at the meetin' place, then somethin' happened to'm." Bubba scratched discolored bumps, bites where the ants had made it a stinging point to attempt to devour him with great eagerness. He intensified his concentration as to where to best position the fatal shot on Rikki.

Hoping to get somewhere with answers, Bubba switched subjects. "When'r we gittin' there?"

"We got a ways to go." C.C. looked over at Theodore (Teddy) Thorne, who had drifted off to sleep, lying across the rear seat, lanky legs tucked in with both knees close to his chest.

His scratchy snoring had become highly annoying to the other occupants. What could they do about it, open the door and throw him out?

"Ain't there no way to quiet'm?"

"Not without killin'm," C.C. jested.

The sight of Rikki taking her last breath, her pulse fading to nothingness, was the only killing that he had in his elementary school educated mind.

"Teddy, you feel like drivin'?" C.C. asked, struggling against his weariness that refused to release him along every passing mile.

Teddy came out of a pseudo coma to comment. "Can't. My license's expired," he said through bruised lips that he received during a fist fight with a just doing her job meter maid.

"Since when did breakin' the law matter to you?" C.C. asked.

"Since never," Teddy verbally assumed his rightful place among society's deviants. "You don't need me to drive. You're doin' fine. Besides, you know this area better than me."

Their car had cleared all remnants of warranty coverage, as it continued past a lemonade stand that had been vacated soon after the children tending to it were beckoned home by worried parents less than an hour after it opened for business. All that remained were the weakened plywood and the poorly designed table—a testament to the money they never earned.

The funnel cloud of debris hung after the weighted-down Plymouth rumbled past it. Considering how fast they were traveling, it was a minor miracle that trees lining the side of the road didn't uproot in the car's wake. In the aftermath of their hurried getaway, a wobbling, metal roadside sign read: Albuquerque Dead Ahead.

THE ARRIVAL
◆

Hookers Elbow Room was a monument, a cornerstone, in the most notorious section of the city. It was built back when standards of decency were a lot higher. Since then, it had become an eyesore, shunned by those who didn't want to see their city fall deeper into Satin's unyielding grip. The building was scheduled for demolition vote by the Council for a Better Albuquerque. The verdict came. The wrecking ball did not.

Inside its dreary old style, swinging double doors, Jack stood hunched over the counter, wiping it down with minimal arm power. Bored and in need of something to do until quitting time, he wiped glassware that wasn't in need of it. Little did he realize that the adjustments to the décor were to be of the variety that he hadn't longed for. In any case, he stayed busy with the interior that was never clean enough to please the fly-by-day field reps from the Board of Health who dropped in to issue fines and unsolicited cleanliness lectures.

To the side of Jack was an old drunk who never gave her right name from the first time she sat on that same stool to watch stale beer suds rise to the brim in one of the before mentioned hanging mugs. There was no one else there.

She would've gone home hours earlier, but she couldn't stand up long enough to do so. Sitting there was the best alternative until Jack could assist her to the bus stop.

The second hand on the circular wall clock marched on, sweeping forward against all wishes from Jack that it do so with greater haste.

"Why me?" he said.

"Why not you?" the woman replied, lifting her head up only long enough to say that, letting it tilt back against the supporting wall.

Out front, the dusty and dented Plymouth sedan—with small amounts of steam seeping from beneath the hood—was parked so close to a fire hydrant that it blocked the view of it—making it impossible for firemen to get to it if they had to. What was anyone going to do, ticket the car? Bubba could only wish that they did-so on paper. That way he could wipe his skid-marked ass with it.

Bubba kicked open the doors that hung unevenly from damaged hinges as he made his way inside. With both brothers in tow, he looked around the musty area, trying to remember when he was last there. In the dreary background, the jukebox played, It's Been A Long Time Coming.

"We're closing in a few minutes, gents," Jack announced to the newly arriving trouble seeking trio.

Bubba's nostrils flared from the plentiful smell, the negative halo of inhospitality that he felt from Jack.

Sporadic lightening flared with no rain to go with it, with multiple thumps of thunder impacting the room, sending walled glassware rattling.

Jack motioned with a bent thumb to the slumped-over woman at the bar. "As soon as I can git her upright, I'll be sayin' good night, turnin' off the lights for the evening and headin' home."

Bubba withdrew a sawed-off shotgun from inside his full length suede duster. The sheer size of it was stirring. It looked like twin invitations to no tomorrow; certain closing costs to whomever it was pointed.

Jack's eyes continued to sting from earlier in the day when he accidentally sprayed an industrial cleaning agent into them. He was unaware that Bubba's middle finger was tightening around the trigger.

The shotgun blast hit the sagging woman, sending her from the stool to be plastered against the wall. In an emotional pile of what was when she was alive, the ex-drunk fell in a heap of motionlessness to the smeared tongue-n-groove floor. Discolored blood had stopped pumping from the gaping hole in a neck that couldn't hold her head.

Bubba was meaner than ever as he loved every second of it. His fiery, bulging eyes danced with unrest as he glared at Jack.

"Care to reconsider?" Bubba asked.

One would've thought that Jack had customer's letting off rounds inside the bar every day. He continued polishing the medium-size imitation crystal glass free of spots as though there wasn't a problem to react to. He had to be calm, reaizing that there was one problem not to be ignored; that trouble stood six feet four inches tall directly in front of him.

Overwhelmed by vastly superior forces, and concerned only for his safety, Jack barely glanced at the woman who lie motionless beneath a slowly revolving, vinyl, stool cushion. Jack wanted to see Bubba in her place. As is the case with most wishes, it wasn't about to come true.

Surprisingly, Jack never thought to trip the alarm button that was beneath the counter to his immediate left.

He worried about calling the police, on account of the lunatics who remained close to him. He knew that had he, there would be a shootout for the ages when the cops showed up to arrest them. Afterwards, a lengthy interrogation was bound to follow. And the last thing Jack wanted, other than, heading into the afterlife with the woman on the floor; was to have endless questions needling him about what went on.

Instead, Jack thought of where he last saw the bleach, a mop, and a bucket of hot water to clean up the mess. If, and when, the police arrived, he wasn't about to let them see all that blood. Holy cow, there was a heckova-lot of it and it was everywhere.

"Take a load off, Bubba. I've always got time to serve friends," Jack capitulated, glossing over the distinct possibility that he might be the next one to have buckshot collapsing his veins, forcing him to cancel Christmas.

Their violent calling card instantly told him that the man standing there was a thorn—in the side of civilization.

Bubba continued to revel in his homicidal masterpiece. Meanwhile, C.C. and Teddy walked past him to one of several empty tables that had the woman's DNA droplets on it; that was in need of a good sanitizing. Suddenly, they feared that Bubba would be upset if they took a seat before he did. So they continued to stand.

"Don't mind if I do," Bubba accredited Jack's invitation, spitting a wad at the woman before stepping over her frayed clothing and body.

Within a few tense seconds after Bubba finally took a seat, Jack made a short man's jaunt to where the imposing brothers relaxed, figuring they'd be gone soon enough. And he could clean up the place. If he was wrong, however, he didn't like Christmas anyway.

"Whudda-ya fellas drinkin'?" Jack asked, trying to be cool.

"Bourbon—J.T.S. White," Bubba drooled over the thought of finally being able to swallow his favorite liquid anxiety easer in five used to be prison years.

"All we carry is the Black," Jack nervously offered.

"Fine by me," C.C. thankfully said ahead of everyone else.

"Make it two," Teddy motioned with a wiggling index finger, feeling that if the Black wasn't good enough for Bubba, he and C.C. certainly would indulge themselves to functioning drunkenness.

Bubba hoisted an index finger, indicating that he'd settle for one. He frowned, swatting a pesky mosquito that should've exited when the men first entered, but chose to be an annoyance, landing on the chair behind Bubba.

Bubba dropped the shotgun, and out came his long barrel forty-four caliber pistol. He placed its iron tip inches from the insect, pulling the stiff trigger just as it flew away.

When it discharged, the powder missed burning him, sending the winged pest to oblivion. The bullet zipped through the opposing wall.

Outside, the heated bullet pierced the Plymouth's radiator, passing through it, barely missing a child who walked while holding hands with his mother. Neither of them knew that the end had almost paid them a visit.

From outside the bar, Jack's eye could be seen looking through the bullet hole, less safe than he was.

"Wutcha-go-n do a thing like that for?" Jack complained from inside the bar.

Actually, he was more worried about the hole in his wall than what happened across the street. His ears were ringing from the firearm's stinging ejection.

"I won't be hearin' nothin' for a week."

Bubba was twisting his index finger in his ear, trying to get it to work again.

Minutes later, he carried four drinks, one was for himself. Upon reaching the frontier west replica table around which the men sat, Jack leaned forward to hand out the refreshments. Just then the glasses began rapidly sliding to the high rimmed edge. Thankfully, they never tipped over.

Having waited long enough, Bubba snatched Jack's tie, yanking Jack's face eye level to his. "Where is she?" he demanded.

"Who?" Jack asked, sentient as to who Bubba asked about.

"The cop who you saw bust me, last I was in here."

Jack hesitated. "She ain't been-round since she popped you tryin' to sell her that beat-bag of coke."

C.C. and Teddy had no idea that Jack was as lying a rascal as could be found. Bubba knew.

The speed with which Jack gulped his saliva showed that he was absorbed by the cold reality of death hanging above him. It was a specter of things to come. Jack was a cowardly, morally deserted, scheming soul. He was someone who would go in a revolving door behind you, and come out ahead of you.

Bubba clutched the tie against Jack's chest, forcing the bartender to stumble backwards, until finally regaining his balance against the same blood spattered wall.

Bubba slammed down his drink to finality, smiling with the last taste of the molecules, standing with his brothers, the three men headed for the exit. Not many steps had been taken, when he wandered behind the counter and took a full bottle of something else. He was still fuming, not absorbing Jack's information well at all. "Hey!" he yelled to Jack. "If you kick-word to that bitch cop I'm lookin' for, I'll be back for <u>you</u>."

Jack's only thought was how does one tell his daughter that a madman is after her? So to ease the conscience that he never had, he decided not to say a word about it.

THE EVIDENCE
◆

It's impossible to establish something when there's no proof.

Rikki had a whole new set of problems to live by. Bubba was out there, and she didn't know where. That made avoiding him—if possible—high on her Things To Do List.

All of this not withstanding, Fat Tony had unmistakable black smoke pouring from both ears when he found out that she hadn't gone straight to the Feds to drop off the evidence.

Rikki wasn't worried who told him. The precinct was filled with brown-nosing squealers, who lived to slime up to Tony with Judas baked, bad-mouthing tidbits of this and that, resulting from out of control aspirations that one day he would reward them with an undeserved promotion in rank. Deep down—to the point of needing an oil drilling team to find Tony's true feelings—Tony liked Rikki better than they.

He wasn't about to look the other way over what she did with the gems unless the 'other way' was in the direction of the gas chamber.

Instead, she made a U-turn in her compact sedan, and drove home to plan her next move. It was anyone's guess what that was going to be.

Early that evening the storm headed east, engulfing and badgering everything in its destructive path, before ultimately glimmering out somewhere over Tennessee.

Rikki arrived at her front door relieved to be there. With sweaty palm discomfort, she wished for home to be somewhere else. On another planet, perhaps. But at minimum, some other setting where she wasn't in so much damn trouble.

The muscles in her arms flexed after carrying overly stuffed grocery bags from the car into her home. The grocery tab was higher than usual. Rikki swore that the cashier rang it up ahead of her ability to keep track of the addition. She aimed the key at the lock and missed, scratching the solid wood door around it.

She was a person who had to have everything in its assigned place. And when one of the grocery bags broke open in the kitchen, sending the contents rolling about the floor, she enunciated every obscenity that she knew; Rikki knew them all.

After a night of surprisingly restful sleep, she snapped to it, in a whirlwind of what the hell was her existence all about?

Through that mental haze she knew that something was askew. Thrashing about beneath pink, imitation satin, sheets—that were originally purchased to lend a feeling of sensuality to her sleep experience—she submitted to the idea that she had to get out of bed and start another day.

"Dad?" came out of nowhere from her into the stillness that surrounded her.

Her worried voice snaked through the pre-dawn air with an eerie silence that shouted back at her.

Creaky stairs reacted to the young woman's light weight being gradually applied to each oak board as is usually the case when a person is sneaking around. Unknowing as to what was so troublesome, she continued onward.

An upwardly sweeping breeze raced inches above the sectioned hard wood flooring, past her and up the stairs. That announced that a window or door somewhere was left open. She hoped like the dickens that it wasn't the front or back door, all too aware of the unsettling likelihood that her house had been burglarized, especially after there had been that rumor of a serial prowler terrorizing the city many months earlier.

Once her bare feet were gone from the bottom step, she realized that the outside air was coming in from the back door.

"Holy shit!" came out like a person who just found out the last day to pay their home electric bill was the day before.

She rushed to slam that door. Then it hit her. And her economy of expletives couldn't express skyrocketing fears. "Fuck!" replaced holy shit. After stubbing her toe, anticipating the delayed reaction for the pain to shoot up her leg, she raced back to the stairs.

It was in her bedroom where horror greeted her. In one motion, she unzipped the parachutist's backpack. That was when fate accentuated the 'D' in disaster. The gems were gone.

How long does it take for a person's life to flash before her eyes? Especially when that life had all the constraints that a grand larceny's tightening noose could produce.

Waiting hours for Jack to return home from wherever the hell he was took more worrying time than Rikki had to spare. She made up her unraveled mind to drive to the forensics examiner's office. Maybe Morty had something helpful, because she sure as hell didn't.

Uncertain as to what that visit would bring, it beat the unlikely possibility that Jack would return home any time soon. Why would he? With the gems in his pocket, or the wad of dough from selling them, Rikki wasn't going to hear from him again. In the face of incarceration, the question had become: What are you planning for the next fifteen years? Prison had such an awful sound. Especially because that was where she sent people—not the other way around.

The middle of the afternoon trek across town was marred by extensive flooding from incessant rains that had left water pooling where the usually dry region had long done without. Even with all of the barricades and alternate route signs, being outside was better than sitting around the house wondering where in the blue-blazes Jack was. And where were those damn diamonds? Why couldn't Erik have taken them from the scene? That wasn't the time for responsibility to be dumped in her ungrateful lap.

An oversized ball bounced in front of her car from behind a tree with connected twin trunks. Heather once told her "When a ball rolls into the street, a child is bound to be chasing after it." Sure enough, a pre-teen popped out to fetch the ball. Rikki sighed from having avoided the furtherance to her problems, by adding vehicular homicide to her present dilemma.

For the rest of the splish-splash drive, she thought of the endless possibilities that might match the man at the lake with a probable cause of death. Her limited history in criminal investigations, coupled with an imagination that could take her anywhere, was the forensics examiner's promise to deliver answers on that hypothesis of how the guy died. Without an official cause of death her case had exposed procedural problems right from the start.

She kept her fingers crossed that the city office complex where she needed to be was on land that was high enough, unaffected by the flood's destructive influence. If not, the information needed to be written on the backs of goldfish—or else it would be washed away.

Pulling into the parking lot, she saw an overabundance of available parking spaces. That was the result of city workers who had the common sense to seize the opportunity not to punch-in for work that day.

Morty's car wasn't in the lot, but that didn't mean that he wasn't there. It was common understanding that he took the bus to work on Saturdays, so his wife couldn't get a direct bead on his whereabouts when he left his office earlier than his timecard said he had.

The elevator ride to the third floor gave her ample time to go over in her head what she needed from him. After slightly jamming, the doors slid open, and she turned right. The target office was at the end of a hall that had no one in it. Rikki had heard about the *"Don't* get caught roaming the halls" rule in that building, figuring that was the reason why it was so empty. That M.O. was contrary to her precinct. There, if you wanted to find a fellow cop, all you had to do was look in the hall.

Seeing anything through the frosted glass was impossible, but she had the correct office after seeing the MORTY'S lettering that was scribed on the door.

"Don't just stand there. I'm a busy man," Morty said from the other side of the door. "Come in."

There was far less trepidation than whenever she came to Tony's door. In ways similar to how Tony wished that he could be calm at work, Morty sat at one of two examination tables with a girly magazine opened to the centerfold. The sight of which had Rikki thinking that she'd stumbled into the men's room at the local bus terminal—as opposed to a professional forensics evaluation office.

"I was just about to give up waitin' on you," he said, seeing her out of breath.

"Why so winded?"

She caught her breath, "I ran the stairs."

"You should've taken the elevator. It's the only thing working right around here."

He sufficiently salivated over the plentitude of photographically touched-up nudes. Then in one of those huffs that only the pampered sound out, he closed the latest copy of Filth Illustrated, placing it within easy arm's reach.

She looked around the area, which wasn't nearly as sterile as she would have had it if she worked there. She swept her index finger along the island marble countertop, rubbing it against her thumb to grind away the grime.

Morty hurried to say, "I gave the cleaning lady a few years off."

She thought there must be something in the genes of some people to make them such slobs.

There was a distinguished crack in his lower back when he stood. The sharp pain reduced the size of his magazine watching hard-on. He walked to the various scientific instruments that were frequently in use with major medical related problem solving, as opposed to the dilemma of how to get in bed with some of the shapely beauties he had just lusted after in between the shiny pages of that monthly edition.

She unsnapped her purse to take out a sandwich bag that she brought from home.

"I got this driver's license from the guy who fell into Conchas Lake."

He sucked his teeth, opening the side of his mouth, "The whole town's buzzin' over it."

He looked at it as though it was essential to translating the Lindbergh kidnapping.

"This ain't really my thing." He squinted, thinking how he left his reading glasses for important looking at home. "Mine is human anatomy crap."

"Fat Tony dumped this case on me. I'm confronted by a series of depressing dead-ends, trying to discover who the bastard is I found in the lake."

"The scuttlebutt's saying the guy bought-it as the result of some kind of a mistake."

"It wasn't one of those things that just befalls decent people," she injected. "If it were—and it wasn't—it didn't happen to a law abiding citizen."

She watched as he fingered open the plastic bag, pulling out a plastic ID sliver.

"I need a check run on this license. Prints, the whole bit."

"Come back in the morning. They'll be ready then."

"What's wrong with now?" she objected.

"Because now's not tomorrow," he explained through a straightforward short answer that had get out while I'm in the mood written all over it.

She sensed that he had an end of the week want to leave, but he wanted her to stay a bit longer.

Rikki stepped it up. "It's not that you got something better to do."

He glanced over to where he had put the reprints of the sex starlets, whom he wanted to help spruce-up his pathetic, middle age.

Rikki's feminine cunning was in high gear. "Pleeease, Morty?"

"I can always resist a pretty face," he said with artificially mustered manly strength. "But never yours." Like air leaving a set of used tires, there went his ability to defy her.

In the building across the courtyard was an overweight cat's throaty whining.

"Damn cat's gonna give me a bigger migraine than I already got. These walls are as thin as my bank balance…A person's only as good as his next door neighbor."

In the hours that followed, she watched him go over the license, processing it through the state of the art computer database that contained the identities of hundreds of thousands of persons who were logged-in over the years. She knew if anyone could make sense of it, Morty could.

She skimmed through a thousand times read National Geographic copy. "This isn't a bad magazine when a person's sitting around with nothing to do."

"A consensus shared by people coming in here to disturb me...Present company suspected."

"This gives us a chance to bond."

He stopped for an instant, "You don't even know what bonding means," watching her fumble through the pages.

"You're right," she opened-up. "But it sure sounded good."

He continued working, being ever-so-careful, calling to her. "Once the prints'r lifted from the subject surface, they're put in the computer for comparison."

"How long before I get my results?"

"Swifter than in the old days."

It wasn't more than an hour later, when he had what looked like promising results.

"I got one usable print." Morty adjusted the focus, steadying his proficient point of attentiveness on the license. "It's smudged, but usable," he said.

"A full read?"

He nodded. "Keep your applause to a polite minimum. It's nothing that any genius couldn't do under pressure."

"You do good work."

"I'm also good at my job," he sexually had to add.

She walked nearer to the instrument that he was using, giving him a man to woman sensation that he didn't have with her when she was on the other side of the room. Using the proper magnification, she was better able to see the full scope of the fingerprint's usable quality.

"There's enough of the index finger for my machine to grab onto," he was proud to say.

She bent to get a better look. He looked down what scarce cleavage her blouse offered, not wanting to draw attention to the fact that he was doing it. He was about to add a crude, sexual comment. The vibrations of desire that he gave-off bothered her. She understood, but what she knew best was that she needed him more than he needed her. That kept Rikki from walking out in a huff.

"We're on company time. And Fatso wouldn't appreciate you coming-on to everything in a skirt who walks through that door."

"You're wearing pants."

"And you wish I wasn't," she knew.

"Adjust this ring," he reached in front of her, to better align her sight into the microscope to best appreciate the image.

Morty knew that he had no chance with her, but it was certainly worth his while to flirt. He watched her arrange the items from the edge of the counter, place them in her purse, and proceed to the exit door.

"When'r you coming back?" he small-talked, anticipating the answer.

"When I need you." With that the door opened. She strolled through, closing it firmly behind her.

He wasn't disappointed. Every officer on the force—except Erik—swore that getting into her little No Parking Zone was an impossibility. But Morty liked trying. There was something about the thrill of the chase.

Rikki was back in the Crown Vic, firing up the sometimes hard to start ignition, sputtering down the boulevard, wondering what was ahead on the road of how did it happen and why?

Disturbing her most wasn't so much where the missing gems were, but how immoral it was to want her father liquidated?

THE DEBT
◆

Minutes later, it happened. Rikki's telephone made its electronic announcement. First, she checked the caller ID to make sure that it wasn't Tony.

"Yeah," replaced her usual level of introductory courtesy, feeling that she should have left it unanswered.

"When do I get my fuckin' money!?"

Her instincts were right.

It was a rough, man's voice. It wasn't Tony. It was the Collector.

"I know I'm late with it."

"Knowin' it don't feed this bulldog," he grumbled. He wasn't shouting, but the rock breaking punishment that his tone offered sure made it feel like he was.

"I've been making the payments. What more do you want?"

"What I want!" he thought to control his volume. After all, he was yelling at a cop. A sense of reserve had to come to the forefront. "Baby girl"—

Why do hoodlums always call women "Baby-girl"?

"You're barely keepin' up with the interest. And that's not considerin' the principal that's risin' every week."

This was a relative debt that was "Jacked" up. The end result being that she had to bear the brunt of someone else who was in over his head. How could she control Jack?

"I get paid this week."

"Then what?" the relentless Collector demanded, increasingly unperturbed as to whom he was badgering. Then he thought to lend an aura of compromise.

When it came to bookmakers, consideration was not in their limited economy of word usage.

"Two weeks from then, I get paid again. I'll be able to cover more of the principal."

It was Rikki whose patience grew short. After all, it was her job to shoot people. "The payment's coming. Now get off my tit!" She jammed her thumb on the END button on the phone.

From behind the steering wheel of his new Cadillac, the Collector stared, perplexed as to what problems he would incur if he had to get more persuasive with a member of Albuquerque's finest. Then his phone rang with a different debtor, with a new and improved lame excuse as to why his payment was late.

Back at Rikki's family's home…

She opened a letter that had no return address. Inside were a series of photographs of people at the company picnic out at Conchas Lake that day. Figuring that Lens finally got around to sending them to her, she slid it to the end of the kitchen table.

She was becoming impressed with the improbable idea that Jack could be the one who had been hitting the jewelry places. Anger is difficult to bring under control especially when it involves family.

Jack's more trouble than he's worth.

Later, Rikki called out for a pizza delivery. She was told that they weren't delivering until further notice since they hadn't found a replacement driver.

It was late into the night by the time Rikki was back behind her home computer monitor. She looked to see how Bubba's escape was performed. She saved the information on a special external drive that required a fingerprint scan to gain access. Suddenly, on her monitor came a sinister message:

I haven't forgotten about you. Bubba.

THE GEMS
◆

The sparkling wonders rested comfortably in an unexpected hiding place.

THE IDENTITY

◆

Tony had put out an all-points bulletin on the department's Crown Victoria that was issued to Rikki. They searched for her all right. It was only a matter of time before someone spotted that car behind the bus station where she left it yesterday.

Out on the horizon the late day sun gave a sad, parting, glow. It was a sorrowful capping off to a bunch of days that were best forgotten by everyone except Rikki, Bubba, and whoever had the gems.

Rikki snuggled behind the steering wheel of an off-colored subcompact. She felt reasonably assured—if that was possible—that no one would be looking for the car that she was in. Her superiors were clueless about it, because it was registered to her niece, a distant relative, who had made it a habit of always asking for favors. Strangely, when it became Rikki's turn for consideration, she came through. The problem was being spotted in it.

A duck and her straggling ducklings waddled past. She watched them with an air of motherliness, reigniting an on and off thought of what it would be like to have had children. Until she had a stable relationship to support that idea, kids had to wait. If she never recovered the gems, freedom would be in line behind having kids. She just hoped that her time would come before her first governmental old-age check, or parole, rolled in. After the ducks were safely secluded in thriving underbrush, she made a daring call.

"Hello," Erik answered, on a cell phone that surprisingly worked, given the battery was well beyond low.

"It's me."

"Where'ya been?"

"Laying low," she excused.

"You probably don't need to be. Fatso's out of state on one of those official conferences."

She gave a mentally exhausted, "Whew." She was free and that's all that mattered.

"Before he left, though, he put out a full alert on your car."

"Figured that."

"You could always turn yourself in." He figured that to be a long-shot.

"There's a thought…But you could've thought of something else."

"One thing."

"Drop it."

"I'm going over to Angles. Wanna come?"

"Appear in public with an all points on me? Ideas that intelligent can wait."

"I said the lookout is on the car, not you."

Tucked away in her thoughts was Heather's voice, "Never drink with people you work with. When they get loaded, they'll say things that will hurt your feelings, under the half-cocked pretense that they were drunk when they said it. Then they'll repeat everything you say to the boss at work the next day."

She staved Erik off, in favor of going home to get sloshed by herself.

"I haven't been sleeping," she replied.

"Fatigue guarantees a cop big problems on the job. A lack of concentration can be costly."

"You're sounding more like Tony every day."

"After the Mayor gets wind of my brilliance, my future in this town will be unlimited," he said.

"That's only if you're monthly cash contribution to his re-election bid is on time."

He adjusted his collar with vertical, professional, desires and pride.

"If anything happens to Fatso, you could be looking at the next chief in this town."

"Dread the thought," she moaned, that the office backstabbing and cutthroat practices will be the bridge he uses. The Albuquerque police force was no different than any other.

"How'd it go with Morty?" he pried.

"I ran the finished print that he lifted from the license," she surrendered.

"I'm listening."

"You needn't be. I came up empty."

"Did you do a complete check?" he asked.

"Thought I did." She hated being told to do something that she had already thought of. If she missed anything, however, this was the time to hear it.

"Never stop at the criminal criteria. Do a legal records check," he notified.

"Legal?"

"There are complete records of each person who ever applied for a state, or federal, job as far back as you need to look."

Rikki wasn't the type to be outwardly appreciative of someone else's ideas, but he knew that she was thankful.

With that she had a brightened path to search for the identity of the man in the lake.

THE EXPLANATION

◆

By late morning Rikki was hard at work, barely blinking, looking at her home monitor. Her racing thoughts could be heard for miles.

Hours later, she scored with the revised data search. Her intensity strengthened, gazing as though she had just won the lottery, she was bursting with the satisfaction that only a pain-in-the-ass fact-finder could have. There was one set of fingerprints that crosschecked to reveal a match. There it was: A photo to line up with the fingerprint.

She looked closely at the man's face that unveiled on the laptop screen, overwhelmed with a resounding sense of surprise.

"It's him," she gasped upon discovery.

He once worked at the Department of Corrections, before transferring to the police department. During those years, she'd seen him portrayed several times as the pinnacle police officer, who he was repeatedly decorated for performance that was "above and beyond the call of duty". She wasn't a cop then, but awareness of the man's heroics was interwoven in the community loop of common knowledge about those types of accomplishments. Somebody had to be from another galaxy not to have heard of Mark Rhett.

She read on to see how the once upstanding police officer had taken a drastic wrong turn. That cop's boat of patriotism and loyalty to duty had run aground in the shallow, slimy, waters of legal and social disfavor. This was a colossal nightmare for the public image of the police department.

She continued to read how crime had displaced his once heightened honor. She changed the screen as fast as she could mentally digest it. The distasteful descriptions of a cop gone bad sank right along with everyone's reshaped opinions of him. She was repulsed by every descriptive New Times Roman letter on the screen.

There were two roads of theory about him that had awkwardly intersected, and neither of them was pleasing to the law-abiding mind.

First, there was the initial perception of a young recruit who was held in upper echelon esteem by his peers. He was a man who had once shown great promise and skill at policing, having accumulated numerous citations for both valor and a steadiness under pressure.

Somehow, his life began to slide. There was his increased poor attendance on the job from heavy drinking, drugs, and carousing the night before. Next, were the persistently plentiful reports of his use of excessive force that surfaced from each arrest. Then came the repeated accusations which ultimately led to convictions. How could it now read this badly? Nothing goes downhill faster than a thoroughbred. Then he was gone.

She put her beliefs aside, conflicting thoughts of what society thought of as improper behavior. Initially, it wasn't personal. The more she hated him, the more he reminded her of herself.

Rikki knew that even in the best of situations people can go bad. She had Jack in the front of her mind as a constant reminder.

Much later, she mustered the courage to call Tony at his sure-fire contact number that he left behind. It was one of those eyes only advances, only for those who needed to know. It was a top secret way to reach him should it be a calamitous emergency.

Tony answered on the first ring. Somehow, he knew that it was her calling. "The rope I ordered just about fits that slender neck of yours."

She was too sheepish to even whisper against him.

"I'm plans as we speak to deploy a SWAT team after you with specific orders to ream those diamonds out of your pretty, used to be a good cop, ass."

Mentally, she'd jumped the track, unable to explain missing gems that were just that—missing. Instead she shifted, "I ran the cross-check on the print taken from the jumper's driver's license."

Tony was riveted to whatever she was about to say. He grumbled, trying to control his temper until after she was finished talking. Public floggings don't really have a timetable.

Rikki delivered news that was best served with a warning label. "He was one of us."

Highly unsettled, he tightly clasped the receiver—not wanting to hear more. "Who was one of us?"

"Mark Rhett."

His face twitched over having heard that name again, and what it brought to mind. "Can't be," he shluffed it off.

"It is," unable to accept no as his reply.

"There's only one problem with your theory." He wiped his knuckles across his jaw.

"What?" She knew that he was about to split hairs, anything to burst her bubble of exploratory achievement.

"Mark Rhett's dead," he supplied. "He was killed in the line of duty years ago…I was there."

She was silent. She had to be.

"We were heading-up a drug stakeout at a warehouse near the University's basketball arena. To make a complicated story short, the suspects made us for cops and started shooting. They ran inside the warehouse. My squad split up, trying to encircle the bad guys. As usual, Mark had to be the hero. Half-cocked, he ran inside the warehouse alone. A few minutes later, we all heard him scream. Then the building exploded."

WHO WAS MARK RHETT?

◆

Could he really be a ghost?

The scoundrels theme of It's Almost Dark Enough To Begin Mugging People Hour was fast approaching, while Rikki sat on the park bench thinking to herself.

Official records indicated that Mark Rhett's remains were never officially identified.

Then it hit her that Morty headed the Forensics Department back then.

Why didn't Erik ever say anything about it to me?

She redialed her phone. Tony picked up.

"Da broad's got guts. I'll give her that," he mumbled before speaking.

"Yeah?" He was less than thrilled to hear from her at all—let alone so quickly.

"Who is Steven Stein?"

"He and Rhett went way back together from their days at Corrections. Why?" The manner in which he said "Why?" was enough to explain that he didn't want to hear her side of it.

"I need to speak to him."

"You can't. He's retiring soon. Everyone who counts wants the party to come-off without a hitch. Then the rummy can wash out of the system with his pension and be out of everyone's hair." His tone firmed mightily. "Hence, you're not going anywhere near him."

Typical Rikki, she wasn't finished. "I only need—"

"Listen to me, Miss is already in enough trouble. Stein's got connections up the yalu. He's protected by the Prince of Darkness. You're staying far away from him. Got it?"

She was again silent, and it killed her to be that way.

He gave in to ask, "What do you need him for?"

"To talk about Rhett."

"I told you, Rhett's dead. Whatever file there was on him has long since been officially closed."

"But—"

"But, nothing." He put in the finale'.

"How does any of what you just said have any bearing my investigation? I need answers."

Tony was sounding more adversarial, leaving Rikki wondering whose side he was on. "Christ, Luckett. The man nearly went mental after seeing Rhett get blown to bits that night. All these years later, you want to dig up a ton of old shit? Give it a fuckin' rest!"

Now he's saying that Steven was with Mark.

She wasn't without sufficient investigative resiliency. "Where's Stein living?"

"Is there an echo in this goddamn line? Wise up. The man you fished out of the lake ain't Rhett."

"Then how'd Rhett's prints get on the license. And why can't the coroner identify the jumper?"

That thought threw Tony.

"Who said he wasn't identified?"

"Morty told me that he can't ID the body because there are no usable fingerprints," she said.

"Everybody's got fingerprints."

"Not my guy. His were deliberately burned off."

"Live up to the salary the tax payers are doling your way, and find out who the real jumper is. Was. What-da fuck ever the situation is." Flustered, he fuddled for the right word, switching hands with the phone before hanging up.

Her attention returned to the work in front of her. Her mind went in circles, always returning to the rogue cop, who Tony was so certain was gone long before that historic night at Conchas Lake.

She cracked her toes. Something she always did when nervousness took over. It was shaping up to be a day of twists and turns. There was one more thing: The address on the driver's license continued to haunt her.

THE HUNCH
◆

Tony was obviously lying about the events that surrounded the stakeout outside that warehouse near the basketball arena.

What really happened? There was something in the manner in which Tony became emphatic about the way Rhett supposedly died.

Rikki, flipped the jumper's driver's license around and around in her moist palm, looking at it for the thousandth time in the millionth different way. At that instant, she was glad that she never turned it in to the evidence locker at the precinct.

There was energy that poured from inside its laminated finish, announcing answers in a language that she couldn't understand. That's when it started mysteriously burning against her flesh.

THE ADDRESS

◆

It was 1515 Cloverdale Road.

Few in their right mind wanted to live there—most notably the people who already did.

The neighborhood had become the living poster example of how a once nice area had ventured down the path of neglect and disrepair. Its residents had multilevel interests in alcohol and amoral behavior. The moral and physical decay was irreparable.

There were empty storefronts and low-rise apartment buildings that the city's derelicts had come to refer to as Paradise Cove. Ruffian mobiles, with the large, over-priced rims, occupied parking spaces just large enough for them to fit in. Those cars just sat at the curb, never going anywhere but around the block, occupied by thugs; to be admired by thug wannabees and their unemployed entourage.

Rikki rechecked the address on the license against the many dilapidated row houses on that block, finally locating one in particular. It was superficially different from those on its flank. A little better maintained—though not enough to notice without a socioeconomic microscope.

Any of that thug element would immediately spot someone who wasn't from there, so Rikki eased farther down the street and around the corner to park the subcompact.

The walk reminded Rikki of her early years on the police force, when she did so clutching her only reliable friends; a hardwood baton, and a thirty-eight strapped to her ankle. Though she survived neighborhoods nearly as bad as this one, this jaunt was still less than delightful; in fact, it was downright depressing. Who wants to be reminded of their past?

When she got out of the car, her watchful eyes scanned all around. For good measure, she pretended to tie her shoe, checking to make certain her Smith & Wesson was in place. It was, and that gave her enhanced confidence to resume walking toward 1515.

She was glad to be in plain clothes. If an officer wanted any answers at all, dressing in plain clothes was the only way. Wearing a uniform in this neighborhood was the equivalent to shouting into a loud speaker for everyone to run like hell.

After stepping over assorted throwaways and smelly garbage that decorated the uneven sidewalk, Rikki trampled the few blades of starving grass that could loosely be referred to as a front lawn.

She reached the front porch, where the building's drainpipes were dislodged at the gutter spouts, producing mold and mildew that hung near a well constructed spider's web.

The steps were rotting planks that termites used as their daily appetizer. They were so fat from it that the insect version of Jenny Craig had to be called in. After leaving the highest level of sagging boards she took another watchful step, routing her focus to anyone inside who might help.

There was a crooked, four button, doorbells plate beside the door; none of the names even closely rivaling in pronunciation to the name on the suspect license that was tucked deep in her front pocket. She pressed the upper bell first, proceeding to the lower ones next. Finally, she gave up and knocked hard at the lower doors. There was no answer from either of them.

Unexpectedly, soiled lace curtains ruffled inside the first floor apartment. That window was positioned diagonally; in such a way that whoever was inside could see out without the visitor discerning that they were being watched. When no one came to open the door to offer an 'Is there anything I can do for you?' advance, Rikki assumed that it was a bad time to have made a tenement call. Or, the place was filled with the lazy, who weren't about to rise from their moth-eaten couch to see who was there.

Feeling propitious in this neighborhood was as common as prosperity, but she did her best to remain upright atop the trash pile of hope; that someone might answer the door in the absence of an official police warrant.

Then something happened. She heard shuffling footsteps on the other side of the door before it opened.

The person standing there was a disheveled woman, who looked much older than she really was. She was another female casualty who had overdosed on too much reality. Within that depressing exterior, her physical shell spoke of being the uncrowned queen of inner city sorrow.

If she ever had good years, she couldn't remember when. Her appearance mirrored physical fatigue that could only be matched with mental exhaustion. By conservative estimates she had to be nearly a hundred pounds overweight; with sloppiness being the least of her concerns. Caught in the entanglement of repugnance and despair, the edges of her mouth had formed a permanent downturn, from the bitter residue that the next day wasn't going to be brighter.

"Yeah?" she asked, knowing that Rikki was probably a lost member of the Census Bureau, a white liberal who promised bountiful urban renewal assistance that would never materialize, serving as bragging fodder at the many political get-togethers that sprung up throughout the city during pre-election time. Or, she figured Rikki to be a research assistant who was going to turn in her paper on inner city interactions; to later receive an appropriate B+ by a falsely sympathetic professor.

The woman's fingernails had been nervously gnawed by teeth that hadn't been brushed since she ran out of toothpaste. It was anyone's guess as to when that was. There was nothing low-key about the jagged knife that she held.

Rikki barely flinched, looking at the rusted, serrated, edges. "Why the hardware? I could be a friend."

"You're not one of 'm."

"How do you know?"

"My friends want to kill me. So they wouldn't knock." The smell of liquor poured from the woman's chapped lips, battering Rikki like a right hook from the heavyweight champ.

The older woman's distrust rushed to the forefront of obviousness. "Before I take a step back and slam the door in yo' face, you gonna say who you are?"

"Detective Luckett, Albuquerque Police."

Rikki expected to be on the receiving end of this neighborhood's unwelcome wagon. It was the usual get-away-from-me standoffishness that was reserved for anyone in a position to flex authority. In neighborhoods like this anything other than congeniality was expected.

"Cops ain't pretty." The woman was in denial over what Rikki claimed to be.

"Want me to apologize?" Rikki was tired of hearing that same comment from different people. Still, it was absorbed as a compliment.

The woman's jealousy was apparent, "It won't help…It's a little early to be going door to door collecting for the policeman's ball. Not that I'd be interested if you wuz. I ain't the dancer I used to be."

She coughed a smoker's cough, spitting brownish saliva beside Rikki's shoes.

"This's a setup." She attempted to further explain her confusion.

Emotionally sidestepping that comment, hoping to do the same by the phlegm. Then she went into her side jacket pocket to produce her badge. "I'm looking for someone."

"Honey, we all are." She strained to summon information about whom that missing person in her life was. She struggled to focus on the face that was laminated on the driver's license that Rikki flashed.

"Your name, Ma'am?" Rikki led off.

"Molly," she grudgingly answered.

"Well, Molly." Rikki used the name as though it was one of several possible aliases that the old woman would've offered-up in a pinch. "May I come in and ask you a few questions?"

Molly wanted to say no. Given that all of her preceding calls to the city's housing authority had been ignored, this was the first city employee who had come within an arm's reach to possibly look into any of her complaints.

She thought that there was an outside chance that her building issues would be heard: the roaming gangs of bandana wearing roaches, the inadequate electricity that barely stayed on long enough for Seinfeld re-runs to roll through to the first commercial, no hot water most of the time, too much cold water damn-near all of the time, and every other inconvenience that a part-time paying tenant could have—and never wish for. Heck, there was a chance Rikki might pass-on Molly's concerns. Maybe this is my day after all, Molly convinced herself.

Rikki saw indecision bounce back and forth in the woman's sagging brown eyes that had seen more than their fair share of tears.

"Whatever you want, keep it short." she said, moving aside to allow Rikki to enter.

Rikki took an energized step forward, into a living room which was obviously mislabeled. The room was for anything but living. It was littered with decaying mold that covered half a sandwich, and a crumbled milk carton that was so old that there was a picture of the kidnapped Lindbergh child on it.

The first thing Rikki noticed was that Molly's antiquated computer was turned off. That was a clear indicator that she had something to hide. Computer people never have it off, unless they're shielding something from a guest. Without the power to effect an arrest, Rikki had to generate even-handed questioning.

Rikki wasn't crazy about sitting, fearing she'd catch some kind of incurable germ that lurked.

"I'm looking for a man named Mark Rhett," Rikki said.

"Ok," she replied flatly, with a who cares tone, wiping her weary face free of strands of frizzy, matted, hair that hadn't had a proper washing, or a required fumigation.

"Does he live in this building?" Rikki further pursued.

"Wouldn't know."

"Have you seen him?"

"Officer, since I ain't heard of'm, I'd be hard-pressed to have seen'm." There was the scent of gotcha in the way she said "Officer."

"Don't make me tell you again, it's Detective," Rikki retaliated with the spear of clarity.

Rikki had enough absorption of the disgruntled woman's grief; to where a little, old fashioned, police brutality wouldn't hurt. Instead, she took out her writing pad.

"Just answer the question."

Molly did, but with something out of deep left field. "You're wanting me to freshin'-up to you with answers like we wuz sisters, ain't helping my wallet."

"Try going to the bank," Rikki injected, having not sufficiently calmed.

"What'd the person you're looking for do?" Molly thought of what it could be, and how any of it lead Rikki to her.

"That's police business." Rikki offered her brand of derision.

"My welfare check's late. If you helped me, I might be able to do somethin' for you."

Rikki knew that the woman standing a few feet from her was filled with contempt, living in a neighborhood where the fraternal order was to be a hating charter member. She wasn't about to alarm Molly into thinking that this was a slight-of-hand raid on her privacy. So smooth was all that was left.

"Tell me about your neighbors. Anything peculiar about the people living around you that doesn't seem right?"

"What ain't right is," she mumbled. "Me being forced to live with the scumbags on this block. To answer your question, livin' in this neighborhood automatically makes a person "not right."

"How so?" Rikki closed the pad.

"When you go outside, take a good look around. Would you live here?"

Rikki was determined to pump up Molly's opinion of the apartment—if it meant lying to do it. "It beats being homeless."

"Not by much." Molly shifted to anything that would add a positive to the one-sided conversation, motioning to a gray, porcelain, lamp. "I love that lamp. Been with me ever since I moved into this dump—from the last dump I was in. It's all that means anything."

She stroked the lamp's base, bringing back fine memories when her day-to-day wasn't perpetually rolling backwards downhill. Within a few seconds, she moved to light a cigarette.

"Don't smoke."

"What'm I, under arrest?"

Rikki conceded, shaking her head.

"Then I'll do as I please." She inhaled, causing the tip to glow before exhaling, making sure that the smoke floated to Rikki's offended nostrils.

Rikki held her breath until the off-white vapors finally dissipated. "There must be something unusual about some of the people living around here that caught your attention."

Passing through a brain soaked in cheap booze were a variety of fast moving mental snapshots, of various people she had seen coming and going in that residential area over the many years since she first arrived. A large number of forgettable transients it was.

That was Molly's chance to get to the point, and she seized upon the opportunity: "What if I did? See somebody, that is," she teased. "In real dollars and no cents, what's in it for me to tell you?" There was the greedy grinding of her index and middle fingers against a receptive bent thumb; that was the hint for a monetary offering from Rikki's forty grand a year deep pocket income to Molly's empty one.

Rikki had to back off. "Vice is the department with the expense spending privileges. I'm not in the position to—"

"Then I don't know nothin'!" she reneged.

"Want to go downtown and talk about it?" The tone escalated from mild to a—I don't have to pussy-foot around, when I'm with the cops—get tougher approach.

No sooner had she finished her sentence, than Molly grabbed a jacket that hung over a nearby rickety chair, slinging it over her sloped shoulders, turning back to face Rikki. Hunger pangs made Molly's decision decisively easier.

"Why not?" Molly yielded. "Cops probably make a heckova-lot better coffee than I do," motioning to a partially full cup of coffee that had turned blacker than the sky when Sonny was fighting the elements to stay aloft in the chopper with Bubba.

Molly zipped up the jacket, ready to roll out the door. "Let's go. Hell, if I tell-I'm what they want to hear, they just might throw in a doughnut."

When Molly took her can't wait to get something to eat steps back, to retrieve that pack of cigarettes, she didn't see Rikki pretending to have dropped something. Rikki had then seized the opportunity to take something from her pocket.

Rikki, straightened before Molly turned around, needing an opening for continued discussion; especially after Molly proved difficult to intimidate. Rikki knew that the only way to win this war of will was to retreat in order to gain victory later.

"We're not going anywhere. I was bluffing."

"So was I," Molly owned up, removing the jacket, tossing it at the chair where Rikki had stooped. The jacket fell in a clump on the floor. "I never had cop coffee. Only heard about it; what I heard wasn't good; besides, they probably put truth serum in it." She laughed, never having made an attempt to pick up the jacket. She sat in a different chair to attempt some low level of comfort.

Rikki had met her match. What was the point to continue to direct an inquisition that lacked results? She reached into her pocket, withdrawing her business card, handing it to her older adversary.

"Take my card."

The woman accepted it, sliding it between the outside of her thigh and the chair's arm.

"I'd like you to stay, but that would prevent you from leaving," Molly snipped.

Rikki offered one last attempt to calm the situation. "If anything comes to you that might be helpful, give me a call."

Before Molly could think to say it…

"In the mean time, I'll see what I can do about getting you a taste of some informant money."

She immediately thought of what lies would pacify Rikki should said money ever materialize.

Rikki didn't hurry to the door, wanting to find the last minute words that would open Molly up. Tilted against the wall near the front door was an unopened envelope. It was near a jumble of writing instruments that were intended to compose another letter of complaint to whoever in city hall would listen. Normally, that envelope would have meant little to Rikki.

Rikki, however, couldn't take her eyes from the letter's return address. It was from the same insurer that the Albuquerque police subscribed to.

Rhett's last address is here. If the old bag never heard of him, why's there correspondence from the police's insurance company?

THE SQUEALER
◆

Nobody likes them.

Yesterday, Tony's subordinates found Rikki's Crown Vic behind the bus station.
Someone spotted a couple of teenagers trying to break into "What looked like a police car" and called the cops. When the proud blue arrived, one of the degenerates was reported to have had a diamond on him.
Repeatedly, they tried to call Tony to notify him of the find. His phone rang and rang with no answer. The whole department got worried, because that was their sure-fire way of getting in touch with him. Not long after that, one of them thought to send out some kind of search team looking for the fat man. It wasn't until he accidentally answered his cell, that it was learned that he had overslept. Few believed that excuse. Tony wouldn't sleep late if he died the night before.
Tony was quick to assume that the gem was from the batch found at Conchas Lake, and that Rikki had somehow left it in the car. The young man's name was withheld due to his age. In the local press he was cleverly referred to as 'The Delivery Boy'.

It had been nearly two weeks since the jumper was dredged from the lake, and a frustrated Rikki wasn't all that much closer to the solution particulars of the case.
Regarding keeping away from Tony's guys, she had one close call already. It was approaching nine one night; when a rookie noticed that her subcompact's

tail light wasn't working. He slowed his cruiser behind her, got out, and walked to her car. Before he could get to the part about 'May I see your license and registration?' she had somehow changed the conversation to a no questions asked blowjob. Where genuine sexual excitement was concerned, her sensuality was running on empty. He came quickly from her talented touch and a few choice sentences of talking dirty, so her lips never had to make the application. She then asked if she could leave. He said "Okay." And she said, "Okay." Okay? Okay.

After that, going home had become too risky. So she decided to take her niece up on a long standing invitation to come over and house sit while the niece was away on a yearly scholastic sabbatical. Until things calmed down—assuming they ever would—she decided to hideout there.

Past her normal bedtime, Rikki was stretched out on the relative's floor. Most of the interior lights were out. She was lost in thought while looking at Heather's finely crafted, mahogany box. During times of fear and distrust, she found comfort holding it. Opening it, she touched some of the carefully folded letters that were inside. It was the last vestige of her mom before her disappearance.

Heather had been a kind and nurturing mother. Without her, all that was important to Rikki had drained to empty, lacking all that only a caring mother's presence could fill. In spite of it, she had refused to become engrossed with hate for Heather leaving. She read the last paragraph of one of the letters before tucking it safely back inside the box—as if it was a life-saving decree—before closing the lid.

Rikki held out hope that one day she would see her again. When that day would arrive was as much a mystery as to why Heather never attempted to make contact to disclose her whereabouts.

If she were around, Heather would try to ease Rikki's grief by saying how bad things can happen to nice people. Rikki wondered why she was the nice person chosen to endure such unparalleled loneliness since that unblessed dawn when Jack told her that Heather had gone out the night before—just after a pizza was delivered—deciding never to return. That was her deepest foible. How could Heather have left?

Within minutes that resembled hours, Rikki drifted into a light sleep that could've been interrupted by a leaf floating to earth a mile away. That was when Rikki met up with Heather in a dream. There she was trying to tell Rikki something.

The following morning there was an annoying ringing on the floor beside her. The ID on the phone was one that Rikki didn't recognize.

"How'd you get my number?" she said, hoping the caller would hang up, leaving her the chance to recoup that dream, to possibly hear what her mom was about to say.

The caller's voice reminded one of sharpened fingernails scratching the side of a blackboard.

"A certain drug dealer is somebody you'd be interested in."

"You want narcotics. I'm in Homicide. After you call the central precinct, dial extension one-eleven." She prepared to hang up.

"Wait!" the caller bawled.

Rikki obliged but didn't want to. That was when she heard: "The connection to the parachutist rests with the guy I'm telling you about."

"What 'connection' is that?" Rikki asked, feeling that there may be something worthwhile here.

"My guy knew the jumper you found in the lake."

"Your guy's got a name? Rikki listened, and wrote while he talked.

The name that she jotted was Rajaan. Then it got really strange.

THE VISITOR

◆

Drugs have a depressing way of capturing one's heart and soul, yielding correct decision making out of the question.

The narcotic that Molly had finished remained inside her fogged head well past the time that the Panamanian pleasure cloud hung in the interior air.

Smoking usually helped her to calm down, but after Rikki left she was unable to do much beyond pacing the unswept floor. She made Rikki for a typical cop, who was only interested in being helpful when something was in it for her. Molly wanted out from under the weight of her dreadful years, and suddenly leaving New Mexico was looking more like the best initiative that she ever had. That is, until a thunderous knocking at the door changed everything.

She fought not to sit and chill, deciding to move to the diagonally placed front window vantage point to look out.

Parked beneath a Don't Walk sign that hadn't worked since the last president was in the Oval Office, she saw a late model Jag that appeared to have someone still inside. Standing inches away from her door; however, was the sinister shadow of a man whose face she couldn't see.

"Hold yo' horses."

She opened the door. It was the Collector. The heated expression on his almost boyish face did more shouting than he needed to. It went without saying, she wasn't smiling.

"You don't look happy to see me," he said with eyes that never inched away from a woman whose head was sobering up a lot faster than she wanted it to.

"You-da-man round here." She sought to inflate his ego. "Everybody's happy when you come-round."

With domineering precision he stepped inside, allowing the door to rattle against the frame behind him. She drew in sputtering breaths, sure that the worst of all possible futures had just marched past her. But why? She hadn't done anything.

Her unsteady hands demonstrated panic.

"You look surprised."

"Bout what?" she asked. "That only happens when somebody's been doin' somethin' they don't want to get caught doin'." Her lips couldn't enunciate nearly as well as she wanted them to.

The smarter man wasn't taking any chances on emitting a clear vocal tone that might jump through the walls into the adjoining apartment. So he lowered his accented voice. "You were talkin' to that cop bout me," he muffled.

"<u>Naw</u>," was all she announced, having been well schooled not to use his name.

He reached into her chair to take out Rikki's business card. He looked at it like a man on death row hearing that the priest was standing by.

"What's this, junk mail?"

With the snap of his wrist, he flung it into her worried and wrinkled face.

Seeing him holding her card was cause for instant alarm.

"You got it all wrong. I'd never talked to nobody bout you. I swear…What we got between you and me is on the Q.T."

Hers were unbalanced verbal rhythms that were orchestrated by thoughts of impending disasters that she was ill-equipped to handle.

"Whatever you're thinkin' bout me ain't true…I'm tellin' you, I ain't said nothin' to no cop bout nothin'. Specially bout you."

Narrowing the space between them, he pressed his imposing advantage, forcing her back without actually touching her. That's when Molly stopped breathing.

He grabbed her throat, stuffing his fingers in Molly's open mouth. "And I'm the dumbest fuck on two legs."

With his other hand he slapped her face to set his fingers free. Then he swept everything from the table to the floor, breaking the gray, porcelain, lamp into more pieces than she could stand to watch.

"Tell me what da-bitch wanted!"

Molly was stressing faster than the seconds elapsed to tally it. "We didn't talk bout a whole-lot, really."

The 'really' was the finishing touch that further stood to convince him that she was lying.

"She asked me if there'r suspicious people livin' in the neighborhood. Not countin' me, of course." She tried to laugh it off with a falsified grin, realizing that he sought more of an explanation.

"What'd you tell her?"

"I said, everybody in this hell-hole is suspicious. But I didn't mean nothin' bout sayin' nothin' bout suspicious nothin'"…Least of all sayin' nothin' bout you."

He wasn't listening. His eyes were shark attack black, reflecting his sadistic soul. "You're lyin'!"

"Me lie to you, and end the best connection I ever had?"

The bugging device that Rikki had planted behind the leg of the chair in Molly's apartment was working. The transmission was terribly slow, with minimal trouble pouring into the small microphone that remained on the floor where Rikki had fallen asleep.

These recordings weren't going to fly past any judge who knew his, or her, way around New Mexico law statutes. But the tactic was all that Rikki had to work with—if she was cognoscente to hear what was being said.

From miles away, there was an incessant on and off breakup in the transmission that made the Collector's voice difficult to discern. Some people have a knack for memorizing the manner in which a person walks. Others can pick a face out of a crowd, who they haven't seen in many years. Rikki's forte was sounds. She could differentiate one person's verbal inflections from another anywhere.

In spite of the fact that he was deliberately altering his voice, Rikki knew who he was. She listened, aware of his tendencies, concerned that he was becoming increasingly violent.

Lacking a wiretap consent from a judge—it would've helped if she knew one who liked her—Rikki realized that none of what was coming through her earpiece was stand alone evidence.

Molly had hidden information when Rikki paid her a visit. She thought that the Collector's presence might bring out something that might be useful to Rikki's investigation.

It was Molly's suffering that Rikki responded to. But the depths to which Molly's chaos had dwindled was for Rikki to soon discover.

Jamison's directive was clear: <u>All available units, proceed immediately to 1515 Cloverdale Road</u>.

One after the other, noisy squad cars raced to park as close to the front porch as possible. There, a growing group of locals had gathered, hell-bent upon channeling their collective anger toward any members of the establishment who they thought caused the problems within fifteen, fifteen. Judging by the size of the crowd, and the heat that registered in each of their outward dispositions, it was palpable that they had blame on their minds.

"Off the pigs!" One of the hotheads yelled.

It was violent jargon that typically had been reserved for nineteen sixties radicals whenever the police were called in to deal with minorities.

After getting word from Erik that Tony's all points on her had been lifted—after one of the Crown Vic attempted car thieves had proved that he bought the diamond that was found on him—Rikki thought that it was safe to show up at Molly's.

She maintained doubts that a couple of small time hoods could have had a hand in robbing her home. With all that in mind, however, she still parked three blocks away; to ensure that no one would see what she was driving.

Rikki flashed her badge to get through the crowd. She visually sifted through them, unable to penetrate the disgruntled personalities of so many displeased residents to see where the incendiary verbiage emanated.

"Let's get out of here, before she says we had somethin' to do with it," said Rajaan, the taller of the two teens, pulling against the bottom of his Phoenix Suns shorts to make them hang closer to the ground, revealing unsightly boxer shorts. As they walked faster to avoid her, it was too late for Rikki to get anything helpful from them.

Having no authority or legal standing to pursue them, she gave up. She reasoned that the best answers to whatever questions that she might later have probably rested elsewhere—with someone more cooperative. Then she headed to the assemblage of police who stood on the sagging, wooden, front steps.

A slouching officer whose legs felt heavy from all that standing at the front door aided Rikki. It was her badge that he was responding to, and pointed. "In there," he said.

Rikki was forced to one side when a foldout stretcher was hurried through the entrance door, by emergency service city workers whom she hadn't seen in a while.

Rikki knew that few people in this neighborhood would ever call the police. If anything, they'd go out of their way not to dial, unless it was to complain about police brutality. So who made the initial discovery here? Feeling that the answers probably were deeper inside the apartment, Rikki followed the stretcher and the men carrying it.

Molly was in the living room, sitting in what used to be her lounge chair, with a syringe hanging from her tourniquet bound, black-n-blue, left arm. Her eyes were wide open, permanently fixed to the ceiling.

When Rikki saw the defeated woman, her confidence had been minced. It was she who had told Molly that it was ok to open-up. Undoubtedly, it was her coming to Molly that ultimately led to this tragedy.

When will my stupidity end?

The dismal smell of death had saturated the bustling interior air. Meanwhile, Rikki continued to distinguish some items of interest from others. It was a cop's job to make mental comparison of a crime scene, to the way it looked before the crime took place. The differences usually led to a conviction. Then there were the workings of the men who had begun to displace Molly from that chair onto the stretcher.

"Can I get a better look?" Rikki asked.

"Sure," one of them said, stopping short of fully covering Molly with the traditional impersonal sheet.

Rikki looked closer at a being snuffed out. It was hard to imagine her anything but feisty and kicking in defiance. That's what happens when someone dies so quickly after having just seen them alive. The depth of it, the permanence of death, takes time to sink in. It shouldn't have been so difficult for Rikki to absorb. She'd seen people die before. When a person works homicide, murder is commonplace. This time it was different. How could doing her job be the same with knowledge of her guilt?

Something about Molly's stiff body wasn't sequential to the way a simple overdose should look. There was a bruise on her face where the Collector viciously slapped her. As with the case of the parachutist, this was no inadvertent death.

"I'm done," Rikki told the two men, meaning the I'm done part more than they knew.

Rikki pressed forward, but was forced to arrive at the same conclusion. She was finished here. Caput. She was greatly saddened, made to feel incompetent. During her period of lax—when she wasn't paying attention to the events that unfolded between Molly and the Collector—she could've arrived in time to save Molly.

"Excuse us, detective," said one of the paramedics, nudging Rikki to get out of their way.

They wheeled the battered woman out into the hall. Rikki walked through the home, kneeling to touch broken bits of the lamp Molly had loved so dearly. Pent-up wretchedness was refusing to budge from within her.

It's my fault, she repeatedly thought with the helplessness that only a failed protector could have.

Solemn bereavement made the air less breathable, thicker, and difficult to pass through lungs that were supposed to signify genesis.

That was what Rikki had on her mind as she squinted in an attempt to hide from her culpability. She wanted to cry, but her tear ducts were reservoirs, water that hadn't been seen in an Ethiopian decade. Through all of this there was one thing yet to resolve. Where was the listening bug that she planted?

Outside, Rikki saw a white slip of paper on the passenger's seat of the subcompact. She slyly took it without drawing attention to having done so, placing it in her pocket. Once down the sparsely crowded street and out of view, she opened the note.

Call me, it read plainly.

The number was so feebly written that it was a strain to decipher the final digit. She took out her cell. After a few rings a male answered.

"Want to hear who did Molly?"

Her impatience mounted.

"You're saying she was murdered?"

"Yep." Suddenly, he sounded more his young age. "I was with the killer."

THE SQUEALER (con't)

◆

Rikki wanted to meet with him just to smash his skull.

She couldn't see the youth wipe his face. He wanted nothing more than to protect his sinking position.

"That was when he told me to stay in the jag and watch-out for the cops." Then his tone got huffy and defensive. "I never wanted her to buy a guest pass to the undertaker. Before he went inside da-crib, he said he was just going to talk to her."

He sounded slightly more articulate than most street toughs whom she had spoken to in the past.

"Why tell me?"

"I'm out on parole. And I ain't in the mood to get busted-back for no bullshit crime I didn't do."

She listened with split thoughts: He was no different than any other jackass who wanted to be the next Al Capone; with simultaneous beliefs that there was something different about this kid.

She sought to best sort out the details, agreeing with him with the usual 'uh huh' inflections, to make him feel more at ease about squealing.

"Seems like, the Molly thing went-down a lot harder than you were promised. That makes you a stooge."

He was in complete agreement, seeking a way out.

"You don't want to take the fall."

Her plan had taken root and it seemed to be working.

On the other end of the line, he was loosening up. From side to side, he raked over the immediate landscape, having realized that the great outdoors was an improved grade over anything that the death penalty offered.

She held her breath that he would provide improved details that would secure an arrest now and conviction later.

"What're you, looking to even the score against the scum who lied to you?

"You got it," he sent back, seeking anything but a confrontation.

She wanted to reprimand him as to the proper way to address a person in her hard fought position, but held back from that tact, unwilling to frighten him away—worse, into silence. She transferred the receiver from an ear that had grown sore.

"Where do we meet?"

"What makes you think I want a face to face?"

"If I were in your shoes, I'd be down for anything that would keep me and a lethal injection from being up close and personal. But—" She verbally stepped back. "I can see you're not interested. Bye bye."

"Hold it!" He collected himself, anxious about his phone card minutes that were about to run out. And that would seal his fate. "Let's talk."

She had him right where she wanted.

"Get it through your head. A, I'm making no promises. B, This dimin' me is boring me shitless. Tell me where your criminal ass's going to meet me."

She listened carefully, writing the location he laid-out, scribbling it in a way that couldn't be deciphered if someone else were to see it. The notion of it ever being seen was remote, but she wasn't about to take any chances.

When the late afternoon hours were needed to last, the unwanted darkness arrived all too quickly, leaving her stellar sense of geographical direction failing.

Where's the damn meeting spot?

After driving in a series of around the neighborhood circles, she somehow ended up at the base of the Andes Mountains.

She felt reasonably confident that the get-together would produce something more than nothing. That was only if the man on the other end of the previous call showed up.

After calming to the fact that revenge upon the informant wasn't going to snare the big cheese, she knew that making a bust wasn't going to do her case any good. Conversely, she sorely needed information that would inject vigor to her hunt for truths about the parachutist, in an investigation that had leads slipping away faster than a greased pig at an Arkansas rodeo.

Rikki's sputtering sub-compact announced itself to anything having ears. A mini plume of smoke was seen coming from its engine, leaving her grateful that it got her that far. She wanted to get the four cylinder looked at, but her most recent payment to the Collector left her short on cash. And if she collared the Collector for murder one, she wouldn't be paying again. There was the unwanted option to charge the auto repairs, but Visa already had hit men looking for her.

After patting her ankle for security, she got out and walked toward a cluster of high hedges. About twenty steps later…

"That's far enough," called her latest mystery man, from the other side of the sturdy green.

At first, she couldn't see his face. Until finally he peeked out from behind the tallest trees. The first thing that she noticed was a black handkerchief tied around his neck, advertising that he belonged to the notorious Boot Hill gang. Instantly, she remembered that their financial mainstay was drugs and extortion.

"Aren't you afraid your colors'll draw attention to you?"

"Never mind Boot Hill. Let's talk about him."

She knew it was him coming through the microphone that she had planted in Molly's place.

"I thought his thing was gambling."

"It was. Since then he moved up to collectin' for the dealers. He keeps twenty percent of every dollar he fetches for them."

Not bad.

"I can't take it anymore. Not after what happened," he said in an 'I'm bailing out' identity.

It's never believable when immorality has a conscious. How atypical.

"You sound different than most street-level types who I come across. It's my guess, you're probably educated somewhere."

He was picking his teeth with a toothpick, a reflection of nervousness that a need for immediate dental sanitation.

"How'd you get mixed up with him?"

"The same way you did," he countered.

That shock was sufficient to make Rikki aware that Rajaan was told things about Jack's gambling.

His shoulders were hunched then down again.

"When I was a freshman at State. I had a job parkin' cars."

Her hand went to her mouth. "If I yawn, it's merely in anticipation."

She saw him float with the short term pride that befits a small-time hood, who tried to make himself out to be more than he really was.

"One night, after a basketball home game against Tech, he came out of the arena to get his car. When I looked at him, his clothes, the way he carried himself, with the expensive jewelry and pretty ladies who dripped from him, I knew right then that I wanted to be like him. He was a man yieldin' influence and power throughout my community."

It hit her that she was at that game, summoning to consciousness that there was a well dressed, gold laced, hooligan type, standing next to her to wait for the lot attendant to come back. That stood out because the college basketball crowd rarely wears much beyond cut-off jeans and their fraternity sweatshirt. She didn't, however, recall ever seeing Rajaan before.

"I'm all goose bumps," she said with authoritative cynicism. "Where'd you and your Shangri-La homicide pal go wrong?"

"He lied to me about his plans for the broad."

Fury filled Rikki when he didn't use Molly's proper name.

He discerned what Rikki felt—through her hate-filled facial expression—and made the needed correction. "At Molly's apartment." Rajaan was street savvy enough to do the right thing, and answer a cop demanding answers.

"Had you known, would it have made a difference? Would you still have gone there with him? Would Molly be alive now?"

He thought for an instant, shrugging his skinny frame. "She was goin' whether, or not, I was there."

Then came the curveball

"I probably would've gone with'm. Not wantin' to see nobody die, but just to stand tall with'm. Learn his ways, for when I got a crew of my own to one day move up and take over from him."

Rikki's sorrow over Molly was being held at bay, by an aggressive defensive posture against everything this punk was about.

"Where does this leave us?" She hinted with hand gestures in an I'm clean, you're filth sort of way.

"He lied to me. Now he's willin' to sit back, chill, while I get the death penalty for somethin' he did. And I want it clear that I had nothin' to do with her murder."

Shifting shadows darkened the features of the immediate landscape, making him less distinguishable.

"You're not spilling all of it to me. Sooner or later, you're going to have to come clean and give me a formal statement. Then when it goes to trial, you'll have to talk-it-up in open court."

Before he could respond…

"If you don't, you're going away with your ass propped up without Vaseline. And that's before they give you the needle."

The fear in his face intensified.

"If you're fortunate. And judging by the situation you already volunteered yourself into, you're anything but that."

He fought to keep his raspy voice lower. "I can't afford to catch another case. With me gone, ain't gonna be nobody to take care of my son."

"You got a kid?"

He nodded with an emotional commitment toward a situation that only he was partially responsible for.

"You should've thought about that before all this went down."

"How could I predict that it would go-down bad?"

Rikki had had enough. "I don't get it with you fuckin' criminals. What'd you think, you could just walk into an innocent woman's home, kill her, and walk out as though you did nothing more than spit on the sidewalk?"

Though she hated cigarettes, she offered him one from a pack that she kept in her purse. It was a spare supply that was reserved for piece of shit suspects and interviewees—anyone she needed information from who might calm down from the nicotine.

One thing that she noticed over the years was that even those who didn't smoke usually took a square and lit up. For some reason, it seemed to calm them, or give them something to do with their itchy fingers.

"By your own admission, you knew that both of you were going to Molly's home." The disbelieving inflection in her voice was obvious. "You also knew of your idol's propensity for violence. Or, did you think he was going over there to gather-round the couch to watch ESPN to get the latest scores from some bet he laid-down earlier?...If you ask me, it sounds like a clear-cut case of first degree...If you help me, I'll protect you. And I'll speak to the prosecutor about cutting you a deal."

He chuckled against his fading will. "Protect me? Like you looked after Molly? Oh, yeah. Great job so far, Detective. You won't mind if I ask you to put a condom over your brainless head and kiss my ass."

The snap kick he got to the groin caused him to crumble in pain. There was no life in his boney legs, and with that he had to remain ground level. She crouched low to get face to contorting face.

"Listen, you murdering piece of left-over dog shit."

He was doubled-over, scratching deep into the ground for traction to stand.

"Now that you're on your knees, you should be the one blowing me." She grabbed his braids, snatching his head back until it sprained his neck. "Tell me what I want and stop fucking me around! Where's the Collector!?"

THE LEAK

◆

When outsiders think of New Mexico, it's the warmth of Arizona that comes to their misguided presumptions. Most days in the fall it is rather cool; barely comfortable enough to sit outdoors in the park.

Rikki's self-defeating thoughts bounced within her cluttered mind like a slap-shot puck in a cheap discount penny arcade, to where she felt a little air might do her good. What she didn't count on was a hacking and sneezing attack that threatened to blow her brains out.

Molly's demise had taken control of Rikki's perceptions about policing, forcing her to question if she had done the right thing—understanding that she hadn't—by not setting up some type of safety net around Molly's home after that initial visit.

Then there was the after-the-fact confession she strong-armed out of Rajaan. She doubted the disclosure that he knew nothing in advance about Molly's killing—given the seedy reputation, and enthusiastic proclivity for violent acts that the Collector had. In any case, the watercourse of information about the case was beginning to take a curious, yet substantial, formation.

Within the realm of possibility was that the case finally seemed solvable.

Erik came upon her and sat at the other end of the splintery park bench. He was properly decked-out in the best thermal wear, a sweater and the whole pre-winter bit, keeping the day's chill at bay.

"You look like you lost your favorite dildo."

"Didn't your mother ever wash your mouth out with soap?" she asked.

"Once. But it didn't do no fuckin' good."

"Even if I lost it—which I didn't—I'm not in need of a substitute." She gave him an arousing grin, looking at his crotch. "Not now, anyway."

Rikki gazed outwardly as he crunched open a paper bag from a popular eating spot, withdrawing two mustard coated hotdogs that were nestled in dual, no longer warm, buns.

He offered one to her, but she declined.

"Jimmy's Eats serves the best dogs in the state."

"If I were a gay man, and saw the way you attacked those hotdogs I'd be afraid to sit near you."

If his cheeks weren't bulging and senses juicy, he'd have spoken to that comment.

She couldn't hold it in anymore. "Don't sugar coat it, you want to hear about the gems."

"Actually, I was waiting for you to volunteer something about them."

"I would if I could. But I can't," she said, wanting to reveal more, but hamstrung to do so.

Her thoughts had gone blank over the inability to get anything right. Her overworked mental hard drive registered T.I.L.T. and there was nothing that she could do to make it any less cluttered.

"You gotta stop torturing yourself about Molly. She knew what she was getting into the day she voluntarily joined the underworld. Snap out of it."

"It's not that easy," she opened up.

This was the hard part. "I gotta tell you, Rik."

She turned toward him, wide open as to what to expect.

"I hear, Fatso's thinking about taking you off the jumper case."

It hit her that he was sliming, underhandedly going to Tony saying that he would be better able to solve it.

"If you steal my case out from under me, I'll—"

"Close your mouth, for once. I'm not the department's policy maker…Face it, what's most important to Tony is getting anybody who can come back to him with answers to his questions. Starting with where are the gems? Then he can lie to his superiors that it was all his idea."

Suspended, she waited. Then he punched out a surprise.

"Didn't you learn nothing about clandestine activity at the police academy?" he asked.

She was lost, preoccupied, about what must've been going through Molly's mind before her death. "Did you say something?" she asked.

He wiped the edges of his mouth, crumbling away the napkin, shoving it all back inside the bag. He was careful as to what verbal precautions to offer.

"Is this conversation off the record?"

She nodded, transfixed that anything he said was part of a professional inquest.

"Your problem is, underneath it all you think you're smarter than everybody else. So what if you skirt the rules. As long as it meets your ends, you're satisfied. Your watchword is manipulation."

"English, please," she requested.

Then he said it.

"When were you going to mention the bug you planted in Molly's apartment?"

Rikki was silent.

"There's one more thing that you might find interesting."

Her expression shouted an unwillingness to hear anything further that he had to say.

"Fatso leaked it to the press that you never turned-in the cash that we found on the jumper."

THE NOTE
♦

Rikki found her way back to the University's basketball arena.

She tried to remember images and faces from the night when Rajaan told her when he first met the Collector. After countless minutes of nothing mentally working, she turned to one side. There she saw a note pinned to a tree.

The handwriting was the same as was on the scribbled message left in her car outside 1515 Cloverdale.

Molly's death was my fault. I can't live with it anymore.

Rikki was filled with confusion. Why would he come right out with such a revelation, when he never said as much during their meeting. Within seconds, her wonderment was clarified in ways that her eyesight was not prepared to accept.

Hanging from a branch of medium height was Rajaan. Laces from his new Nikes were wrapped tightly around his swollen neck. His eyes had bulged to nearly popping out from their sockets. There was a subtle afternoon breeze that pushed him to slowly twist.

It was barely possible, but when her cell rang it managed to interrupt her staggering chain of thought. When she answered it was Thelma was on the other end.

"Slow down," Rikki said. "You're talking too fast."

Her garbled words made enough sense. The extent that it got to Rikki was effortlessly discernable.

"What do you mean, the police came to your house asking about me?"

THE FUNERAL

◆

"I couldn't come up with this many people to be at my funeral, if I plucked names out of a phone book," Rikki said.

In the worst part of the poorest section of the city, near enough to where Molly caught her last breath, there was a steady stream of people saying goodbye to Rajaan. The turnout was inordinately large for a small-time hood who was only good at one thing. Failing.

There were more white people paying final respects to Rajaan than someone in his social circle would normally command. The motorcade was lengthy. The string of nice cars stretched for over a mile, snaking through red lights that were ignored by those in the precession. He would have liked the manner in which he was sent off. The sight of it made Rikki gag.

"He was a popular bastard. I'll give'm that," Erik complained, feeling a cramping in his lower back, accepting the binoculars.

Later, the string of cars stopped in front of a plush church service that exaggerated Rajaan's good points while minimizing the rest. Those who chose to speak recited nice, yet rehearsed, fabrications about him. But heck, that's what funerals are all about.

Didn't anyone realize that they were speaking about a man who was on the wrong side of legality since he was ten? Something about death manages to wipe clean nearly everyone's life slate. Those on the inside at the Albuquerque police department knew that overall Rajaan wasn't even a nice guy to be around from far away.

"We've been squattin' here till my ass hurts like a fag's after his first gang-bang." Erik's discomfort was developing into a major distraction. "Of all the times to leave my pain pills home," he winced.

She took out a camera, and started clicking away, capturing the pallbearers who carried the casket out from the church. She rechecked the amount of space that was left in the compact flash memory card. She made certain that everyone in attendance would be clearly photographed. One can never predict whose face will end up to be important.

"You're sure this is legal?"

"I doubt it," she answered.

Erik saw that Rikki was taken by a disturbing thought.

"The Collector got wind that Rajaan talked to me and snuffed my credible witness."

"He's the kid you promised to protect? Your chase is costing lives. If you turn out to be wrong, you're gonna need to be fitted with a lightening rod."

She turned red with embarrassment. Her frown of self doubt spoke volumes. It was the second time that she extended her powers, and was unable to provide the security blanket that she had promoted.

"Do me a favor," Erik said. "Don't offer to protect me."

For Rikki, that remark hurt. "I promise not to," She meant every word of it.

Erik scratched his head, realizing she couldn't take his humor. "I'm sorry."

"No, you're not." She knew that he was on target.

"Let's get out of here before someone down there looks up and sees us." He demonstrated that her camera use might attract unwanted attention.

They ducked as they stumbled down the rocky embankment away from the church to Erik's unmarked sedan.

THE CLUB
◆

By nightfall, Rikki had an unfulfilled craving to get downright drunk.

She put on a disguise and headed to where the hip-hop crowd waited impatiently outside of the popular out of town nightclub called Angles.

Hundreds of eager young people fidgeted, talking amongst themselves, waiting to get in. Everybody was there; few of them were allowed entry into the on-the-up club, where fun seekers—old and young alike—just had to go.

The wig and coordinated outfit that Rikki wore would leave anyone wondering who she was, as she sat crunched in her sub compact. She needed something to take the uneasiness from her troubled mind while watching the who's who of hopefuls standing outside waiting to be admitted. Those closest to the hand carved, double-doors did so beneath a distinguished, colorfully marked canvas awning, where an over-sized doorman/bouncer stood, powerful hands clasped in front of him, waiting for the slightest inkling of trouble, so he could use said hands to disassemble whatever problem came up. After a dozen minutes, Rikki climbed out and walked inconspicuously to the entrance.

"You got an invitation?" the doorman asked, with enough gold front teeth to show, signaling a self-satisfied smile, proving that he really did put his money where his mouth is.

His shifty, beady, browns slid up and down on her like a rolling pin in search of dough to make smooth. The outfit that Rikki had on was downy enough to make a Hugh Hefner talent scout assume a posture of fascination over her.

The doorman liked what he saw, but that wasn't without the standard, "Lady, this's an invitation only club."

What she needed was something that was guaranteed to alter his nobody's getting past me stance.

She looked away—as though all that waiting had made her hot—to slyly undo the top two buttons on her silk blouse. When she snapped her head around, he was fully appreciative, and compliant with her plan. That sight had him bursting with pleasantries—ahead of anything the swelling crowd that waited uneasily to get in had promised.

All night, some of the young girls, especially the underage ones, tried to coax him with offerings of this and that. He managed not to listen to any instincts that would land him in more statutory trouble than his past failures to pay court-ordered back child support already had. The mere mention of underage girls wasn't something that he was about to tread near.

"If there was something in it for me, I might understand better."

She slipped him her phone number. He took it.

"Sometime, I make exceptions," he said.

She stepped forward when he disconnected the rope barrier. She glided past him, sure that she would see him again before the night was through. There was no telling what that interaction might bring. He certainly wasn't her type; which would've been news to him. If he telephoned her, she could always spring it on him that she was a cop, and he'd better back off.

He returned his attention to the others, those jockeying to enhance their position in a line that wasn't moving nearly as fast as they wanted it to.

On the crowded dance floor, where tight fitting, low cut, tops that revealed everything the wearer wanted. There was an opium cloud hovering above the people, instantly reminding Rikki of the reason why she wore clothes that could easily be washed once she returned home, something that she learned while growing up after hanging around countless smoky bars where Jack worked. Her flaring nostrils brought back the awareness of her past getting high daze. It's not so funny how some senses never leave a person.

Fewer than a hundred seconds later, Rikki found a chair that was, for the most part, comfortable enough to sit on. It was comparable to being harpooned by Erik's billiard stick that he called a penis, with far less pleasurable consequences.

It was then that she spotted a lanky, olive skin, waitress wearing booty pants that more resembled a wide, black elastic band. After seeing Rikki's page, she walked closer.

The scantily clad server asked, "What're you drinking, hun?"

"A double scotch," Rikki said.

The waitress swayed away. There was another beauty walking around the room, taking videos of the crowd. Rikki looked out over the spacious dance floor, searching each face for clues, with improbable expectations that she might see someone of interest. Then it happened.

There he was, a ghost having returned from the dead. Cosmetic surgery had altered his facial appearance greatly from the images that she'd seen. But it was him, all right. There he was, in the flesh. Mark Rhett.

Complete with leather everything, right out of any low budget S & M movie that had an expensive wardrobe budget. He figured that Rikki was looking at him. What was the big deal? All the girls did. That really didn't matter to him. He had no idea who she was.

"Aren't you afraid there might be cops in here?" asked Sharon, the streaky brunet beauty, accompanying him.

"Do I look worried?" he answered, lightly chewing on her lobe, sticking his long tongue deep enough inside, wanting to lick her brain into agreeing with every sexual idea that he had planned for them later.

"You always got everything figured."

She admired his ability to spot trouble coming. If he was relaxed, so was she. Then she pulled his mouth down to her open one, kissing him without restrictions. He gave her all the tongue she could handle during a lengthy mouth to mouth.

The waitress appeared at Rikki's table, placing the water atop the club inscribed coaster.

Walking away, her buttocks nearly popped from her partial bottom covering, treating Rikki to that little extra visual delight that's all part of the cover charge.

From a discrete distance Mark continued transacting more than sexual conversation with various men with whom he came into contact. He was oblivious that Rikki was near. He didn't care about much past making money. His uncle was the architect of the place, so he knew every secret passage in and out of the building in case trouble raced in his direction.

Sharon then whispered something to Mark of a vastly disturbing nature, prompting him to slyly pivot his neatly combed head of hair toward Rikki. That was when he made her for the cop, and wanted no part of staying. Slyly, he moved out of sight.

Not many minutes later, Rikki moved past the coat check room, to a darkened area. There she pushed hard against a stubborn door. Finally, it flung open into an alley behind the club.

Many yards ahead, she saw Mark running past a flat-black Corvette in the direction of a tenement building about seventy yards away.

"Mark!"

In that instant, he stopped to look back at her. Their eyes locked. She took off after him, brushing past the Corvette, noticing a silvery-white ash on its tread, stepping over countless dollar bills that he dropped in his wake; for anyone chasing him to be forced to stop and pick up the money. Mark was smart enough to realize, nobody can pass-up free cash.

"I just want to talk to you!"

She wasn't gaining on him, though managing to maintain visual contact, until he slipped into that building, a structure that used to be the Bashon Morgue. Just then, Mark Rhett was lost.

Many from inside the club came outside to see what all the shouting was about. They were astonished by the money that was lying around. The screams followed from those panic-stricken people in the alley as they scrambled to pick up the bills.

A blast from inside the old morgue followed, propelling glass and bricks at breakneck speed. Shredded paper and limbs were flying.

The evening's show was over. Rikki was face down, unable to move.

THE HOSPITAL
◆

"Can you hear me?" a man's soothing voice petitioned, amidst an environment that was whirling in a kaleidoscope of unfamiliar sights and faintly stimulating sounds.

Someone was shaking her. At least, that told her that she was alive. Barely. None of it was the least bit recognizable. She couldn't be sure how long she was unconscious. Days. Months. Even years. Finally her vision cleared sufficiently to see a man in white standing over her.

"What happened, doc? Have trouble finding a parking space big enough to fit that Bentley of yours?" she complained through the miasma.

His smile added to her painful dilemma.

"You could've taken the day off. I'm fixing to check myself out of—" she strained mightily to get her distorted bearings, her head fell back to the overly tight pillow, "wherever the hell I am."

The confinement of lying in a bed with high walled, metal rail, sides helped her not to fall out. But at least then she'd have expectations to make it to the elevator, and out from this sterile place.

That was when it hit her that she must be in a hospital.

Rolling over, she sighed. "I've got to get back to my case." She barely had energy to say that much.

"That's not the way I see it," the physician said. He held up an X-ray film to the light, pointing to explain to someone with a limited medical background.

"You're ahead of the game to be breathing without a respirator. Or, breathing at all, for that matter."

"The only way I could feel thankful would be if somebody was reading me my last rights."

"Wait till you get my bill." His approach went from medical helper to a parent with kids needing a ride to dance lessons. "I hate working weekends."

She tried to adjust her position, but muscular inability prevented her from doing so more than fractions of an inch. She watched him jot notes on a fold-out pad.

"First off," he instructed, "The pain in your side is from a cracked rib from the bricks that were flying from the blast...In the ensuing mêlée you were trampled by the people trying to get out of that alley."

She still had work to do. A cop is a cop is a cop—often too much of the time.

What protest she wanted to mount was short lived. More important than the pain that she was in was him being correct about the situation.

"This ought to help ease your discomfort," he said, using a bedside manner that left little to complain about.

The length of the needle that pierced her skin was anything but pleasant. When he withdrew it, it hurt all over again. After disposing of the syringe, he took notes on a pad.

"I'm putting you on mandatory sick leave."

"You can't do that."

He closed the pad. "I just did."

Time seemed suspended until...

Rikki's undisturbed stillness, her blackened chasm, was stirred by shuffling around her. Fat Tony was never one who could move without being heard. That was when Tony started coming in and out of focus.

"What happened?"

"You were chasing some guy throwing money in the alley outside Angles when the place blew up." He leaned closer to bring her around. "What were you doing there anyway?"

When it finally hit her that it was Tony standing there, she was suddenly overwhelmed with the need to be silent.

His voice got very sturdy. "Let me tell you this one time." He leaned to her ear, continuing, "You fucked-up everything. My undercovers have been working that club for months, passin' me information about drugs flowing in and out of there. Then Miss Pain-in-the-ass created a scene that left the whole goddamn operation unsecured."

Mark Rhett had become a once promising lead. She learned that he was probably seen in that club before. And nobody said a word about it. She was aware that the police used criminals to do their bidding. But the thought that coworkers were working both sides of the law turned her already restless stomach even more. Again, she was behind square one. Flat on her back without a good leg to stand on.

"Don't think about any of it now," he said, barely able to contain his rocket fueled anger.

"There's nothing to think about. You're telling me, my suspect's gone...I'm left with nothing."

"You're alive."

"Gee, thanks," she quarreled.

"You need plenty of rest."

She tried to move, feeling the soreness throughout every part of her; in a furious race to see which pain impulse would win out in the race to her rattling brain.

"Says who—about the rest?"

"The doc, for openers," he remedied. "He's calling the shots. Right now—not counting me—he's the closest thing you'll ever see to God."

"I don't get it."

His lips almost touched her ear, to give a poignant whisper. "Listen, pretty. If it weren't for the Doc barkin' orders that's keepin' you laid-up here, I'd have your ass spread out on my desk reaming the shit out of you, till I get <u>my goddamn diamonds back</u>! You got that?" He calmed a bit, patting her forehead. "Shut up for once, Rikki, do as you're told."

His smile gave her reasonable assurance that she wasn't going to get fried just yet.

"When the Doc gives you medical clearance, I'll put fishhooks through your nipples and pull those luscious tits off on account of the missing gems."

"Where're you going?" she muttered.

"To round-up anyone who was outside Angles last weekend. Maybe somebody'll tell me what I want to hear."

"I've been here a week?"

"I got to find out more about what they saw."

"Keep me posted," she coughed.

"Will do," he said, fingering the brim of his hat, acknowledging her request before leaving. His frustration toward her about the diamonds made it unlikely that he was going to cool off any time soon.

Rikki was trapped. She no longer had any compassion for those who were deprived, because she had joined their ranks. To add incapacitation to irritation, the mattress was as comfortable as a freshly laid bed of nails.

That was when she noticed traces of a silvery-white ash on the floor where Tony had been standing.

THE ASH
◆

When it came time to evaluate her to be discharged from the hospital, it was difficult for Rikki not to react when the doctor pushed and pulled at her busted rib. If there was a bullet to bite to control the pain, she gladly would have.

It hurt like hell. But if she revealed the degree to which it did, she could've counted on a more lengthy stay in the third floor ward. Instead, she nearly bit a hole in her tongue, saying how the ribs felt "Damn-near like new."

The doctor didn't buy any of it. He concluded that she needed to remain under his watch for at least another week. Hardheaded, she wasn't about to allow common sense to disturb her motives. So, when the night nurses came on duty, out the side door Rikki eased.

Fearing that there might be irrevocable damage to the morale of young spendthrifts who adored Angles Club, the owners decided to reopen it.

The Revenue Department wasn't about to allow the Planning Commission to permanently close down the huge tax base for what the Commission called "Countless building code violations." Morals are just that, but money runs every city.

Calm was quickly restored in the alley near the Bashon Morgue. Everything seemed back to whatever normal was supposed to be. It would've been easy to say how it was all over but for the shouting. However, the riotous screams that awful night were all too eternally vivid for anyone who was there. Even with her hands over both ears, Rikki could still hear them scrambling for their lives.

Far from where Erik waited impatiently in the car, there was a barely noticeable patch of silvery-white ash on the ground that police investigators had missed. It rested partially hidden, beckoning Rikki to see it. When she knelt to finger it, she couldn't imagine what significance it would later have.

THE GIRLFRIEND
---◆---

"I shouldn't have answered when you called me," Erik said.

Miles down the road, he and Rikki stopped at a hilltop, greasy-spoon roadside eatery. There people sat in their cars, waiting for high school age servers to come out on roller skates with piping hot orders. It was a wonder that customers went there at all. From the rise in antacid sales, many wondered how the cook escaped international judgment at Nuremburg.

"If Tony finds out you checked yourself out of the hospital without doctor's orders, he's gonna bury you in an unmarked grave."

"He'll never learn about it," she tried to calm him.

"How's that possible?"

"Cause I won't tell'm…I had a thought."

Erik said, "It's never a good sign when that brain of yours starts working."

"Thinking is a crime?"

"When you're the one doing it," he glowered, turning to her, waiting for the next syllable to trill from her very kissable lips.

"What if…Never mind."

"Don't leave me hanging."

She lightly squeezed his crotch. "Then you'd be unarmed."

He waited for Rikki to return to the previous thought that she nipped.

"What if Rhett's out here somewhere watching us, while we're bustin' our asses chasing the wrong suspect?"

He was sorry to have waited. "Now it's 'we'?…Mark's not coming back from wherever the devil took him."

"You're convinced he's dead?"

"Aren't you?"

"That's just it," she said with a new found enthusiasm. "Maybe we shouldn't have been at that funeral."

Dejected, that this was all going to bounce-back in his face very soon. "Yeah, we should've been at mine." He held his head, thinking of more interesting places he could've been. But no, he had to listen to his penis, and tag-along behind Rikki—who wasn't giving him any loving anyway.

Something about the whole day had him reconnecting to the fact that there was an utter lack of prosecutorial possibilities to go on as the result of this waste-of-time spying. His bachelor eyes wandered to the street below, seeing several parked sports cars. He always wanted one, but could never quite fit their cost into a fifth year cop's income.

"What if Mark was around somewhere, looking to see who came to Rajaan's funeral, to scope out whose on his tail," she explained.

"He'd have to be one slick sonofa—"

Rikki thought. "Had Mark ever been arrested?"

He shook his head. "Investigated, yes. But not formally arrested."

"How many criminals so deeply entangled in the upper levels of crime don't have a rap sheet?"

"Very few," he admitted, not fully able to absorb the depths of Rikki's supposition.

"You've got nothing that conclusively connects Mark to Raheem."

"Rajaan," she corrected.

"What-da-fuck-ever his name is." He strengthened to best pinpoint what he quietly wailed about. "Assumptions don't count when presenting a case to the District Attorney."

"What is it with you?" She wondered why he wasn't sounding more supportive of her position.

"The cuckoo asks what's wrong with me?"

"Why don't you think what I've told you has relevance?"

"It doesn't matter what I think. It's a judge who you have to convince."

She sulked. "I guess, you're right."

"Good guess," he replied with a flatness, suggesting that she should've surmised that.

"No matter how anybody slices it, he's on tape talking to Molly before she was killed."

Erik battled to see how strong her side was. "Killed, schmilled. She was a fiend who OD'd. Until you get the coroner to change what he wrote on his official cause of death, hers was an accidental death. The likes of which happen in this city every week."

From behind came the sound of a high performance car engine nearing. That hot rod sound belonged to a flat black Corvette. It popped the cobblestone parking area, finally stopping next to the passenger's side of Erik's car. Out of the corner of her eye, Rikki saw the driver staring at her in an on and off fashion. The woman in question was very stylish.

"She's not your type," Erik said.

Rikki shunned his comment. "Must you notice everything?" she asked with noticeable, yet manageable, annoyance.

"Have to. I'm with the cops, remember?"

Sometime, I wish I could forget that I was.

A mild bladder area grumbling told him, "I have to use the little boy's room. Back in a flash." Within seconds, he clicked-open the door, slid from under the steering wheel, heading toward the door marked MEN.

The woman in the Vette made sure Erik was out of earshot before quietly asking, "Got a minute?"

Rikki was trying to ignore the woman's good looks, and the monster diamonds on her fingers. Rikki knew that the woman was on to something. Then it hit her.

The woman leaned back, shaking her head Rita Hayworth style.

"I was talking to Mark the night you chased him out into that alley…Then I saw you and—" she motioned behind the wheel where Erik was, "that guy up on the hill watching Rajaan's funeral. I figure, one or both of you are cops."

"We're going someplace with this? Or, is this designed to help my food digest better?"

The woman continued looking straight ahead, not wanting onlookers to see that they were talking to each other.

"I can be of help to you."

"That's nice," Rikki said, uncertain if that was workable.

The dirty blonde sipped. "It's a darn shame to be sitting here talking about funerals."

Rikki repeatedly glanced to the restroom to see if Erik was on his way to the car.

"My partner'll be back any minute. I want to talk with you." She made a point of saying talk with you. And not talk to you. She wanted the verbiage to be two-way. "Where can we make that happen?"

"If I let you come to our house, promise you'll leave behind anything that's mine? I mean, stuff that's got nothing to do with whatever reason you're investigating Mark."

From nowhere this young woman had become the break that Rikki was looking for. "Deal," Rikki agreed, wanting to give an assurance of hocus-pocus, to snap her fingers to make her disappear before Erik returned.

They weren't about to shake hands. There had to be Mark's customers lurking nearby. After all, fast food joints were the hangouts that his brand flocked to.

"Meet me around the corner tomorrow, seven AM," she outlined to Rikki.

"Why so early?"

"Mark worked his business from here. I'm known in these parts…This place doesn't get crowded before ten am. None of his customers will be here at seven."

Rikki couldn't help but say, "There's no need to behave like we're strangers. We've been pretty friendly here."

She spit across the gap between cars, catching Rikki's face flush, sending a vastly different message to anyone who may have been looking or listening.

"Leave me alone!" The woman shouted loud enough for Erik to pick up on upon his return.

Nastily, she tossed a few wrinkled bills out the window to the ground for whenever the server returned, throwing the Vette into reverse, pulling back onto the street, burning the tires through the sparsely crowded business district.

That little—, Rikki thought, remaining in her seat to minimize any attention from watchers.

Rikki's wristwatch swept its second hand past the five in 7:05, and still there was no sight of the woman.

Drowsiness was setting in as she concluded that she'd been outwitted again. This time by a criminal's girlfriend. Hmmm, she thought.

Perhaps, I'm not the detective that I think I am.

If this was where Erik had been duped, it would've been a lot more amusing to Rikki.

Seemingly out of nowhere, the woman quietly approached on foot, opening the door to the subcompact, sitting down in butt first then drawing her legs in, secretively closing the door. Whew, Rikki had survived a night of worry.

Let's go," the woman said, ducking to refute anyone who may have had a clear view of them. Though that was unlikely, she wasn't about to take that chance. In that part of town, detection could be deadly.

Rikki pulled away without drawing attention to the vehicle.

Miles away…

"It's safe," Rikki said. "You can come up for air, whatever your name is." She took another three-sixty look around. "Nobody's around."

"The name's Sharon."

Sharon raised her head above the dashboard, complaining, "Could you drive any slower? I thought I was ridin' with Miss Daisy."

Rikki waited to hear something more meaningful, but absorbed it for the simple laugh value it represented.

Sharon knew that her parting, spitting, shot back at the drive-up eatery had to be explained.

"Sorry about the face…Had to make it look real that we weren't connected."

"Let's hope the rouse stuck," Rikki rubbed her cheek. "I'd hate to have to re-enact it."

Sharon took Rikki's hand, kissing it.

Rikki didn't feel anything special toward the kiss, interpreting it as a goodwill gesture that was bound to ease any possible tension between them.

Sharon reiterated, "You're staying with our agreement that I get to keep my stuff in the house."

She pressed on the gas, careful to stay just below the speed limit.

"Anything else you can add about Mark?"

"Other than underneath it all he was an asshole?"

Rikki lacked confidence that there was more usable information to follow about him. Wanting it and getting it were two vastly different prospects.

"Don't get me wrong, he treated me good. Bought me everything I wanted."

"Why slam his character?" Rikki followed up.

Sharon thought back on the entirety of her often stormy relationship with Mark, with a diamond on her left hand that was the size of any woman's pinky nail. "He treated me like a thing, a possession of his, instead of the real woman that I am." She rolled the ring with her opposite hand. "I'm nobody's 'thing'."

They continued driving, Rikki heard the tale of how Mark approached one of his customers, to switch identities with him.

"At first, he was hesitant to sell his identification papers, figuring that Mark was setting him up for some kind of fall. But fifty thousand dollars later, Sonny went along with it, taking Mark's money as pretty as you please."

"Did you say the man's name was Sonny?"

Rikki was struck by that name, remembering that was the second name of the license that was found on the jumper.

"That's right," Sharon answered casually, not feeling the heaviness of Rikki's question. "Mark checked up on him, to make sure that he didn't have a criminal record. That way, Mark could operate with a clean slate." She thought more about Sonny. "What a strange guy."

"Then he bought a costume disguise from Mark…Mark was big on always changing the way he looked. He used to say, ain't no tellin' who's watching me."

"Strange, huh?"

"It was his fingers. The horrible way they were burned. Mark said he got that way from an accident when Sonny used to drive a gasoline truck for Acme Oil…I didn't think a whole lot of it at the time. Too busy being absorbed in the lifestyle that was my everyday with Mark." She sighed. "I figured Mark knew what he was doing. But later I wondered."

"What about?"

I thought that Mark was arranging up some kind of vanishing act…I never said anything to him about it. He had a strict rule that I couldn't ask him about his trade. But I knew all along that he was planning an exit route in case things got too hot. A dumping ground—to unload me like he's done with all the others. That was why I never wanted to go there with him."

"Where?" Rikki asked.

"Vegas. That was the drop-off point for all of Mark's girls. Nobody dumps me." She said it with a woman's grit and determination, feeling unsteady because Mark had disappeared on her.

During an investigation sometime the smallest things can be the biggest. Rikki was finding that out.

They drove three quarters of a mile until…

"Hang a right at the next corner," Sharon pointed.

Arm over arm, Rikki cranked the steering wheel, looking at upper middle class surroundings that Sharon and Mark rolled in. And why the hell not? How many people like Mark live below the poverty level? One look at the home, and Rikki knew that this was on a higher underworld level than she had suspected.

"Nice."

"It outta be. It's in my last name, Richberg. But he paid cash for it."

"Didn't that draw in the IRS?"

Rikki thought about her tax problems, and they were far less than the multi-million dollar property that she was looking at. Why couldn't the IRS take time to take notice this house? How was he able to skate by—to this magnitude—without anyone on the police force getting curious about his dealings? He was pretty smart, all right. Linking him to jaywalking—let alone serious crime—wasn't easy.

"Mark had a way with money, to make people not suspect him," Sharon said. "Especially people who he paid-off to look the other way…The realtor never seemed to care, as long as she got her cut of the action."

That caught Rikki's attention.

"Realtor?"

"He called her Hildy somebody." Sharon thought. "Again, I didn't ask. But she told him that if he was worried about anything, all he had to do was buy the house in my name, and make the payments in increments of under ten thousand dollars. That way, the I.R.S. wouldn't get wise to what was going on."

When the car jerked to a halt Rikki knew that she wouldn't have anyone to confide in when it was all over. Certainly, not Tony. As far as she could tell, he was somehow in on it. In for a penny in for a pound, they always say. This case shaped up to be no different. In the movies crimes get solved in sixty minutes or less. Not so oddly, real life was always dissimilar.

Outside, Rikki saw the initials M.R. on the mailbox. Once inside the lavish home, she immediately began putting on her gloves.

"It's ok to touch stuff. Your people've already dusted the place," Sharon assured.

Rikki thought it odd that Tony hadn't said anything about it.

"You look surprised."

And Rikki was.

"Don't cops tell each other what's going on?"

"Sometimes more than others," she bounced back, curious about that very question.

Then again, she never spoke to anyone about her non-stop troubles with Jack. So keeping silent on matters of official importance was a heap easier to comprehend.

"I'm going upstairs to wash off this day," Sharon smiled.

Rikki watched Sharon sway as she ascended up the winding, imported wood, staircase.

If I only had a body like that, I could've made the police officer's calendar.

Less than an eternity passed before Sharon returned, wearing only sheer-black panties and a stomach open T-shirt with the word Punk written high across the front.

"I've always had a thing for cops. Especially the ones who look like you." Sharon seductively shared, brushing past Rikki—gracing her forearm against the small of Rikki's back—en route to the refrigerator.

Rikki walked behind her, keeping a modest distance. Once in the kitchen, against the backdrop of the freezer's chilling sting, Sharon whirled and kissed her hard on the mouth.

THE JEWELRY STORE
◆

Half a block away, Rikki walked past a costume shop that had assorted knick-knacks in the window. It was a store for those who like dressing up to look like somebody else. She, however, hadn't the time to stop and peek, because a bit farther away was the real cause of interest.

There was something about the feeling that a woman gets when looking at jewelry that she can't afford. It somehow provides her with a type of synthetic orgasm that nothing else can duplicate.

Only those with lots of discretionary income could afford to go in to browse. That was hardly the instance when Rikki entered the renowned dome of endless glitter named Sparkles Jewelry.

An attentive man, wearing a stylish shirt with matching pants, tending to a couple that had arrived about fifteen minutes earlier. They'd come in only after the woman had proclaimed that she was tired of being single; if her latest version of Prince Sometimes Charming didn't come across with an engagement ring, she would have to put her always charming pussy back out in the street to snare a different unsuspecting bachelor.

The owner's turn around "Good morning" gave Rikki the artificial feeling of being a welcomed regular there. It wasn't true, but she thought about it nevertheless. "One minute," he assured.

"Take your time," Rikki replied, seizing the chance to gaze in awe at those things that she used to only marvel at.

That's the way it continued until the owner separated from the couple, to make a bouncy line to Rikki.

"I'm sorry to have kept you waiting," he pleasured her with his tact.

"I'm Detective Luckett, with the Albuquerque PD."

"But of course."

There was a whew, instantaneous relief, in his reaction; he relaxed after she identified herself. His smile had become more genuine. It was one of relief.

"I'd like to ask you a few questions about the robbery that you had a short while back."

That caught the collective ears of a young couple who slowly moved from one display case to the next.

Rikki continued reading from her pad. "At the time of the robbery, you weren't able to provide a clear description of the perpetrator."

The owner's face tightened in a having to re-live the ordeal all over again feeling.

"Now that time has passed, have any mental images of how the robber looked come to your mind?…Sometimes it takes a while for the doer to materialize in the mind of the victim."

Struggling, he fought himself for a face to offer Rikki's inquisition.

He pointed. "I was standing over there talking to a customer."

His arm swung about the interior where it happened.

"I heard the viewing case over there open. At first, I paid it no mind because the customer was in front of me; I knew it couldn't have been him doing it. That's when the entrance door opened by itself. For some reason, it struck me to check the case. Then I noticed the diamonds were gone."

"The whole time, you saw no one?" Rikki asked, wondering if she had just heard the truth, or something out of Disneyland, a fairytale from a confused victim, unable to come to grips with what had happened to him.

"When do I get my stolen property back?" the owner pleaded.

The nearby customers uneasily looked over. Fearing that there was a problem, he took his girl by the arm and together they shuffled out the door. He was the king of stalling, relieved that he didn't have to fork-over premarital money that he really didn't have to spend considering how low his funds were to begin with. Gosh, he thought. Women are expensive; on the other hand, she was thankful to have not wasted anymore time with him. So much for true love.

After the couple was back out on the street, the robbery event had the owner perplexed. How could his eyesight that day have failed him so miserably?

"It's like the robber was invisible."

Rikki wasn't overflowing with confidence with his story. In the absence of Stevie Wonder being the owner, it was virtually impossible that someone could've entered an interior that small without being seen.

He saw her face go flush with disinterest and disbelief. "If you don't mind, I've got work to do," he grumbled, turning away, certain that his stolen inventory from that day was gone forever.

"Does this look familiar?" she held up a plastic bag that contained sprinkles of the silvery-white ash.

"Where'd you get that?"

"Never mind. Do you recognize it?" she repeated.

"That's the ash that was on the floor the day of the robbery. I paid no mind to it. But looking at it brings back that dreadful event."

She dropped the bag back in her purse and headed to the door, stepping on a crumbled and faded business card for Hildegard Realty. The agent whose card it was happened to belong to was a man named Michael Tellata.

In the background was a radio report that spoke of the continuing mystery surrounding a helicopter that crashed in Las Vegas a while ago.

Rikki was back at the lake, sitting there starring at the water. She mentally reenacted every movement that she and Erik had the morning when they were both recalled to the scene. There was something that she was leaving out of her pattern to place the pieces properly into place.

Her cell rang.

Rikki's "Yeah" sounded like a person in the middle of doing something when interrupted by a pesky ringing cell phone.

"Snap out of it," the caller said, never considering that someone could be engaged in activity more important than talking to him.

The distraction had Rikki struggling to place the caller's voice.

"The answers you want rest with the key you found on the parachutist…If the deputy guarding the evidence locker discovers that the key has been removed…Well, I promise not to mention your name."

"Why don't I believe you?" Rikki asked.

"Because I'm lying."

THE KEY
◆

Niguel Hargrove was often heard bragging about having been a fierce front line soldier during the Korean War. In reality, the closest thing that he ever saw to combat was on the outskirts of Chattanooga, fighting with his three older sisters over hand-me-down clothes he was to get.

The locksmith shop where he worked—for upwards of twelve hours a day—had been passed down from his great uncle, through his dad, to him. That was fortunate, because he had never thought to do anything else for a living.

Locks were all he ever wanted to be bothered with, except for Lilly, his wife, who had a lock on his never wanting to stray heart. Given how fast he made a habit of going straight home to her after work, it was fortuitous that the shop's burglar alarm hadn't been turned on by the time Rikki got there.

Hargrove moved his chubby fingers from already having begun typing in the alarm code.

"I need you to take a look at something," Rikki said.

She extracted the out of the ordinary key, handing it to Mr. Hargrove.

With the alarm not having been set, she entered the age-old shop looking, scanning everything about him. After all, it wasn't the jewelry store—with all of its twinkling things—so the sight of the masculine owner had to suffice.

He blew off what dust lingered on the key before handing it back, saying, "It's a flight key. I immediately recognized it." He pointed to it, "See the N-number embedded in it?"

She nodded. How could she not have been taken in by it? It was that stand-out feature that initially captured her attention; as something different than the run-of-the-mill keys that most people are accustomed to.

"Give me a minute."

"Sure," she complied, watching him reference a book that was beneath a short pile of other reading material.

Within a fast few seconds he began, "That key is from a helicopter."

He handed her a piece of paper on which he had scribbled numerical notations about the manufacturer.

"The one you're looking for was sold at that aircraft dealership listed there," pointing to the paper. "It's on the outskirts of town."

She continued to listen.

"Can I tell you something?"

She nodded, thrown off guard by his somewhat secretive manner.

"Earlier this morning, another man was in here asking about that same key number. Granted, he didn't have the key with him. But somehow he knew all about it—even before I started telling him what I just told you. Didn't say who he was. One thing stood out."

"Let's hear it."

"He was fat."

The store lights went out.

THE HELICOPTER MANUFACTURER

◆

The heralded Sikorsky flight school was located behind the showroom, stretching the entire length of the two story, prefab metal building—where sounds freely travel.

A man approached Rikki with a welcoming hand, amidst this world of financially extravagant purchases and limitless flight potential that she had only experienced through films and fantasy. Rikki produced the key in full view of him.

"I was told that this key belongs to one of your helicopters."

"May I?" asking to hold it.

She obliged, pressing it into the crease of his wide, working man's, palm.

It didn't take more than a few carefully scrutinized seconds before he returned it. His "Follow me" was one that had intrinsic meaning; the full extent of which she was uncertain.

Like the earlier visit to the locksmith, this Q & A had interesting points of interest that would hopefully be revealed later.

After passing several helicopter models, they turned left and walked through a newly varnished archway that was more befitting an exclusive private home. A dozen feet away was a bent over man who did precise work on a lathe, until he was handed the key from the first man. The second man then began fingering it.

"She," the first man pointed to Rikki, "said it came from one of ours."

He returned it to her then went back to his task, pausing, "I remember it...That one was different from the norm. It was altered. Fitted with multiple, larger, fuel tanks for extended travel."

THE PHONE CALL

◆

Getting comfortable on the couch was as difficult as trying to inhale a breath of fresh air at any airport. But Rikki was determined. Her bubble popped when she heard Sharon answer the telephone.

"Some guy wants you," Sharon called from the other room, before coming into view.

Rikki found herself being drawn closer to Sharon. And it was much more than an experimental, physical, attraction. That aura had worn off many weeks ago. Nope, this was turning out to be a deeper feeling of commitment, something that she had never felt, nor wanted, from Erik.

"Tell-em I'm not here."

After sucking her fingers free of leftover pancake dough, Rikki's answer was cut short when she heard a highly agitated, bossy, voice come through loudly and clearly through her speaker phone. It was Tony.

"Whatda-fuck are you tryin' to pull!? The Doc gave strict orders to cool-it, until he releases you from his care, and gives you the okay to get back to normal."

She figured it was as good a time as any to break it to him. "I'm taking a few months off."

The harshness in his voice was evident. "If you don't produce the jewels you might just as well take the rest of your life off!" He switched, not wanting to pay attention to anything more that she had to say. Then he finally calmed, "Tell me something I don't want to hear."

"I'm going to the circus."

THE MAN CALLED TINY

◆

Las Vegas, there's no place like it.

Eyewitnesses near the crash site at Circus Circus Casino told police that the fiery helicopter event looked like the second coming of September eleventh.

Immediately, that gave the authorities the antiterrorism suspicions from which they immediately acted—in the wrong direction.

Rikki considered all of the official descriptions of the helicopter crash that she raked in from the Internet, tracking a straight line flight path from Las Vegas, backwards through Albuquerque, southward. From that she was able to determine that the chopper had originated somewhere in Latin America.

Wind filtered through the rental car, scattering Rikki's hair, as she battled fatigue while speeding along the highway heading to the Nevada state line.

Many exhausted hours later, Rikki entered the brightly flashing Vegas strip with a severe case of asphalt vertigo. On the way, Jack had called to say that he was all right and he would be home as soon as he could. He added that something had come up, and he would explain when he saw her. Not once did he volunteer anything about the gems.

She was drained of any real concern about him, only that he give back the diamonds. Given all of the situational dilemma, she was somewhat relieved that he sounded safe—until she got her hands on him.

It's a given that the strip never sleeps, but Rikki's sense of time was different. Squeaking front struts announced themselves as she drew near the hotel's entrance. She was never one for long car rides. That day was no exception.

She wanted to check into her hotel room, with enough time to relax to possibly enjoy a once in a lifetime room service meal. Since her life consisted of being the head cook and bottle washer for Jack, it was a pleasant thought to have someone wait on her for a change.

"Welcome to Circus Circus, Ma'am?" said a dwarf bellhop, who welcomed her with a professionally plastic, Las Vegas touch.

As she twisted to get her luggage from the back seat, the hustling hop had already opened the rear door to remove it.

"Allow me," he volunteered.

"You're sweet," she said.

"That's why I get the big money."

He labored ahead of her to the grand entrance. Until the year before it was just another small time Vegas sleepover. Then came an influx of cash that was willed to them by a former guest—a man who got the lay of his life there some ten years earlier. Anyway, the place has since been the proud recipient of a facelift that was sure to attract a higher level of clientele.

"You had a pleasant trip?" commented the front desk clerk.

"I got lost three times on two different highways," she shook her head. "Or, was it two times on three different highways?"

He took it all in as coming from yet another weary traveler.

"To top it off, my air conditioner didn't work."

"Bad, huh?"

"The worst," she answered.

He focused his attention on the sign-in ledger in front of him, reading her signature. Then the desk clerk tore-off the confirmed reservation sheet, handing her a copy, along with a piece of plastic that was her room key.

"You're in room eight seventeen. The elevator's right over there," he pointed past incoming guests and workers alike. She struggled to get a clearer view of it.

It seemed to take forever, but finally Rikki was in her one hundred and twenty dollar a night room, with a friend's coupon that she thought had long since expired. After sliding shoeless feet across the limited edition, low pile, maroon carpet, she wearily plopped on the tightly made-up double bed.

Finally being able to enjoy the sense of 'whew', she stared at the limitless patterns of stucco on the ceiling. She thought about what being in Las Vegas could mean to her investigation, so long as significant answers were forthcoming about that helicopter.

Just then, she reached into her purse. It hit her hard when she realized that she'd forgotten to bring her debit card. Given her financial woes, Sharon had volunteered to give her money that she pinched-off from Mark's underground stash. Rikki declined, wishing that she had let Sharon give her some of it, especially since Mark could be dead; he'd not be apt to come back looking for it anytime soon.

Daylight hours faded, leaving behind a closed window to get anything accomplished by way of the investigation.

During sleep Heather appeared. She was suspended, wearing a never before seen expression of fulfillment. All that was disturbed when a man came upon Heather from behind and started choking her.

A knock at the door made that vivid nightmare sanitary. For Rikki, she wanted it gone forever.

She hurried to fluff-up her hair, making hastened steps to see who was in the hall, reasoning that it must be one of the hotel personnel who obviously forgot that she had already tipped them; returning to collect the gratuity, giving her a second chance to make-good on an already concluded financial restitution.

Once she got within a few feet of the latch she asked, "Who is it?"

"Tiny Sox," came the pounding, male, baritone from the other side.

"Is that name supposed to mean something?" she asked.

"I got better things to do than stand out here wastin' my goddamn time. If you're not interested in that chopper."

The door opened, and Rikki stood small in front of a muscular mountain of a black man.

Her badge best explained who she was. He barely flinched looking at it. Not the typical minority, who normally contracted hyper behavior syndrome in the presence of the cops. Not this guy. No, Ma'am. Nothing short of a SWAT team was going to get his attention, frightening him was impossible.

"Got wind you were in town."

She leaned against the door's frame, listening with newfound comfort.

"There's a guy who's hip to what you need." Out went his upwardly turned thick hand. "For a price."

"Why'm I palming you, if you're not the guy with the info?" she asked.

"Cause without me, you'll never see him."

"I'll get my purse."

He couldn't have picked her from a registry of newly arriving guests, to decide that it was Rikki to sham. Feeling confident that the proposed meeting was worthwhile, she rushed back inside the room, returning with a twenty. He took it, turning it over to see if there were more bills beneath it.

"That's eighty you owe me," he grumbled. He pointed down the hall, past the ice maker and soda machines, with an index finger that equaled her wrist. "Meet me down there at ten o'clock."

She leaned. Trying to see around Tiny wasn't the easiest of chores.

"If the eighty ain't the first thing I see when I roll back here, I'm forgettin' I ever saw you."

He eyed her tight and tired body, admiring what he saw. But money counted ahead of sex, ahead of everything. Then he lumbered away with his wide back getting smaller with each step away. This was a costly out of pocket fact finding mission, when considering her budget—if one could call nothing left a budget. She had to call Sharon to get a wire transfer of money.

Passing hours had turned late afternoon to middle evening, with Rikki in the hall feeling left out of the information mix. She thought back on all of the times when someone was supposed to meet her to deliver on something, only to abscond with her holding the sinking feeling that she'd been had. Perhaps, things would be different with this Tiny character. Dragging minutes would either confirm or deny.

Peering up, then down, the lengthy hall, Tiny was nowhere to be seen. He seemed to be a man of his word—if "The eighty better be the first thing I see when I roll back here," is any indication of sincerity.

Why wasn't he there? Given she had just met him earlier in the day, there was no basis to assume anything positive was in her immediate future concerning him. If he did present himself, she was determined to find out from him all that she could.

Where's that over-grown primate?

For someone accustomed to having dealt with the worst criminals that New Mexico had to offer, Rikki nervously shuffled.

Tiny appeared from behind her. "Didn't think I'd show?"

She was upset at having been kept waiting. "I knew you would. It was a matter of what year."

He looked around, seeing no one taking exceptional notice of them standing in the hall.

"The rest of my dough?" he demanded in a voice that could crack cinderblock.

She extended a hundred dollar bill. His mammoth hand enveloped hers when he took it, before retracting to stuff it in his pocket. "I knew I wasn't wastin' my time with yuz."

Was there a hint of New Jersey in his accent?

He turned and walked toward the stairs. At first, she thought that was the end of the conversation and her money, but when she followed she realized otherwise. Being with him on those dark stairs, Rikki should've been in fear but she wasn't. Instead, she reached to hold onto him for stability. Within minutes, he shouldered an emergency exit that had been painted shut.

Once outside they saw a second, a much thinner man standing alone. He was the nervous type whose head pivoted like an owl on night watch, managing to look at Rikki only long enough to look away at anything else that he thought to be a potential threat.

It's no wonder, she thought. Anyone who'd wear those baggy green and yellow Bermuda shorts and a clashing top had to be uneasy about being recognized. Instead, his body language deferred everything to Tiny.

"Don't worry about him. He's my cousin. He's down with info about that chopper."

Her interest peaked.

"Tell her what you told me," Tiny instructed the frail man, not mentioning that Rikki was a cop, which surely would have produced memory loss in the other man.

Has he been informed that I'm a cop?

"What about my taste?" the cousin asked.

Without a monetary incentive, he was more in the mood to vacate.

She looked at Tiny, getting nothing back but a 'You heard the man' return glance. She palmed the cousin a face down twenty—thanks to Sharon utilizing Western Union's speed. He greedily took the bill.

"I'm hip to who owns the chopper," the man blurted, feeling that was enough to earn the twenty; then it was time to scram.

"You're sure?"

"What's this, a freakin' quiz show?"

He reacted as though he could be speaking into a microphone that Rikki might be wearing, until Tiny gave him the okay nod to continue.

"Last month, when I saw the chopper's tail, I knew it was his. All his flyin' toys got that same markin'."

She looked anxiously and heated. "I need a name."

"I never heard his real name. I called'm Sonny."

Bingo, she thought.

"Don't know nothin' else bout'm," the cousin went on. "In this town, askin' questions can get a fella filled with hot lead."

With that he left with a typical want-to-be tough walk, leaving Rikki and Tiny standing without him.

Within seconds, Tiny separated from her. Rikki knew that there had to be more, even though what she had was already enough of a justification for having come to Vegas in the first, second, and third place.

"You can't just leave me here," she complained.

"Watch me."

"Stop, damnit!" she blurted.

Tiny was surprised that someone so much smaller would dare to shout at him. He pivoted—in the time that it would take to show a lengthy Super Bowl commercial—as would an asteroid, casting an ominous shadow over the entire hemisphere. He began to feel that he was being detained against his mighty will.

I need this ass-hole more than he needs me.

"Where do we go from here?" hoping for positive results.

He looked to the sky, as if answers to that ridiculous question hovered. He huffed mightily, with enough blowing force to push a sailboat through the Panama Canal.

"There ain't no us. There's me and a sexy cop, who's gonna get me capped if anyone in this big ears town finds out I've been talkin' to you."

"How'd you know I was a cop?"

"It's your perfume. Moon Over the Precinct."

She broke down, allowing feminity to take a step ahead of her job. "Do you really think I'm sexy?"

In tough-guy fashion, he snatched his head away. "Only when you're movin' away from me."

The helpless look in her face was more than he could ignore, continuing to hold his position on the slightly uneven sidewalk.

"Damnit," he sulked. "Come on."

She resumed following him. He snapped around sharply.

"Keep your distance behind me. Remember, I don't want no—"

"I got the flavor," she assured. "You don't want anyone thinking we're together."

The feeling of being lost is difficult to explain unless a person's been there. Yet she felt confident that she was finally on the right track. To where? She could only guess. This time she had a solid lead to pursue, and a confirmed identity to go with that helicopter.

She learned how Tiny was plugged in. With his meddling in everyone's affairs, he kept on top of all the local goings-on. Even if he wasn't helping Rikki for money—and he was—he would've been doing it as a hobby. In the dictionary under busy-body, there needed to be a shrunken photo of Tiny. If not made smaller, his picture would have spread across two pages to fit him in. She knew that he had more information in that massive head of his than he was letting on.

It was all heating up. Her once far-fetched theories about the circumstances leading to the man in the lake had taken on a curious shape that any District Attorney would love to present in court. Well, almost. It was clear that this saga was only beginning. She was getting closer, to what she wasn't sure. In any event, she needed to be ready in case Mark wasn't really dead.

THE INTERROGATION
―――――◆―――――

It took several crisp wraps from the hall side of the door for consciousness to arrive to Rikki.

She struggled to sit up, nearly teetering over onto the floor. If tossing from one side of the mushy mattress to the other could be thought of in terms of meaningful rest, she was sleeping.

He and his relative have been paid. What does Tiny want?

She was missing Sharon more and more, yawning while putting on the monogrammed bathrobe that the hotel expected to see in the room after she checked out. Staggering to the door, she was unaware that that was a terrible oversight.

When she opened the door a swift, stinging, breeze forced Rikki to tighten her robe. To her left, not more than five yards away, was an open window that sucked the stylish pale curtains outside into the honking horns and chattering people night air.

Initially, she thought nothing of that window, until screams from the street below pulled her closer to the slightly tinted, double glazed, glass. Careful to maintain her balance at the opening, she saw a crowd gathering around a man who was sprawled on the cement. She couldn't see his face. What stood out was the baggy green and yellow Bermuda shorts.

"Holy shit!" she gasped with hand to mouth.

In the distance were the growing sounds of emergency sirens racing to the scene.

"Look!" someone yelled from the street, "Up there!" pointing to the window where Rikki stood.

Why are they looking at me?...They can't possibly think that I—.

She backed away from the window, but it was too late. They had already seen her. She was instantly knee deep in whatever had gone down—quite literally. Her catastrophes were branching out like a well watered vine. Legality's pit was getting deeper, with another death around which she was centered.

"Look! Up at that window. There she is!" someone in the crowd yelled.

Unlike the man in the lake, this guy did his Peter Pan with hundreds of witnesses who quickly shouted that Rikki caused it. She didn't see herself as a suspect. Let alone the prime one. Wrong!

With her palm prints on the window sill, Rikki fled to the relative safety of her room, fighting that overflowing want to be back within the mountainous confines of Albuquerque.

"How many times do I have to answer the same goddamn question?" she complained, to one of three, shirt with loosened tie, plain clothed, police who stood menacingly around her. They were lecturing her, spewing unpleasant droplets of saliva with each threatening word that they cast.

"As often as we tell you to answer," the tallest of the three said. He was Victor Saint, Victor felt encouraged, and consternated. He was a good man and even better cop, who—more often than not—thought of himself on being the last of his kind. Honest.

In years past, he'd entertained the idea of pursuing the office of district attorney, but could never muster enough political support for that to eventuate. There was never a large Third World voting block in Vegas. For Victor to stand a chance, that crowd had to register to vote, then go out and actually do it. That meant coming out in the open, and there was little chance of that happening.

He then stepped away from the others, aligning his Latin twang to better aim at her.

"If you don't mind, detective," he added, in full command of the first wave of his verbal bashing.

The way he said 'detective' hinted that he disliked her rank within the policing society, and was spiteful of a woman having it.

"I did some checking."

"Keep it to yourself," Rikki said, confrontationally turning to face him in a stare-down of wills.

"You made detective in less than two years."

"If my C.O. were in town, your balls would be in a vice for dragging me down here for this bull session," she guaranteed, referring to the rough way in which Victor and his boys were treating her.

She sucked her pearly whites, disdaining both him and the manner in which he was conducting the investigation. "I'm innocent."

"Innocent is a relative term." Victor continued, with patience that was wearing thin—as if he had any appreciable levels of tolerance before the backroom gathering began. "What did you do when you first heard the knock at your hotel room door?"

"I've answered the same question eight thousand times," she said.

"Humor me."

Victor leaned closer, so she could make no mistake as to who was running things. "Make it eight thousand and one."

"I heard loud knocking, and got out of bed to see who was there."

One of his cronies, Barnes—the undersized one—spoke out of turn. "You thought it was that nigger come callin' again, who you were hanging with earlier in the day?"

Though he wasn't crazy about the way that was phrased, Victor allowed the question to stand.

"<u>I figured</u> that it was some drunk who was out crusin' the bars, got oiled-up, and staggered back inside the hotel to the wrong door."

"What happened next?" asked Victor.

Rikki added, "I asked again who was out there, and got no answer."

"Then?" asked Ernie, the third detective. He was still in training, but Saint demanded that he be in on the Q & A. He didn't mind being there, so long as Victor didn't break anything on the suspects—arms or legs, as had been the case on more than one occasion. In fact, he couldn't care less what Victor did, so long as he wasn't the only witness to it.

"Answer the question," Victor insisted.

"I opened the door."

Victor went on with disbelief. "You're in a strange town, late at night. And you just opened the door?"

Rikki adjusted her position in the crackling, wooden chair. "I've been more than clear on that point."

"Where I get hazy!" Victor stormed.

Ernie touched Victor's arm to calm him. Instead, Victor sharply snatched it away, defiantly proving that he was under control. But he was far from it.

"Were you holding your service revolver?" Barnes injected to interrupt Victor's anger. If left unchecked, Victor' thrusts might disrupt the flow and integrity of the questioning. After all, there was a fellow cop sitting in front of them. Practicing everything in this session by the book was of the utmost importance.

Rikki shook her head, unclear if she had the weapon in hand at the time.

Barnes supplemented, "Your answer is, you didn't have your revolver with you when you went to open the door. Or, you don't remember?"

Victor's was a curious disbelief. It was obvious that his doubts on Rikki's forthrightness had risen to the forefront. "A reasonably experienced female cop" (One had to hear the way he said 'female') "opens an unfamiliar door, under pressure circumstances, in a strange city without her weapon drawn?"

"I'm here with no legal permission to be armed, I felt it unwise to carry my piece in plain sight."

Barnes joined the verbal target practice. "A second ago, you said you didn't remember carrying it."

Rikki fired back, "I was unarmed when I got to the door."

Victor jumped back in to accuse. "Then who pushed the man out the window?"

"Ask him."

Just when he figured to give her enough space between them, Victor was back in Rikki's face.

"We can't, detective!" There was that word detective, and the way it pained him to call her that. As though the mere thought of Rikki having attained that stature made his stomach turn and head pound.

"When were you going to tell us about the diamond cutting paraphernalia that was on the chopper that hit Circus Circus?"

She was silent.

"I guess you never saw this either?" Victor said, holding up a baseball cap that had Little Ferry Cubs inscribed on it.

The three men broke away from her to conclave. They whispered with their not so unique brand of western strategy to attach her to a spit, and roast her over hot coals of situation and suspicion.

"Are you going to charge me?" she spoke, unable to contain it further.

"When we're good and ready," Ernie said, determined to be a good puppy dog for Victor.

She listened to them continuing amongst themselves, but couldn't precisely make out what was being said.

It was then that a desk cop opened the door from the hallway.

"I told you not to disturb me!" Victor snapped at the man who opened it.

The desk cop was unwilling to stick anything inside the room other than his pronounced imposition of a material fact.

"There's a Captain Fatino calling for you," he said to Victor.

Finally, he calls.

Victor looked at Rikki; as though she had something to do with that call. He then broke away, pointing to her get-me-out-of-here face. "I've decided to let you go back to the hotel."

"Bout time," she said, standing without specific permission to do so, feeling as though the cavalry had arrived.

Victor gave her the last word. "I don't like you. You give policing a bad name."

Rikki felt pain as her circulation swam downstream past both stiff knees.

"When I'm done with whatever he wants, aren't you going to talk to your chief?" Victor asked her with a hidden curiosity.

"And hear him demand that you keep me?"

The other two men repositioned themselves, with the interrogation having been concluded.

"This ends this part of our investigation," Victor concluded.

Rikki stretched both arms high and wide. "I figured that," she mumbled, leaving the emotionally charged room of epoxy painted concrete with matching flat paint.

When she reached the door's handle…

"Be where we can find you," Victor demanded, above the sound of Barnes rat-tat-tapping recently repaired teeth—a dental partial—that he had not fully paid for.

"You want me to leave town?"

"Not soon enough to suit me," snapped Victor, struggling to calm himself, feeling his plain white collar getting tighter. "Until such time, behave yourself." He had to say it kindly, because of her higher-up police connection to the south of Nevada.

She opened the door and paused. "Tell Tony I said thanks for dropping a quarter to spring me."

When she was gone from his sight, Victor stewed at having been out-foxed by an out-of-town woman.

Why didn't Tony ask to speak to me?

THE DIAMOND CUTTER

♦

After those boring hours of sitting in front of Victor and his henchmen, Rikki's attitude had deteriorated, lending to a growing feeling that she needed to be out of town before anything worse found its way to her.

She walked the crowded sidewalk, sidestepping everyone from street hustlers, to vacationers who flew in to get rich quick before scampering back to the airport to resume lives that they were able to temporarily forget. What Rikki needed was a basic cab.

She knew that returning to the hotel was a waste of time, because her room was probably bugged. When it hit her that she was being followed from a discrete distance, she decided to take the snoops who were pulling up the rear for a stroll. Her steps quickened.

After what happened back at the hotel window, she got the bothersome feeling that she'd as soon find fortune waiting at the roulette wheel than locate Tiny. After the guy hit the concrete outside her window, making it the talk of the strip, doubtlessly Tiny knew that Rikki was to be avoided at all cost. She gave up ever seeing him again. That mattered little, though; she had accomplished what she came to Vegas for. Information on who owned that chopper.

"Taxi!" she wailed, seeing an endless stream of yellow pay-for-rides passing by. She wanted to annoy the local police flunkies, who kept close order drill behind her on foot patrol, by forcing them to hop in their cars if they wanted to stay close. Afterwards, if she ever made it safely back to any semblance of hospitality, she would soak ten sore toes in the warmest water that the desert's bright lights town had to offer.

The amber street light turned red before a frustrated cab driver could dart through it. That gave Rikki the opportunity to hop in.

"Where to?" the burly driver asked, flipping a glance to the rear seat.

Rikki's initial thankfulness was interrupted by a voice she wasn't apt to forget any time soon. Her head jerked up. "You're a man of many talents," she complimented.

Tiny never turned around, choosing on-n-off, eye-to-eye, peeks.

"I'd say, drivin' this thing is earnin' an honest buck, but it ain't. Who in their right mind wants to earn an honest anythin'?...I heard about you gettin' grilled downtown. All us guys on Victor's opposite side know he's a real prick."

Her neck pressed back against the rear headrest, exhausted, relieved to be under Tiny's protective wing. She didn't know how long, and she didn't care.

His sharp, beady, eyes zipped between both side view mirrors, constantly re-checking to see, not who was following them but how many?

He snatched the steering wheel, dashing the wrong way down a one-way street, exposing any previously unidentified cars that might be in pursuit.

Rikki was on to his technique, panting, fearfully hiding behind fingers that were barely parted; to see if Tiny's efforts worked to shake their tail; while at the same time trying to assure herself that she was still alive.

"Fancy driving," she complimented.

"Old bodyguard stuff. My ex-boss was a rich, paranoid, skitzo who was always convinced that someone was followin' him. So he had me get this drivin' technique down-pat."

"Do I ask whom that boss was?"

Tiny was silent, justifying the obvious answer.

I figured as much.

"Did you shake whoever was on the street back there?"

"For now." Tiny half turned, keeping his sights on the constantly changing traffic patterns ahead, concerned about what it was that got him drawn into this mess. "Girlfriend, why so much interest in an empty helicopter?"

"One of the cops said there was something important on that chopper, and that I knew about it."

"Do you?"

"Sorta."

She worried about what would happen if Tiny were discovered helping her, and how that would impact Victor's theories about all that he claimed Rikki knew about the helicopter.

She was thrown hard against the side door when the cab roared down a narrower street, before the car bounced back out onto a road that far fewer cars traveled on. He hawked the rearview mirror to make certain that no cars were behind him, before making that driving dodge. He probably had lost the chasers. But that supposition was probably one of transitory certainty.

"Why'r you doing this for me? There's got to be more to it for you than the chance to stick it to cops."

Whatever his reasons were, Tiny was keeping it to himself. "After I show you what you need, you're gonna have to find a way back to the hotel. Can't afford to backtrack right into'm."

"After that, where can I find you?"

Again he was silent.

She settled back, searching for answers to the many possibilities about what was to come next.

Five miles past the last series of pulsating neon advertisements—that drew the greedy attention spenders from all over to the gambler's capital of the world—the taxi rose and bottomed-out along an off-road, sometime sinking into weak dirt, making traction everything except easy. Bad brakes had the cab stopping a rarely used football field away from a rusted, aluminum, building.

The building in front of them, however, shared none of the Vegas twinkle. It was more akin to Molly's old home; where every window was boarded-up with half-inch plywood that was cross-fitted with two by fours, making looking inside impossible. The shed wasn't so far that they couldn't walk there. But that meant leaving the cab out in the open, alerting anyone that there were unexpected visitors to the property.

Tiny got out and Rikki followed suit. His long, ponderous, steps were difficult to maintain stride with.

They came to an entrance that was hidden behind a sizable pile of fifty-five gallon drums, put there by a local contractor, who didn't have the money to properly dispose of them. He was sure to remove any markings that would lead anyone who found the drums, back to his business. Penalties for illegal dumping in Nevada were costly.

On that door was an old-style combination lock. After scanning the building for anything that resembled burglar alarms, Tiny went to work on getting inside.

His wrist popped as he turned the dial. With his ear touching it, he listened as the tumblers fell nearly silently into place. He heard different sounds that were connected to the sequence of numbers, alerting him to reverse the dial, until the numerical grouping was aligned.

"And they say big men lack a delicate touch" he said, pulling the Master lock from the chain that held the barrier closed, tossing it to the ground in a rattling clump.

Before they took another step, she said, "In case there's somebody inside to greet us, we got to keep our lies simple."

She knew that the first mistake criminals make is not coordinating their stories. This happens because they never envision getting caught.

"Why'r we here?" she asked, preparing him for the questioning that would surely follow in the event that they were caught.

He couldn't pass-up the chance for a verbal jousting. "We're looking to buy a house, and figured this's as good a place as any to raise a nice, interracial, family."

His silent reaction shouted, ask a reasonable question, and you get a typical idiot's answer. "Gee, why didn't I think of that?"

She assured him that she was in order, with a friendly peck on his cheek.

"I already thought of that," he said, responding to the kiss.

The skylight was heavily caked with dirt, resulting in a dark interior, making it nearly impossible to discern one shadowy object from another. At the southernmost corner of the building limited light danced in from outside, showing that there was no one guarding the entrance.

There were a few metal tables and chairs, depicting that some level of activity had gone on there. The amount of dust on each thing there showed that whatever it was had transpired some time ago.

Tiny found an old style, kerosene lantern. He lit it with a short stroke of a cracked stick match that he dug out from a crushed box in his front pocket. The flame wiggled inside the curved glass, illuminating the interior in a creepy way, everything that she was not supposed to see.

"Got to be careful with the flame. No tellin' what's in all of these drums," she whispered, looking at an assortment of fifty-five gallon drums that dotted a good portion of the interior.

"Anything you touch will tell folks we're here. So be damn careful."

The hand held swaying lantern cast its flickering influence into adjacent rooms as their cautious, step by step, search continued.

In one of the rooms, she saw magnifying glasses of varying intensities and of ranging strengths. There were also several scales, and an assortment of packaging equipment. That was odd: Being inside a building that from the outside gave the impression of never being considered for such production type activity.

She took out her over-priced, digital, camera from an imitation leather purse, aiming it to capture everything of interest. Since she initially had no idea what to omit, she continued clicking the shutter in rapid fire succession to get it all.

Tiny tried to cover all bases, to eliminate the possibility of something arising that they weren't prepared for. He wasn't about to leave something behind that would potentially lead the authorities back to him.

"I want to see the finished pictures before we separate tonight. If there's anythin' in that camera that looks like my face, you won't be seein' New Mexico again. Not breathin' anyway." He continued his usual tough-guy, "I ain't goin' away to jail from nothin' incriminatin' that you did."

She took him at his word, feeling his guarantee that he didn't want to go away and never see his family again. Unafraid, she touched him on the shoulder, lending a measure of assurance to an otherwise tense situation, unwilling to make it a standoff between the two of them. Considering she would surely lose that confrontation.

"Not a chance of that happening."

"Better not be," he verbally thumped.

That was when she spotted an industrial conduit that crisscrossed from the wall to the ceiling. Its buzzing sound meant that electrical current was flowing. But to where?

She pointed to the electrical supply. "That box's pushing juice somewhere in here."

Distantly, a man was mumbling to himself, and that quiet echoing alerted them that someone else was in the shed with them. That realization had them walking in a crouched manner to the northern side of the musty interior.

They progressed closer to a far corner where an old man sat. He was beneath the glow of a lamp that was similar to ones that Rikki had seen strewn in other places across the interior.

This area was different. It was well lit, with assorted tools that were within easy reach of a man who sat hunched. He was leaning over, closely examining something small that he held with experienced, nimble, fingers.

Tiny's pistol was drawn, ready to shoot at the slightest provocation. Rikki took in a restricted, fearful, breath.

"You didn't tell me you have a gun," Rikki said with alarm.

The senior was quick to respond to Tiny's advance with a meek reaction. "If you were more observant, you'd have seen that I'm not a threat to you."

A metal on metal sound where he sat drew curious attention to the shackles that connected him—via a chain and handcuffs—to a steel ring that was bolted to the floor.

Rikki stepped toward the captive man. "What are you doing here?"

The man tried to ignore them, continuing to examine what appeared to be a diamond.

Tiny wasn't overwhelmed with sympathy, wanting to rid the gun's chamber of hot lead. He shrugged in his usual who-gives-a-shit manner, thinking of a way to get back to the cab for a timely exit before anyone of consequence came around.

In addition to Meyer's tools for doing fine work, there were assorted glass containers, an oscilloscope that was fueled by the electrical power from thick cables that lead up the wall to the conduit, and that silvery-white dust.

Rikki pointed to the dust.

"What's that?"

"It's the flakes from my cutting," Meyer answered.

She noticed that it was the same consistency as what she had seen inside the parachutist's belt bag, on the Corvette's tires, and where Tony stood beside her bed at the hospital. She reached down, grabbing a handful of it to deposit in her rucksack.

On a fragile plastic hook was a clock that had Johannesburg posted below the time.

She studied the handcuffs that bound him, bending to closely inspect the locking device.

"They said if I help them I'll be set free."

From a crack in the roof came the ear catching, almost disturbing, sound of water trickling. The monotonous drip…drip…drip made for an annoying backdrop addition.

"Help them do what?" Rikki went on.

"Cut and prepare their rough gems. Diamonds, to be exact."

Tiny's eyes widened considerably, suddenly wanting robbery to be his calling ahead of being a lowly compensated do-good gofer for Rikki.

Spiders sucked in water droplets that rolled along their webs.

"When were you going to tell us about the diamond cutting paraphernalia that was on the chopper that hit Circus Circus?" Victor's question rang truer than when it was asked of Rikki earlier.

"Why the chains?" Tiny asked, finding it almost funny that white people could be slaves.

"When I didn't agree on the nominal money that they initially offered, I was reduced to the posture of involuntary servitude."

That was when Tiny's slave scenario faded from any humorous plateau, and into the valley of it could happen to you scenario. Rikki aimed her camera at Meyer.

"When they couldn't get you to work on the cheap, they made you their slave."

"Fraid so." He tugged on the chain to accentuate the point.

A new form of trouble was lurking, leaving Rikki and Tiny part of it.

In the fresh air outside the building's rusted walls, they heard a fairly new pickup truck crunching the pebbles in the driveway, grinding to an abrupt halt mere yards from the entrance. A once full moon was being covered with thickening clouds, producing a gradual darkness that gave an eerie flavor to what once was a clear view of that entrance.

"We're <u>leavin</u>'," Tiny took Rikki's arm as she prepared to photograph Meyer again.

"I'm not done shooting," she protested.

"You are now," Tiny said.

Again, someone talking with Rikki has placed his life at risk.

Meyer trembled over what would happen if his captures returned to find him talking with strangers.

"Do as he says." Meyer whispered to her, "Please go. Then the men will remain convinced that I'm still here alone. Only then do I stand a chance to be set free."

Her ferocity caught hold of Tiny's plans for a two person escape. "Meyer's coming with us."

Tiny was in mid turn when he pivoted back to Rikki. "Like hell he is."

Ernie and Barnes got out of the pickup truck that couldn't have been police issue, considering it was stolen last week from a used car lot on the outskirts of town. They walked with distinction on their turf, past the ground level windows to a different entrance.

"Somebody's been here," Ernie said, seeing Tiny's heavy footprints leading to the shed. His nostrils flared with a bloodhound's style, "I can smell'm."

From behind a propane tank Rikki lifted her elbow, sampling her underarm, having just heard what Ernie said. "The odor can't be me."

"Broads," was Tiny's confirmation of feminine vanity.

A horizontal, negative jerk from Tiny's massive head indicated that they stay low, to follow him laterally to an alternative way outside to the cab.

On hands and sore knees, they shuffled to a slight opening in the wall that wasn't far away. They doubted every inch of the way that they would make it out in the same physical condition as when they arrived.

A pronounced click from a light switch illuminated the full interior from one steel support beam to the next. Rikki was certain that the only way she was going to leave was in a pine box.

"What're the odds of us getting out of here?" she asked in a depressed mumble.

"Four thousand one hundred and sixty to one," Tiny answered.

Rikki looked at him with disbelief, that a hood could never be a math wiz. "How did you—"

"When I was in high school I helped a local bookie make-up the weekly spread," Tiny elaborated. "We did it based on how many kids were absent from school that day."

"Four thousand to one?" she asked quietly.

Tiny added, "If you'd hurry, maybe it'll increase our chances to see tomorrow."

She didn't need that extra motivational boost. Living in and of itself was stimulation plenty. The only way out was making them unwilling participants in an unfunny game of marksmanship where they were the target.

"There they are!" Barnes shouted.

He aimed his semi-automatic pistol, squeezing the trigger. The muzzle flash repeatedly discharged, aimed to pierce Rikki and Tiny, instead hitting all around them.

"Die, motherfuckers!" was his demented, cackling, christen.

His wrist jerked from the kick of the gun, making a straight aim difficult. A round of shots roared from two pistols that blazed.

"Ahhh!" Tiny screamed.

He fell against one of the support columns, tearing a deep gash in his leg. His failing sense of balance had allowed him to stabilize himself with one hand. Pure adrenalin had him desperately trying to get up. The blood that poured from his shredded leg was the result of a major artery having been hit.

If the shooters didn't initially know where the trio had moved, they knew with audible certainty that Tiny had caught a hot round.

A hanging light made the place a complicated, moving composite of dim, side-to-side light of perpetual up-and-down shadows.

More shots followed, hitting the lock holding Meyer, springing it open. That metallic pop was something that he longed to hear but had thought impossible. The weight of his panic to get away had him tipping to the floor like a child would after crashing a tricycle. Looking across the silty floor, he saw scarce remnants of Rikki and Tiny fleeing.

They're not leaving me, he thought, failing to catch his huffing breath. He squirmed, scrambling, to right himself to stay close to them. They were the liberators, random elements leading to his freedom. He was going to maximize on the opportunity to leave with them.

The shooters took up combat positions, having moved to get an improved viewpoint on their marks, to lower their stance for improved accuracy. More shots exploded, hitting the fuse box, silencing the lights throughout the building, making visibility a memory.

The attackers reloaded, snapping closed the bullet filled metal jackets to their death devices, ready to resume firing.

Tat-tat-tat-tat-tat-tat-tat-tat-tat-tat…

Large caliber shells ricocheted, blazing to make everyone's next step an uncertain costly one.

Tiny managed to take control of his pain as he stood. He gripped the rusted steel beam so tightly that his hand impression remained behind. When the agony shot through him like a hot knife piercing thin plastic, he caved in—like a sandcastle having been kicked by children who couldn't wait to run back into the water. But he fought on.

Rikki tried to catch her breath, to compose herself to speak quietly enough that only Tiny could hear her. "What're you doing?" she asked, trying with all of her limited weight to hold him down.

She functioned without the burden of having to think. She tried to lasso some shred of calm if they were to make it out.

Tat-tat-tat-tat-tat-tat-tat-tat-tat-tat!

An industrial propane tank burst into leaping flames, sending a fireball out in search of skin to broil.

Determined to allow courage to surface past his alarm, Tiny peeled Rikki from around him. Finally, standing upright, he charged a wooden exit door, thrusting his powerful shoulder against it, breaking it from its frame.

Rikki dove out the window after Tiny, falling on top of him in an exhausted human pile of temporary relief, having escaped to relative safety. Outside darkness had fallen, making it impossible for the assassins to get their bearings. Burning pellets of death dented the concrete and asphalt around them.

He mumbled through his pain, feigning with a man's locker room humor from her being on top of him, "Not now, Honey. Wait till we get to the bed in your hotel."

Instead of being filled with an erection, his pants were soaking with his blood. His pain was unrelenting.

"If you let me die, you'll never get back the twenty that I owe ya," he yelped.

Meyer found Rikki and Tiny by tumbling to the ground beside them. If he ever had a preferred place to die this certainly wasn't it. Oh, God, Meyer thought.

Beneath the protective veil of night they ran to where they thought they left the cab.

"You need a doctor. At the rate you're leaking, you're not going to make it."

Tiny turned to her, wanting no part of that analysis. "Can I see your medical degree?"

She searched the front of herself. "Must've left it in my other pants." She tried to make a joke, but nothing was funny.

He wasn't in too much pain to look at her crotch. "Anything else in those pants?"

Men can't stop being perverts even when they're bleeding to death.

Express rising heat inside the burning shed forced Barnes and Ernie outside in search of their victims.

"Over there!" Barnes shouted. "Finish-em-off before they get away!"

Tiny's once controlled stride had diminished to one that desperately needed assistance, leaving distinct markings of murky blood which oozed from him on the ground. His trail was easy to follow, especially by way of the flashlights that the two shooters held.

Rikki said, "We got to get to the cab," in a weary voice that weakened in strength as she valiantly kept Tiny moving. Meyer pulled up the rear, and the three of them slid down an embankment of loose earth before finally reaching the taxi.

Meyer opened its passenger side door. Tiny could barely stand, falling against it.

She looked to Meyer. "Are you good with directions?"

Meyer nodded.

She came out of Tiny's pocket with the keys, tossing them to Meyer.

The car's metal and glass were perforated, when a string of semi-automatic weapons fire, made imitation Swiss cheese of it. The unmistakable hiss of the punctured tire left little doubt that driving on it would be a true test of anyone's roadway skill.

With keys in hand, Meyer dove into the cab head first. Waiting was the last thing on his mind. He started the car, seeing the two killer hopefuls approaching in the distance.

Tiny coughed a wad of blood, gagging to catch his growling breath, kicking the front seat. "What d-hell are you waitin' for!?"

Meyer floored it, and away they sped from beneath a shower of bullets that promised their demise. When the sky finally saw fit to deliver, the rains began washing away the car's zig-zagging tracks.

"You're the worst fuckin' shot I ever saw," Barnes complained.

"Me?" Ernie defended. "I'm not the one who got all those marksmanship awards…Lotta-good it did you here."

The wheezing men could do nothing more than watch their prey get away; finally vanishing into the inviting Nevada horizon.

Meyer did his level best to drive normally, with the car constantly pulling to the side of the flat tire. When the galloping trio was within a few miles of the strip, Rikki saw that Tiny's bleeding had slowed from the tourniquet that she applied. His pulse was also at a minimum to sustain life. Once dark and shiny skin was pale, with fading hopes of making it to tomorrow. That was when he defied medical probability and spoke.

"Where are we?"

He doesn't recognize the Vegas strip.

She snapped, "We can't drive around all night. Where can we take him?"

"They've got to have your hotel room staked-out," Tiny whispered.

"My place'll have to do," Meyer volunteered.

The night grew perilous while the yellow cab with one flat tire limped along their un-merry way. Finally, on the outskirts of town Meyer found his street.

"I'm home," Meyer announced as the three of them entered his unassuming, lower middle-class home.

They were overjoyed to be alive, and it took a sizable amount of time to be assured that they actually were. Completely bloody below the waist, Tiny fell from their grasp, hitting the floor like a lump of clay.

Meyer heatedly complained while watching the blood seep, "Do you know how much this carpet cost!?"

Meyer's wife, Marta, made haste to get down the short flight of stairs to greet them.

"Did it ever occur to you, that a wife of thirty-five years wants her husband to be home?" She caught sight of Tiny, immediately wanting to call nine one one, wishing that she had it on speed dial.

Totally out of sequence with what was depressingly transpiring before her, Marta thought of the old days, and her first date with Meyer...

Back then, he seemed like such a nice, clean-cut young man. Look at him, she thought, fighting back her sorrow. He's Robin Hoodlum with these people.

Perplexed, she leaned on the curved, wooden railing. Looking at what he dragged into her home, she cringed.

"Close the drapes," Meyer ordered her.

Without thinking she stayed. Because had she given it consideration, she would've run for safety. She raced to the curtains with arms flailing Edith Bunker style. With a single yank, the lace verticals covered the window.

Why'm I doing this for that black guy, she thought. No doubt, he's packing problems that will only suck my husband and me into whatever trouble he caused.

She knew that Meyer had a kind heart, too much for his own good. A biproduct to her nostalgia had her uneasy feet nearly riveted to the floor. Tiny was minutes from his end. Perhaps, deservedly so. But she didn't want it happening in her home.

Meyer pulled out all the stops, adding a hurry-up to her unappreciative tempo. "This man's dying from saving my life. We have to help him."

Rikki had torn away Tiny's shirt, retying it tightly around his upper thigh.

Meyer leaned to Tiny's cloudy ear to whisper. "When Marta's done with me, I'm gonna kill you."

In an inner battle against the pain, Tiny mustered a faint smile.

Meyer reached for Tiny's pocket. "In the mean time, I'm taking my new carpet money out of your wallet," Meyer added.

Tiny's smile evaporated, watching the bloody bills being extracted. The three of them then went to work on Tiny's wound, barely succeeding.

"There's no waiting for a doctor," Rikki joined in. "He needs one now!"

"Doctor Angie," Marta blurted, willing to say anything that would have Tiny removed from her home.

What Rikki had hoped to absorb was clarity. With desperation she asked, "Is that a man or woman?"

THE BUNGLERS
◆

That's when it hit the fan.

The message board lit up inside the Las Vegas Central Precinct, more wildly than a room filled with birthday cakes and all of the candles they could handle.

Victor's not always trusted team of apprentices, Barnes and Ernie, had lost Rikki. That was the depressing news that he chewed over before the flashing telephone LED's distracted him. What else can go wrong, he thought.

Victor sat with a clinched fist solidly pounding the edge of the standard issue, metal, desk contemplating his next move. The electrostatic paint job initially made the desk look new. For a while afterwards, that had him feeling better about his office. But the rigors of the stressful job, the collective incompetence of Barnes and Ernie, quickly brought him back to the reality of his daily routine—that grew bleaker with each passing year.

He was at a loss as to what to do next. He wanted to put those two bozos out of their combined misery, with a planned push over the side of the Hoover Dam. Sadly, that would've only partially relieved Victor's concern. He still had the problem of Rikki being gone.

Sure, he'd heard of Tony Fatino. Who in the southwest law enforcement community hadn't? But this Latin law enforcer wasn't going to allow Albuquerque's top cop to interfere. Not if Victor could help it. That was until Victor's desk cop later told him that Barnes had asked for the caller ID to Fat Tony's incoming call.

Though he couldn't prove it, Victor knew that somehow Fat Tony had circumvented Victor's local authority and gone straight to Barnes and Ernie with some kind of personal directive. It showed in the two men's faces shortly before they separated from Victor and left the stationhouse.

Victor also couldn't prove that Rikki was connected to that helicopter. What he couldn't prove and what he knew to be fact had a canal between them that Moses couldn't close.

Victor yawned, but taking a rest had to wait until he located Rikki. That was when he heard the shout from that same desk cop.

"Victor, you got a problem!"

Alarmed, Victor's piddling fingers froze as the desk cop continued articulating how deep the methodological hole had gotten. The desk cop stood at the door with a partially crumbled sheet of paper in hand.

"Vegas FD is on the outskirts of town, at what they're calling a suspicious fire."

"Their union just got a pay raise." He mumbled, "Something ours couldn't get." His vice got louder. "Whatever they found, it's their setback."

Victor snarled, thinking about how sweet that raise would've set with his bank account. Especially with the holiday purchases that recently stood out on his most recent VISA bill.

Victor readied himself for this latest interruption. "Go on," he granted.

"The fire investigators at the scene identified Barnes and Ernie as possible suspects."

"Suspects?"

Victor was again lost with the happiness that only Hoover Dam could bring.

"They actually called them 'suspects'?" He wanted the answer to be anything but yes.

"No," the desk cop answered.

Victor was relieved.

"He called them "prime suspects."

Victor was at a loss asking, "Anything else?"

"Isn't that enough?"

He shook his head in disgust, as only a boss can, motioning for the man across the room to go back to whatever he was doing.

"Morons," he mumbled to himself.

He often talked to himself. When he first got the job, fellow officers thought he was a bit touched in the head. Later, they all would learn that talking to one's self is a common byproduct of policing. It comes in handy when there's no one around who will listen.

This time, however, he thought to himself, there's an outside chance that Barnes and Ernie won't say anything until after I speak to whoever's running things at the Fire Department.

Then he knew of the unlikely scenario that would allow that to happen.

On the outer edge of Vegas, the fire raged inside that used-to-be frequently used, metal, shed. Whatever was in those fifty-five gallon drums was reacting wildly to the fire.

A second fire truck had to be called in, to help fight the chemical reactions that were going on inside as the result of the intense heat.

Barnes and Ernie did their best not to look at each other, thinking that would be a giveaway to the fire investigator, Paul, who stood in front of them stroking his chin. Typically, police and fire never saw eye-to-eye on anything that had to do with either procedure, or the pay that resulted. He was one of the few in his department, who didn't have a rooted dislike for the cops, figuring "We're all in it together" was the best motto.

"What you're telling me doesn't add up," he said to the two out of uniform police.

Paul was a beleaguered forensic criminalist of many prominent years, who continued scratching his leathery cheek, dissatisfied with the independent—yet similar sounding—lies that Barnes and Ernie had recited not two minutes earlier.

He pointed to Ernie. "You said that you saw who started the fire."

Barnes absentmindedly nodded, unaware that he was doing so, not realizing that made him appear to be in on the falsehoods being enunciated.

"But—"

He pointed to Barnes.

"You told me that that both of you got here after my fire truck."

Paul wanted to believe in the goodness in civil servants, though his confusion mounted.

"How can that be?"

"Paul!" shouted another firefighter, standing beside the puffing, diesel fire truck.

He was having noticeable problems turning one of the water wheels.

"The pump's stuck. All my guys are in the building. I need your help!"

"Damnit, Paul!" the firefighter insisted, against anything that Paul was thinking to do about the two policemen.

Paul yanked himself from them to get back to the truck. There he saw its hoses tangled. But not nearly to the extent as the twisted tale that he just got finished hearing. None of it was making a dime's worth of sense. Police are trained to uphold the law. He knew these cops had just done something. Through it all, he was unable to take his eyes from the silvery-white ash that was on Barnes and Ernie.

THE DOCTOR
◆

Rikki's head snapped forward, yanking her to an improved level of awareness. She couldn't relax. That was hardly something new. Such was the case while she sat in the after hours waiting room, not many yards from where Meyer's no-questions-asked doctor worked feverishly on Tiny's life threatening wound.

The outer hall was chilly and dreary, absent of any of the physician's office added extras befitting one of the top surgeons in the west.

Rikki was foggy as to why a man in his position would risk it all to help Tiny, someone who was constantly on the periphery of illegality. Tiny wasn't worth exchanging the upper echelon of Vegas society circles, to get dragged before Nevada's ethics board, to hear why he should be stripped of his well earned medical license. There had to be a reason why this doctor wanted to walk both sides of the fence.

It wasn't easy to see the hour on the wall; that was probably for the best. Had she been able to, it would have been a constant reminder of what was needed to get done. She had hoped to get more useful answers about Meyer and the chopper.

"Ahhh!" Tiny wailed a masculine scream from behind a wall that wasn't thick enough to fully block out that which streamed from the suffering man on the other side. He was lying there thinking how death might even-out a life that had turned out much different than he ever thought it would. His last breath might clean-up all of his past wrong doings.

Rikki promised that if he lived through it, she wasn't going to remind Tiny of his begging episode.

She had fallen asleep by the time the doctor came into view. He wiped his hands, weary from too many hours on his feet. He felt like a not ready for stud racehorse, having finished just outside the win, place, or show money.

"Well?" Rikki asked, having rebounded from the barriers of daydreaming to minimal awareness.

She wanted any type of encouragement; even if the doctor could do nothing more than shell-out a bucket of empty promises.

The expression on his face, however, said it all. "I did what I could."

Rikki's imagination was getting the best of her, while pulling her mood down rapidly. Every movie that she had ever seen had the doctor giving bad news that the questioner was never prepared for.

"He's in shock from the massive blood loss."

Her depleted morale was at subterranean levels. "Is he gonna pull through?"

The doctor inched his head from side to side, dropping it in pursuit of his downcast spirit. "I doubt it."

Rikki's mouth opened refusing to close. Her tongue that couldn't enunciate feelings that attempted to pour to the surface.

The doctor added, "From the little that I knew about him, he seemed like a loner. Did he speak of having any family that you can contact?"

"May I go in and see him?" Meyer asked, unable to wait any longer to revisit the subject of his ruined living room carpet.

The doctor nodded once, not wanting the visit to last. Then he removed his gloves and sat beside Rikki. "You're with the police."

"Albuquerque. But keep in mind, Doc. I'm not even here."

"Understood." He lowered his Charlton Heston voice, "What did Meyer tell you about me?"

"He said if anyone could save Tiny, it's you."

"I've been friends with Meyer and his wife for years." His words were quiet, head jerking to where Tiny was. "By law, I'm required to report this."

She wanted him to look past that requisite as she continued to listen.

"There's no reason why I need to immediately. If he pulls through, get him out of here before I phone-in the incident. By the time the authorities get here, he'll be a memory...Is there some place where you can take him?...If the police see him before I file my report, it's bye-bye medical license."

* * *

Two mornings later, Tiny gained full consciousness in his apartment, coughing with a harshness reminiscent of an eighteen wheel Kenworth starting up on a cold South Dakota morning.

He thought that he had been sleeping for a thousand years, straining mightily to turn over, struggling to focus on Rikki and Meyer who stood looking over him.

"This can't be heaven. You two are here."

"Try not to be too disappointed." She leaned forward, unintentionally partially exposing warm breasts—courtesy of an unexpected cleavage—to wipe the drool from the edges of Tiny's swollen lips.

"You're going to heaven?" she asked with all the disbelief that money could never afford. "Not even under a quota system."

That made Tiny hoot, sending pain throughout his bullet ravaged leg. With no strength, he accepted a few sips from a cup of lukewarm coffee that Meyer had handed to him.

"Thanks," she told Tiny with gratitude, indicating that the bullet he caught was heading for her.

"Don't get mushy on me. I might throw up."

"You already did," Meyer said, producing a receipt for the new carpet that Marta had delivered the day before.

"Get out of town," Tiny said. "If push comes to shove, the Doc's close enough," he assured. "I'll be ok," he winced.

She took out a piece of paper and wrote, speaking to Meyer.

"This's my number. Call me if anything happens."

She bent to kiss Tiny's wrinkled forehead, holding her hand on his.

"Don't forget about me," Tiny said.

"Consider it a contract." She contemplated her next move, wondering how to get out of Vegas without being seen. Then it hit her. She hadn't checked-out of the hotel figuring that should keep Victor and his goons positioned there waiting. It was decision time and hard choices are always that.

THE EXIT

◆

Everybody needs one.

Rikki was half-way to making it out of town with her life in tact. That was a near miracle if she ever saw one. In her short life she'd seen few. One thing about being on the run, everybody looks like the pursuer. It was a scary proposition.

As she walked the station's padded strip everyone's eyes seemed to be on her. That continued the full run of the concrete floor. Rikki couldn't take her mind from Tiny, and the pitiful way that he looked when she last saw him.

With all of his below grade habits, others had to be aware of where he lived. His sexual appetite for the hookers throughout the city all but guaranteed that it was common knowledge exactly how many steps it was to his never made-up bed. If there was one thing they'd spill their trashy guts to the police for, it was for reduced legal charges against themselves. That explained the common practice for police for frequent streetwalkers for information.

"Eight Twelve for Albuquerque is now ready to board," resounded over the bus terminal's difficult to hear public address system.

Rikki hated when things were over, but hearing that announcement she managed to step faster. Her blouse was sticking to her as though she was born wearing it.

Not long afterwards, she moved by yet another bus terminal employee, who did her best to look ten years younger. For the most part, her beauty strategy worked. There was one little extra that stood out to make this person different.

It was the listening device in her ear that was not well hidden by hanging strands of semi-curly hair. Rikki was certain that she had been followed.

Passing through the last in a series of conspicuous metal and weapons screening devices, Rikki was in the aisle of the rapidly filling bus.

Removed from countless travelers who squeezed past her seat, uttering the usual "Excuse meees," she managed to drift into a deep REM sleep. Centered amidst her dreamland were misty patterns that always returned to the one person whom mattered most. Her mom.

TONY'S TALE

◆

Rikki was back in Albuquerque, but for how long? Compared to the dry sweltering heat of Las Vegas the temperature wasn't all that uncomfortable. If the weather was all that Rikki had to be concerned about, that would've been enough. The late day atmosphere was stiff with the one, two, three progression that high crime case solving produced. Her next point of unanswered concern was why did Tony spring her so quickly from Victor's embrace without learning why she was being interrogated?

She walked past the plainclothes officers who stood at the exit. The two police maintained a demeanor that didn't lend any hint as to why they were there, or whom they were staking out. In any event, she walked past them with no fanfare.

And what was Meyer's role in all of this?

She remembered the way he looked when she first saw him. It wasn't until later when she considered that his wrists weren't nearly as chaffed from the handcuffs as they should've been. A man who was supposedly shackled for as long as he claimed to have been, should've had skin as red as the fire engine that idled near Barnes and Ernie after Paul called Victor to report the duo as suspicious.

Was the Vegas trip really worth it? What new and binding evidence was there for Rikki to go on? All that was certain was that the gems were still missing. Until they turned up, Rikki was going to need a damn good lawyer.

Once outside the Albuquerque Bus Transportation Center, she was as nervous as could be, given this was where they found her car not long ago. She hoped that since this was where they located her car, it might be the last place they'd expect her to turn up.

She walked with haste outside, not so much as to attract unwanted attention, to her substitute means of transportation. She was relieved to be back inside the subcompact and the relative safety that it offered. The instant she closed the door…

"Surprise!"

Having come out from under the driver's seat, she snapped to her left with pistol aimed. Her heart raced to the beat of the Greyhound Detroit diesel engine that had delivered her from Vegas.

"I thought you'd feel left-out if nobody was here to say welcome back," Erik said.

"You're a fuckin' idiot."

"I was hoping to be fucking you," he smiled, bending to kiss the glass at the height where her cheek was.

"You're begging me to shoot you," she panted, perspiring. Slowly, the pistol's barrel went below the door's height and out from his sight. A slow click released the cocked trigger from its prepared firing position.

"How did you know about this car?" she asked.

"Last Halloween, you were in this car with your niece, trying to fix me up with one of your dog pound relatives."

He straightened to stand, protruding his butt to anyone pulling up behind him.

"Fatso'd like it if you blew me away. I'd be gone. You'd go down on a second degree. Two fewer cops for him to yell at when he had nothing better to do."

She started the car, making the window glide down, sorely in need of fresh air to clear her anxiety. She needed any distraction to cool her nervousness over Erik's games.

She pleaded, "Do you mind standing between the headlights?"

"Can't. Tomorrow's payday. I've got tons of bills. The day after tomorrow, I'll consider it."

It had been a difficult week, and she just wanted to get the days over with. "Let me drop you back at your car."

"That won't be necessary."

He walked around to the passenger's side door. She reached to unlock it, allowing him entry, feeling that what was to follow was surely to be something out of line with anything that she considered to her advantage.

"If you're setting me up for a 'By the way, I've got nowhere to sleep tonight. Can I crash at your place?' Forget it."

He can't be that dumb.

"Now that you mention it," he whined. "Can I?"

He's that dumb.

After seeing the helpless, puppy dog, look that he wore, she reassessed her grip on disapproval to change the subject. "What'd I miss while I was away?"

Erik had a blanketed sense of disheartened silence.

She tried to decipher his expression, and what had caused the sudden downward turn in his mood—beyond her sexual rejection. "What'd I say?"

"You didn't hear?"

"Nobody tells me nothing. Even if they tried, I've been incognito."

He shifted to qualify. "In spite of you thinking that I was only out here to get into your pants—"

"Make your point."

"Another jewelry spot was hit…Tony circulated word around the precinct that you had something to do with it."

Whatda-fuck did I just hear?

"He said it's no coincidence that you left Albuquerque right after that store was robbed."

THE ATTIC

◆

"You had something to do with the jewelry store robberies."

Erik's words about Tony couldn't have sounded worse if a judge had recited them to her. Maybe that's why he had Victor release her. Then again that didn't make sense. If she were truly a suspect, he'd have had Victor detain her longer.

Later, a mystified Rikki was mentally spent after dropping Erik off at his place. That whole meeting with him was out of whack. Even the sex wasn't all that great. After the incident near the lake in the back of his car, he promised to "really make her cum" once he got her on a bed. She came today all right—to the conclusion that she never should have returned to Albuquerque.

When Rikki reached the front door, her hand missed the lock with the key, scratching the wood around the brass fitting. It wasn't an extensive wait before she got inside. When she did an indescribable odor rushed out to greet her. The sensory discomfort from it gave her a piercing pain that clobbered the side of her head. Just that quickly the smell was gone. It went away so fast that it was probably the imaginary bi-product of her problematic life that was slipping away from any fixed point that existed pre-man in the lake. Somehow, however, she had an extrasensory feeling that the odor was somehow real.

Inside her house there was a light hammering sound, lifting Rikki's attention to the plaster ceiling. Never once did she think that someone was in the house with her, reasoning it to be some kind of subconscious reflection of years gone by. Jack used to do a lot of carpentry work in the attic, and she was sure that was what she wanted to hear, anything that would bring him back.

She dropped a short stack of unopened mail on the kitchen table, still soaking up the sights of home sweet home. A manila envelope read, "PHOTOS DO

NOT BEND." She wasn't about to take the chance of having her mail stopped at the Post Office while she was gone. Not many can boast about having a mail carrier who can keep a secret. While he neatly stashed her bundled letters, he never mentioned that he was holding them for her until she returned. One letter in particular stood out. It was from the Social Security Administration office—addressed to Heather.

The upstairs noises continued to penetrate her head like a tainted memory that she couldn't shake away. Too bad, people can't control their dreams—day or night.

She dropped her purse, quickly making a fast track trip to the attic. The only way there was through the closet. When she bent to see through the small swinging door that led up there, she saw the uncertainty that only darkness can bring. When she pushed the door slightly wider, she saw Jack.

Right away he clicked off the bare light bulb that hung from the low height, A-frame, ceiling.

"Yes," came his muffled, agitated, delivery.

She was puzzled as to why he was doing carpentry alterations in the dark. It seemed odd that he took an otherwise docile Saturday to do work in the attic, considering how Jack was the laziest man she'd ever seen, or why he courageously returned home at all.

Suddenly, Jack began to dissipate, thinning out before her disbelieving eyes. He was never there. She wanted to see him so badly that her imagination was the only way to make that impossible visualization occur.

With thoughts that could no longer be relied on, she dragged herself back into the main body of the house to worry. Her cell went off, jolting her from the daydream. The vibration nearly sent her through the roof. She noticed the number had a Las Vegas area code.

"A couple of cops named Barnes and Ernie'r swarming all over. They'r madder than hell that you got away," Meyer said. "What I was too scared to tell you then, is that they were the two who kidnapped me."

Damn.

"I'm pinned-down. Rita's scared shitless. Keeps telling me we have to get out of town, fast. I've got to find a way out of here."

He peered through the Venation blinds, seeing Barnes and Ernie across the street. They were speaking to each other in hushed tones, before stepping from the curb, headed towards Meyer's home.

Rikki frowned at not being able to hear anything. "Meyer, are you there!?"

The line went cold. Rikki's palms were soaked.

THE GOGGLES
◆

The next morning a lizard carefully crawled along the windowsill, unaware of the possibility of being swooped-up by someone, and carted off for shipment to a variety of pet shops across the country, or being spotted by a hungry owl and carved-up for dinner. Just that quickly it leaped away, after missing a fly that buzzed close. Rikki felt like that reptile.

On the other side of the screen, Rikki watched the results of an Internet search. Various lines of highly sensitive, police eyes only, information rolled up in front of her. Reading on, she thought about the lengthy sequence that had stretched from the lake, to the crashed helicopter in Las Vegas, to Meyer. That was when something of profound interest appeared.

The night vision goggles found on the jumper were U.S. Army issue, and only used by governmental special forces units.

Methodically, she read through the serial numbers affixed to the night vision goggles that had been manufactured solely for the Army over the past five years. Finally, she got a match to the number on the pair found in the parachutist's bag. That pair had been warehoused at Fort Dix, New Jersey.

THE SEX
◆

Angles Club finally reopened with a socially stimulating, underground, impact. It was like a cold slap on the face, sharply inviting, seeing it's grand doors swinging wide to accept properly screened guests again.

The highly anticipated excitement levels knifed the sounds through its deco walls out into the street, playing leapfrog with everything that got in the way. Dozens of customers again waited for their chance to be patted-down for illegal anything—by the same bouncer who was noticeably better presented—before they went inside to enjoy what was easily the best after-hours, plaster cracking, music in the city.

At the midpoint between the hostess podium and the back wall, Rikki nursed a glass of icy water, thinking about the last time she was there. The club's physical makeup had changed. But inside it was still Angles, the funkiest place to be.

In spite of the nonreciprocal oral sex that the bouncer offered—and Rikki declined—she managed to get the best booth for people watching.

Earlier in the day, she had seen Erik. Thankfully, he chose not to pester her about what she was doing later. She was beginning to want something different from him, though lying to keep her distance from him wasn't something that she savored. Sex with him used to involve feelings of greatness, but immediately after she stopped squirting she felt empty, longing for more. Someone more like herself.

"Mind if I join you?"

Startled, Rikki looked up to see Sharon who was also in need of something other than the superficials that the social club represented.

Rikki's affirmative nod was enough. She sat and barely looked at Rikki, choosing to see who was on the dance floor, bouncing her head to the thumping sounds that the energetic band performed with enthusiasm while giving energy a new definition.

Sharon managed to fit in, "How'd your trip go?"

Rikki sipped the water gingerly.

"Learned enough to make it worthwhile. And you? How-bout that guy I saw you with the last time I was here?"

Sharon wasn't about to let on that she knew that it was Mark who she was seen holding onto.

"Haven't seen'm since." She nonchalantly looked away, then, decided to give it up. "It's been lonely." She felt it was futile to conceal the obvious. "The good thing is, it only bothers me on two occasions."

"When might that be?"

"Day. And night."

Sharon motioned for the waitress to come over. She wanted to guzzle and feel the effects of any booze she could wrap her sexy lips around, anything to chase away the blues.

"A tall glass of wine."

The waitress waited for Rikki's order.

"I'm fine," Rikki said.

The waitress wrote the order on a minuscule piece of paper, compressing it in her palm and walking away.

Sharon looked at Rikki's water, and the polite manner in which she was idle with it, "You've got a long way to go to be a lush."

There are some aspects to one's personality that we think will never change. Sharon had taken a liking to this conversation. It was something that was impossible when she was riding high, coat-tailing it, with Mark.

Rikki noticed that Sharon wasn't sniffing, as was the case when they first met. "There's something different about you."

"I stopped gettin' high…Don't ask how that's been goin' for me." She pouted, "Because it hurts."

"Why'd you stop?" Rikki sipped. "I hate enduring pain. Unless it's—"

Sharon caught the sexual innuendo. "Had to, if I'm gonna score a real job."

The queen of luxurious fast lane get a job?

"Sounds like a healthy start," Rikki encouraged, feeling that it was unlikely that Sharon would ever work a straight job.

"I need a clear head for a battle that's brewing." The waitress returned, placing the glass in front of Sharon, who reached into her purse.

Rikki said, "I got it," indicating that the payment was taken care of.

"Thanks."

The waitress took the bills from Rikki, and off she went to scour the room for anyone else in need of internal lubricant to keep them company for the night.

"I inherited a problem," Sharon said.

Rikki never considered one that could top hers.

"Mark was a stickler for details, except when it came to payin' his legitimate bills on time."

Rikki thought of Jack. "There're a lot of people like that."

"I got a letter from the city tax people, sayin' our house is in arrears six months. If the debt isn't caught up soon, and I'm talkin' soon, the crib's goin' back to the city's ownership."

She gulped, leaving droplets on the edges of those lips. Rikki took a curious notice.

"It's money I don't have forever to come up with." She twirled her glass before chugging. "If I don't pay-up, the highest bidder gets the deed, and I'm out on the street."

She felt embarrassed before turning to Rikki. There was nothing that Rikki could do to help ease her dilemma. She had opened the verbal flood gate of financial want.

"Then me and the sidewalk are gonna be on a first name basis." She finished her glass.

"Easy with the drink, will ya?"

"Why?"

At the rate Sharon was going, chronic bent elbow disease was sure to be in her near future. She went to light a cigarette. Seeing the match burn made Rikki repulse, giving her a fiery, back alley blaze, flashback. Sharon blew it out.

"Even cigarettes don't even do it for me anymore."

"What does?" Rikki asked.

"Having someone to talk to who I trust. Even though he rarely listened to a word I said, I could always talk to Mark." She sighed with recollection. "Even with that, I never really trusted him."

Rikki couldn't help guessing what that meant. "Why'd you stay with him?"

"Money. Excitement. Stupidity. Take your pick...It really doesn't matter now." The more she thought about it, she was only sorry to see Mark gone, because of the excitement that his money brought to her.

"What about you?" Sharon asked, unsure if a truthful answer would follow, sliding her feet out of casual footwear, placing them flat on the floor closer to Rikki's. The chill on her soles gave her a distraction. "Havin' any fun in your life?"

Except for a once-in-a-while freelance sexual fling with Erik, she was empty when it came to having someone to call on for what counted most. Companionship.

"You could list my friends on a piece of confetti."

She thought of Tiny, desperately wanting him to be safe. Because it was her fault that he was suffering. He was probably hanging on to dear life, while she escaped to a nightclub, talking the evening away as though all was right with the world.

On the subject of having someone to call, Tiny was long overdue getting back to her, as to his end of the fallout after she left Vegas.

She felt Sharon's bare foot lightly touching hers. Figuring that it was probably by chance, she floated with other considerations.

"Mark's profession had him away from home a lot...Now that he's never comin' back, I don't miss him as much as I thought I would."

Her rarely ignored fingernails contacted the artistically etched tabletop.

"One thing's sure true about him not bein' around. It's a heckova-lot quieter at the crib. No more cops snoopin', wire-tappin' all our calls, somebody goin' through our garbage lookin' to dig-up any evidence they could against him." She wanted to exclude Rikki. "No offense bout the cops thing."

"None taken."

Sharon was uncharacteristically sad. "It's just me there alone to catch the hell aftermath he caused."

The waitress returned. "Anybody want more?"

Sharon requested, "Another for me."

"Another it is." The waitress added to the order, thankful to see additions made to the bill. The server's bylaw is: The more the bill the more the tip, unless the customer was a cheap bastard. In which case, the more the waste of time it is bringing her anything other than a map showing the way out of the club.

Despite being fundamentally at odds with the woman sitting beside her—Rikki being the searcher and Sharon the subject—Rikki began to feel more at ease. Heck, the investigation was going on forever. Maybe Erik was correct when he implied how Rikki was chasing the unknown and the unproven to her own undoing.

The change of pace that Angles offered was something that was absent from Rikki's social register for quite some time. It was harmless relaxation. The second drink arrived, and was properly placed on the lace-trimmed coaster that was directly in front of Sharon.

Sharon hoisted her chilled glass to Rikki. "Bottoms up."

Rikki acknowledged that with her water held high before swallowing. Some of the water spilled across her blouse. She was aware that Sharon was looking at a mouth that savored a good licking.

The rest of the time there was spent with the two of them exchanging semi-idle conversation about their short-term futures. Amidst the eye wandering and head turning, Rikki didn't see something dissolving in her water.

All Rikki could see of the digital clock was the first numbers before the colon. From that she gathered that it was six something. What was lacking was the day of the week.

Her mind spun in the haze over what had been placed in her drink countless hours earlier. Was this another dream in which the mystery woman would appear again?

First of all, the covers that she was under weren't hers. Neither were the over-size, custom, bed; or full apartment size room in which she lie. Wetness between her legs had her convinced that something had gone on, though she wasn't able to fully figure out what. She tried to think through remnants of the post sex haze that swam upstream against the once mighty currents of intellectual reasoning and discretion.

The morning light that flashed through imported, in glass, blinds did so in such a way as to cast a diffused hue throughout the well appointed room. In her home, were the old fashion kind that refused to stay down over the window once they were pulled. Rikki craved knowing where she was. Her head couldn't stop gyrating to allow for clear thinking. She was resigned to keep questioning thoughts silent until more strength and mental awareness arrived. Repeated questions weren't going away: Why was her nose sore? Who was in bed next to her?

The person's face was hidden by a series of evenly matched designer pillows, the variety she could never afford. This was further proof that she was in someone else's home. The hairless arm belonging to the person next to Rikki flopped over her stomach strongly hinted that it was a female. The stranger's unconscious moaning announced that whatever went on in that room was still in that woman's thoughts. There was a pounding nervousness surfacing from deep within Rikki's untapped soul. What used to be the fantasy of being with another woman had changed to the reality of what had already occurred.

Uh, no.

Rikki rolled with a quiet stillness away on the queen size bed, with whoever it was beside her inching closer. Standing in the nude, she searched for pants.

"Where-ya goin'?" the young woman asked with a voice that purred from beneath the covers.

"Work," Rikki answered. That was the last place that she wanted to be other than in front of a judge explaining her side of the missing gems.

It was then that Rikki recognized the voice.

"It's Sunday." Sharon yawned, suspecting the past evening's fun was over, wanting it not to be.

She wondered why Rikki had to go so soon. Sharon pawed to draw her back. She longed to be held since the day Mark was nowhere to be found. She believed that Rikki staying longer wasn't so appalling.

"Aren't you hungry?" the kitten asked of her departing guest.

With that, the satin covers slid off. Sharon lifted her T-shirt to show more, rubbing her palm across each to make them talk out loud. Leaving the best for last, she exposed soft legs wide with invitation.

Stunned with a rekindled curiosity, Rikki's heart revved like a race car's high octane pistons. As sexual intrigue overcame all lingering traces of professionalism, she climbed back in bed to lie on top of Sharon's warm, receptive, heart. She really didn't want to leave, especially when she heard that it was time to eat.

"That's my little girl," Sharon complimented.

They kissed with a mouth-watering fill. Both women ravaged the other's open mouth, with a ferocity that could only be rivaled by one who had been removed from food for weeks on end. Theirs was that passionate junction where loneliness met company. It was an interlocking of bodies and ambitions.

In the basement laundry room, two pair of subtle print pants were grinding in the washing machine, cleansed of orgasmic fluids from two desperate women who sought something that—before last night—their lives had failed to satisfy.

Wearing only a sheer bra, Rikki stood in front of the bathroom mirror liking what she saw more than usual. When she opened the medicine cabinet, she saw an array of makeup that was more befitting of a movie actress. There was also something strange. It was a tube of glue. For that instant, she thought that she had seen an identical tube in the window of that costume shop.

The kitchen ceiling fan clicked-on to lazily twirl. It circulated the air, but didn't ease any of the rising heat from the oven. Entwined in those temperatures were the distinctive fragrances of simmering sweet rolls. The familiar ping from the oven timer signaled the breakfast chewables were brown and ready.

"When were you told that you have to move out of the house?" Rikki asked to no one standing there.

Sharon came in from the den, floppy sock covered feet dragging across the hardwood floor. Her see-through nightie had its naughty stitched edges stopping at the lower curve of her tight, rounded, buttocks.

Sharon reached for, then bit into a crisp apple. "I got the note not long after you visited here the first time."

"There has to be a way to stall the proceedings against you," Rikki said.

Sharon sat close enough to touch her, thinking better of it, considering Rikki's preoccupied stare.

"Are you ok?" she asked.

Rikki nodded with a complete understanding of what was being asked.

"Don't worry. When I was with Mark, I made a lot of acquaintances. Most of them when the jealous idiot wasn't lookin' or listenin'…Somebody I met back then is bound to let me shack at their place til I get my own roof."

She sighed with noticeable apprehension and anticipated sorrow.

"I wonder what I'll have to do to get one of those low-life friends of his to make me an offer."

THE GRAND JURY
◆

It was a little past 4:05 in the afternoon, on a day when easier decisions could've been made. That was when the Grand Jury voted to indict Rikki Luckett.

THE QUESTION
◆

Rikki was running out of time. That was when she sought the telephone to bail her out. What she didn't see then was that she was headed straight into destruction.

"Warden, can you tell me if Bubba had any visitors?"

She was one of the last people that the Warden wanted to hear from. The absolute last was the Director of the Bureau of Prisons. Why? Because Bubba was nowhere to be found. With any shred of promising leads drying-up faster than fresh fruit in a sweltering sun, he wasn't filled with verbal openness.

"It's rare for long term cons to get visitors. Mostly because this is their final stop on the legal system's up the river guest pass. Face it, who wants to be bothered with convict scum that has been exiled here?"

Disgusted, he sucked in bitterness, wanting to discourage whatever she had to say—syllable by syllable. He counted the seconds for her to hang up. She didn't, forcing him to continue.

"What difference does it make who came to see him? Even if somebody did, visitors do all they can not to fill-in their correct names when they sign-in." With much more on his overtaxed mind, he wanted out from the conversation. "Will that be all, Detective?"

He was convinced that Rikki was somehow connected to that darn reporter, the one with the reputation for having the platinum stroke with a pen to ruin everyone in her path. The one who tried to trash his upstanding reputation a while ago. That never sat well with the Warden, because anyone who ever interviewed him was getting kicked-back money to write only nice things.

"Warden, it's important. Think. Was there anyone who visited Bubba?"

I see how she made detective, he thought, against his will to hang up on her. She probably pestered her superiors till they caved-in and promoted her—just to get her off their backs.

"Now that I think about it," he recalled.

"Yes," she listened with peaking enthusiasm.

"There was a Sonny somebody."

THE AMBUSH
♦

Things were heating up to frightening measures—not by temperature, but in the degree of intensity. It all added up to making the present day sacred. It was a special time to be alive. But there was no telling if tomorrow was coming.

Coyotes howled in the distance. Like Bubba, they were in search of prey. Much like certain unsuspecting folks who were unaware that their collective sovereignty wasn't going to last much past the time when they would first see Bubba.

Late that pesky afternoon, Bubba sat atop an edgy boulder that had finally come to rest in the center of the road. He watched four protruding human legs scuffle dust from beneath the smoking Plymouth. Its hood was open, emitting smoke that rivaled the extent to which the outdoor temperature had risen. It was a day when being free didn't mean all that much.

C.C. and Teddy were shoulder to shoulder under the car, straining, working feverishly, beneath an engine that could barely maintain a shaky idle.

Bubba snarled, "How much longer you boys gonna need before we can git the hell outta here?"

C.C. twisted to crawl out first, removing his red headband, wiping sticky fingers that were covered with grime. Looking into a blinding sun, he squinted painfully, trying to adjust to Bubba's ominous silhouette.

"No tellin'," C.C. answered. "That-there rock slide cracked the radiator." He covered one nostril, blowing out remnants of dirty mucus. "It's shot-to-shit."

A high pitch hiss sounded from the radiator that yanked Bubba's attention to it. He had no understanding about cars. The little he managed to retain from his mechanical training—that he dropped out of a week after the Warden granted him permission to attend—was that cars can't run without a radiator.

Bubba spit to one side, barely missing his shoulder, hitting a bug that wanted water but not nearly that bad.

"Teddy!"

The other brother contorted to make himself seen.

"You backin'-up what Chowder head's tellin' me?"

Teddy saw this as his chance to finally be heard. "Ain't much of a chance that we'll get this thing runnin' agin'."

"What'r we gonna do for a ride?" C.C. calmly asked. "No tellin' how far it is to the nearest repair shop. Even if it was right over yonder, this thing ain't gonna make it."

In the ever shifting distance a wavering image loomed. It looked inviting. It was a mirage that appeared to have a chance to come true. Against the deafening silence that only the desert can manufacture, Bubba saw a station wagon getting closer.

From miles away, it passed thirsty cacti, creating streaming debris that kicked-up behind it as the unsuspecting vacationing family sped towards them.

Bubba said, "This-here might just be our guardian angel come to rescue us poe-folks."

Bubba checked his pistol to make sure that it was fully loaded, snapping the chamber back into place. With a mean temperament fueling his pride, he tore away his prison issue shirt, revealing a **Born To Lose** tattoo that was splashed— with many poorly drawn colors—across his hairy chest, typifying the spirit of the possessor whose confident smirk said it all.

Why not attack the station wagon? Each of them knew that they were already in so much trouble that another crime couldn't add anything to a sure-fire life sentence when they finally got caught.

"Do we have to kill'm? All we need it their car." Teddy's going soft approach wasn't well received.

Bubba pointed his gun at him. "If I have-ta tell you one more time to shut that mouth."

Bubba wouldn't really shoot him, but neither of his brothers were ready to bet that he'd show either of them any rarely seen mercy.

Pure meanness wouldn't allow Bubba to take his sights from the intended prey that streamed towards him.

"They ain't gonna know what hit-em." Bubba instructed, "Battle stations, boys."

Quickly, C.C. and Teddy climbed inside, rocking the chassis, settling in for the upcoming fight. Each secured his weapons, ducking beneath the window's height to remain out of sight.

Bubba slid his pistol in his pocket, then picked up a wrench to make it appear that he'd been working on his car under the unfair heat all afternoon.

"Quiet!" Bubba graced the bulge in his pocket, wanting mercurial speed to get to his pistol to fire when he needed it.

The station wagon got within range. Bubba began waiving his arms in a 'My car's broken-down' frustration.

The other driver saw him. Deciding it was unsafe to risk stopping. Instead, he floored the accelerator. As the speed neared its high RPM peak, the assailant's readiness turned to action. The ambush was on.

"Now!" Bubba shouted to his brothers, stepping out closer to the dusty roadway's center line. He dropped to a three-point stance and peppered away. The car's windshield shattered. The brothers fired from inside the Plymouth at the swerving station wagon.

There was a plentiful discharge of bullets as the car passed, hitting it and everything else in the surrounding geography. Animals and insects of every conceivable size that valued their lives ran for cover.

In an inverted pattern of escape, the station wagon skidded, zigzagging, before finally flipping over, spilling the occupants out onto the cracked, uncaring, ground. From inside the car came the hanging sounds of a toddler crying.

The three men ceased fire, rising to admire what they had done. Around the car there was choking, black, smoke that stayed right there, never thinning out. The mind-blowing smell of blood, and the finality that only mass murder can bring made the trio relish in what they had done. The three brothers looked at the car with its slowly turning wheels pointing to the dimming sky. It was then that the baby stopped crying.

"The car's no good to us."

C.C. added, "Least, we got in some target practice."

Bubba's face twitched. "Shut up."

Not far from them was a sign that read, Entering Albuquerque.

THE TAPE
◆

When the gloom of night arrived to the desert it was anything but a hospitable place.

Overwhelming warmth that was so prevalent during the day had vanished, to such a drastic degree that the rough-n-tumble flatlands hardly seemed like the same place. It was as though the sun was somehow offended, chased away to hide until the following day when it was safe to re-emerge. Everything that once scurried to burrow in to keep out of the daylight had the opportunity to explore nocturnal interests.

Rikki had not the time to check her email to see if Sharon had sent her the particulars on the impending expulsion from the house that she shared with Mark. She was probably busy, Rikki assumed. Then again, who is too busy to look after their own house?

She spotted a cassette tape that was wedged between the refrigerator and the counter. She couldn't understand why she hadn't seen it before.

She took her time to play it. But when she did she heard a scratchy, poorly recorded, voice that sounded like Heather's. Her words spoke of love, and how she felt that she'd been a burden to Rikki and Jack over the years. It closed suddenly by saying that she was gone and never coming back.

Rikki dropped it to the floor. The tape burst open, ruined forever. That was when it hit her that everyone she ever cared about had abandoned her.

THE FLIGHT SCHOOL
◆

In the background was the whining sound of a twin engine, 427 Bell helicopter, whirly-whirling while preparing for liftoff. There was a heavy drizzle that it sprayed, creating a waterspout effect that was interesting to watch, but not to be caught in.

The trailer turned office vibrated from the Bell's engine, behind a smattering of trees that leaned severely. The mechanic on duty used to take side bets with the students as to when the trees would fall. The over/under was six months. Rikki arrived there on the twentieth week.

She was outside walking about, raking her hair through a dry washcloth's cotton fibers, sponging away nature's elements of silt.

"Got an interest in flyin', do-ya?" called a man from behind one of those trees.

"This is your flight school?" she asked.

"The last time I looked." He readied to introduce himself. "Prestis Server's my name."

"Albuquerque Police. I need to talk to you."

Together, they went inside the office. There he walked past a stack of papers that were the entry level student signup application forms.

The unstable weather grew increasingly threatening. He parted uneven drapes, to see the 427 having great difficulty with wind sheer as it rocked on the helipad. Ultimately, the doors opened and the occupants got out and walked away in disgust. So much for being able to make their daughter's wedding on time. They had to find another way to be in Tuscaloosa by nine o'clock tomorrow morning.

Prestis felt badly for them. "One thing about the wind. It makes short work of the best flight plans."

Unbeknownst to Rikki was that he was referring to a time when he nearly didn't come home, after a rocky ride from a deep sea fishing trip off South Padre Island.

Prestis backed away from glass that had been cracked, when a child of one of his students was outside hitting rocks with a bat. Rather than simply pay for the glass, the embarrassed student abruptly changed flight schools. Prestis shifted his attention to Rikki, hoping that she might be interested in taking lessons in the near future. That would be a good thing, considering he hadn't sold a lesson in well over a week.

She pulled out a computer enhanced photograph of the parachutist. It was a digital correction that removed all of death's negative facial influences from the man's face.

"Word has it, this guy trained here."

She was bluffing. What other choice did she have? There were no other helicopter training schools for hundreds of miles, and she figured this one had to be it. The rising price of gas had her hoping that she'd strike results here. Plus, she wanted to somehow put pressure on him to open up if he knew anything that might be helpful to her.

Prestis reached into his overstuffed breast pocket for bifocals that were as easy to look through as that cracked window pane. He placed them awkwardly on his face before nodding.

"I never forget a paying customer. Especially one who always paid in cash."

He rubbed the imitation cue ball that was his head.

"He had one of those Wild West names...Six something."

"Sixkiller?"

He snapped his fingers, pointing to Rikki. "That's it." He always flew with a man named Rhett...The two of 'm were darn-near inseparable."

There was further confirmation of the link between Mark and Sonny.

The glasses came off. Prestis never liked the way he looked in them. His wife always said, "If you can see in'm, what difference does it make? It's not like Hollywood's looking for the new Clark Gable."

Then Prestis got worried. "Sonny's not in any kind of trouble, is he?"

"What makes you think that he might be?" Hers was an instantaneous look of accusation.

"Sorta makes sense, don't it? When the police come around asking bout somebody, they usually did something wrong."

She wasn't letting on to give away her position. "When was the last time you saw him?"

He winged-it from memory.

"It's been a while. Early last year, maybe."

He bit-down on dentures that were cheaply fashioned by a fly by night dentist.

"You're sure."

His certainty was amplified by his nod.

"That was when Rhett came to me one day, saying he found a heliport to lift-off from closer to where he lived. And he wanted to thank me for all I dun for the two of'm…I thought it was darn nice of'm to sign-off that way." Then he thought about the parent of the child who broke the window. "Most times, folks just up-n-go elsewhere."

"Do you have a picture of Rhett and Sixkiller together?"

He turned back to that short pile of papers; learning how to work a computer at his age wasn't going to occur.

"I keep track of all my students this way. After 9/11, the Feds said that they want photos and information on everybody participatin' in flight trainin'."

He fingered through an unevenly arranged pile of manila folders, sliding out the one marked February of the preceding year, causing the others to slip from his aging grasp, spilling onto the floor. From the one he held onto, he took out a single photograph then handed to Rikki. It showed the slightly taller Mark with his arm around Sonny—in an "I'm the leader of this duo" manner.

"Had to scrap with those fellas after I took the picture."

"Why?"

"Rhett offered me a fair amount of money to give it to'm."

"What'd you do?"

"I ain't no dummy…I took the money."

That greatly annoyed Rikki, having assumed Prestis to be on the positive side of that which is right.

"What then?" she asked.

"Rhett crumbled the picture. Said, it didn't do'm justice. Said, he'd pose for another one the following day."

"Did he?"

Prestis sucked air through upper incisors, shaking his head. "That was the last I saw of either of'm."

She gazed at the picture. "If he didn't return, how'd you get the one I'm holding?"

"My camera takes two pictures with each click of the shutter…Dem boys never knew it."

Rikki smiled at a job well done.

"I may look stupid, but pulling a fast one on the U.S. government is another story. No Ma'am, not me. Make sure you mail that picture back to me. I need it for the Feds. In case they drop by."

She tucked it safely away, and he followed her to the door.

In the car, Rikki sat thinking how before that day all she had to show as results was effort, and that wouldn't have been enough to please anyone. Suddenly, there was a definitive connection between Mark Rhett and the man in the lake. Not to mention, that they took helicopter lessons together. See what happens when a person gets the energy to leave the house? Results.

Prestis's eyes grew heavy seeing her drive off. He went back inside the trailer, paining that he hadn't sold her a flight lesson. He was feeling old and poorer at the same time, and that was a difficult combination to accept.

Rikki sat riveted to the photograph he had handed her. Mark had befriended Sonny—a man who damn-near looked just like him. That way, in case anything went wrong, he'd have a replacement corpse that the police would think was Mark. And having no usable fingerprints to trace from Sonny, the positive ID on it being Sonny seemed a lock.

THE REALTOR
◆

Sharon said, "Mark called her Hildy somebody."

Increasing, Rikki's suspicions about Tony were his insistence that Mark had been killed in the line of duty many years earlier. Unable to decipher why he was so strong to insist that misleading falsehood, she went out in the daylight to give herself a better chance to think about it.

Many of the city's upwardly mobile, the socialites, were out in droves that day. It was their showy exhibition of we're tired of being cooped-up, and we're determined to retake the open air for ourselves.

Along the sidewalks, couples and singles alike enjoyed coffee, tea, and whatever else made them feel good about warmer weather that finally arrived. They chatted lightly about a variety of things, ranging from business, to that which was purely social, to meaningless nothings. Comfortably seated in one of those outdoor café's, on a spongy chair that had a non-adjustable back, was Hildegard (Hildy) Stein.

Hildy was a hefty, third generation German, who thought her ancestors lost WWII, by virtue of a quick-count by the conspiring assemblage of international referees. Her flaming red hair brought to mind the myth that women of that hue had attitude problems. Regarding Hildy, they were correct.

She was the eldest daughter of Ethel and Lawrence Stein, who migrated from Dresden after the war, to find new roots in a town called Buzzards Breath, South Dakota.

Ethel treasured sacrificing for others. It wasn't an eternity before she landed a job teaching at a local elementary school. Not long afterwards, she started a small Bible study group in the basement of the local Lutheran church. Everyone warmed to her as she had to them.

Lawrence—never call him Larry—wasn't equally disposed in the direction of ever seeking gainful employment. Before Hildy had reached the age of ten, Lawrence was killed in a botched robbery at a local check cashing establishment. Unfortunately for the Stein family, he was the thief. The Stein's took a terrible social beating after that. Not many months afterwards, Ethel took ill. Eventually, she died from a chronic case of loneliness and despair, over the compiled dishonor over what her husband had done.

That left Hildy in the care of the grandmother. From then on, she was raised with unbending discipline that bordered on abuse. The resulting imbalance from the lack of family warmth left Hildy to erect an emotional fence between her and others. Instead of having friends, she had books. She knew that in the long run, that would someday enable her to raise herself to become a somebody. Then she would never be in need of anything, or anyone, again.

At sixteen, she was an avid shortstop. That is, until a wayward throw from a player on the other team struck her in the left ear while she ran to first base. The result was permanent sensory loss in that ear, leaving her with persistent headaches. She was also cursed with recurring, incurable, constipation. That fact made her full of shit in more ways than a thousand.

She graduated from an advanced learning program at the University of New Mexico. With both grandparents gone, there was no one at her graduation to share the experience with her. The bitterness of having to be part of such a festive occasion—with other students happily jumping around with loving others—never went away. From then on she was a one woman presentation.

In spite of a few opportunities to do so, she chose not to marry. Though some of the men in her social climbing life had demonstrated more promise than others. The sticking point was that she had few equals. She was a go-getter. They were not.

Except for an un-crowned prince who—after a rather brief time together—proposed a future life of elegance. The "Will you marry me?" contained more showy language than any demonstrated ability to pay for the engagement ring that she picked out.

Then there was the laid-out wedding ceremony that was more for public pretense and advertisement than a representation of true love. The likelihood of matrimonial bliss soon evaporated beneath the blanket of financially rational practicality, once she learned that his title was more distinguished than was the soon-to-be groom. It went without saying that the marriage plan remained on the wedding planner's list of deposits returned.

Since then hers was a productive life. Someone once asked her how it felt having never been married. She was rarely caught at a loss to explain. "Compared to what?" she would answer. In the recesses of her mind, she knew that there was always time for it if the right husband scenario came along.

She was an uncomplicated battler in need of space to punch back at people who got in her way. Her personality told anyone not paying her to keep their distance. It was the way that she informed others that she was of better quality than they were. It was the condescending manner in which she made it comprehensible how catching up to her socio-economic status was best left to another's hopes. If it was business, however, Hildy was all charm.

She was influential and physically imposing, resentful of any mention of her physical mass. Mostly, because she figured negative remarks about her came from those with complexes of inferiority. Her haughty, puffed-up, style was the aftermath of an exaggerated impression of her sense of importance. Make no mistake about it, she was hot-stuff in every section of New Mexico's commerce community.

It took a noticeable amount of daring to be at her side. Few could boast to have the courage, or the interest, to do so for very long. That is, unless it meant riding her clout to gain some measure of financial advantage for themselves.

By mid-morning that uncommonly warm day, Hildy's irritation deepened as she watched Rikki take a seat near her. She immediately knew that it promised to be less than a positively anticipated interaction between them. Hildy had an innate ability to locate those who could best serve her needs. Rikki, on the other hand, was neither required nor desired.

"Try asking to sit beside me like everybody else."

Rikki tweaked, "I was hoping you would've lined up something a little more formal for my arrival."

"Indeed," Hildy snipped, looking at Rikki with rising doubts that this upcoming verbal jousting would hold any meaning. "Long time no harass, Detective."

"Don't sugar coat it. Tell me what you really think."

She couldn't help noticing Rikki's face. "How'd you get the nose? Did she close her legs too tight?"

Rikki was taken by the question, figuring it unlikely that she knew about Sharon. But Hildy was plugged in, and it wouldn't have surprised her if Hildy's span of gossip intake had that far reaching ability. Hell, Rikki didn't care. She was in pursuit of her own ends.

"What's the matter?" Hildy felt in control of the pipeline of inside information. "You don't think I hear things?"

Hildy sipped her espresso, then was forced to look back at Rikki.

"As I would've predicted, this conversation promises to be less distinguished than the espresso." Hildy poured her cup into a small flowerpot at the table's center.

Rikki smiled, "Very well, then. Where shall we drink?"

Hildy held in her chuckle.

"There's got to be a better reason for you to come to my table than to discuss the pleasant old times we never had."

Beneath the cloud of important business appointments that Hildy had lined up for later, she wasn't comfortable with Rikki occupying the chair that was reserved for several clients who were expected at any minute.

"I'm here about the sale of the Richberg property," Rikki said.

"You mean, foreclosure," said the magnate of southwest real estate, finally having discovered the real reason why the two were speaking at all. "My sources tell me, the property's going on the auction block at the end of the week." Then came the condescension. "I think it's a little beyond your financial means. So why ask about it?"

Rikki shook her head to indicate that Hildy was in for a shock. "I can handle it."

Surely, that got Hildy's attention, causing her open mouth to remain so.

"You see, the house that you originally sold to Sharon Richberg isn't going anywhere, until after my investigation is finished."

For Hildy, what was the point of this endless banter? She wasn't about to let something as inconsequential as legality get in the way of making a good sale. Hell, she had her own problems. One of which was the second installment on her pre-retirement, preconstruction cost, condo in South Beach that she was already two days late mailing.

Hildy continued with Rikki's inquisition, ignoring anything but her own side of it. "I've got five buyers for that bottom of the deck dealer's place already lined up. That's without the interior renovations that I'm going to make once I get the title."

Hildy got a cell call, filling her with hopes for anything that might persuade Rikki to feel that one important call was company, three—which included Rikki being there—was a crowd.

"That's my carpenter calling me with his estimate to redo the Richberg place."

Hildy waived Rikki off, speaking briefly to the caller in coded responses before hanging up.

Rikki held her ground. "You've been feasting off repo'd property long enough to know that evidence in a police investigation can't be altered prior to the official unveiling of the facts at trial."

Hildy's shoulders slumped, as did her disposition, realizing that this time she couldn't outmatch the above-board process—in the absence of a bribe. Such illegality had landed her in trouble more than once before. This was hardly the occasion to reconnect with her past arrests.

"What'm I supposed to tell my buyers? When they hear the place is frozen from sale for over a year, they'll turn-tail and find another realtor."

Hildy was sinking fast in a sudden daze, having lost the sales commission that she already spent.

Rikki's mouth puckered, edges turning downward, in a demonstration of 'what can I tell you?'

"In spite of your buyers being associated with you, they're probably nice people."

Rikki tried a more workable approach, motioning suggestively in the tense conversational climate.

"You can't be down to your last property…You'll think of something." Then came the sarcasm. "Being such an honest person and all."

"You're any better?" Hildy regrouped, cutting her eyes at Rikki.

That broke Rikki down, forcing her to wonder about her own character and failures with the case. Still, there was a chasm of mutual respect—friendship was exceedingly unlikely—before any assurance from Hildy could be secured.

"Is Michael Tellata still working for you?"

"Not anymore." Hildy was curt with her answer, sharp as to not promote any follow-up questions from Rikki.

"The problem with him was, our business ethics didn't jive. He had an ill-mannered way of making promises to clients that I simply couldn't sustain…I had to cut him loose."

What bothered Hildy was that she began to notice similarities between herself and Rikki; that was a regrettable bi-product of their conversation. Hildy continued to maintain a pleasant tenor in her sentences, while keeping a professional distance.

"You need my help," Hildy assumed.

Rikki noticed an original artwork on the floor beside Hildy. In the lower corner on the plain, brown, wrapping were initials M.T.

"Who's interested in buying that house?"

"That's significant to your imaginative investigation?"

Rikki generalized with a silent affirmation, mute about the details.

There was derision in Hildy's tendency. "Skirting the rules is a poor procedural technique...Are you in the mood to tip your hand by telling me the game plan?"

"Fraid-not."

"Why would I grant your request, given that it'll come back to bite me in the proverbials?" Then it socked her as to what was going on. "I get it. You need someone to blame when your policing malfeasants hits the fan." She chuckled, feeling as though she figured out Rikki's M.O. "What you're doing is sure to put you on a collision course with a mistrial."

Hildy was keen to those types of questionable policing methods and Rikki knew it. But Rikki needed her, and Hildy knew that.

"I'm not asking for favors. I needn't tell you, the governor's backing this," she bluffed. "From what I understand, when he's in a good mood, the Governor has realtors for breakfast," Rikki stabbed.

"That's funny, I heard he's on a diet."

Rikki leveraged, throwing the Governor's weight around as though it was hers. "You're willing to part the Governor's hair the wrong way? With all that's on the line, if you come out on the losing side you might be reduced to selling life insurance. You're standing in tall weeds with some pretty big dogs...You didn't graduate from Dakota State with scholarly honors being a dummy."

"That's riiiight."

When the tough get going was when Rikki revved up. "No more Miss Nice Guy."

Hildy was strategically backpedaling. "What's that supposed to mean?"

Hildy's resistance firmed. A once promising financial outlook in the Richberg house had been lowered into the mire of this unfortunate mini roundtable summit.

Hildy wanted an end it. "Is that all you wanted to see me about?"

Rikki rubbed her palms together with a sense of intrigue over the next thing that Hildy would utter.

Having been distracted by a moving thought, Hildy rose from the table, shuffling to grab her purse. She constantly shifted her stance that stressed one leg then the other.

She reached to grab Rikki, tugging convincingly to bring her along.

"Move the nice shoes of yours."

Rikki strained to have to move so hastily, and on such short notice. "Where're we going?"

Hildy groaned, "Not to have fun."

THE PLUNGE
◆

At first, it made no sense.

It was getting late. The expectation of that event was impossible to contain.

There was something soothing about the refreshing sights and sounds coming from the Rio Grande River that ran far below the elevated speaker's platform.

The stage was put together mere minutes before the first guests had arrived. Some of the volunteers who did the hammering and riveting thought deep down that it would not hold the weight of more than one person at a time. None of them spoke out, because if they did and something bad were to happen, they felt theirs would be the blame that followed.

That congratulatory night was carefully orchestrated to commemorate the retirement of a particular twenty year employee. Everybody who was somebody in the state and city hiring systems was in attendance. Former co-workers, who had permanently left their civil service jobs, made it their business to return to pay tribute at this well thought-out farewell.

Chauffeured limos were parked bumper to bumper, up on what was newly cut grass, making it difficult for those who arrived late to slide past them. There was no doubting that this would be the best party that most of them would attend all year. The exclusive send-off was for Steven Stein.

There was a musical ensemble that provided the pleasant backdrop. It was comprised of a commercial insurance adjuster, a musical child prodigy, named Kathy. She fiddled at fiddle—all pretty as you please, four feet nine of her. She once found lifting weights, and a gentleman truck driver, to be her after hours joy. But in the end, it was music that sent her heart flying.

In the months preceding—after she inexplicably drove away from the driver—she had salted away a few bucks to afford a new dress that she desperately wanted to be noticed wearing—by any single gents in attendance. Bless her heart and a petite body that was packaged so well indeed.

Then there was Jasper, the retired plumber, who was eager to return to musician stuff on more than a part time arrangement, having endlessly tinkered in his basement with tonal musical strategies. Then one day his wife, Ann, demanded that he return full time to something other than pestering her hour after hour—over having nothing better to do with his free time.

Gertrude Potter was the drummer. This county clerk liked taking out her frustrations hitting something other than her head against the wall at home each time her grandkids emptied their ant farm in her living room. The sight of the insects scattering every which-way was driving her crazier than the child psychologist at the pre-school thought the kids were.

Henderson O'Reily was a standup widower, who stroked a mean stand up bass. After grueling years of making bedpost bolts in Bayonne, he finally gave in to Gertrude's calling, to give their endless emails a rest. That left him to go out for a year-end, potentially romantic, visit to see her. The southwest had a subtle appeal, and it didn't take much coaxing before he sent word back east to the moving company, to bring the remainder of his belongings to New Mexico, so the two of them could shack-up together. Later, it was the first frost that converted him to understand that the Albuquerque weather wasn't all that most non-residents assumed it to be. And then there were those darling grandkids....

The musical group was well rehearsed in the classical tunes that they played, and though their step and a half, two-step, dance tempo was the speed of molasses; nevertheless, it allowed for happy feet to dance.

Many yards away and off to the left, Rikki was confused about Hildy. Not a few miles back, they were nearly at each other's throats. Then came the forced invitation. Why didn't she have a date for such an important event? It couldn't be because of her coarse personality. After dispensing with that doubt, Rikki rearranged her thoughts to enjoy herself. She was in Rome. And to behave in any other way was un-Roman-like.

Hildy was the epitome of appropriate behavior at those types of functions. It wasn't uncommon for Hildy's commanding voice to be detected above all others. This time, she wanted only Rikki to hear.

"If I could yawn with my mouth closed, these people would never know how boring they really are."

"They don't seem that bad," Rikki quibbled.

"First, they'd need a pulse."

Tapping her toes to the band's waltz, Rikki was caught up in the mood to have a good time.

"I once redeemed a free coupon at a local Fred Astaire's Dance Studio. That's got to count for something…Care to dance?"

She offered her hand to Hildy, right palm up to receive. Together, they eased to the edge of a designated area of hard-packed dirt that had been previously flattened with a squeaky asphalt masher. The result was better than dancing atop quicksand, but not by much.

Rikki and Hildy moved with the beat in an arm-n-arm's length distance. Over Hildy's shoulder, Rikki saw a man wearing an out-dated dark blue, pinstripe suit. He walked in their direction, bent forward at the waist with a sideways lean.

He had an unyielding need for a high percentage alcohol liquid that wasn't helping him walk any better. No sooner had the man finished his vodka and tonic, than he greedily grabbed a gin and water from a passing waiter.

The waiter's bushy beard appeared almost as crooked as the drinker's walk. Anyway, he periodically pressed the hairs against his face in what appeared to be a bumpy manner. He didn't possess the usual straight back rigidity that most servers held as their routine working posture. Something was different about him. For one thing, he never seemed overly concerned about dolling out food.

His serving tray was speckled with tasty looking miniature sandwiches, and even nicer napkins beneath each. Soreness at having to be there had taken up residence in his resentful soul. But working that evening meant a lot more than just money. There were certain dynamic points of interest that had to be properly set.

Guests joyfully helped themselves to scrumptious imported delicacies that were on every server's tray, with taste buds that craved to eat more of them faster. Theirs were valuable munching minutes. They swallowed quickly, reaching to add more culinary delights to miniature plates that never seemed to hold enough.

"Here he comes," Hildy said to Rikki, nudging her, displeased with both the drunken man's clothes, and the teeter-totter manner in which he carried himself closer to them.

"The straight line he's not walking is a corkscrew," Rikki said in a dimmed voice.

"If you thought you weren't having a good time before, you didn't realize when you were well off," Hildy manufactured, delivering a fake grin for the archives.

She played the Saint of Fine Acting as the distastefully suited older man drew nearer. Despite that, he mingled easily. It was the schmooze. He pretended to socialize out of true feelings of pleasantness, rather than the booze ordering the commands. When he stopped beside Hildy, she paused to show a closeness towards him ahead of what she actually felt.

"Rikki, I would like you to meet the pride of our family and of local government."

"Steven Stein. Rikki?" She stumbled for the word. "For the life of me, I forgot your last name. I'm so busy calling you by your title."

She minimized to her, turning to Steven, "Call me Rikki."

Steven spilled some of his drink when he said, "Hi." His mouth opened and pure toxicity rushed out, in an earnest attempt to gag anything in need of oxygen. Those nearby were nearly decapitated by the fumes. His breath was a blast furnace, a black hole searching to destroy all living things.

Rikki and he accepted each others introductions, reacting as comfortably as unfamiliar persons can.

There were bundles of seconds for Hildy to notice how the two interacted with each other. For the most part, she saw nothing significant between them—by way of their mannerisms. Then came...

"Hi-ya, Hawkdegrade." Only Steven could mangle his own sister's name.

"How does it feel to leave your twenty year nine-to-five?" Rikki asked.

"It feels Oooo-K," he slurred.

Asphyxiating gas began to overcome everyone within his suddenly expanded, practically lethal, thrust.

As Steven turned away he stumbled, barely catching his balance. It wasn't very hard to ascertain that something was troubling him—well past the point of being able to simply forget about it. To look at him was to complete the question of what the problem was. An out of control alcoholic is easy to spot. Too bad. Because that night was supposed to belong to a happy man and not the inside of a rotting, human, bottle of booze.

He was on the periphery of the furthermost perimeter of sanity. His emotional tram had jumped the track long before the revelry had begun, with collision's impact coming at the next turn of dealings. In the eternal words of H. Ross Perot, "It was sad."

He fought to straighten from a posture of self-pity that snowballed from the time that morning greeted him. Any salvage attempts to rescue his attitude were too much, too fruitlessly tardy.

"That job made me hate life," he established. "If I had it to do all again, I'd as soon tongue-out a democrat than have worked there."

"He hides his problems well," Hildy attempted to mask.

Rikki looked around, refreshed about her own level of happiness. "Glad, somebody's got the holiday merriment," she whispered to Hildy, poking fun at a situation that was far from amusing.

Feeling hungry, Rikki took a doughnut.

Steven watched her go at it. "After more of those, you'll soon need to be rolled out of here."

Self conscious about getting fat, Rikki stopped in mid chew thinking instead to shove a powdered sugar coated one up his ass.

Many yards in front of them, a dazzling comedian wore a goofy expression. Unrelenting, he pranced across the stage, exciting the crowd with each of his clever witticisms. The audience roared with his every gyration, wanting the non-stop laughs to continue. There's nothing like a funny guy who can keep it all going.

Steven verbally headed elsewhere, focusing on the emcee. "I love comedians. They always make things better." Then he started to cry.

"Is everybody happy?" the funnyman with the microphone asked, with an enthusiastic cheer that affirmed his intent. Occasionally, he would bend to converse with those in the front row. He went on to make them enjoy their feeling of 'Oh God, the comedian's embarrassing me' time.

Hildy needed something to brighten Steven's dismal outlook. She wanted to inspire him above his feelings of sorrowful self-absorption. "Bad things happen to upstanding people. Often for no good reason…Ease-up. Stop being so hard on yourself," Hildy told Steven.

For Rikki, the seconds had begun to pass in a manner befitting days.

Steven hoisted his crystal stem to make a drinker's toast, "Mahafkan."

Rikki overheard that comment, mentally filing it away, to be retrieve at a later time if she needed to.

Steven returned from inattentiveness, that thousand yard stare, to grasp yet another drink from a server's tray, downing it with haste and no discretion, or concern for his diminished capacity, or the ability to get home.

The bushy bearded waiter took it all in.

"Pardon my brother. He's in a gin-induced fit of remorse," Hildy said to Rikki.

"Fit of revenge is more like it," Steven lived up to Hildy's initial remark about him. Then he got louder, and that pushed out the fumes, risking future sinus capacity for those close by. "I should have gone down with the ship," he garbled.

Those standing nearby were dismayed by his drunken babble, choosing instead to move away and into individual pockets of group conversations.

Rikki's immediate thought was that she could've just as easily visited Hildy tomorrow than today at that café'—when Steven's sadness would've been a forgettable non-memory. She never should've asked Hildy, "Where're we going?"

She wasn't about to make that mistake again—not that she'd ever get the chance. By then, she sorely wished for an alien abduction to take her away.

Steven's slide into regret had taken a respite in the ward of the common man's philosophy. "Money changed me into something I could no longer stand to look at in the mirror. Sure, I could've gotten out. But I stuck around—only to get stuck."

He dropped the empty glass onto a serving tray that wasn't there, unaware when it fell, breaking into a thousand pieces at his feet.

Standing out of sight behind a row of hedges, the bushy bearded waiter was scarcely seen in shadows that were created from portable lighting towers. Its posts weren't built to handle such heavy loads at their tops. They began to lean harshly, suggesting that they might topple with the slightest push of the wind.

The waiter watched with eyes that pinpointed Steven, distinguishing him from others in the crowd. He was never an exceptional shot. Initially, he had thought to use a blowgun. It was silent. But he had to stand a lot closer to have the slightest chance of hitting Steven with the poison dart. As it stood, it would've been a miracle to nail him with a blowgun at his present distance.

The waiter knew that Steven was a nervous-Nelly who'd sell out his mother if it meant saving his hide. Looking at Steven, he thought, I'm reading Steven's lips. I'm boiling over what I'm hearin'.

At the ceremony, Steven held his stomach. The booze was kicking back at him. By then, everyone who remained near him had turned away, pretending that there were items of pressing interest, or assorted who gives a damns, to tend to.

Steven continued aimlessly, "There was so much money lying around I—"

Having heard enough, Hildy kicked Steven's ankle to make a definitive statement.

"Hush," she reprimanded. "You don't want to bore these nice people."

Hildy patted him across the shoulders, with orders to "Stand up straight."

He fulfilled that directive as best he could with such a limited physicality.

She adjusted his tie to hang better.

"Get out there with a speech that'll have everyone talking about this night for months to come," she promoted.

Steven's strength of mind perked with vigor, as she hunted for anything to talk about that would lift his outlook.

"You're right." Steven belched in her face. The intensity nearly blew Hildy's wig onto someone else's head.

Hildy coiled, fanning his bad vapor breath, anything to thin the noxious fumes.

"There's a great hangover cure. Just wish there was a cure for the mentally ill," Rikki uttered to no one listening.

The comedian on stage continued, struggling to talk above the cheers that greeted his every punch line. "Without further ado, let us pay tribute to tonight's guest of honor."

The crowd accepted his direction, and focused on the area where Steven stood. Rikki and Hildy stepped to one side the instant before the spotlight hit Steven.

The comedian continued his verbal prelude…

"At the beginning of his tenure working for the state of New Mexico, Steven wasn't certain if he'd made the right career move. After leaving Oklahoma's Bureau of Prisons, he figured convicts never moved-up, so why should it be any different working here," the emcee joked off-color. He got forced laughter. "Seriously folks," he rolled on. "Before us is a man whose dedication to service has made him a pillar amongst his peers. He's someone who we all want our kids to be like when they grow up."

He waived Steven on to join him at the microphone. "Please give an inspiring round of applause for Steven Stein!"

The emcee lowered the microphone from his lips, tucking it beneath his arm to clap, watching Steven amble toward him.

Strangely, Steven didn't look all that drunk anymore. He was controlled and well meaning. Or, so it seemed.

Steven graciously bowed at the waist to the captive audience. For once, he appeared to be organized. His feelings were locked in; no one could prevent him from doing what he felt was best. He was free from other's ferocity. At long last, he was empowered.

Hildy spotted it, and was worried about what it all meant.

Many yards away, the bushy bearded waiter's own life flashed before his eyes, as his rifle aimed at Steven's head. Steven had to be silenced.

Steven had begun shaking. The cool exterior was rapidly wearing off. He stood sad and ashamed, believing that the collective applause was appreciation for someone who didn't deserve it. With each passing second, he drifted mentally, glancing at all of the dissimilar faces.

Why are they here, he wondered.

After many strides, he reached the stage. He took the microphone from the emcee, lifting it to his quivering mouth. There was enough sand in his throat to make the entire Middle East jealous.

"One thing about history," Steven cleared his throat. "By the time a person tries to make up for all the bad he's done in life, it's far too late."

Hildy feared that shock was forthcoming—for she knew not what. She could only feel it, and didn't like the sensation.

Rikki, on the other hand, felt disillusioned. She looked down to curse her feet for carrying her to Hildy's Jaguar—to be driven to this dreadful event.

"You should've left me at the café," she said to her ten pedicured toes.

Hildy overheard that, thinking that Rikki was talking to her. "We'll both stay. Maybe go somewhere and rent a video," Hildy answered back.

"Any in particular?" Rikki asked.

"Die Hard." Her answer was fatalistic.

Steven continued, "While doing time in Catholic School, an old Nun told me that most sin can be corrected if restitution is made with the utmost sincerity. This is why I stand before you tonight. Not as a man to be congratulated, but a misplaced soul to be scorned."

An audience mood that had peaked long ago began to fade like the horizontal hold on TV sets during years gone by.

The waiter steadied his aim with the rifle.

"Ladies and gentlemen, for years something's been eating away at my insides."

Everyone gasped while collectively holding their breath.

"Please, allow me take the opportunity to cleanse myself of this sin, and all the trouble I caused to innocent others."

His constricted throat barely allowed his confession to continue.

"During my day to day duties at the Bureau of Prisons, I was privy to more than I could handle. I did my best to turn a blind eye to all that was going on around me. But it was the forgeries, the payoffs, the rip-offs, and the things I wasn't supposed to see that had become too much to bear."

The audience squirmed in their seats, spellbound, quietly talking, holding out optimism that this was all some sort of a distasteful skit. For them, this had to be something that the comedian put Steven up to, that the crowd would get a hearty laugh from before the night was over.

If Steven's words were true, however, they were in for the revelation of a lifetime. Together, they held on that this was all part of a not so well rehearsed comedic bit.

Steven nervously patted his forehead with a drenched handkerchief, showing pronounced water marks under his arms.

"Then things got way out of control," Steven went on. "Temptation stared me in the face, until my morality fell through the cracks like water through a sieve."

Hildy was ravaged in the crosshairs of guilt by association. More than anything, she wanted to rush the podium to shut him up, then dash to another hemisphere before Steven attached her to his wretched tale.

Some in the audience stood, alarmed, scurrying to step into the aisles, to leave before he said anything that would make them more ill at ease than they already were.

"Why the stroll down Amnesia Lane?" Rikki asked, not wanting to offend Hildy, remembering that she needed Hildy for a ride back to the café' to get her car.

"We're about to find out," Hildy unwittingly whispered.

Steven's disclosure widened. "From H-Unit at McAlester Prison came hundreds of thousands of dastardly dollars that got me in over my head."

Unfortunately for everyone in attendance, he became more relaxed.

"I can think of no better way to clean the slate as a symbol of my born-again honesty."

People are honest? Rikki was perplexed that that might be a remote possibility.

Steven reached to produce a bulging shoebox, holding it out for the crowd to bear witness to.

"This is my share of the kickbacks. Ninety thousand dollars. It's every illegal bribe I accepted. Had I not foolishly done so, many convicts wouldn't have been prematurely released. If it wasn't for me, society would've been so much safer."

He opened the box, revealing the bundled cash, struggling for the strength to continue.

"Mercy never came without sacrifice. Forgive me."

In one motion, he vaulted the railing behind him, plunging the full length of the sheer drop to the rushing water below. His screams went on forever until the raging water silenced him.

Pandemonium ensued. People were commanding orders to everyone else, seeking prompt decision making for that which the order givers had no solutions.

With weapon in hand, the waiter seized the chance to make great haste into the surrounding woods.

Rikki heard someone sneeze. That was when she saw a man with a balding crown running with the waiter into obscurity in the hazy distance.

THE VISITORS

◆

That morning brought mating crickets too close to the side of Rikki's house where Sharon slept. The ratchet-like chirping may have been a welcoming sound for some, but Sharon hated it. Adding to her overall discomfort was that living in someone else's house caused Sharon to stray from her usual day-to-day activities. She was constantly groggy and cranky. The last time she felt reasonably fresh was hours before Rikki chased Mark into oblivion outside Angles Club. Time was racing by, making that night seem like a lifetime ago.

In spite of it all, she wasn't about to dismiss the celebratory good news that was the cause for a controlled uplifting in her spirit. It came when Sharon got a letter from the city's revenue department, saying that the forced foreclosure of her house had been put off indefinitely. The tax office was frozen from evicting her, due to the five thousand dollars that Rikki had put up as payment of the past due tax debts. Somehow, she was able to reach into her pension and withdraw enough to cover that tab. Sharon had told her that it might be impossible for her to ever repay the money, but Rikki did it anyway.

That action left Hildy's greedy fingers virtually taped together, precluding any future sale, until after all of the legal proceedings were satisfied. Even then, the property might still remain with Sharon—as long as she remained current with all future tax payments.

It was late morning when Sharon stepped into the outdoor hot tub, lowering herself in the soothing hexagon of bubbling water. It was a great way to temporarily escape the disturbing reality of her figure-eight pattern life in Albuquerque. Hers emotional travels always revolved around one thing.

Trouble. The city was changing for the worst. And there was nothing that she could do about it.

Fully immersed up to her neck with both lobes touching the water, she hoped that Rikki would be coming home soon. She had so much to thank her for. Sharon knew that Mark had no real friends, who would lift a finger to help her in time of need. They were all a bunch of drug and gambling heads, who could see nothing past their individual wants. The point was, she never had to go begging to them, only to hear "No" flying back in her measly direction.

The next thing on her agenda was holding onto a job. Make no mistake, Sharon hated that idea more than losing her home. She couldn't stomach real work, even when someone else was doing it.

The tidy sum of untraceable currency that Mark had buried in their backyard was supposed to be for urgent situations. His. Lately, notions concerning the dough had been summoned to the forefront of Sharon's financial woes. The word emergency was spelled immediately—with all capital letters.

She had been terrified to go near it, because if Mark wasn't gone for good—as Rikki's evidentiary scenario had intimated—Sharon would surely windup on the coroner's table, insisting that the parachutist move over. If Sharon were to gather sufficient courage to return to her house and dig-up the unmarked, rubber banded, cash, she might have a new home all right, with her confined bedroom being strikingly similar in stature to the palace that Bubba had recently escaped from.

The non-stop worrying pressed her to sink deeper into the water, covering both ears. The noise from the pulsating bubbles pushed through the turbo charged water, leaving her unaware of the threatening sounds from nearby crackling twigs. Unannounced intruders had come on to the property. She left hesitation for someone else. It was hammer time. The chance for aggression to take over. And Bubba and his brothers were yielding semi-automatic hammers.

Many yards away, they couldn't see her. They were just outside the visual scope of the backyard.

C.C. knelt, whispering, "You're sure, this's where she lives?"

Bubba scowled, "When you two left the Elbow Room, I snatched the address from our pal, Jack."

It was Jack's pay stub that displayed his home address. After memorizing it, Bubba gave it back to Jack. Bubba was a homicidal lunatic, but to say that he was an out-n-out thief was a little strong.

Teddy nudged C.C., in agreement that it wasn't all that socially out of line to be on a stranger's property intending to kill her.

Bubba's eyesight shifted, darting as would a frog having just spotted a fly.

Sharon's head had risen from having been submerged in the fluid solitude that only chlorinated, hot tub water can bring. Refreshing water cascaded down her face. Her nipples began to harden when she sensed that something was different than had been the case when she first got into the tub.

When her criminal sixth sense kicked in, she slyly clicked-off the patio light. That left only unreliable shadows to operate in, reducing visibility from a full moon that had suddenly been covered by intensifying clouds.

She repositioned her glistening body inches higher to get a better vantage point of the landscape around her.

Maybe Rikki's here, she thought.

Within that sphere of thankfulness for Rikki's help, and wanting to see her, Sharon felt that her street-wise instincts had somehow failed her, giving off an uncommon false alarm. She slowly lowered back into the water, letting it rise to grace her top lip.

"Did you see that?" C.C. whispered after seeing Sharon's luscious, nude, body above the rim of the hot tub before she lowered. "Like she stepped right out of one of dem-dare sex movies."

"I'll show her what a real man is like before I kill her."

Bubba salivated at that thought, never certain which he liked more, rough sex, or watching someone die by his rough hands. He crouched behind the hedgerow that separated the side lawn from the rear yard.

The three needy men had a superior view above the natural partition that Jack had installed. Its sole purpose was to keep street level passersby from looking in on him when he and Heather wanted to be alone behind the house.

The distant sound of a police car's siren echoed, ringing too close for their comfort, limiting the assaulting concert to hold their devilish positions until the threat went farther down the street. Then, they desperately wanted safer places to hide.

Sharon, too, was alerted by the four-wheel enforcer's call. As an underworld lord's companion, she was trained to react sharply to that alarming charisma. Mark had always preached that she needed to be ready to move quickly on a moment's notice in the event of impending doom. His catch phrase was "Always have your escape planned."

To one side, she spotted what looked like someone doing a bad job of hiding behind the tightly knitted foliage. Quickly, she wiped her face free of the water, rapidly blinking. Just that fast, whoever she thought was there had gone—if anyone was there at all. She couldn't be sure, but she was never one to take a foolish chance.

She remembered Rikki telling her about a hidden compartment in the bottom of the tub. Instinctively, she reached to pull the drain plug. The water emptied as fast as her thumping heart pounded, but with a quieter, stream-like, sound.

Bubba was squat, livid with the prospect of being unbalanced on ground that had become increasingly soggy from the hot tub's rush. If he was to be successful, he needed to get off a good shot when the scene presented itself. Sex with the soon to be victim had to wait. Killing had again stepped to the front.

For Sharon, there it was—that now or never pinnacle of unfortunate circumstance.

Silently, she unlatched the watertight panel. Inside was a 9mm pistol zipped within a sealed plastic bag. Rikki told her that it was there for when uninvited, revenge thinking, criminals chose to stop over for a little help themselves.

Confident with those military maneuvers of escape that Mark's Sergeant friend had demonstrated to her and Mark a short while back, Sharon belly-flopped over the side of the tub. With pistol in hand, she snaked on her stomach to the sliding glass door at the rear of the house.

To their collective dismay, the three men leaped out from low to discover that she was gone from the outdoor spa.

"Da-hell'd she zip-off to?" C.C. asked, heatedly looking around, trying to cue-in on any moving shadows that would reveal where Sharon had gone.

They still thought that it was Rikki who they were pursuing.

Sharon had made it inside the house, closing the glass behind her. In the TV room, she quickly put on her clothes. Without wasting a second, she moved to the bookshelf behind the big screen plasma, rummaging her hand behind the collection of rare books that filled so many shelves. Rikki was a studious reader, thinking that one day she might become a mother, wanting her kids to be literate. Until such time, the novels were there just for show—when guests came over, but those on the character level of the Thorne's.

Acting on pure adrenaline, Sharon found the silencer that Rikki had hidden behind her favorite hard cover volume. She hoped that it would screw onto the gun that she held. How badly she wanted this to be the ideal opportunity to give a series of lethal, hot lead, presents to the men who were outside. She never questioned who they were, only that they meant her harm. Why else would they sneak onto the property in the way that they did? Leaving hesitation to those who were lost, she tiptoed to an upper floor window.

"She's gotta-be inside the house," Teddy supplied.

"She ain't out here," C.C. indicated in hushed, yet projecting, tone.

When the canvassing clouds parted, the moon's glow cast itself upon wet footprints that lead away from the tub to the sliding glass doors.

"That-a-way!" Bubba said louder than he wanted to.

He placed an index finger to his closed lips, indicating that peaceful utterances were for all of them. Loud people fail to realize that they're that way.

Suddenly, a piercing, arrow-like, zinging sound came from inside the house.

Teddy never saw the muzzle flash, nor the hollow-point bullet that sliced into his head, fragmenting once inside. He dropped to the sloppy ground in a clump of bone, tissue and worn fabric.

Bubba and C.C. were up ahead, unaware as to what had happened behind them.

"Wait," C.C. said to Bubba, hinting that Teddy was lagging behind.

They needed their third member backup for a thorough assault on the rear of the house. C.C. carefully made his way back through the nearly impenetrable blackness, ultimately tripping over Teddy's leg.

"There you are." His worry instantly turned to disgust. "Bubba's gonna be pissed as hell if he sees you sleepin.'"

C.C. was couldn't recognize that Teddy would be silent forever. Nor was he aware of the flowing, crimson, blood that oozed from Teddy's head announcing the man's demise.

Bubba had lost the patience that he never had, unable to figure out what was taking the other two so long to catch up to his position of attacking readiness. He was convinced that his two cohorts were back there wasting time, doing something other than helping him with his not-so-well thought-out undertaking. He figured one of them was goofing-off, and the other had stumbled over him.

Mark taught Sharon to be highly skilled in the art of nighttime pistol shooting at moving targets. With that confidence, she wanted to make C.C. like Teddy. When self-defense had become her favorite words, she was thankful to Mark for all that he had taught her.

Another shot from the second floor window ricocheted from a flat stone, catching C.C. in the knee. He dropped his pistol, crumbling to the ground overcome by uncontrollable pain. Unwilling to give away his position by screaming, he bit a hole in his tongue, writhing in the mud beside Teddy.

C.C.'s begging, wrenching, sounds made Sharon feel powerful, almost God-like. All of a sudden, she had the ability to decide how much each of them would suffer. She squeezed the trigger again, hitting C.C. in the chest.

Her trigger-happy gratification dimmed with the sound of that police siren having drawn within a half mile.

Damn, my fun's ruined, she thought.

At once, nothing mattered more than hiding that pistol. When the siren rounded the final corner, Sharon took a chance to go out into the blackness to the hot tub. There she opened the secret compartment, replacing the 9mm in the floorboard slot, turning on the water to refill the state of the art spa. Then came the front doorbell ringing.

Being gazelle-like, she ran back to the house to put the silencer behind the row of books. When she arrived to open the front door she was breathing deeply through her nose, so as not to draw attention to her panting.

"The siren wasn't you?" she asked, looking around Rikki onto the empty street beyond.

Rikki thought about what it was that seemed to be bothering Sharon, to where her skin was noticeable shades lighter.

"It was a black-n-white heading to a B & E on the next block," Rikki explained.

Sharon's uneasiness slowly subsided. It was a sheer twist of fate that a squad car had blared so close, hopefully to chase away the intruders. Then a quick calm came over her.

"Black and white. B and E." She threw her arms around Rikki, bending her leg upwardly in a huggy, schoolgirl, manner. "I just love when you talk technical."

She let herself be wrapped in the feeling of protection that Rikki ushered in.

Rikki saw patterns of wet spots across her polished, wood, floor.

"I was outside in the tub." Sharon volunteered. "That reminds me, I have to turn off the water."

Breaking away from their secure embrace, she moved with haste to the rear door to cautiously run outside and turn off the tub's water. There was the fear that someone was still out there. A bigger concern for Sharon was that Rikki would eventually go outside and see Sharon's victims. Dashing ahead of her was a chance that Sharon had to assume.

Rikki walked to the living room, continuing on through to the family area. She plopped on the sofa to enjoy a brief rest, with no interest to see what Sharon was doing in the backyard.

When Sharon saw C.C.'s fingers twitching her fury heightened, because she didn't have time to watch him bleed. After carefully stepping over him, she returned to where Rikki was. She had no idea that she had just missed him making a final reach to grab her ankle.

"You're jumpy about something," Rikki asked. Her years of interviewing people made her an expert on being able to spot unsettled behavior in someone.

"It's just nicotine withdrawal…I finally got the strength to stop smoking," she faked a cough.

"Wow." Rikki genuflexed in prayer over the news.

Sharon was glad that she had mustered the energy, but was truthful when adding, "Sure wish I had a cigarette."

Rikki nestled into the couch, feeling its cushiony absorption. She broke the silence to take out the threatening photographs that she got in the mail. One by one, she placed them on the coffee table.

Sharon snuggled beside her. Their thighs rubbed against each other in a sharing body vibes manner.

"What'r we looking at?"

Rikki was pressed to explain. "A bunch of pictures somebody sent to me. Some of them were taken inside Angles the night Mark disappeared."

Sharon's curiosity peaked at some of them.

"What's the big deal?" Sharon spoke before focusing on the subjects in the photographs.

Rikki's delivery became tentative. "So far, disaster struck two of the people. Rajaan's dead. And Mark's gone."

Sharon recognized Rajaan in one of the pictures—not saying so—nervously looking at the other images.

"Who's that?" she motioned to a picture of Morty.

"Somebody who is helping me with the case."

Sharon minimized the faces, more concerned with the men in the backyard. That was much more threatening than anything that the small color snapshots could generate. It was then that she picked out her face in one of the pictures. Suddenly, she felt isolated.

"Are you saying I'm next?"

Sharon gasped, resisting having to reformulate her thinking about the possible briefness of her young life.

And what about the two bodies strewn outside? She clutched Rikki's upper arm, wanting to burrow-in for security.

"This is why I came home early. I had to warn you. To shield you."

Sharon's prevailing wish was that Rikki wasn't too late to rescue her future. A tear trickled from the corner of her welling eyes, downwardly along her cheek. Rikki stopped it with a bent thumb.

She knew that it was impossible for Rikki to soak-in that the dead men outside were the result of her right of protection. Then there was the issue of using an illegal silencer to do it. Feeling that Rikki would buy none of it, Sharon fixed it in her mind to dispose of the men as soon as Rikki left the house.

Rikki eased to scoop up the photographs, putting them in a short stack. Sharon continued to hold onto Rikki, like a child to a favorite stuffed animal.

"With Mark out of circulation, I think there'r bad people out there looking to score on whatever he left behind. Drugs and whatever else they can find."

She lifted Sharon's chin with the underside of three supportive fingers, thinking about when Hildy hinted about Rikki nose, and how Hildy must have known it was Sharon's knee movements that inadvertently caused that bruise.

"It all includes you, girlfriend. And the fact that we've become an item of gossip."

The sound of the word 'girlfriend' had a deep meaning for Sharon. It had been so long since that word was applied to her with any type of lasting meaning.

Rikki needed a plan of fortification that would work, something that would keep outsiders out.

"For the time being, it seems unwise for you to go home."

"What's my next move?"

"Stay here until the dust settles."

There were items of sobering interest that had to be resolved: Who was out there shooting at Sharon? How soon would they return?

All of a sudden, she feared living alone.

"What about your dad?"

Jack's vanishing act had bothered Rikki less and less. "He's gone."

Sharon left it at that.

Rikki's pager chirped. She pinched it to see who was calling.

Sharon took that moment to get up and go into the kitchen. There, she took a Pepsi from the fridge, wanting something a lot stronger to ease her troubled mind. Not more than a few minutes passed before she was back on the couch. Rikki had since dissolved the pager's entry as to who just called.

"I gotta check something out." Rikki said.

Sharon wanted to appear understanding that Rikki had to leave, but she couldn't muster the dramatic ability to make it believable.

They stood and began walking; across carpet fibers that regained their rightful stance after Rikki and Sharon moved past a turned down, framed, photograph of Rikki and Jack. When they reached the door…

"You're gonna be all right? If not, F da department's rules, and I'll stay with you."

Sharon jerked. "You can't risk your job over my insecurities."

"Why not?"

"Why so?" Sharon asked.

"Because I've fallen for you," Rikki said, fighting to regain her professionalism. "Plus, I need my star witness in one piece, if my case ever gets to court."

Sharon purred with the need that only emotional deprivation can bring.

Rikki pivoted to her. "Want me to bring you anything when I come back?"

"Your warm pussy."

Rikki was unable to move, on account of Sharon's secure grip on Rikki's crotch.

"Got any weed in one of those evidence lockers that isn't doing anything? Seems like forever since I been high."

Rikki didn't turn around while walking out the door to the replacement car. Down the road Rikki heard a single, muffled, pop that she ignored.

Not far from the hot tub, Sharon had gone to no trouble to put a single pistol shot through C.C.'s temple. Maggots and ants had already found Teddy.

Within an hour, Sharon had dismembered the two men. She then placed their parts in black, heavy gauge, plastic garbage bags for the sanitation men to pick up the following morning during their duly appointed rounds.

The day after that, Sharon reluctantly moved in with Rikki.

THE BASEBALL CAP

---◆---

It was an afternoon unlike most. That was when Rikki walked into a charming memorabilia shop in downtown Albuquerque. In the window were skillfully arranged items of sporting interest that anyone passing by was helplessly drawn to.

One step inside, and she was immediately taken by the vast collection of baseball caps. They were everywhere. Though she wasn't a fervent follower of sports, there were countless insignias that she immediately recognized.

"Im-pressive," she mumbled.

"Thank you," replied a man of Mexican descent, who was outfitted in mixed sports garb. In any other setting it would have signaled an undefined fashion deficiency. But inside that store he looked right at home.

"You must be the charming lady whom I paged the other night," he said.

Finally, a gentleman who appreciates a woman.

She continued to take-in the sights and placements of various sports related items. She knew that if she were to bring her elementary school age relative there, she'd be hard-pressed to get him to leave.

"Sports memorabilia is a tight-knit profession…On your behalf, I made several inquiries. I found a shop owner in New Jersey who stocks the specific baseball cap that you asked me about when you returned my page."

That caught her attention. "Where, exactly in New Jersey?"

"It's in a town called Little Ferry."

THE SUSPECT
♦

For the first time in his life, Michael Tellata was really scared.

At his feet was an empty, manila, envelope. His mind was locked, unable to waver from the pen-n-ink drawings that he held. At street level, the commercial courier Honda had just sped up the nearly empty street, looking for the next delivery.

One of the drawings was of a man, bound with arms above his head. His throat was being cut, with a brilliant yellowy fire coming from the ripped gash. The second illustration was of the Pyramid Hotel. It had that yellow flame darting from an upper floor window. That was the same rendezvous that he often frequented during extended sexual lunches with Lorna. From the looks of things, someone had sent Michael a message to silence him. It was plain that whoever sent the drawings wanted to illustrate what happens to those who talk to the police.

Around the house his wife, Joy, wasn't her usual upbeat self. Maybe she got the same drawings? He doubted that. If she had, perhaps Joy could possibly have shed some light on the subject, starting with what it meant?

When Michael asked her what was wrong, she simply shrugged it off as nothing more than residual feelings that were associated with her moody, menstrual, monthlies. She knew that topic was sure to keep him from intruding further into her emotional doldrums.

What sealed her decaying marital enthusiasm was when she finally had irrefutable proof that he was having an affair. It would've served Michael well not to have left the hotel's telephone number in his pants pocket—when Joy went through them before dropping them off at the cleaners.

Though he left out the area code—a way to disguise its location—Joy immediately recognized the number. For years, her sister worked there in housekeeping while in high school.

The resulting sexual cold shoulder that Michael got was on the predictable order of "Not tonight, I have another headache." That could've easily been recited as Not tonight—on the advice of council.

What bothered Joy most was that she somehow blamed herself for her husband's straying. After all, had she not been out on maternity leave, from working at Michael's company, none of this would've happened. So she thought. The result was that Michael had to use his two callous hands for what Joy's talented mouth used to expertly perform.

For Michael, that was not the end of his problems: There was the text message from his daughter, who informed him that she was at a male schoolmate's home with no parental supervision anywhere to be found. The Veterinarian, who said that it would cost over two thousand bucks to remove a growth from the family dog's stomach.

He just wanted to go home and let his woeful worrying hover, suspended to allow an influx of tranquility to pour underneath. He needed some type of distraction that this day had not provided.

* * *

News from the memorabilia store gave Rikki's spirit a long awaited reason to rise. But she still needed to establish the linkage between Michael and the man in the lake. For that she needed to go to New Jersey—wherever the hell that was—to get it.

The very idea of getting close to an answer was alluring, despite all of the dangers that were around her. The dark city streets took on a different aura than during the relatively safe daylight hours. That was when those who were violent came out in droves.

So it was as her replacement rental car sat silently beneath the recently power-washed façade at the entrance to Tellata Enterprises.

Behind the wheel, Rikki adjusted her investigative stress to concentrate on the mysterious night vision goggles that the jumper fell out of the sky with. In one movement, she realigned her sights to see Michael moving from one front office window to the next, nervously looking out. It was as though he was expecting someone, while hoping not to see anyone—both at the same time.

When Rikki finally got the chance to speak with him, she hoped to get more than a politely packaged single sentence of nothing; equal to the limited number of answers that Joy had to tell—when Rikki stopped by their home earlier in the day. What a secretive little hussy, Rikki thought about Joy.

Suddenly, the car Rikki was in rocked hard. It was as though someone had suddenly jumped onto the trunk, hopped up to the roof, proceeding to the hood. Then without notice the jolt was gone, returning the car to steadiness. Maybe it didn't happen. Probably, it was only Rikki's overly active imagination again getting the best of her. One thing was certain. She saw no one there. It was as though whatever it was carried invisibility.

At once, dark upper floor windows brighten. That was when someone entered the corner room in Michael's office. She couldn't make out details in the person's face, but it had to be Michael.

"I'm here to see Michael Tellata."

The young woman seated in front of Rikki closed her compact mirror with a snap, only her eyes tilted up to see Rikki standing over her. She huffed, having been counting the time until she'd be on her way to the elevator for the final time that day.

Hearing Michael's name gave her a bag of mixed emotions. Initially, it was one of the subordinate hating the sound of the boss's name. While at the same time, she knew that he was her sugar daddy, and keeping up the submissive, sexual, front was the proper wave to ride.

In the back of her mind was how she'd rather have been spreading her early twenties legs for him—even when she wasn't in the mood—than sit behind that awful desk. When they raced off to screw, he usually brought her a gift of some type, and that beat having to wait two weeks for her direct deposit to land. Amidst all that, she was weary from a work day that was littered with unscheduled visitors—starting earlier that day; when that man with the bushy beard got out of a Honda to deliver a manila envelope.

"Mister Tellata didn't authorize me to interrupt him."

Rikki held up her badge as the strength, the muscle, behind her visit. "This is your permission."

She dug in her shoeless feet into the carpet to roll her chair six inches closer, leaning forward to better see Rikki's credentials. To hear the hourly employee behind the desk tell it, she was paid to answer the telephone, not to read.

The intimidated post high-schooler huffed, then pressed the same intercom button twice. She maintained a straight-back posture.

"Mister Tellata. There's a Detective Luckett here to see you."

A minimal amount of nail biting passed, before the cadence of alligator shoes against stainless linoleum flooring sounded. There stood Michael. He was solidly built, standing uneasily. Rikki could tell.

The negative expectancy of what the questioning might produce gave him caution. That, coupled with the marathon sex from his sexual sideline had already made for a full, two hour, lunch.

"What's this about?" posturing that he was above reproach.

"I've heard a lot about you," Rikki said.

He shrugged, "Maybe, we can still be friends."

"That's unlikely," Rikki apologized.

The young woman snickered with a 'he is only friendly with me' chuckle.

Michael looked down, unwilling to expose the hired help to information that might prove difficult to explain when Rikki was gone.

"Fortunately, I've got an unoccupied conference room where we can talk."

They sauntered away, leaving the receptionist alone and still seated. Michael turned back to her.

"That'll be all for the day, Lorna."

Blood pumped into his penis when he spoke her name, but not enough for a full fledged hard-on.

Out of Lorna's earshot, he gave Rikki a scanning glance, "You're the one who visited my house today—after I left for work, pestering my wife with endless questions." His tone was laced with edginess. "Joy almost missed her salon appointment thanks to you."

They made the turn from the hall into the spacious meeting area about which he spoke. Always the gentleman, he watched her sit before walking to the far side of the room. There he grasped a golf club.

He lined up a put of noteworthy distance. Taking aim, he launched a short stroke at a tilted cup where the white ball rattled in.

"Among other things, I'm investigating a recent robbery."

He needed a sidetrack line to throw-off her strategic alignment. "What brings you to me?"

"Crap rolls downhill."

"That still doesn't answer how that necessitates this conversation."

The glare from the diamonds on his Rolex made her squint, bringing Meyer to mind. "Your name," she corrected herself. "Actually, it was your business card at the scene of a certain jewelry store heist that peaked my interest in <u>you</u>."

She produced the card.

Without touching it, he looked at it with minimal regard before returning its importance to her.

"That's an old card. I stopped working with Hildy a long time ago."

There's that word 'with'. Hildy made it seem as though he worked for her.

He sucked in his slightly protruding stomach. Rikki glossed-over the small-talk end of it, nodding slightly.

He continued to explain away that business card. "From time to time, I shop at Sparkles for my wife. That by itself shouldn't be cause for alarm."

She was surprised that he voluntarily placed himself at the scene of a recent crime.

"It's the only jewelry place in town that I trust to sell me the real thing."

"You're from New Jersey," she speared with an accusatory flavor.

"Given the pollution, it should be a crime having to live there," he answered, calling her bluff. "Yeah, I was born there."

"Ever hear of a town called Little Ferry?"

His eyes sprung to show acceptance of that question. He only wished that she would've asked a different one.

"Jersey's not that big." His palms went up to surrender. "Of course, I've heard of it. Why do you ask?"

"No reason."

"If you're going to lie, perhaps I should oblige you with tales of my own."

"I'll save you the trouble. Jewelry sellers across the state have been getting hit."

"It's in all the newspapers."

"The robberies have happened often enough for me to think that it's more coordinated than coincidence. To such an extent, that I'm convinced they were pulled-off by the same person."

"Or persons," he supplemented.

"There were subsequent things that happened concerning that crime that brought you into the less than illustrious mix."

He was open to hear more, hoping that she would add nothing that would implicate him. He was the matador, not wanting to be gored by the sharp horns of her probing questioning. He took a seat, to see her without having to sit directly across from her.

"Go on."

"In what was probably the getaway helicopter, there was diamond cutting equipment, and a baseball cap that had the Little Ferry Cubs written on it. And you're—" she pointed to him, "from New Jersey."

"Being familiar with a town's existence, and me being involved in any criminal activity are miles apart…If you can find a judge with as wild an imagination as your own, to grant you a warrant to search my home and office, you'll see the happenstance is nothing more than that."

"What makes you think I'm getting a warrant?"

"Apples and oranges still mix in every police department around the world."

"That they do," she offered a sly grin.

He uncrossed his legs, feeling a pinch under a knee that should've been operated on long before he ever heard of Albuquerque. He was suddenly reminded that the workday was over long ago.

"Why don't we finish this conversation in the morning over a round of golf? You're bound to think of added questions to prod me with the second you walk out onto the course."

He again stood, thinking that sitting would prompt her to make hours of this quasi interrogation.

"Why not formulate your Q and A tonight. Then we can finish it out in the fresh air."

Fresh air. There's something in short supply in New Jersey, he thought.

*   *   *

The Bedford Hills Country Club was where hard core little white ball chasers wanted to be. The century old facility sat perched on prime hills. Its lush greens, fast fairways, with minimal sand traps, made it a favorite among golf enthusiasts from all of the surrounding counties.

Rikki, Michael, and two of his regular outdoor buddies stood several paces from the eighteenth hole. Rikki looked on with boredom, wondering how the well-to-do actually consider that to be fun.

Watching Tiger on TV was okay in a 'who gives a crap?' sort of way. Rikki figured that hitting a diminutive white ball over hill and dale, then walking after it—with faint hopes of ever finding the damn thing—couldn't possibly be interrupted as recreation. One thing that dominated her thinking was questioning Michael in more detail.

Michael eyed his next golf shot. His ball had landed too far from the stick to make it with a simple stroke. He squinted, kneeling then standing, to best position himself. He disliked using the pole to mark the hole, but from that distance he wasn't certain if he could sink the ball without it. Either way, he felt more at home here than living with Joy. Nothing made him relax as did a good round of golf. Not even sex with Lorna.

One of his pals called, "Come on, Mike-eee. What're-you, gonna take all day to hit the shot?"

They had grown tired from waiting for Michael, but never from the sight of Rikki. Each time she bent over to place her ball on the T they basked in their middle age thrill.

"We've got something else in the fire. It's called the rest of our lives," called the impatient fourth member.

After I nail this hole, they'll wish they never rushed me, Michael thought.

He readied himself, knees slightly bent, head down for the ultimate in concentration. In situations like this, he liked to imagine that there was a million dollars waiting if he hit the shot. Meanwhile, Rikki had a million reasons to see him behind bars.

His address to the ball was flawless, causing it to rapidly advance, traveling until it collided with the pole, dropping into the hole.

The course had all but emptied of participants, those whose tomorrow was work, and the real-life responsibilities outside the tempting course.

Michael turned to see her standing in the distance, her stare knifing through his intellectual protective barrier.

"I've been thinking about your questions." His head went from side to side, finally coughing-up, "I told you everything."

She took out a squeeze bottle of water, intentionally missing her mouth to douse her head, with droplets falling like mountain snowflakes on Christmas Eve.

"How long were you in the National Guard?"

He knew that was coming. "Two years."

She took out a pad, opening it, keeping the pages away from the cascading water to begin writing.

"Check that," Michael corrected.

She observed that his instantaneous answer had to come with a qualifier.

"Two and a half years." He swallowed past filaments of partial truths.

"The Guard has half-year hitches?"

"They authorized my leave of absence, after I told them about my problem."

"What 'problem' was that?" She figured that he'd make this good.

"Gambling."

"That's why you relocated out here? To be closer to Vegas," she equated.

"Nice try."

She was on to him, but he had space to maneuver. He countered her rapid-fire questions with an equal verbal badinage.

"You're wrong."

"After moving, you didn't get around to re-upping with The Guard—as per your military contracts," she implied that something had gotten in the way of his armed service obligations.

He hadn't forgotten about the letter from The Guard, outlining that he was supposed to report to the local Guard branch by the end of that first month after moving to New Mexico.

She waited for an answer that wasn't forthcoming. She then switched to an end-run battering.

"Tell me more about what went on a couple of years ago. Specifically, April of that year," she narrowed.

"You're talking about the burglary at Dix." He mentioned that, trying to make it out to be an inconsequential event. "There wasn't much to it. Local cops were called in. After labeling it a simple B & E, they dusted for fingerprints, asked a bunch of questions around the base that nobody had answers to, and left...Eventually, the suspects were caught. Pretty straightforward stuff. Open-n-shut."

"Be more specific as to what was taken." She had a hard to detect facial twitch.

"None of my superiors took time to itemize to me what was missing. Army people explain everything on a need to know basis, leaving me out of the information loop."

"I figured that nobody would've directly told you what was stolen. So try to remember the scuttlebutt that floated around the base after that."

Her patients weakened.

"A couple of pistols...A few boxes of ammo."

I knew he wasn't going to mention the goggles.

"And some goggles," he added.

"Goggles?" She sounded confused. "What kind?"

"The type used by construction workers," he padded. "Ever since the first Gulf War, there were always construction projects of some kind going on overseas. The workers there were constantly afraid of chemical attacks, and wanted eye protection."

"May I speak candidly?"

From her lead-in he knew something was about to come out that he didn't want to hear. The profundity of her pessimism was surely to sting, but he hung in there.

"I don't like you," she said. "Scum bothers me."

So much for hanging, Michael was free-falling. A man in his position rarely heard such harshness said to his face.

"I'm in possession of a series of photographs that include a man wearing a baseball cap from your home state."

She was dying to see how he reacted.

"Sorry to disappoint you, but I wasn't in that chopper."

I never mentioned the helicopter.

"You were an accomplished pilot in the Guard, until the casinos in Atlantic City got in your way."

Michael gave her the touché sign, feeling that she had nothing on him. Still, he wasn't done. "You said photographs plural. What's in the other pictures?"

"People who are winding up dead," she added, turning him limp.

He regained his strength of stubbornness. "Explain it step by step. Make it easy for me to follow."

"Three things about my case are coming together: One. A man loaded with enough diamonds to bankroll a small country landed dead in a lake very close to your home. Two. On that same man were U.S. Army night vision goggles that were stolen from an Army base where you were stationed at the time of that theft."

She intentionally left out the fact that Mark bought his home—in cash— from the realtor who Michael worked for. Through the intimidation of suggestion, she sought to entice his help.

"I was hoping that you'd be a taste more obliging, if for no other reason than to save your own skin."

"If you're looking for Sammy The Bull, I hear he's doing twenty to life…Besides, I'd rather be home with my family than be a rat."

He knew that his comment wasn't going to cut short any of her inquisitiveness. Throwing it out there, he sought to put a little distance between himself and her.

"Which of your families are you talking about? The one you took marital vows to remain part of? Or, the cute, busty, thing I met in your office?"

He wasn't completely startled that she knew. "Such a cheap-shot remark. Even for a cop."

She wanted to punch him with words that would knock him out. She closed her note pad, hoping to have gotten something more from his body language than the movie star composure that oozed from his pores. His answers were slimy with multiple coatings of caginess.

He stood to escort her, pausing. "You said you're investigating a robbery…What's the third thing on your mind?"

Rikki wasn't about to answer, to give him insight into the way the pursuit of him was going.

Later, she sat in the parking lot which was on a boomerang path to the country club's pro shop, watching Michael getting into his never to be paid for Mercedes, leaving with the last of his golfing buddies.

Her car's interior reeked from the pot that she swiped from the evidence lockup. The infectious smell in the two-seater car resided comfortably beside the slipperiness that was Michael's when Rikki tried to corner him.

It wasn't so much that she was giving drugs to someone who she cared about, it was how she had done something that she often criticized other cops for doing: Going into the evidence lockup, taking out illegal items of interest— that they used to plant on suspects, to arrest them on additional, trumped-up charges. She had gone from bad-mouthing those borderline cops, to being like them.

Before she started the car, she flipped open her cell phone to read a startling text message. It was one sentence that changed everything.

There's a certain warden who has a friend who hates to shave, the tipster said.

THE BOMB
◆

With the rope fibers hat cut into his stretched hands, the man with the bushy beard pulled himself from a rowboat up the side of the Raritan River Bridge.

Once on the catwalk, he was careful to remain in the secluded recesses of the thick support beams. No one expected him to be there, so there were no security measures in place when he arrived with explosives, and a can of gasoline that had Acme Oil on its side.

THE FORT

◆

Rikki's once promising policing career had jumped the tracks, leaving her with countless ideas of how it could've progressed. She had decided to leave the force when, and if, her case ever made it to court. The only unattended aspect to her life was how to best start a new one when the guilty were led away to prison. Whenever things didn't go Rikki's way at work—and they rarely did—she'd fantasize what it would be like to have a real job, where life and death wasn't always hanging in the balance.

Rikki knew that Tony had the airports covered, with cops looking high and low for her. The only way she figured to slip out of town was to take the highway at night.

Undaunted, she pressed the accelerator to head to New Jersey. Looking ahead, she could only think of what was to come. Something kept telling her that it might be the final time that she saw Albuquerque.

New Jersey was different than she had imagined. It wasn't the smog capital of America that everyone said it was. Not counting New Mexico's being out in the middle of nowhere, the two states were very similar.

The northeast roads were lined with trees that had fresh greenish hues that hinted of the coming of spring, with hidden buds that were ready to sprout, with nary a spec of crud lining the asphalt. And when they did, there were chain-gang clean-up crews out to maintain the roads. Only an idiot creates litter to bring that bunch around.

Once she crossed the line into the Garden State, she was trapped behind a box truck that streamed pollution, tempting Rikki to change her mind about the smog.

The ride along the Garden State Parkway was pleasurable, until she was encroached by the time-killing traffic, from a car fire that had all the vehicles backed up long before she approached the Raritan River Bridge.

After an eternity of waiting, everyone was moving along its incline to the crest. A single shot pierced the air compressor on the side of the box truck. Immediately, all breaking pressure was lost. Its spring brakes engaged, dragging it to a complete stop beside the can of gasoline that was left near the guardrail.

From afar, the bushy bearded man quickly lowered his binoculars, after having seen Rikki's car stuck behind the box truck; then he moved toward the radio triggering device that was on the ground, having gotten a late jump to set it off.

A raccoon staggered toward him in a manner depicting that rabies had invaded its body. The deranged animal sniffed the remote control box.

"Rikki's going to get away," he grimaced.

Coordination of the attack had reached its critical mass when he dove for the remote control. The raccoon bit his hand. He yelled, frightening the deranged animal back into the surrounding woodlands. He knew that the opportunity for attack was fading.

Rikki heard a shattering blast beside the truck, causing the bridge to vibrate out of control. Cars around her began to shift, sliding, colliding into each other and against the guardrail. The once mighty bridge was collapsing. One by one, huge sections of steel, cables and cars were pitched downward into the river. During the horrifying journey straight down, Rikki could only think of Sharon and her mom.

*   *   *

Historically, military bases have had an uneven pattern of activity. Sometime, there is a hustling and bustling that rivaled the nation's most heavily traveled airports. Other times, total boredom dominates.

There had been on and off references to Ft. Dix Army base when she was at the police academy. After a ferocious dip in the waters that ran beneath what used to be the Raritan Bridge, she finally got to see where so many recruits had marched non thoroughfare streets never to be seen alive again.

Having hitched a ride on a vegetable truck, she was let off on the main road that was fifty yards from the wrought iron lift gate entrance. After what she had just been through back at the bridge, she walked with a pronounced limp, trying hard to carry herself as normally as one could—given she was glad to be able to walk at all. A steady passage of military vehicles, most getting suited for an Iraq tour, made it difficult to be heard; when a soldier, outfitted with many medals of distinguished service, came out of the guard house to greet her.

"Where do I find Sergeant Stern?" she asked, showing civilian permits of her own.

"See that barracks? Most likely, he'll be in there."

The entire way, she could feel ghosts all around her, marching in close order drill from previous decades. They were innocent nameless faces there to warn the living.

He watched Rikki walk away, wishing that more females on the base could look like her. When the last of her disappeared inside the building it was back to the order of the day—guard against the unexpected.

She stopped with a raised fist, ready to knock. Before she could, Private Marks was there.

"Ma'am?"

"I'm here to see LeRoy Stern."

"Please wait here," he politely replied.

The private pivoted, never changing his pace to return inside the building. Within a few minutes, there was the unpleasant aroma of a save-a-buck cigar that introduced the onset of the Sergeant.

He clasped both thumbs to his belt buckle, palms against his abdomen, in a rugged John Wayne stance. He sucked in a gut that hadn't seen nearly as many sit-ups as he demanded daily from younger soldiers.

The sight of him immediately struck her that he was one of the people in the batch of photographs that she showed Sharon. With that in mind, she made formal her introduction. "Rikki Luckett. Albuquerque police. I'm here to discuss—"

He huffed in an authoritative, let's get this over with tone. The cigar rolled from one side of his thick lips to the other.

"Who sent you to me?" He wasn't about to reveal how he knew that someone had.

"That name's here nor there."

That answer annoyed him.

She had a special gift of avoidance, that irritated countless people who tried to get answers from her—most noticeably, Fat Tony.

Resigned to the fact that she wasn't going to open up, Stern demonstrated with an extended arm which way for them to proceed.

"This way, Detective."

Meanwhile, Private Marks had eased closer to overhear all that he could. But when they walked beyond his listening range, he was shut out.

Inside their destination she saw a wall filled with assorted historic artifacts.

Aware that military types aren't of the time wasting variety, she got to it. "The night vision goggles that I asked your superior officer about were stolen from this base."

He puffed, making minimal effort to keep the smoke away from her. He wanted it to aggravate her to the point where she would cut short the intrusion and leave the base.

"My intelligence people in New Mexico have verified it."

She mentally backtracked, having stretched that just a bit. Intelligence and those with whom she worked were rarely thought of in the same sentence. Then she wondered what to do if Stern denied that the theft had actually happened.

He relit the cigar, making it glow brighter. He chewed on the tip, leading her to think that it was about to fall out from between his stained teeth.

"Is that a fact?" There was no confusion in a growling voice, that placed him on the level of appreciation with digging ditches, or twenty mile hikes.

"I need to find out if the serial number on the goggles that I have matches those from the batch that were swiped from here," she said, willing to butt heads with him if need be, intolerant of any stonewalling.

"Not sure if I can get you that information."

"Why the runaround?" she asked with mounting frustration, determined to get what she needed.

There was no way that she came these many miles, having stayed in so many crummy motels, nearly having fallen to her death on that bridge, to be roughed-up like so many underlings that he frightened on a daily basis.

"I'm just following the first rule of the Army," he advised.

"And that is?"

"Never volunteer."

It killed her to accept that, but she appreciated his frankness. "We've got a similar rule in our department," she added.

"Which is?"

"Follow the Army's lead."

The Army mentioned in any way tickled his fancy. "It bothers me that we have something in common."

"The feeling's mutual."

He lightly touched her elbow. This time, feeling more relaxed. "Let's go."

They exited Building Six to a more fortified structure that was set apart from the others. It looked different, in that it was absent of the usual military markings, making it appear inconsequential. And that was what the Army intended the perceptions to be.

At that entrance, Stern pressed his forehead to look into a retina scanner. There was a pronounced click that opened the door. He was somewhat amused by her silent, wide-eyed query, loaning a benign smile that said how he had everything under control.

After passing a guard who was so rigid that he seemed to have been there since the building was built, Rikki and Stern moved to a self-contained room of steel and concrete. Inside were two restrooms, and a high-tech video camera and an infrared protection system that spotted everything. The area quieted when the scanner shut off the motion detectors.

The air was stale. It was as though turning on a fan was an express route to a court martial. Given the high level of safety measures surrounding its contents, the interior had to be kept free of openings that weren't absolutely necessary. No one was taking any chances to let someone sneak inside. About that time, Rikki's claustrophobia set in.

"This is the records building. Or should I say, the classified records building. There's information here that can sink a bathtub full of battleships." He motioned. "What you need is in this file cabinet."

He touched it as though it was a hard to get along with newcomer.

"We call it the hernia cabinet. Many a soldier's lost his nuts trying to open it."

He stepped away, remembering the strain the last time he tried to manage it.

"I'm warning you. It ain't opening without Mister Universe coming in to do it."

She noticed its sides had been impacted by something, producing a concavity. She took hold of one of the drawers, finagling the handle with a female's nifty, crafty touch, jerking it from side to side before tugging. It glided to widen easily.

"They must've requisitioned a new cabinet without my authorization," he grumbled. Like so many in charge, he was incapable of understanding when he was wrong.

With anxious fingers she twiddled, searching through countless papers for answers, essentials that were key to her burden of proof in the case. She took out a flashlight from her purse to better see the pages. Initially, nothing of interest jumped out at her.

"If you'll pardon me." With that he turned away, with steps that were a bit heavier than when they first came inside.

Time wasted was an opportunity lost. The instant he was gone, she whipped out her miniature camera and photographed the pages that she deemed important. She had to work quickly because it wasn't going to he long before he'd return.

She continued to read, comparing the serial number on the stolen night vision goggles to the one that was found on her jumper. Bang. She got a match. Then she saw something that she hadn't envisioned to be there. It was the name of the person who telephoned the Army base claiming to be from the insurance company, and that he needed an inventory check. This all happened before the goggles were stolen. That person signed the name Mark Rhett.

From one side, Stern returned. She was caught far off her guard, not having heard him coming. That was when she knew that he had set her up with the ole' footsteps trick. Get'm used to a noise level pattern. Then throw'm a curve, and come back quieter.

"Back so soon?"

He passed gas.

To convince him that she didn't see anything past what he wanted her to, she was re-reading the same documents that he originally saw her going over before he walked away. With a maneuver of her own, he had to be steered from thinking that she may have been up to something while he was gone.

"Is this all that pertains to the theft in question?"

"It is," he answered, wanting her mission completed so he could be rid of her.

"I reckon, that'll be all for now."

"Don't tell me, you're coming back. Sorry," he adjusted his presentation. "If ya-do, I'll be mighty glad to have-ya." He wiped his out-of-line mouth. "I'm a busy man around here." He was less enthused with the prospect of ever seeing her again, than military protocol would allow him to come right out and say.

"Too involved to help law enforcement? I don't think so." She closed the folder, placing it back in the drawer before closing it, nearly slamming his fingers in it.

They walked to the exit. She was somewhat relieved to have found another answer to her crime cracking puzzle. As she passed through the door an alarm sounded. She figured that her camera had set it off. He looked at her curiously.

"Why didn't it go off when we came in?" She appeared calm.

"We don't want things getting borrowed," he glared at her with natural misgivings, "without authorization."

Surprisingly, he pulled out a remote control device that cancelled the alarm.

"I'm the only one with clearance and the ability to disarm the detector, to get in and out of the building without the alarm going off," he minimized.

His was an easy press of another button on the remote. Through the door they went without further interruption.

"You're commanding officer will get the word if I need anything more," she instructed.

"Why go through my C.O.? What's wrong with talking to me?"

The silent reaction from her answered his inquiry.

After shaking hands—as do fighters after a heavyweight bout—they walked in opposite directions. He thought to turn to look back at her, then figured the hell with it.

At her roadside motel, Rikki was again on the internet. She extensively read about the usages associated with those goggles. She learned that they were primarily used by construction workers; that jived with what Stern said, and the descriptions that were on the sheets that she photographed from that file cabinet. Still, it didn't make complete sense. Somehow, Stern had tricked her.

It was obvious that the parachutist wasn't into the construction trade. How could she have been misled into thinking that construction night vision goggles were the same ones on the jumper? She looked closely, and saw the name of the manufacturer of the goggles in the corner of one of her photographs: Denton Prescott Incorporated.

The next day, she was at the side of the road at the entrance to the New Jersey Turnpike, dialing.

"Denton Prescott," the operator answered, having arrived to work from a vacation that had passed much too quickly. She was swept-up in the first day of the citywide transit strike, leaving her dismayed as to how she got to work at all.

"Give me customer service," Rikki requested, rolling up the driver's side window, cutting into the roadside noise.

Rikki had but a scarce few seconds to wait, before a different woman came on to speak. "Customer service."

"I have a question about your XD-17 Goggles…What are they used for?"

The woman said, "Are you speaking of the XD-17? Or the XD-17N?"

"What's the difference?"

"The XY-17's are carried primarily by construction contractors. The 17N, however, isn't sold to the general public. They are for governmental issue only."

Rikki felt it necessary to get closer to the root of the dilemma, by identifying herself and the official police capacity in which she functioned, and why she made the call to Denton in the first place.

The woman on the other end was in full compliance. "The XY-17N has infrared night capability. It is used primarily for night surveillance."

"You've helped me tremendously."

"Thank you for calling Denton."

Rikki knew then that Sonny wasn't at that Vegas meeting. It was Mark Rhett, using Sonny's name. There was no way that Mark was traveling under his real name. Still, she couldn't let go of the thought of who would be the next to die.

With Jack gone, there was no way to be certain if breathing was part of his daily routine. Or, if her problems with Jack were somehow connected to facts that Tiny was helping her section together.

Feeling alone, she was returning to Albuquerque, desperately wanting to see Sharon alive. That's when it hit her.

The buddy who hated shaving was the man she saw at Steven's Stein's send-off.

WHERE'S BUBBA?

◆

Sharon had grown increasingly paranoid about getting caught, worrying to the point where holding food down was a feat unto itself. That would explain her recent weight loss. After changing her mind about getting rid of the two dead bodies in Rikki's backyard via the Department of Sanitation route, she had opted to dispose of them in the desert.

While Rikki was away, she watched an infinite amount of whodunit, forensics, TV crapola; where the slightest missed detail by the illegal actors managed to always lead to an arrest. Sharon wasn't about to make the same idiotic mistakes that those bonehead criminals did.

On top of all that there was a third man in Rikki's backyard when she was in the tub. No doubt, he was out there somewhere thirsting for payback.

THE TELEPHONE REUNION

◆

To confirm her theory about that Las Vegas meeting that Mark had, Rikki discovered that Mark wasn't on record as having flown out of Albuquerque. There was no telling exactly where he had gone, or if he flew commercially at all. One thing was certain. When he kissed Sharon adieus in Angles, he was a man who was constantly on the move. It went without saying; he was still very much alive.

A brief series of chimes from Rikki's resuscitated cell phone alerted her.

"Hey, white girl," the caller huffed with a crackly voice of friendliness.

Instantly, she recognized it.

"Figgered I'd have to die before you took time out from your precious-ass day to even think about callin' me," Tiny said.

Doing her level best to contain her animation, her glee of relief, over finally hearing his voice, she went on to defend her position.

"I'm dodging goblins on this end. And you're saying I haven't had you on my mind the whole time? Well, I have. It's interfered with everything that I'm trying to get done."

Tiny hadn't changed. Feeling the sexual additives, "Want to learn what I'd like to get done?"

"Quiet that," she snuffed, inwardly wanting to allow him to say anything that he wanted. As long as he was alive and kicking, she didn't really care.

Then again, there was the investigation.

"The three police who razzed you at the precinct paid me a visit the other day."

"How'd that go?"

"Bout as you'd expect."

They were rougher on Tiny than he was willing to disclose. Tough guys tend to be that way.

"Victor was the lead hard-ass. When he wasn't snapping-around those two under-idiots of his, he was on me about: My connection with you. Where are you? When was the last time I saw you? The usual shit…Woman, you must've really steamed his clams."

Before she could interject concern that he may have spilled the beans by saying too much to them…

"I went on talkin' to'm for a while. Never enough to satisfy'm…Victor's convinced that someone helped you slip out of town. And he couldn't stop thinkin' it was me…Haven't seen hide nor hair of Meyer since we busted'm out from the shed. Heard tell, he and the wife vanished. There's a chance Victor's henchmen got to'm. If they did, it's sayonara to Meyer. I ain't been outside much to check into it."

She was back in his good graces and wanted more. "I need another favor."

"Forget it!" he snapped, wincing from his shouting.

"That was quick," feeling put-off.

"Not quick enough," he added, damn sorry that she asked.

"Whatever happened to the Tiny who said, "If you ever need anything, don't hesitate to ask."

"I meant, don't hesitate to ask someone else."

Her moping was because he was under no obligation to help, but it sure would've been nice had he decided to.

"Take this in the right spirit, kid. You're unlucky to know."

"I love you, Tiny," she coaxed. "It's just a little favor. It's not like I asking you to cut off one of your legs, for Christ's sake."

He inched to one side to inspect a bandage that was still gathering blood and fluid discharges. He was a lousy nurse, and it looked more and more like the infection, and the pain, wasn't going away as fast as Angie said that it would.

"Whaddya-say?" She had the hook. What she lacked was enticing bait. "I'm paying five hundred."

Forget food. It's money that brings people back to the table.

"What I got to do to get the five?"

Suddenly, his interest was ripening.

"Locate where they're keepin' the wreckage of the crashed chopper. Take a few pictures inside it. And find out if a man named LeRoy Stern ever booked a room in Vegas."

The enormity of her request had settled in on him. "You want me to do what!?" he bellowed.

She extended her arm, keeping the cell from her ear, minimizing his volume.

"How do you expect me to get close to that thing without gettin' my balls blown off?"

"Look at it this way. You swore to Victor that you're not involved with me...If you get caught, they're gonna shoot you on sight. So you won't be needing your balls anyway."

She thought that was darn humorous. It went without saying that he didn't.

"I found out something else," he added.

"What's that?"

"Ever wonder why Victor released you so quickly after they popped you?"

"My Chief called'm."

"Did it ever occur to you that somebody told your chieff where you were?"

She was caught in the feeling, the sticky web, of perplexity.

"Your chief had you released, to have you and me followed by Barnes and Ernie immediately afterwards."

The way he said, "and me," expressed how sorely he wished that he had never picked her up in that cab.

"That's why they chased us. To later kill you inside that shed, making the resulting fire look like that's what did you caused...Watch it, my dear. You're getting close to answers that nobody wants out in the open."

She wanted what she wanted, and his explanation wasn't about to alter her objectives.

"You're the one with talent. Figure out how to get close to where they've got that chopper." She felt that her proposal needed financial strengthening. "Do this for me, and make my payout seven-fifty."

Suddenly, his pain wasn't as bad as before. "How do I find you to collect?"

"Easy."

"Broads," he mumbled. His past came to mind all too hastily. "Everything's so damn 'easy' when it's what they want." His were sentences taken from the bachelor's by-laws.

Though he had taken a modest liking to her, he wished that he would have committed himself to the local nut house, ahead of continuing on with a woman who had gotten him into more trouble than anyone had before.

"How dumb do I look?" he asked.

"You're a cutie. Especially when you're angry?"

Her end of the phone line shook from his growling.

"If you run into any trouble, I'll ride in to your rescue," she consoled, even though she had no way to back it up.

"I already found trouble. Should I say, trouble found me. And you're grim reaper was drivin' that trouble, to cash-in the chips I don't have!"

She was sorry to have been the one who brought about his misery. But she needed him—more than he needed her.

Three days came and went, with Rikki figuring that there had to be something in the wreckage that would help her identify who was onboard that helicopter. Then as only pure chance would have it, she got a return call from Tiny.

She was silent.

"Last April, your boy, Stern, booked a room—in a local dive, where my hookers get in for half price…I came across phone records from that motel, showing on that same day there were several calls made to Johannesburg…Then the next day, Stern and some guy named Rhett, who had been overheard talking about a guy with burned fingertips, and a woman named Conchita Contreras booked a flight going there. Does any of this mean anything to ya?"

"It's starting to." She switched. "Enough with that stuff. Tell me about you."

There was also something that Angie told Tiny. It was that Tiny probably would never be free from the wheel chair that he was sitting in. The bullet had bounced off his hipbone, fragmented, and hit his central nervous system. One thing was certain, he wasn't about to tell Rikki.

THE STERN SIGNOFF
◆

There was no logical explanation for why Sergeant Stern was out at that time of night. Those closest to him said that it wasn't uncommon for him to want to puff his favorite stogies in the late night air. What was a complete surprise was when the man with the bushy beard came upon him from behind.

Down the block there was only an abbreviated yelp. It would not be for another six hours before Stern's body was found with his throat cut.

THE MASK

◆

Minutes turned to hours, to days, then to weeks. It was all worthwhile when Rikki got the news that she had waited with earnest to hear.

Tiny had emailed her with pictures from inside the crashed chopper. One of them in particular struck Rikki. It was the picture that showed a clown's mask that had bits of tinsel inside it on the floor of the aircraft.

Instantly, she remembered the Warden saying "Yesterday, some clown in a chopper swooped down and sprung'm d-hell out of here."

The Circus Circus chopper was definitely the same one that carried Bubba out of prison. Also, there were fragments of tinsel stuck to the parachutist's neck; not to mention, the controls were set on autopilot, which explained how it managed to continue on to Vegas with no one aboard to fly it.

Tiny was a miracle worker. The remaining issue was how to tell him that she'd be late with his seven hundred and fifty.

THE GOOD-BYE

◆

Sharon was gradually getting the hang of living with Rikki. But it was that day—when she never stopped stirring her scalding cup of tea, watching Rikki enter the kitchen—when she had a creepy feeling that unpleasant information was about to erupt.

"How was your day?"

"Like every cop's: Stomach churning, the public hating me, with minimal results to show for my hard work."

The grind was getting to Rikki. All semblances of her emotional strength had faded faster than good news on Wall Street.

Rikki wiped her face with a dry palm, wanting to be rid of her past, leaving only a clean page to follow from that day onward. A new beginning with Sharon seemed further away than at any other time.

At the same time, Sharon sought the protectiveness that was absent when Rikki wasn't around.

"I think I landed a real job," she mumbled, not expecting anything good to come from that disclosure.

"That's great."

Rikki's reaction wasn't all that explosive. When a person goes to work each day, it's not that big a deal hearing someone promise to join in the workplace rat race.

She wanted to react in an upbeat sort of way. Though she was never one to feel good without sufficient proof—the cop in her. Optimism was in short supply as Rikki settled in to be surprised.

"Doing what?"

There was a hint of luminance in Sharon's face. "Being a receptionist."

"Where?"

Her worst suspicion was that Sharon had latched-on to be a bag woman for a local drug dealer.

"Tellata Enterprises."

Hearing that was a striking kick in the teeth.

That bastard's using her to get to me.

"What's wrong," Sharon asked. "I wanted you to be happy for me."

"I am," she covered up. "I'm curious to hear how you found that company." She was tongue-tied with worry, unable to voice the full scope of her concerns about Michael, and the connection he'd made between Sharon and her.

Sharon's face had changed to a flushed shade of red. "Funny thing is, he contacted me."

I knew it.

Sharon thought of how to best tell the story, to make the details come out in the correct order.

"Earlier today, I took the bus into town. When I got off, there was a man standing there. He didn't look like he was doing much of anything, until he spoke up. At first, I thought he was hitting on me. Then we got to talking. After a minute, he said how he was sorry to hear about what happened to Mark."

Rikki stopped her eyes from moving about, gluing them on Sharon.

"That hit me as odd, especially since he came out of the blue to say that…Then he asked me if I knew anybody who needed a job."

"I told him that I had experience as a buyer, but he said he recently fired his old receptionist, and needed a new one."

"You didn't tell him about your 'buyers experience' with Mark, did you?" Rikki asked.

Sharon merely shook her head, wondering how stupid Rikki thought she was, to have mentioned such a thing.

"Actually, I was a buyer for Johnson and Johnson Corporation in New Jersey. That's where Mark and I first saw each other. We were at a party at Cook College. He was meeting with one of his gambling connections. We talked and kinda hit-it-off." Her tone saddened. "Wish I could've been warned that it would lead to a full-time wanted by the cops existence."

Rikki was sold on the idea that Michael planned to use Sharon for information about the man in the lake. How did he learn about her relationship with Sharon? Maybe he didn't, and this was a by chance meeting, with a legitimate job offer. Sure, and the Black Sox didn't fix the 1919 World Series.

Sharon continued, "He didn't say I definitely have the job. He's going to get back to me in a day or so, after he flies to New Jersey to attend an old Army buddy's funeral. Then he has to check my references. Blah. Blah. Blah...You don't mind that I put you down as a reference, and gave him your phone number. I had no other choice, after the phone company cut Mark's off."

Stern got his throat cut after I paid him a visit. He was another person who had to be silenced. Who is going to be next to die?

When Rikki said nothing to the contrary about either the issuance of the telephone number, or using her as a reference, she took it that Rikki didn't mind. Then she leaned closer to give her a small kiss to seal everything.

Rikki hated hearing every word of it. Michael had an inside route to find her. "No problem," she said with anger headed in the direction of wherever Michael was.

Searching for something to uplift Rikki's apparently downtrodden mood, Sharon hoisted her cup for a toast. "To us."

"To your new job," Rikki added with artificial cheer.

She touched the back of Rikki's hand with an, 'I'm in high spirits that you are here' mannerism.

"My case's taken a turn."

Sharon's mood plunged, sensing that the impending news wasn't going to leave her feeling the way that the new job prospect explanation had. She nestled within a protective layer with unbridled apprehension.

Rikki went on, "I've uncovered things that'll have me out of town for a while."

Sharon again felt exposed to whatever consequences would happen during that absence. She put down her glass, pouting. "Can't we ever get five minutes alone together?"

Rikki slid closer. "Don't look sad. It won't be forever." She immediately sought to pump air into Sharon's deflated morale. "Maybe you should come with me."

She wanted to, sounding morose. "I'd be in the way, weighing you down...You need to travel light."

She gathered strength to add, "I'll be okay," though that possibility was far-fetched.

There's more inside Sharon than she's telling me.

"Has anybody been asking around about you and Mark?"

Sharon could only reflect upon when red-hot ammunition was flying in the backyard. She wrapped her arms around Rikki, holding her with designs never to let go.

Rikki needed to say, "I worry since word got out about Mark, that people would go to great lengths to find what he may have left behind, anything that they can get their hands on."

The fret in Sharon was rising like a volcano that had been dormant for decades, which threatened the entire social landscape.

"That settles it," Rikki concluded. "I'm not going."

Sharon began to unbutton her own blouse. She gently pushed Rikki's head lower, for her eager mouth to travel to where the bra was. She caught the elastic in her teeth, pulling it up and away. Sharon obliged, allowing the coupled, non-padded, C cups to tumble to the couch then the waiting floor.

Rikki wasn't finished with her. Her snakelike tongue flickered to catch the hard, fleshy, receptacle. She took a hand full of Sharon's hair, gripping it tightly, pulling her head slowly back, fully exposing a long neck that begged for Rikki's aggressive, erotic, attentiveness. She moaned from Rikki's touch, wanting no end, needy for repeated beginnings.

Then it became Sharon's turn to demonstrate just how much she had missed Rikki. Her nails scratched across Rikki's bare back. She hoped to leave a lasting impression, something to signify their eternal union.

They were joined. More than physically, their emotional interlocking had blossomed into something that the two of them had only seen in old movies. Finally, true happiness had arrived for both of them.

Darkness had fallen upon New Mexico like pulling the covers over an infant's inquisitive face. By that time, the first metal latch had snapped closed, on a suitcase that had been over-stuffed with every female necessity that Rikki could have possibly thought to take with her.

"Don't forget anything." Sharon figured that was highly unlikely, wanting the passionate hours that went down earlier to carry her through until Rikki returned. What chance was there for that to happen?

"Looking at your suitcase reminds me of how Mark never wanted to bring me along when he left town for whatever reason he skipped out."

She saw Rikki struggling to lift the timeless American Tourister, straining from its awkward, unbalanced, weight.

"Let me help," Sharon chimed-in.

Rikki's boundless confidence in Sharon was enhanced, seeing her eager to lend a helping hand. The occasion when someone actually wanted to help Rikki do anything was such an oddity, that Sharon's gesture was warmly absorbed. Rikki liked the togetherness, the teamwork aspect of it, given that Sharon didn't feel obligated to assist.

"Nothing's too big for both of us to handle," Sharon offered a manufactured smile. Considering what had happened with those backyard shootings, she knew that her protection would be gone when Rikki stepped outside.

"I shouldn't be away much past a week. Ten days, at best."

Sharon wasn't certain what to think about the explanation of a timetable. All she could soak in was seeing her lover leave in a time of significant, defenseless, desperation.

"Don't leave loose ends wherever you're going, that you'll have to go back later to clean up."

Rikki's agreeing nod was the answer that Sharon sought.

"Still don't feel like telling me where you're going?"

"Johannesburg, but I never said that. Above all else you can't breathe a word about this trip to anyone. Sure, there'r people whom you trust to tell. But in no way can you trust who your friends trust. Gossip is free-wheeling, unable to stop until it gets to the wrong person."

Sharon was left to utter, "The only friend I have is you."

"Hopefully, none of Mark's old contacts will come around."

Sharon's internal fear of whoever she had buried in the desert haunted her. Then she pressed her lips closed with a stiff index finger as a sign of promised silence.

"I can count on you. Niggling is the cop in me. Ignore it."

"What time's the flight?"

"Midnight."

"Mark said that's the time that draws the most attention."

"The very reason I'm taking it. I'm supposed to be a big-time, illegal, diamonds merchant. I want to be on a flight that very element arrives on."

Sharon thought better of that strategy, but knew that Rikki was stubborn, and was determined to do it her way.

Rikki dropped to one knee, Sharon followed. Together they recited Rikki's favorite prayer aloud, asking that Rikki return safely. Sharon wanted more.

"I need to get high," Sharon began to cry, caving-in with old desires that never seemed to have left her weakened ability to endure.

"Nothing bad is going down while I'm gone." Rikki touched her down turned chin.

"How can you be sure?"

"Cause I'm with the good guys. G.I. Josephine, remember?"

Rikki tried to believe that everything would be fine. What bothered her most was that the case had taken control; to the point where solving it, proving her theory against Mark, was everything.

Sharon knew deep down that this was the end of their relationship. This was another Mark-like move. It was the big kiss-off.

Sharon said, "With the short time we have left, let's get in bed."

Watching Sharon taking off her clothes, Rikki realized that Hildy had told Michael about Sharon. Or more frighteningly, it was the other way around.

THE TEXT

◆

Erik became a believer.

Rikki was bothered by a low battery alert from her cell phone. And since she forgot to bring her charger, calling anyone from the road was going to be very short lived.

Then she saw an incoming message. She was forced to pull off the road onto the shoulder to read it. She was getting close to something, and the last thing that she wanted was to land back in the hospital from a car accident—trying to read a text message.

The words were horrifying.

Morty's dead. Last night, the cleaning crew at his job found him at the bottom of an open elevator shaft. Out of nowhere, Tony was the first one at the scene. He's gone on record, saying that it was an accident. He said the elevator's has always been faulty, and Morty should've known that. You've opened-up a can of worms with this investigation of yours. Everybody helping you ends up dead. I'm running for cover. What the hell have you done!? E.

Rikki knew that the "E" was for Erik. She did all that she could to get that text message off her troubled mind. But she was knee-deep in it with no way out.

She crossed her fingers for Erik's safety, but not ahead of for herself.

THE TRIP

◆

Everything was for sale, starting with the lies.

Thieves see who drives into every airport's long-term parking lot. Or, they have an inside person working as attendants, to relay back what cars come in. Then they run a check on the license plates. If it's an out of state plate, forget about the owner seeing that car again. The owners of in-state cars can count on their homes being broken into when they return from wherever they flew. It's sad that the perpetrators never used their ingenuity to get a legitimate job. Theirs was an outright waste of ability.

Household valuables can easily be replaced, but Sharon couldn't. That was why Rikki left the subcompact in the driveway, choosing instead to have a car service drive her to the airport. The intent was to throw-off anyone spying on her movements. She wanted potential prowlers to think that she was home, or perpetually very near by.

Rikki walked from the curb into the main terminal. During that time, she held tightly to the idea that this back and forth across the country hunt—which had escalated to a worldwide search—was about to yield the long sought after results. Did someone say, Detective of the Year?

Missing the sound of Sharon's sexy voice had Rikki reaching to call her.

"Hello," Sharon answered.

"That's a good sign when you're calling so soon," Sharon joyfully acknowledged.

She wiped away tears that had refused to leave a face that finally began to regain its natural complexion.

Airport security came upon Rikki, taking her by the arm.

"Ma'am, I must be certain that yours is a working phone and not an explosive device. These are times of high security concerns. Please understand. I need to hear someone talking on the other end of that phone," he insisted.

Rikki extended it to the man, who listened to Sharon say, "I can still taste your cum in my mouth."

The embarrassed security guard became apologetic while handing back the phone. "I prefer to be safe than in a million pieces. Waking my wife up to come down here to identify my remains might take some doing."

Rikki continued to the departure gate. Unknowingly, she passed the man with the bushy beard, who stood on an elevated section watching her from afar. Behind the thick hair on his twitching face, he looked noticeably worse than was the case at Steven's farewell. His hands shook from the effects of the rabies.

"Are you there?" Sharon asked, through the cell phone that Rikki had all but forgotten that she held. Then the battery died.

Rikki rethought her game plan, demanding of herself to carry it to the finish—even if it meant dying. All that she sought was success. First, she had to think of where to begin.

Ahead, she saw an airline assistant collecting boarding passes. The woman seemed comfortable, considering she hadn't been off her feet in over nine hours.

"Good evening," she smiled to Rikki.

"It'll only be that when I'm in my seat sleeping," Rikki huffed out of breath.

The woman split the ticket, keeping the important half with a fist filled with others.

Rikki walked past her to the mouth of the gangplank to enter the plane. She was greeted by a flight attendant who wore the same stereotypical beam. Squeezing past her was easy. Then it was on to the more difficult chore of finding her seat. Finally, Rikki shimmied across wide, leather, chairs to get beside the window. Even though there was nothing to see outside except darkness, she still felt more at ease to begin relaxing for the flight.

Most of the late night sky walkers were already tucked in, by the time Rikki pressed her upper back against the recliner. Some were reading, others piddled to pass the hours.

It wasn't too extensive a wait, before the jet revved its mighty engines and rolled out onto the tarmac to rocket down the runway. Its final, mighty, burst lifted the loaded-down 747 off the ground. Within minutes, the jumbo jet glided through light turbulence into what was the beginning of a peaceful flight.

"Can I get you anything?" Rikki was asked.

She strained to focus on the neatly arranged beverage cart in the aisle.

"Sanity," Rikki delivered.

The attendant was gracious. "If I had any to spare, I'd have placed it in my overhead storage compartment for safe keeping." She switched back to why she was there. "We have a wide assortment of drinks that you might like."

With brainwaves that were as clear as London at dawn, Rikki said, "Just water."

After receiving the chilled bottle, Rikki looked lazily through the window into the blackened, non-threatening sky. She imagined what it must have been like that windy night when Sonny tumbled out, then down into the lake. As rotten a person as he turned out to be, she wished that he was frightened out of his dim wits. Then she presented no resistance when conquered by sleep.

Hours later, she was stirred by the screeching sound of burning tires, and creaking metal couplings that announced that the plane had touched down.

She and countless others stretched in their seats, eagerly anticipating finally being able to deplane. Children had trouble remaining still, as their parents scolded, or coaxed, them under control. It wasn't easy for the little ones to behave, except for those whose parents were from the old school of discipline. For those kids, the options to exist outside the lines of the rules were limited.

The final cabin jerk came from the outside, when the portable stairs banged against the aging fuselage. The unfasten seatbelts sign flashed. That prompted the passengers to stand, most ducked, to file into the aisle, to gather their carry-on belongings, bidding farewell to mini space travel. Finally, everyone prepared to leave after such a lengthy trip.

Very few people found the pre-dawn hours friendly enough, to be there to greet the arriving passengers. On watchful patrol, however, was a smattering of sleepy, undercover police, who lacked the dishonesty to have called in sick. That was mostly because they couldn't find a corruptible physician to write a convincing note explaining why they couldn't be at work. Make no mistake about it, the day shift was more difficult. But the degree of complexity in fighting crime can sometimes be on a par with fighting sleep.

In charge of only the name of the woman called Conchita, a partially crumbled email confirmation for the hotel room, Rikki proceeded to the baggage claim area. The chance of her connecting with Conchita was on a par with the timetable for hell freezing over. Given the incalculable odds for success, she gladly would've settled on the chances of when pigs fly. In any event, she was grateful to Tiny for finding out that much. When it was all over, she had one heckova thank you for him. First, she had to solve the case, get back to

Albuquerque alive, and find the gems to keep herself out of prison. And that was far too tall an order to process.

Rikki reached between others, who uneasily waited to grab their luggage, from a carousel that turned much too fast. Rikki, on the other hand, was cognizant to snatch hers.

If I run into trouble, nobody'll ever find me this far from home. And to make matters worse, I don't have a phone to call.

Rikki's sense of inquisitiveness was stirred by attention-getting winds that swept past the terminal's exit. Standing outside, she wondered if English was going to get her from point A to wherever she needed to go.

South Africa has inspired media-driven images of eternal racial strife. Placed into a wider historical context, this part of the world has had a proud tradition; with its spectacular natural beauty and its rich history was for all to boast. With the tourist's dollar stretching much further, this country's oppressive past seemed all but forgotten as Rikki took in deep breaths. Amidst all of that, however, there was the underlying feeling that the whole place remained strongly anti-American.

Johannesburg was everything the modern tourist wanted it to be. For the not-so-ordinary traveler, it was a safe place to hide money. And a haven away from worldwide scrutiny, where people on the run flock, thinking that no one will ever find them.

Rikki felt the country as quite cool, yet breathtaking; with energizing, breathable, air that allowed her ever-changing thoughts to settle-in for the long haul. Should all else fail, this would be a splendid vacation spot with Sharon.

Outside the hotel, she paid the driver with the local currency that she got at the monetary exchange booth at the airport. He felt slighted by the amount she handed him, taking it with a twist from disappointed lips before speeding away. He left thinking that all Americas are all the same. Cheap.

Rikki bent to hoist her suitcase. Once upright, she proceeded along the stone lined path to the low profile, yet well tended, entrance.

It was the beginning of the International Jewelry Show. The streets were bustling with small shops that opened to the expected cash and barter flow that the celebration drew in each year. Rikki was convinced that if she were to have a chance of spotting Conchita, it would be here. Many yards away, the man with the bushy beard watched.

* * *

This wonderful South African city was bustling with people and their situational interactions. Even though the haves and have nots were noticeably far apart, it didn't stand out as was the case in the United States. Here, their coexistence seemed quite doable.

Hoards of children rushed to Rikki, convinced that all Americans have money in excess, and are willing to dole it out to anyone who asked. The once manageable crowd quickly swelled, drawing the ire of elders who were situated at many residential windows. From their perch they questioned what the commotion on the street was all about. Anyone reading Mickey Spellane's novels, thinking that Americans can hideout in other countries without being noticed had better give it a different reflection.

"You speak English," Rikki remarked to a dirty face child, who played on the ground while adults walked around her. It was miraculous that she hadn't been stepped on.

The girl reacted as though her limited intelligence had been infringed upon. "I didn't spend two years in the third grade for nothing. Of course, I speak English."

She eyed Rikki holding her stomach. "You deserve a break today," she remarked, mocking the McDonalds commercial, "So don't eat out here."

"Funny," Rikki complimented.

"I do a comedy act out here every day at this time," she pointed to a bent and rusted limited run, iron railing behind her. Rikki fixed that in her memory, in case she planned to find her way back at some future time.

"I might stop back to see you," Rikki replied. Hers was a spontaneous utterance with no validity.

The child figured that, hearing it from so many people each day. She came to understand that adults were all terribly insincere.

Later, Rikki waltzed down the cluttered block, finding nothing of particular interest on side streets that were wide enough to accommodate only one car at a time. She sought anyone who looked shady; someone who was in need of gems the old fashion way, illegally.

She moved purposefully to blend-in. From all reports, if an outsider wanted to meet with certain death, all they had to do was ask about the underground trades.

"Pssst," someone called in a hushed tone.

Rikki turned her head with a undefined conduct to better see who issued the cat-call. There was a young man with long arms and untied, canvas, sneakers not too far away, who made his advance obvious. Using police sagacity, she wanted to see if anyone else was part of his forward move. He appeared to be alone. His body language was shifty and untrustworthy.

"Looking for something?"

Her stance was relaxed. His was anything but that. She wasn't about to let him walk away without first trying to ascertain more, to flush out his intentions that she suspected were questionable.

"What if I were?" she went on.

He rubbed his knuckles, with eyes that seemed to look in all directions simultaneously. Then suddenly, he fled.

Unperturbed, Rikki wasn't ready to abandon attempts at fact finding. Instead, she wanted to soak up more of the socioeconomic landscape before retreating to her pay by the day living quarters that were less than a mile away.

A few hours into the walking expedition, she became disillusioned at having found nothing of particular interest that would lead her to feel that she was in the right country—let alone the correct city.

At the hotel…

The front desk clerk seemed like a nice enough sort, given the degree to which his simple "Hello" sounded as genuine as the previous two dozen that he uttered that same afternoon. Management and guests alike spoke kindly of him, in a way that made them feel comfortable and charmed when they came near him.

"Good evening, Miss Luckett. You had a nice get-around across our fine city?" he initiated with an older man's warmth.

His was the variety she used to wish for—from Jack while growing up. Realistically, a person can pray only so much, then it becomes nagging.

She looked to see the lobby free of the children who earlier had pursued her on the street.

"Where'r my little buddies?"

"The truant officer got wind of their whereabouts, and inadvertently came to your rescue," he said.

He continued to arrange items that didn't need it, dusting where spotlessness had existed earlier. He loved the hotel, considering it his home away from home, never growing tired of keeping it ageless.

She shuffled along a floor that far and away beat the walkways that she had been on for the better part of that day. It was then that she saw the dirty face girl walking inside the lobby's entrance with her raggedy doll. Rikki's commitments had changed while watching her draw closer.

"Olga wanted to thank you." the child answered, preoccupied with the partially broken doll that she held.

"What for?" Rikki played along, looking at the doll as if it were human.

The girl held the doll to her own ear, before turning back to Rikki. "She isn't sure."

Rikki looked around for the nearest adult who might be this child's parent. There were none with any interest in the small one at risk. One would have thought that kids her age walk those mean streets alone every day. The more she thought about it, that's probably the way it was.

"What's your name?"

"Sabina."

Rikki heard a subtle growling from the child's stomach, suggesting that it had been quite some time since she last ate.

"Now listen to who is hungry."

Sabina continued talking quietly to her doll that had a lack of cleanliness to rival the child's.

"Where'r your parents?" Having to ask the question was troublesome enough, fearing the worst anticipated answer.

Sabina shrugged her shoulders. Rikki took that to mean that the parents were simply not around. Or, Sabina had no idea where they were.

The child said, "I live there" pointing through the floor to ceiling glass out onto the street beyond.

Rikki had a new major concern. Coming to Sabina's rescue was the sudden calling.

"Let's get something to eat."

That brought an awkward half-smile to a child who hadn't felt a full stomach for far too long a period.

The task for Rikki was how to get a child with such grime into the upscale hotel dining room. There had to be a dress code in place. Circumventing it wasn't going to be easy.

At the dinner table Sabina was a sight to behold. Her mouth stayed jammed with food that she couldn't chew fast enough to keep from choking. The meal left the plate in a straight line to her small receptive mouth at an alarming rate of passage.

"Whatever this is, I love it," she beamed, reaching to her throat that began to hurt, from solid food that went down in portions that were hurried and too large.

The sight of the child finally being able to do away with hunger pangs gave Rikki sufficient reasons to feel useful. Youth is never an easy road to jaunt, especially when extreme poverty dominates one's daily theme. Suddenly, it wasn't all about the investigation.

"I'm finished," the little one said with a potbelly soreness that wasn't all that bad when she thought about it. In fact, it was different.

Rikki was a bundle of exposed feelings. "Wipe your mouth. Good table manners are a must."

"This sure beats looking through garbage cans for food."

That further broke Rikki's heart, forcing her to realize how growing up with Jack wasn't all that bad after all. Then she had the unenviable task of what to do with Sabina. It seemed immoral, bordering on barbaric, to simply walk her back to the dusty street where they first met and disconnect with her.

"I'm ready to go," Sabina yawned. The pint-size one stretched both her arms, and those of her doll. "Olga and I are getting sleepy."

That placed Rikki on the edge of tears, when Sabina suggested her own return to a sewer hideaway.

"What's wrong?" Sabina asked innocently, trying—as many children do—to make the adult feel better. "Don't worry. The street's been my home since I was a kid." She wiped her face, adding a layer of courage to make her proclamation more believable. "I can take care of myself."

Children are so naïve. Wanting desperately to help, Rikki realized how helpless she was to save this child from her reality of circumstance. How sad the truth really is.

There but for the grace of God go each and every one of us on a daily basis.

When Rikki looked down from a distant stare into the dispassionate face of truth, Sabina wasn't there. Rikki's neck hurt from jerking her head, trying to ascertain how she could've gone that fast.

"Did you see which way that little girl went!?" she asked of restaurant workers who stood near.

Each shrugged dispassionately, preoccupied with their children and those problems inherent to their own child rearing.

With countless narrow streets into which Sabina could've fled, finding her was unlikely.

Perhaps, Sabina thought that Rikki was about to remove her from the only environment that the child ever had. And that was too much for her small heart to bear.

Having slid from prime focus was that slight chance of finding the mysterious Conchita.

It wasn't long after her wakeup call from the front desk, that Rikki was out on the streets with both eyes finely sharpened, looking for a child who could be anywhere.

Many hours that yielded no results had moved late afternoon to evening. Rikki was back at the bent and rusted railing. People walked by, with no interest having been paid to those peeling, iron gates. Rikki's frustration was not being appeased.

On a path away from the secondary road, Rikki saw a limited group of shabbily clothed boys who were off by themselves. Some were sitting, a few standing.

They were smoking atop a mattress that had been discarded farther up the street months earlier. They had since dragged it into their den, as an add-on to the makeshift trimmings for the gang's meeting place.

Nearby, there was a crane. Its steel cables held a mixing vat for concrete. There was no wind, so fortunately it didn't sway.

Rikki was composed at the sight of the boys, despite their behaviors that demonstrated they were indulging in something other than cigarettes. When she dared to walk closer that much was obvious to her nose. She'd been outnumbered before, but always managed to talk her way out of it when things got out of hand. One difference here was that she was without protection. Her nine millimeter friend was in Albuquerque.

The walk toward them encroached their line of "we're on this side and you're on the other" demarcation.

One of the boys snarled, "Get lost, lady!"

The others laughed at her, but still they were uncomfortable with her getting closer. She outlined to herself that he was the spokesman.

"I hate working weekends," she added with a quip of one-upmanship to show that she wasn't afraid.

Rikki was collected, aware that one of them seemed to have taken a curious interest in her. He was the one who stared through her.

He's got the answers.

The spokesman continued, "Why'r you here?"

There was confusion in their faces as the stench of meth singed her delicate nostrils.

The others turned away, more concerned with getting high than continuing idle chit-chat with a lost outsider, who could just as easily turn-tail and be back on the main street.

Her silent admirer licked closed another tightly wrapped joint, showing uncommon generosity when he offered it to Rikki.

By the way the others gave him space to operate, she knew then that he was in charge. Though he was still a youngster, he had an unsentimental face that had seen similar pains of everyday life that were beginning to shape Sabina; however, she was still young enough not to have her youthful appearance chiseled as was the case with him.

Rikki took the joint, rationalizing that partaking was merely the means to an end, which was somehow getting closer to finding her way to Sabina or Conchita—whichever came first.

"Don't let the joint waste away, sister," the leader said, as he watched it burn away in the breeze. "Reefer costs money."

To exercise her prerogative and leave would negate any opportunity for them to warm-up to her, to disclose anything that might be helpful. Backwards reasoning, it's true. Again, what choice did she have? Her inhalation filled lungs that were in no way prepared for the saturating effect that the drug had.

Her inflamed chest burst the smoke into the leader's street hardened face. He hated when anyone did that, but sucked in the floating white, to hopefully get an additional contact euphoric influence.

"Good stuff." She tried to convincingly act the part of an experienced drug head.

The leader's thoughts of her being undercover with the local police began to fade, but he hung on to that suspicion.

"Ask her what does she want?" said the young man with long arms and untied sneakers, taking a self-preserving, half step closer to her. He looked at the leader. "Earlier, I saw her snoopin' around town, asking a bunch of questions."

The leader was made extremely tense by that comment. "Is that right?"

By that time she had difficulty concentrating. The drug's influence was hitting her hard. She felt light headed, floating, mentally drifting, and struggling valiantly to maintain concentration on why she was there.

Her hope was that she wouldn't say something that would have her swallowing a hot lead sandwich. Her ability to make decisions was fading. She was trapped by the drug's assault on her senses; nonetheless, she continued to draw on the tip, to receive the full strength of the near lethal chemical mix.

When the glow nearly burned her fingers, her thinking was to the north of Saturn. A fact that didn't go unnoticed by the delinquent band of gang brothers. Carnal thoughts of domination had overcome their otherwise carefree, seventh heaven, manner.

Whatever concoction the boys had rolled in that smoking paper was far stronger than Rikki's ability to think through it. Her mannerisms had changed in a gesticulation that ran counterclockwise to all that was apt, against anything that resembled positive mental health.

She'd forgotten why she had approached them in the first place. Then she figured it best to walk back to the street to hopefully clear her balmy head. The hour for desertion, however, had grown short. That's when they surrounded her.

"She wants to be with us for another reason," one of them said, aching from the sight of the defenseless woman.

They, indeed, wanted to feel her western body. Imposing thoughts of sex had dominated their thinking.

"I…I got to get back to my hotel," Rikki garbled.

The leader pushed aside the few boys who remained seated on the mattress from its surface of exposed springs.

"Make yourself comfortable here," he directed more than suggested to Rikki.

Erik? Tony? Where are youuuuu?

The sex-glazed look in the leader's glassy eyes harbored plans of carnal assault that quickly hatched.

She continued to retreat; when she tripped, they sprang to action. Their eager hands groped her everywhere at once. Her physical resistance and shouts of protest fell on twelve deaf ears and egos that had one thing in mind—self-satisfaction. This was their collective call to dishonor.

They captured her, demanding all that they could. They pulled and held tight, making it impossible for her to budge or speak another word. She did her best to fend off the attackers; she was no match for their numerical and determined evil advantage.

In the ensuing tussle they dragged her to the mattress, plunking her hard onto it. That was when they all joined in. They tore away her clothes. Each nastily waited his chance to seize her for his demented brand of uncontrollable pleasure conquest. Her efforts to oppose collapsed beneath her drug-induced ineptitude and physical battering. Sadly, her drained campaign was lost below a pile of twisted, juvenile, savagery.

Her spirit died that day. Her clothes were gone, tossed to the side as one would the day's refuse. The unbearable pain was inadequately dulled by the drugs in her system. It was the worst of everything having come together in a splash of unforeseen, flaming, misery.

When it was at its worst, the man with the bushy beard stepped out into the open, saliva dripping from the edges of his sagging mouth. "Finish her!" he yelled.

A sharp bash to the side of her head did just that.

Well past the hour when most of the city had settled in for the evening, Rikki's senses finally began to come alive. It sure wasn't much. But ten percent of something surpassed a hundred percent of nothing—with the 'nothing' being death.

The mesh of vivid colors, saliva spraying breaths and rangy violent sounds were gone; to where silence dominated the confined, trashy, landscape. She could barely hear, from eardrums that had been severely damaged. Near complete silence was all that she had.

That wasn't to say that she was at peace, not at all. Hers was a restricted, inner city, hell; into which a special invitation had been issued by the devil himself. It was to reward her stupidity for being in the right place for the wrong results. One eye tried to coax the other to focus on what she hated seeing, herself.

Rikki's exposed flesh was needled by the sudden coolness in the unsettled, African, air. Her spinning brain fought to overcome crimson blood that heavily trickled from her skull.

After connected minutes of forcing herself to realize that she had to get out of there, it was time to begin a body systems check—the transmission of data to her whirling brain, to ascertain how badly she was hurt. She needed a way out of this.

Seeing retaliatory justice return to those who attacked her hours before wasn't important. That reprisal would hopefully come at some future time. Meanwhile, she had to get to safety before they returned. She was convinced that the attackers had a perverse, unfinished, torment for her.

Then there were the rats that climbed over her. The needle-like feel of their claws assured Rikki that her nervous system still functioned. That was a hale and hearty beginning to a sickening aftermath.

The sun's enriching rays poured between the low-rise buildings on the street beyond, seeking to uplift the bleak climate within her. Where were the elders in the elevated windows when she needed them?

"Stop the car," called a woman from the rearmost seat of a recently shined passing four wheel coach.

The only reason why it wasn't a stretch limo was that it would have drawn unwanted attention, in areas where getting in and out as quietly as possibly was the chosen means. Neutral was best. In any case, the toy for the rich hurriedly approached. The woman in the rear banged on the interior window to again alert her driver.

Woman to woman, there was Rikki lying in the dirt. Something quick had to be attempted for her rescue.

"Yes, Ma'am," the driver obeyed. He was Maurice, a man not to be messed with.

He pressed the brake pedal to conclude the lengthy vehicle's advancement, never so much as to lend the slightest jerk to the rider while doing so.

The woman's head of freshly made-up hair was fixed to the gruesome sight that was Rikki, who was many yards away unable to get up.

Rikki was on both scarred knees, fighting away the lice covered rats that bit at her to defend their turf. She screamed from the additional pain.

"We'd better be getting on," Maurice said, not wanting to get involved with anything that wasn't part of his scope of responsibilities.

His milk of human kindness had evaporated many years earlier, when he came home to find his entire family murdered. Street level tones said it was on orders from a powerful industrialist, who felt that one of Maurice's family members was about to testify against him in a bank fraud case that threatened to level the business climate for the entire city.

"We can't be late," he stressed.

She had warned him numerous times about giving his opinion—especially when it didn't jive with hers. Their destination was with ranking international dealers who, if kept waiting for an instant, would be quick to dissolve their association with her.

Maurice was a loyal employee who had to do his job to the fullest, even if it meant breaking past rules not to offer his proposals. He was one who had to insert his opinion. He felt that failing to do so was doing his boss of many years a great disservice.

"It took quite a bit of energy for me to get everyone to agree to the meeting." The possibility of missing that arrangement was something that he wasn't willing to entertain.

"That woman," she pointed, "Over there. She needs help." Soaked with unexplainable reasoning, she was able to feel Rikki's perspective.

His want to help strangers was less than exemplary. "Many in this part of town are in need." The 'Who cares?' in his tone was apparent. "Must I again remind you that our prospective partners are waiting? The last thing we want is to demonstrate any level of unreliability."

"Yes. Yes," she minimized with increased annoyance at his slowness to move. She thought only about Rikki, and how desperately she was in need. "She requires our help."

That came from a woman who'd order Maurice to sideswipe Mother Theresa if it meant making an extra dollar.

A moving gesture from her left hand gave him no choice but to hurry.

"Go to her."

With her scratched and bleeding back against a brick wall, Rikki struggled to gain leverage to stand. Her unsteadiness appeared to be drunkenness.

Maurice thought the woman needed a place under a shady tree to sleep it off.

He opened the weighty door. With tamed frustration he left it open, allowing the late day coolness inside the vehicle, to irritate the commanding woman without making it look like he did so intentionally.

His cautious trek seemed to take forever. His size eleven shiny alligators advanced those risky yards to where Rikki had again collapsed.

In Rikki's post concussion haze, she saw Heather. Her mom was wearing the startling, blue, dress that Rikki loved. Heather stood on the curb, above a low running surge of water in the street from an earlier rain, ready to greet her only child. When the elementary school bus rolled to a halt, it opened its squeaky, folding, doors. Heather was the best that any child could ask for.

As the bus's door unwrapped to let Rikki walk down the short run of steps to the sidewalk, Heather began to disintegrate right before the seven year old's eyes. Her arms, torso, and legs shredded to eventual evaporation.

"Mom, don't leave me!" Rikki shouted to the fading vision. "I'll be a good girl," she cried, watching the last of her mother dissipating, filtering, to nothing more than a memory.

Maurice turned back to give his boss the 'I told you she's a mental case' look. His reaction was met with a look from the woman who sat on the tailor fitted, ultra-suede bench seat. That look told him to do as he was instructed.

His immediate inspection of Rikki prompted him to project back. "She's badly hurt!" He thought that would prompt his employer to seek the better of trying to be an untrained lifesaver, and order him back into the limo, to hurry off to that meeting that was of the utmost business importance. If all went well with the waiting group of expert others, hers would be an advancement of promise and enriched power. How often does all go well?

He sighed, disgusted over not having taken the long way to the meeting, a more conventional road that would have never had them see Rikki. But no, he had to be the expedient one, and take the straight line travel route.

That'll teach me, he thought. Few things are as bad as self blame.

Rikki's blurred vision had two thin men standing in front of her. Immediately, she thought that the attackers had returned to secure more from her ravaged remains.

The sight of her blood-stained garment repulsed Maurice, pressing his conclusion to scatter, leaving her to be tended to by the next—has nothing better to do—person who wandered by.

"Who are you?" he asked, believing that Rikki's incident was obviously of her own choosing.

She was aware of nothing other than her indescribable suffering, only able to guess with minimal certainty that safety might lie elsewhere.

From one of several storage compartments in the rear of the luxurious import, the woman located a pair of opera glasses, to better view the exchange between Maurice and Rikki.

"Lady, let me get out of here," he whispered to Rikki. "I'll give you fifty dollars to say that you're okay."

Rikki was doubled-over, coughing, wobbling upright only to fall atop vomited, bloody, fluids.

"Bring her to me," the older woman directed, with a commanding tone that bounced from the uncaring walls to nearby buildings, conceivably alerting anyone who previously hadn't noticed the dire situation before them. Few residents peeked out. Those who did were unable to care enough to continue looking past the few seconds that it took to leave their suddenly un-preferred vantage point.

"Yes, Ma'am," Maurice answered back to the limo, hating every bit of having to satisfy that command. "We're on our way."

Maurice grabbed Rikki under her arm, holding her steady. Together, they slowly headed to the limo.

"Hurry!" the woman in the rear seat bellowed. She knew the area well, and was aware of how quickly safety can be altered in this section of town.

Maurice had all he could do to support Rikki's weight, dragging her from the ominous pit. Once out into the dimness of the street's lights he felt somewhat safer, especially when the rear door opened, and the woman slid over to allow Rikki to climb inside.

"Wait!" the woman in the rear of the limo called. "She can't come in here smelling like that." She indicated to Maurice with a twiddle of her slender fingers, to disrobe Rikki, discarding those soiled articles of clothing.

Rikki's was an abbreviated protest, initially feeling that they weren't there to help, but to further harm her. Then she calmed, rationalizing that if they were that, at least, there were only two of them.

Once inside the limo, Maurice floored the accelerator. The limo's burning tires filled the air with a sickening rubber vapor.

Out of nowhere came the man with the bushy beard. Rabies had caused his nervous system to no longer follow his brain's commands. With pistol drawn, he fired with a shaky hand.

The bullets shattered the windshield. Maurice swerved the limo towards him, striking him. The man was knocked high into the air, landing on the hood of the limo. Rikki's mouth dropped, seeing the man so close. For that instant, Rikki thought that she recognized him, then that thought withdrew in the face of her own startled agony.

Maurice jammed the limo into reverse. Rear tires burned, snatching the luxury vehicle backward, tossing the man to the ground. In doing so, the car crashed into the crane. With one last gasp of strength, the man saw straight through to the rear of the limo. He aimed to fire at Rikki.

The crane's support arm bent, fraying the steel cable before it snapped free. The giant steel bucket holding the concrete fell fast. As the man was about to pull the trigger to send a bullet through Rikki's head, the bucket severed his shoulder.

"Go!" was Maurice's order to vacate.

Maurice yanked the shift into drive, and away they sped. With each mile per hour increase, he hated Rikki for being the cause of these problems.

The attacking man was on ground—that recently had been so hospitable to Rikki—bleeding profusely. He didn't have long to live. His bushy beard was on the ground next to him, having been ripped away. The glue holding it on to his lacerated face was stretched to its limits, unable to do the job anymore. Finally, he was free from the dual identity illusion that he'd gotten away with for so many tumultuous years.

Also spilled out on the ground beside him were two drivers license. One said Sonny Sixkiller. The second one more accurately identified him for who he was. Dead, at last was Mark Rhett.

THE HOASTESS
◆

She had style.

Within range of surveillance cameras that were everywhere, Rikki spent the remainder of that week in the guest room, sloshing in an ocean of her sweat, blood, and awareness of only one thing, a willingness to be gone from this earth.

She finally awakened, considering she never really slept at all. Her purpose in life had faded in the haze of who and where she was. Never completely alone, there was always the pain, which kept her company at all times. In spite of her hearing finally returning to normal, she was totally deaf with purposelessness.

Maurice tended to her basic needs, hating every minute of it. Fraught from the weight of it all, he wanted his duties as a wet nurse to come to an inglorious end as quickly as possible. Only then could he get back to being a full-time advisor and bodyguard.

That day, he wasn't gone from her more than a few minutes, before Rikki saw a shadow moving beneath the door. Seconds later, the door re-opened. Standing there was the woman who was instrumental in getting Rikki out from the den of torture.

The woman of such giving kindness entered the room, sitting beside the well-appointed bed. She wiped fallen hairs from blackened circles around Rikki's puffy eyes.

"Feeling better?" the woman posed.

"It only hurts when I breathe."

"You've got a sense of humor," she observed, thinking that some progress was in the works with her newfound patient.

Rikki smiled from some memory of what politeness was supposed to be.

When Maurice returned, the woman motioned to fractionally open the blinds, shedding light into the gloomy interior where recovery was to facilitate, though at a snail's pace.

Streaming beams raced inside, bouncing from the top of a magnificent, imported, dresser to splash onto Rikki's swollen face. It was all too much too quickly, forcing her to turn away to shield her eyes.

"You defied probability just being alive."

Rikki was at a complete loss for a response. She felt anything but fortunate.

"In that dreadful alley there was nothing around you except garbage, the remnants of the beating. Inside your purse there was only a used tube of lipstick, no identification to tell me who you are."

A puzzled Rikki shook her head. She wanted the cobwebs of memory loss to dissipate, to return her identity, restoring her to completeness.

"Allow me," the woman said.

She helped Rikki to reposition herself on the bed, with both feet dropping to the feathery, carpeted, floor. Her soles were delighted to touch something other than the moist bed linen. She slid her feet inside guest slippers that had been left beside the extraordinarily comfortable bed when Rikki first got there.

"Maurice, leave us alone. I'll summon you when it is necessary," the woman finalized.

Outwardly, he appeared eager to remain. Yet he was glad to be temporarily free of both maudlin women.

Outside, a stunning atrium was centered diminutive size residential cottages of assorted heights that seemed to peacefully rest there since the inception of time. The all-encompassing parkland that made dreams intersect with reality was the mystery woman's everyday life.

The courtyard was really something special. Splendid was the description that hardly did it justice. Its grass was never more than a millimeter too high. There were hedgerows, flowers, and decorative mini trees that were not only beautiful, but their soothing influence upon the human spirit was what made their simple viewing an eternally treasured event. The manner in which the gardening crew kept them so neatly arranged was mind altering in the smoothest way possible.

There a man stood alone at a thick, plastic, cutting table. He precisely trimmed an assortment of fresh fruits, placing the cuts in a professionally decorative manner on a platter for a deliciously fashionable presentation.

Meanwhile, around him were domestics, who scrubbed the stone patio, making sure that they didn't miss any flaws that their boss would later notice.

Having minimal strength to support her weight, Rikki leaned on the window's sill, looking out onto the peacefulness that swallowed-up anything that threatened the calm. Wherever Rikki was, she knew that it had to have been precisely sliced from bliss. Around her were the uplifting sounds of nature. Her initial thought was that whoever owned the property must be extremely wealthy, or doing a pretty good job of faking it.

"Come," the woman motioned. "It's too nice a day for you to be cooped up inside."

Sprinkled throughout the cheerful, green, lawn was tasteful outdoor furniture that persons with social ranking would proudly have in the interior of their homes. To view the lavish estate was to see a real life postcard that was in the hands of private ownership. This place could easily be used on the cover page of any upscale travel brochure.

A warming sea breeze swept in from the west, the pleasantness of which alerted Rikki that perhaps she had a chance at life's wholeness. By that time they had reached the man who had finished arranging the fruit. Being amidst all this made Rikki's throbbing begin to diminish. Not much, but any relief was fine.

"Sit," the woman said in an authoritative, yet pacifying way.

Rikki did, with muscles that pained during her attempt.

"Try the oranges. They were brought in fresh this morning," the uncommonly kind woman said.

Rikki reached for one, peeling it. Wide mouthed, she bit into it. The act sent streaming juice outwardly and inside her mouth at the same time. The sting was welcomed to senses that had been dormant for too long.

"What do I call you?"

The woman who had earned a PhD, if for no other reason than to prove how everyone else was beneath her intellectual capacity looked around. No one really ever called her doctor, but she liked the superior scholastic fit all the same.

"I am Conchita." She extended her hand for Rikki to kiss.

Rikki's pursed lips graced its back before it was withdrawn.

Her name did nothing to Rikki, ringing no bells of remembrance. It was as though she had seen a leaf blowing past in the tropical breeze. Zero. The name's mere sound popped into Rikki's head as striking, different in tonal quality, but that was all. In no way was she ready to associate it with the reason for her being in South Africa.

"That's a nice name," Rikki smiled.

"Strength is of the utmost importance. You're going to need it." Conchita had plans that were a ways from explaining. That was evident by the speck of bossy that appeared on her tongue.

While Rikki sampled other eatables, Conchita talked about a variety of light-hearted topics that neither of them cared much about. That was Conchita's attempt to build a basic level of communication, linking them with degrees of common reasoning. How else could she get her new guest to do her future bidding without a trusting bond having first been formed?

Rikki reacted well to the compassion bestowed upon her, in a thankful way that recovering patients usually express. It was impossible to predict if the attention would ease her back into any degree of understanding about herself. This was her chance to be calm, something that she was unaccustomed to, since the night she almost died. Finally, she was beginning to handle the intricate patterns of normal life.

Many frivolous subjects later, Maurice appeared. He stood off to one side, impatiently waiting to disturb them. Ultimately, he had to repeatedly clear his throat to draw attention to his presence.

She tilted to Rikki in a girl-to-girl fashion, "Just when we were having such a nice conversation."

She looked to Maurice, forced to acknowledge him, wanting him out of her line of vision quickly afterwards.

"What is it?" she griped.

"There's someone in the holding area desiring to have a word with you," he said.

He bent at the waist to whisper. She seemed mildly surprised, and more concerned than before.

"Is that right?...Very well," she capitulated, "Transfer him to the sitting room."

He left, walking faster than when he came to speak to Conchita.

"Excuse me," she said to Rikki.

After seeing Conchita leave with Maurice from the backyard sitting area to the main body of her flamboyant address, Rikki turned her attention to multicolored butterflies that were mating atop similarly designed flowers. She admired how they were free to come and go, flying away, returning when they saw fit to do so. She was saddened that they lived the life that she could not.

In that instant, she wondered about the forces of nature, the manner in which one person's life is so greatly different than that of the person standing next to her. She remained unable to understand why she had been cursed by being attacked, leaving her with no facts about herself upon which her life could be rebuilt.

The downtime allowed her mind to wander, as to why Conchita was being so very kind to her. The plethora of unanswered questions left Rikki more confused than ever. There seemed little way out of this newfound maze. Her heart which once raced—to a threatening pace of self-defense in the face of incalculable attacking forces—had at last slowed. Without warning her pain began to subside.

Conchita's undersized steps hurried from the estate's back door, making varied weaving patterns along the winding, paved, paths through the enclosed yard. She had returned to pierce the engulfing silence.

"That didn't take long, did it?" she asked.

Rikki's head inched from side to side to affirm that it had not.

"Unexpected guests require more than a casual hint as to when they should make themselves scarce."

"That must include me." Rikki rose from her chair.

"Don't be ridiculous," she comforted, gesturing for Rikki to regain her seat. "Where were we?"

Rikki was frustrated over not being able to recall anything past a few frozen minutes before. Short-term memory retention was all that she could direct, prompting her frustration to mount.

Conchita extended herself further. "When you're feeling better, let's say I buy you nicer clothes. What you had on when I found you was badly torn, to the degree that it required immediate disposal." Her sense of smell was greatly offended. "Saving everyone's nostrils a journey into the unpleasant."

Rikki looked down at herself, unimpressed with what she saw, oblivious as to what she was supposed to look like. "There's no way I can—"

"Consider it a gift. There'r other ways you can repay me."

The word 'repay' came out in a more business-like manner than did any of Conchita's initial verbal offerings. This time she was different. Her outgoing manner continued to shield what rested within her plotting soul. Conchita's pleasing smile was intended to promote a lasting calm between them, to keep Rikki in the dark about the future.

Rikki finished the remainder of her fruit drink, feeling weak. She thought to stand, but lightheadedness had her reconsider. Holding her forehead, she thought it wise to wait to gather more energy.

"I need to lie down."

"Of course." Conchita snapped her fingers, for the servants to hurry to clear the table free from food articles.

There was a foundation of friendship to install. Conchita wasn't about to waste time doing that. Rikki was in the preliminary stages of preparedness.

THE DREAMS
◆

The nightmares roared with a vengeance that told Rikki not to pay attention to anything else.

She was afraid to awaken that morning, fearful that those hours would be as unbearable as when she slept. After an extended wait of apprehension, her eyelids eased wider, leaving her unable to identify patterns and faces that swirled within her tormented soul during the preceding night. That was when fatigue and fabrication had arrived to conquer her, to drag her into the unstable world of the subconscious. If she were able to learn more about those demons it would surely frighten her to death.

Earlier in the day, an unexpected barrage started. The endless pitter-patter against the seven foot tall panes of glass in her room was a symphony in itself. Nature's repetitive splashing sounds reminded Rikki of the gun battle that she, Conchita, and Maurice emerged victorious from to save her. She was shaken by a series of real-life screams.

At the other end of the hall, Conchita had bolted from her bedroom with both arms flailing. Down the stairs, out the door she ran toward the barn. Hers was a feminine storm of emotion.

"Maureeeece!" Her silk nightgown streamed behind her like Wonder Woman, sprinting, unable to lift-off.

From her window, Rikki saw Maurice in off-white pajamas, hopping in one shoe and the other being put on, doing his best to follow her. He stopped to pick up a tub, filling it with boiling water before continuing after her.

The floor of the barn was where Conchita and Maurice knelt. Between them was a black and brown Rottweiler. It had already given birth to six slimy pups, with another peeking its trembling head out to see a world that it surely wasn't ready for.

Each of the pups jockeyed to find the best nipple from which to suckle. They made whimpering sounds, intent upon getting the attention of their mother. She was too drawn-out to differentiate anything past her fatigue. The dog's eyes rolled back with exhaustion, needing to be alone with her young.

The spectacle had Rikki considering the attractiveness of nursing one's young.

"You have children?"

Her pessimistic impulse was to think not.

"My daughters are away in boarding school," Conchita bragged. "They'll be returning in a few months for summer vacation…I travel to England three, or four, times each year to see them."

"Why so far away?"

"I placed them in school there, to be away from what's going on here…With children it's a day to day proposition. One day they're a joy to behold. Then they're something you wouldn't mind packaging and shipping off to anyone dumb enough to take them."

Conchita's tearjerker explanation was confusing.

"As I get older I have more time to reflect upon the little things in life that'r most important," she exhaled noisily to accentuate her feelings. Then it was back to the same ole' Conchita. "But money is money; raising kids inhibits making more of it."

For Rikki, it was increasingly unambiguous as to what Conchita was getting at with those remarks.

"You're still young. One day, you'll be able to realize your full potential as a woman." She mumbled, "Hopefully, with kids who are easier to manage than mine."

Why is she talking about me having children?

Conchita wasn't finished.

"Take a ride with me. I have important matters that need tending."

Rikki was relieved to have the strength not to have to hold onto something for balance. She followed Conchita back out into the sunlight. There the brilliance made it easy to see the tall grasses bend with the demands of horizontal breezes that swooped across the plains and upwardly to the mountainous peaks in the distance.

"This is all so beautiful," Rikki said.

"It is that," Conchita agreed.

THE BUSINESS

◆

The South African countryside was as advertised. The majestic absorption of the sights had Rikki's blood pumping with a new vitality. With each passing mile, she took pleasure from inhaling the untainted air. Her eyes were treated to that which she'd never seen. She distrusted the effect of exhaling, thinking that she might never be able to take in such splendor again.

"Foreigners who come here find it unfair that they can't take the scenery home with them."

Rikki immediately wondered where her home might be.

From the outside of the Range Rover, Conchita was heard saying, "Taking the limo up here isn't the best idea. Many of the roads haven't been properly cared for."

The Range continued climbing the mountain road, along a winding thoroughfare that defied gravity. Maurice drove steadily, speaking in subdued tones into the intercom, assuring Conchita that they were on schedule.

"What'r you thinking?" she asked.

"Nothing, really," Rikki answered.

Rikki felt that her life had begun here, hoping that it would last forever. There was a certain category of contentment, the suspension, to walk the tightrope, removed from the common cares of everything—beyond what Conchita wanted done.

Dense clouds hung low that day, adding a pillowy frosting to the low mountain terrain. The natives had a long held belief that it was the sign of high risk, at minimum vast uncertainty. They would prove to be correct.

The Range hit a few bumps, jostling the occupants, testing a state of the art suspension that made those inside as comfortable as possible without whiplash. For the next thirty minutes, they rode the steep incline to the pre-arranged destination.

She reached into the flap behind Maurice's seat to take out a small blanket, draping it over her shivering guest.

"It comes in handy up here, where it tends to be a lot cooler."

Rikki casually grasped it, feeling better about the drive when Maurice sent added heat to the rear seats. The car finally pierced the mist, landing them on a higher plane. Not many minutes later, they spotted an armed man who stepped out from a narrow guardhouse at the side of the road. There was a crisp preparedness to him, as he steadied his Mac10 machinegun from over his shoulder to aim it at Maurice. This was the vortex where travel met trouble.

"Why'r we stopping?" Rikki asked, uncertain as to why Maurice hadn't floored the accelerator.

"To avoid being killed," Maurice assured, from a vantage point that allowed for the best view of the gunman, understanding that Rikki had no experience with type of situation.

Scared took on a new and improved meaning for Rikki, when she asked Conchita, "Shouldn't you call someone?"

"We're in the crevice of the mountains. Transmissions from here are impossible, even with my satellite phone."

Rikki didn't want to ask, "We're trapped?"

"I'm known here." Conchita lowered her smoked window to let the man see those who he was aiming at.

"I'm known here" rang in Rikki's brain, feeling as though she'd heard that phrase before.

The guard snapped to attention. "Just being sure, Ma'am," he calmed. He had no alternative, given he was looking at a woman who had widespread retaliatory powers.

Conchita gave assurances to the bulletproof vest wearing man that his attention to readiness was well appreciated.

Having done his job, the sentry cranked his free arm in windmill fashion for Maurice to continue on. Rikki was safe, assuming that she remained beside Conchita.

"I've got the best protection on the continent." The female master was proud to have it, though saddened to need it.

The expensive, all terrain, vehicle continued along a road, constantly filmed by numerous hidden cameras, in case anyone had the suicidal notion to crash the clandestine fortress.

About a mile farther, the car stopped again. This time the three of them got out.

"Now we walk," Conchita said.

She's got to be kidding.

That was when the day turned from strenuous to leg crunching.

"This is why I had you wear flat shoes."

Rikki then changed to be a silent malcontent. But she was relieved to be able to get out and stretch legs that had been cramped for hours.

During the walk, which more than equaled a week's worth of anyone's treadmill footwork, Rikki felt that the older woman must do this often.

Look at her. She's barely breaking a sweat.

Rikki couldn't figure out her own identity, but she spotted superior fitness in Conchita. Gosh, the older woman seemed to be able to walk around the earth and never once stop to catch her breath. When they reached the point where two paths made a 'Y', Rikki turned back to look onto a marvelous lake in the valley.

If God were to ever cry, his tears would've poured there. The light that filtered through the trees was obviously borrowed from the sun just to add thrill for everyone living there. It was a heart-warming sight to behold.

She could see a string of huts that were made of some type of masonry material, centered in a clearing, at the edge of a respectable size spot of standing water. It was a lake of merit where the only drinking water for miles around could be secured. The distant scope of it all resembled the miniature visuals in Macy's windows at winter holiday time.

Remaining high above with the traveling trio, were armed men who had taken up positions on cliffs, allowing them a perfect view to destroy any intruder's life should anything go wrong.

From a nearby jagged peak came a single ringing gunshot. The sound of which echoed across surrounding hills. Conchita's confidence was quite apparent.

"They'r signaling to each other that I'm here." She peeked at her specially designed Movado. "They're eight seconds late in doing so."

The irrepressible Conchita wasn't sure how long Rikki's training would take before she would be a good mule. With the proper instruction, it would be time well invested.

The hike had Rikki's legs feeling as anyone's would on the last stage of the Boston Marathon. Her chin dropped to her chest. She gasped for breath in the thin air, wanting the walking to end.

"Breathe deeply through your nostrils, to get air to your lungs faster," Conchita instructed.

Doesn't she care that I'm gonna pass out?

Maurice took out a flask of cool water, offering it to Conchita who chugged it. Rikki was left out of the liquid satisfaction mix.

At Conchita's behest, Rikki had to rough-it. She was in boot camp, getting used to learning under thirst's fire, how to survive along the full length of the tricky mountain path.

Up ahead were two men who also held large caliber machine guns. The expressions on their survivalist faces showed an enthusiastic willingness to use those weapons. That left any provocation toward them completely out of the question. That was when one of them swept Rikki with an electronic detection wand.

"They leave nothing to chance. Consider it a safety hurdle." Conchita knew that she was a marked woman, who had enemies lining up to see her out of their way.

After Rikki was deemed non-threatening, the sweeper motioned to his left.

Out from the seclusion of the woods came a man with a wooden leg. He hobbled closer, without introducing himself. He then positioned his lips to kiss Conchita on both cheeks, stepping back waiting to be properly established.

"This is Slinky," Conchita said of the man. "He also works for me."

Rikki was at a loss as to what to think about him or the situation—other than he whispered English better than Rikki could another language.

She clung to the thought of her mouth filled with quenching water. She wanted this get-together to lead to a drink, anything that would ease the tightness in her desiccated throat.

They proceeded an additional dozen yards inside the well hidden entrance to a narrow mouth cave, past two Bloodhounds that sniffed the entrants, in search of explosives that one of them might be trying to conceal.

The boulders that hid the cave's entrance had tumbled from high above to finally rest there. Those inside the cave were shielded from anyone from the outside who might be trying to gain access to the cave.

Slinky again leaned to whisper to Conchita.

"Wait here," she initiated to Rikki.

Rikki felt more alone than ever when the three of them walked deeper into the cave and out of sight. Around her she heard bats chirping. Tasteful pen and ink etchings on the walls that more resembled an avant-garde gallery in So Ho rather than where she was, virtually buried alive, elevated, in the middle of the mountains.

When the others returned they marched on. This secondary trek ended when they reached an imbedded laboratory facility. Rikki was not allowed inside. Theirs was more of an in depth inspection than a simple walk by. Rikki was hazy as to what this place was used for. Being so far from the society below the hills, it was obvious that Conchita didn't want anyone pinpointing that location.

Conchita sensed the hour was sinking into lateness.

Maurice was ready to get home to work on the limo's engine. It hadn't been running right since the crash when they found Rikki.

"We'd better be going," Conchita said. "With the array of unsavory thugs roaming at every turn, one can't be too careful."

"Would you like an escort down the mountain?" Slinky offered.

"That won't be necessary." She looked at Maurice. "Will it?"

"I think, not," he answered in a got-it-under-control tone.

"Call me when you're safe," Slinky politely added.

His words silently suggested to Rikki that she had heard a woman somewhere say that. But where? Her buried subconscious was trying to tell her something.

* * *

Finally, Rikki was able to maintain keen attention to the days. That wasn't much to brag about. But it was something to latch onto. A handful of seven day batches had passed since Conchita had instructed Maurice to fetch her from peril.

In spite of the hospitable treatment that she had been showered with, Rikki knew Conchita's extension to her wasn't simple courtesy. Something within Conchita's plotting mind was brewing. It had become apparent that she wasn't the type who did things for others without getting her efforts back ten fold.

"Join us," Conchita shouted up to the guest room from the bottom of the curved, imported, wood stairs.

"Be right there!" Rikki's answer through the adobe walls was muffled but heard.

She was beginning to understand why Conchita had been so comforting to her. That shouldn't have been a problem, but it was a concern for Rikki—given levels of split personality that she'd often witnessed in Conchita. Increasingly, that aspect of their relationship had become a worrisome element.

When Rikki came downstairs—which was never fast enough—Conchita was waiting, fidgeting.

"Late sleeper?" The irritation in her question was apparent.

"Not really. Just sitting on the bed thinking about stuff," Rikki answered.

When Rikki slid her chair, it put a scratch on the cement. Strike two on her 'Conchita, how's the morning going so far?' count.

Conchita's poorly disguised frown answered that. The next time Rikki moved the chair she lifted it so as not to make the same mistake. Finally, they prepared to eat.

"After breakfast there'r a few things that I wish to go over with you."

Rikki nodded, feeling more the hired hand than the guest that she was setup to be.

"Good. We're in complete agreement," Conchita said, not waiting for an answer, dabbing the edges of her mouth with the napkin to remove bits of her favorite pastry. She was never the last to leave the table.

Maurice's sixth sense distrust continued to have him edgy about Rikki. Though he never spoke to Slinky about Rikki, it was interesting how two people who didn't interact with each other would have identical beliefs about Rikki.

About fifteen minutes after the last of the dishes were removed by the cleanup staff, floor boards creaked as Rikki and Conchita moved to a more secluded area on the ground level within the main body of her home. It was her game room, where she had every conceivable highly specialized electronic gadget that a techno geek could crave. That was when Rikki heard...

"This is where the world comes to me."

Rikki was silent with what further to add.

"Mine is a far reaching, global, enterprise. Some might call it an empire. I prefer to think of it as a profitable hobby."

Nice hobby.

"You're probably wondering why I'm explaining it to you."

It crossed Rikki's mind. She, however, was quickly learning her rightful place within the sinister empire. Most times, silence with regard to questioning Conchita, was the preferred route.

"I demand complete loyalty from my employees."

It didn't take long for me to sink from the supposed level of a friend to nothing more than a common employee.

"The people of South Africa have been oppressed for far too long. For me not to come to their need was something that I couldn't defy. To that end, I have taken in a few diamond miners to assist me, while they in turn help themselves."

"Being on your payroll," Rikki assumed.

"That is correct."

"Additionally, my responsibilities have grown too great for me to handle by myself. I need a proverbial second set of eyes. Yours."

She looked at Rikki as a needed underling.

"Mine?"

"Precisely." Conchita was as sure of that as she was of the fires in the part of hell that she ruled.

This conversation was the precursor to where their motivations had begun to cross, with Rikki wanting to be set free from her. If ever wish fulfillment could be secured, it had to be for Rikki to be somehow sent back to wherever she rightfully belonged, anywhere but alongside the wicked one and anyplace other than in that alley.

Rikki was perplexed, ensnared in the haze of what her life was, unwillingly propelled into what she knew to be an uncertain future.

"How can I help you?" Rikki felt outclassed in the presence of one so powerful. "You've got it all."

"I'm glad you asked."

Mine was just an expression. I wasn't volunteering.

"Don't just stand there," Conchita reprimanded. "Come closer."

Rikki did so, nearly rubbing elbows with her.

"In the world of high finance, they call it creating the demand for a product. Then reacting to it."

Conchita took out an eight inch gold plated serving platter that was covered with a black velvet cloth. On it were several sparkling diamonds resting beside a wire rack that held a vial filled with a murky liquid.

Rikki was intrigued, watching Conchita drop three small, uncut, diamonds into the glass tube. Then Conchita removed the vial from its holder and began to shake it until the diamonds disappeared, blending in with the liquid.

There's got to be a reason why she did that.

The vial got very hot, with fluffy smoke oozing from its top. Unable to hold it, Conchita placed it back in an upright holder until it simmered to a touchable coolness.

"This is a diamond elixir."

Rikki watched with a childlike curiosity. "Such a strange look to it."

Conchita continued, "It's not how it looks. It's what it does…When a person drinks this it makes them invisible. They're able to move about without anyone seeing them. Their freedom is made undetectable."

The word 'invisible' bounced in Rikki's head, ricocheting from one side to the other, attempting to rattle her to an awareness that someone else had said that very phrase to her at some earlier time. In her mind she kept hearing a man's voice say, "It's like the robber was invisible."

The words reverberated resoundingly. Something within her was again desperately trying to call out.

"There's just one catch," Conchita continued. "When the person is in that invisible state, they must move about with slow, deliberate, steps. A fast pace will over stimulate their molecular structure. That excessiveness will cause their body to overheat from within. The added friction will cause them to burn alive."

Her voice dipped with reflection. "A while back, I showed another American this, and somehow he spilled some of it on his fingers, badly burning him. When he returned to the United States, I never heard from him again."

"Doesn't it burn to drink it?"

Conchita shook her head. "Oddly enough, no."

"Amazing," Rikki thought more than said it.

"Several governments are willing to pay a tidy sum for my formula."

Rikki watched as she picked up the vial, placing it to her mouth.

"What are you doing!?" Rikki shouted.

Within seconds after swallowing, Conchita began to dissolve right in front of Rikki's disbelieving eyes. At least when Heather went away, it wasn't in front of Rikki's crying face.

When nothing remained of Conchita, Rikki knew that this was her real life bad dream come to life.

"Conchita?"

The concoction actually worked.

There was no sign of her, only the commanding "Yes."

"I don't see you."

"What better way to demonstrate how it works," the imperceptible one assured.

Then came the heavy switch, aligning Rikki more to the point of why they were talking.

"Soon, you'll be dealing directly with Slinky. You are to report directly to me. He's up to something," she firmed.

A frown overcame her wrinkled face. Rikki sensed something in Conchita; it didn't take an eternity for it to bubble out.

"It's not that I don't trust Slinky."

She paused long enough for a luxury liner to drift through the multiple locks in the Panama Canal.

"It's that I don't trust'm."

That had to wait until she felt more prepared to fully get into the particulars of that comment. Anyway, she switched…

"Naturally, your efforts won't go uncompensated. For starters, you'll be given your own living quarters here at my compound. It will be a marked step above the guest room in which you've been staying."

I didn't plan to stay with you much longer. I guess, all that's changed.

For the better part of an hour, Conchita went on to explain the many dimensions of the precious gems underworld, specifically diamonds, and Rikki's new role in the transportation of them. Listening was easy; retaining all that was required of her took more concentration than she had the ability to sustain. There were the names of the different people with whom Rikki would have to meet along the way, gain their confidence, with the expectation that they would deal with her the way that they had been accustomed to with Conchita was a stretch to hope for. But with Conchita's backing, it might just work.

Rikki knew nothing about the gangland life. In the end, she would wish that she had never met Conchita.

THE TRAITOR

◆

Rikki learned more about the precious gems trade than she ever wanted to. She was no longer in it, but not of it. Inadvertently, she had become part of the very criminal fabric.

What was most disturbing was how shadowy images of a young woman continued to appear in Rikki's slowly surfacing consciousness. There was never a sound, or a name, to go with the similes, but increasingly Rikki knew that the streaky brunette in her thoughts was someone from the past. It was those subliminal suggestions that reeked havoc on Rikki's every waking hour.

She felt the need to pay closer attention to them. When the wavering female subject came to her the next time, she hoped to better concentrate, somehow holding on to those thoughts until they made sense. It was interesting how that woman used some of the same phrases that Conchita did.

It was a motionless Sunday when Conchita wore an uncommon expression of genuine sincerity, one of those rare instances when business didn't appear to dominate her inflexible protective shell. Much like the Cone of Silence from the old Get Smart, black & white TV days.

Conchita swiveled her chair to face the door as Rikki occupied the open frame.

"How did it go with the neurologist?"

"He said that I didn't appear to have sustained any permanent brain damage from the attack."

Conchita perked in a self serving way. "That's good news."

"He also said that my memory might never return, barring another head injury," she berated herself.

"Don't look sad. It won't be forever," Conchita sought to assure her.

A vision overcame Rikki. Again, there was that streaky brunette woman. This time, she sat where Conchita was. But it wasn't Conchita. It was someone else who Rikki couldn't identify. Conchita noticed the way Rikki looked at her, dismissing it as that which confused people do.

"You mustn't let it get in the way of your responsibilities to me."

It didn't take long for human sentiment to drift to the rear of the line.

Rikki plunked her purse on the end table, continuing to securely hold a platinum trimmed attaché in her other hand. Her moist grip on the attachés handle had weakened, as she waited for Conchita to take her key to release the lock that connected the carrying case's handle to Rikki's sore wrist. Gosh, how that metal clanging stirred shadowy memories of an elderly man who worked while seated at a table. That man was also wearing handcuffs. He, too, was nameless and virtually faceless.

She led Rikki to sit at a circular marble table. She then began massaging Rikki's wrist with cream to relieve the soreness. When Conchita was a girl, she worked in a massage parlor. That explained her physical technique. She was quick to have someone killed if they knew about her past.

"Most things forgotten aren't worth holding on to."

She gave her boss the 'whatever you say' expression of patronage.

"I want you to get proper rest. You must be alert for your meeting with Slinky."

Conchita stopped rubbing Rikki's wrist, then extended to open the attaché. The sight of the carefully wrapped bundles of hundred dollar bills made her hazel eyes flutter.

Rikki took that as her cue to leave the room, and find something else to do while Conchita counted, then stashed the money.

Later, Maurice saw the two women sitting across from each other, intensely staring at what few chess pieces remained on the board in front of them. His resentment increased, with hatred for Rikki rising uncontrollably to his emotional surface, because she had replaced him as Conchita's sole confidant.

"Chess is a wonderful game of calculation and skill. It's about control—one of life's must haves," Conchita told her.

Conchita carefully castled her king and queen to hide in the corner to avoid being threatened. Rikki countered that move, inching her pawn one step closer to a rook that had to move or be taken. At the opposite side of the black and red board, Conchita watched an opposing knight, which was too close to her queen. She made the most of the opportunity to surround it.

"It's about entrapment…With no surprises."

Conchita said the word 'entrapment' as though it was her desire to boast of that influence over all people. Rikki had always suspected that character trait in Conchita.

"Your move."

Rikki slid her knight into proper position to instigate a capture. "Check."

Conchita was in a pinch. How she hated being boxed in. She eyed the board in search of evasive opportunities—of which there were few. Instead, she repositioned her queen up and away. That preparation was briefly enjoyed.

"Check. And mate," Rikki reconstituted.

Conchita was madder than a wet hen.

Surprise!

* * *

Rikki was stretched out on yet another lounge chair that was more suited to be indoor rather than an outside furnishing. The inviting sight of the recently completed negative edge swimming pool, with its pungent smell of chlorine, was tempting. She watched it's gently rippling upper crest roll off the side. She wasn't sure if she could swim, preferring to watch, opting to take her liquids internally.

The air produced certain chosen scents that attempted to jog her dormant memory. Each time it failed to signal an end to the recollection fog that she aimlessly waltzed through. It was then that Conchita came upon her, with the reactions of an angry feline who had her canary cornered.

"Again, I caught Slinky pulling a fast one!"

Her pitch was spiked with vengeance. It was a specially cultivated reaction that dominated her judgments. Especially evident in that regard was when she kicked a chair out of the way, to allocate a closer stance near Rikki.

"Something has to be done about him," she concluded, with an unabashed sense of 'the time had come'.

Conchita was renowned for having a brute-force approach to problem solving. Even in her rare happy times, extremism was her pump.

"You once trusted Slinky," Rikki said through sunglasses that buried her eyes from Conchita's keen, critical, analysis.

It was apparent that Rikki wasn't the cause of Conchita's unsteadiness. Nonetheless, she liked being to the side of Conchita's multi-pronged retribution.

Just that quickly, Conchita attempted to reach into her shallow reservoir of calm. "At one time, I did. But that was when I needed him to go into the ghettos and recruit the mine workers, to come out from working underground—for such miniscule wages, I might add—with my diamonds in their stomachs, bringing them to me for processing later."

"Don't the mine owners have ways of detecting diamonds inside a person?"

"That problem was taken care of, when a certain Army Sergeant showed me how those recognition devices can be altered to reveal nothing; when the workers pass through mechanical screening devices after they leave the mines."

Then her anger towards Slinky re-emerged.

"As of late, there's been a detectable difference between what I tell him to do, and what I later have discovered he has done."

Rikki tilted down the UV protection to look her eye to watchful eye, courageously asking, "What's spinning in that brain of yours?"

Heck, Conchita wasn't mad at her. So she had nothing to worry about. Not yet.

"The Slinky problem is something that I refuse to ignore any further. The problems with him have become too much of a distraction…My sources have told me about a series of events, financial shortcomings, against me that he has profited from."

A commercial jetliner roared overhead. That should have signaled to Rikki that it was high time to leave South Africa. Rikki was absorbed by Conchita's anger, completely unaware of any significance that the plane had.

"Tomorrow, pay close attention to how he handles his end of the diamond mining and refining…He's been told to expect you. He'll try to prod you on why you've become more deeply involved in the business. It goes without saying that it'll bother him to no end that you're looking over his shoulder…The only real way to flush him out is if I'm not around. Only then, he might slip-up and say the wrong thing…Tell him just enough to quiet his questions. Reveal nothing of consequence to him. Above all else, you'll report directly to me. Is that clear?"

What could Rikki say? Who is dumb enough to ram heads with a rhino? She felt morally compromised, at a loss with what to do next.

Rikki's confidence grew from the early morning crowing from several roosters that trotted about the complex. Having been elevated to being a trustworthy member of Conchita's inner circle, Rikki would've preferred to delegate her newly assigned duties to someone else. Mostly because she regretted being around cutthroat criminals day after headache producing day, especially those who would want her dead, once they discovered that she acted in a quasi double-agent capacity. It was that very element of sadism that Rikki found herself surrounded by, turning her stomach more than her head.

By the time Rikki had reached the peak of the treacherous and complicated climbing course where she was to meet Slinky, her legs didn't hurt nearly as much as they had the first time they were introduced to this business motivated exercise.

"Your arrival came without incident?" Slinky asked, appearing out from the surrounding rocks, with an approach of welcome that could only be maintained by the ever-present pressure that Conchita exerted on him.

He hated everything about Rikki, starting with her presence.

"You were scheduled to arrive much earlier."

Complaining was his way, and that was how he ran his end of the business. His stare delved to her core, looking for a cue that Rikki was someone other than who Conchita thought she was. Then he could run with that discovery back to Conchita, regaining what he considered to be his rightful place within her powerful wrecking ball domain. He tightened up to spot anything about Rikki before it was too late for him.

Rikki wanted her delivery to be more conversational, while deflecting blame from herself. "Conchita's the reason for my tardiness. If there's some problem with that, I'll express your sentiments when I see her."

"Not at all," he reshaped. "I appreciate exactness."

Slinky had to back off, figuring her explanation to be a bunch of crap. Conchita had never been late in the whole time that they had worked together.

He nodded as though he understood. But he knew something else was in the works. A methodology that was certain to go against his position that he worked so hard t achieve.

With a Nazi-like click together of his hard heels, he extended his hairy arm straight ahead to lead Rikki inside the cavern. "After you." He smiled, but didn't mean it.

"As it should be," she said softly, yet confidently.

That's why he never meant the smile.

After walking through a different entrance than what Rikki had remembered, Slinky brought her into a more spacious area. There, a dozen workers wore surgical facial coverings, looking through magnifying glasses, working diligently with instruments to do precise work.

"What goes on here?"

Her question made Slinky even more paranoid. He couldn't stop thinking that she was part of some kind of backstabbing scheme to move him out. In no way was he going to let that happen. But he had all he could do to keep a lid on his emotions. There was no need to have his reactions get back to Conchita. Walking the plank above Conchita's ability for retaliation was a risk that he wasn't about to rush to.

She watched a muscular black man walk in. His ebony flesh had an over abundance of sweat that waxed him to a distinguished shine. He emptied a pintsize canvas sack onto a table in front of one of the seated workers. Out spilled the uncut gems about which Conchita had lectured. Their luster was virtually non-existent, but Rikki was sure they were diamonds. The workers immediately began chipping away at the unrefined edges.

"This is the processing stage where the diamonds are brought in to be cut and polished."

He put an iron veil over his thoughts to continue. "That area is where the elixir is refined."

The black man didn't stick around. Immediately, he turned to walk to a separate workstation not fifty feet away. There he removed his drenched clothing, to put on drier items. She looked at his taught, muscular, body. She began to feel wetness, deep arousal, from the sight of such a virile specimen.

Professionally forced to turn away, she watched others carefully dipping the diamonds into a slimy liquid, which ultimately led to the final drying stage. She was resigned to take in as many visual observations as she could before following Slinky out of the area.

"What are your impressions of a people starving for their rightful place in a democracy?" he asked.

"None that I'm at liberty to discuss with you."

He gritted his polished, white, teeth, believing that he wasn't worthy of Rikki speaking to. He was determined not to say anything that Conchita would disagree with.

Going through Rikki had become distasteful. He peered at her with distrust, because he'd no longer be dealing with the boss. He took strong exception to that. No one of stature wants to go through intermediaries. He also knew that something was in the works that didn't include him. Ever-present bitterness was rising without any possibility for containment of such rampant feelings. Nobody takes kindly to stepping down. The backseat is never as comfortable as up front.

She adjusted her jacket lightly across her shoulders. "Unless there's something else, I'll bid you farewell until next time." Then it hit her, adding, "Conchita wanted me to ask you about the growth of her toy."

Her eyes lowered for a second to his crotch, which he took as a hint, a possible invitation. His hatred for her turned away what could've been a flow of lust. He simply ignored it. The slight tip of his head meant that she was to again follow him.

Their route wasn't in the same direction as the entrance. This one consisted of snaking walkways into even smaller exit stages. She was disposed to fear, thinking that this was possibly leading to another sexual trap, the likes of which she experienced with the gang that dreadful day.

Many yards ahead, were dozens of welders whose torches brightly flashed while they worked in the blazing heat.

Slinky was preoccupied with anything other than talking to her. To break the proverbial ice, she pointed to a cigar shaped hull that was in the early stages of construction. She was hesitant to assume that the vessel would join the other cigar boats in the harbor that she had heard Conchita speaking about days before. After a few seconds, she pieced together that it was a full-scale submarine being built in the mountains. That was real money being put to work.

He walked ahead of her, running his hand the full length of the inches thick, reinforced, shell. He did so much as a bachelor would, making the rounds in any new car showroom.

"The big girl should be sea worthy in less than six months." He couldn't be certain, but said it anyway.

He then assured nervous, imported, skilled German workers who looked on. They knew the ocean like Conchita knew control. They were unsure, however, about the interloper standing beside Slinky.

Many of them flopped their eye shields back over their faces, keeping each identity a hard fought secret. Between carefully plotted weld points, they still peeked out through openings to take notice of her—many in a man wanting a woman sense.

Curiosity had her out on a limb to ask, "Have you figured out how to transport it down the mountain without damaging it? From what I gather, deep water is many miles from here."

"Leave that to me," he said from his egotistical perch, having something to hide.

"Here's your payment," she vocalized, entrusting him with a plain-white envelope that she took from identical others.

He figured, the next time she arrived to pay him, she just might get robbed and killed on her way back down the mountain. Out here all alone, no one would ever find out who was responsible.

THE DOUBLE-CROSS

◆

The extravagant, multi-level, opera house was state of the art. It was an out of this world treat for anyone to have received a grand opening invitation.

There were creature comforts and sensory delights that left no one in the packed house wanting more. It had elegant restaurants, fine drinking bars, posh smoking lounges, well attended restrooms—all trimmed with shiny gold furnishings. Everything to sit on was exquisite and soft.

On each side of the stage were two twenty foot high, multi-colored, video screens that pulsated with on and off still images of the international megastar who pranced with endless energy. The assorted lighting schemes made the world famous entertainer larger than his glamorous everyday life already was.

Rikki was astonished, having never been privy to such sensation. "The screens are so big and clear."

Conchita's inward pride came from a woman whose fortune financed the multi-million dollar arena. It was going to bring big time entertainment to that part of the hemisphere for decades to come. She pointed to the stage below, through tinted glass that enclosed her booth.

"I saw to it that the acoustics were vastly superior to everyone else's," she sipped from her scarcely touched bourbon and water.

"The key is to give people something more than a place to come in and sit their fat asses. They want a life experience that'll force them to return again and again." She sipped. "Blessed be the consumer with the ability to pay."

While the beaming musical amusement was still going on, Conchita had relocated to her executive study. She sat hunched behind a mahogany desk, reading. The array of numerical combinations on her notepad had her highly frustrated. To the side of her was a perfectly matched porcelain cup of once steamy coffee that had since dwindled from its original intensity to room temperature. When those rare times arose when Conchita didn't have her coffee, something of paramount importance had to have been in the works.

Her calculating intelligence was overworked, trying to decide if Slinky was worthy of being permitted to continue living. She silently starred at the squiggly paper that streamed from the adding machine, disliking every number on it.

It was the results from the previous week's numerical summations that Slinky had provided to Rikki on her most recent visit to the mountain factory.

Rikki cautiously entered from one side, careful to silently close the door behind her. Conchita was very busy, so Rikki waited before speaking. Conchita looked in her direction.

"When you didn't return to your booth I got concerned, and came to look for you."

"What's on your mind?" Conchita took timeout to say, distracting Rikki from her own worry.

Rikki was stuck in a web of continuing confusion about who she was. "A thought just popped in my head, only to disappear equally quickly."

"If it was important, it'll return."

She came closer to concentrate on what was expected of her, seeing Conchita's face frowning from the results of the displeasing additions that were in front of her. Rikki thought that she and Slinky had a constructive meeting. Then again, Conchita was the real judge of all final numbers.

"Why the look? From what Slinky said, we had a good month. I mean you had a good month," Rikki corrected.

"Horseshit!" Her rage was plainly detectable. "Stop being so naïve…More than ever, I'm certain he's working against me…That cockroach will soon pay with his balls. His are not accidental inaccuracies, but deliberate intentions to keep hidden how much he's been stealing from me."

Emotionally, Rikki raced to Conchita's defense, wanting to volunteer something that she wasn't competent at, or brave enough to pull-off without getting caught. Instead, she remained silent without any verbal response.

The boss closed her writing pad. "The weight of the diamonds that Slinky says the mine workers brought in isn't adding up. My mole in the mine keeps me posted on how much they're stealing. That total weight is constantly different from that which Slinky reports. Slinky's been feeding me a lesser amount!"

She turned to Rikki. "There were only three people who had access to those shipments. Me. Slinky. And you. It wouldn't be stealing, nor would I be complaining, if I took it."

Rikki wasn't worried. Conchita was keenly aware of her every movement since finding her in that alley.

"This's why I've had you increasingly involved with my operations. I'm grooming you to take over his role in the company."

Smoke all but streamed from both ears, while her serpent-like tongue flickered.

"I should've left him in that Latin American shit hole when we first met…I guarantee you, he won't see his next birthday."

A look of personal sanction came over Conchita. It was something different than Rikki had witnessed before. The issue was settled. Slinky would soon meet his end.

Conchita peeled a banana, exposing its bare shaft, which she took a full mouth of.

"Come with me."

The two of them walked outside where her favorite trotting horses were. Rikki immediately saw the look of tranquility that overcame Conchita at the mere sight of the stallions. They were being trained by several hired hands, who took great care to instruct them as to the proper ways that trotting horses should behave.

Rikki and she continued past them into the shade. There they sat. Conchita spoke, while watching the trainers working with the horses.

"I need to tell you about our upcoming traveling arrangements…I received an offer by a head of state, who is willing to bid for my elixir…I want you to accompany me."

In the distance, one of the horses reared back on its hind legs, only to be calmed by the enthusiastic horseman.

Rikki wanted it to be a busy trip, one where there wouldn't be a lot of time for dreaming.

THE TRAIN

◆

You don't know it's the end of the line until you get there.

Capital Park Station had a spooky, cavernous, interior. It was an aesthetic lesson on how to build a metropolis commuter hub to last throughout the ages. The solidly cemented mortar made the multi-story building one that was likely to hold up for centuries—barring terrorist activity.

In that vein there was a collection of evenly moving protestors who walked in an oblong formation outside the entrance. Their demands included everything from rising ticket prices, to the government's inflexibility toward lowering ever-rising energy costs.

In spite of the commotion, riding the rails aboard South Africa's fabulous Blue Train was the finest land riding experience that anyone could have. The look and feel of it was only surpassed by the service, and the attention paid to the traveler's every whim. The traveling episode promised to be nothing short of memorable.

That was why Conchita paid handsomely for two seats, instead of journeying on a much faster airliner. Maurice found it odd that there were so few people inside the unsoiled train station that day. He suspected something was unkindly out of line, but was not certain enough to say something to Conchita about any perceived risk to her safety.

Standing in a line that barely moved had taken its toll on Conchita. Her optimism had become heavy, as though she carried an anvil with each mini step forward.

"I was hoping to simply board the damn thing, and go right to our compartment," she complained.

Rikki released the steamer trunk's handle, allowing it to drop to the marble floor. She flexed her hand, opening and closing it for better circulation, over having dragged it from the parade of picketers—where Maurice had left them. Normally, he would have carried the bags inside, but he told Conchita that there was a mysterious unattended errand that he simply had to perform.

When Rikki's head went back to roll her neck, she gazed at the ethnic wall etchings that led to the wooden connections at the upper vertex of the structure. There ceiling fans circulated warm air, in an effort to make it fresher for those people waiting to step aboard the renowned multi-car train.

Though memory loss prevented her from realizing it at that time, Albuquerque never looked so good. And when yet another person stepped on her feet, Rikki felt the annoyance from the line's lack of progression. Her skin was sticky, brought on by an unusually humid day. She motioned to black and gray pigeons that flew past many picture frame windows. She fantasized, wanting to be rescued from the confusion by one of them, taken to some other place. Somewhere cooler, perhaps.

Rikki and Conchita hoped for brief chatter from a ticket handler who was far more gabby with prospective customers than he needed to be.

"Ten thousand words or less," Conchita carped about the verbosity of that worker.

People ahead of them shunted each other, shuffling forward toward the barred, cylinder shaped, ticket booth; where the seller bowed and scraped while servicing each person who came to the slotted opening.

Conchita and Rikki were five customers away.

"Next!" the man inside the booth mandated.

Conchita squirmed. "There's got to be a women's room around here somewhere."

Finding one wasn't important to Rikki. How could it be? She didn't have to go. "We're practically there. What difference can it make now?"

That advice wasn't received well. When it was Conchita's chance to confirm their reservation, she dashed.

Rikki had problems with the fact that she ran away just when it came time to confirm their tickets and board. She saw Conchita raise her hand, indicating that a rapid return was forthcoming.

Within seconds, a man wearing a railroad messenger's cap appeared. His movements were shifty and untrustworthy. That was when she saw Conchita returning.

* * *

Outside, beneath the suffocating African sun, August Byrd walked beside with the latest in an indistinguishable list of new track inspectors. This day's loser was a recent add-on named Stagger-Lee Ivory.

Both men were in standard, brown, jumpsuits. Their cadence was a sign of how August was more willing to tackle a full shift of gainful employment than was his younger assistant.

Back in the day—when hiring blacks wasn't dared—August was the first one who Blue Train Rail Lines saw fit to put on their payroll in something other than the usual subservient capacity.

In those times, not many rushed at the chance to apply for a job where they stood no chance of being accepted. Since August's was a life filled with rejections, he had little to lose when he filled out the job application that first day. Reflecting upon those darker times, it was his gumption that got him in; his stick-to-itiveness kept him there. Since then, he has put up with many a substandard worker, about whom few kind words could be enunciated.

Periodically, a homesick Stagger-Lee looked into the distance behind them at the rail station. His thoughts drifted to his history of one contravention of rules after another. To move with a purpose and inspect the tracks at the same time wasn't one of Stagger-Lee's specialties. That came as nothing new, given he had difficulty walking and chewing gum simultaneously. When a company is short-handed the bizarre can happen—even hiring Stagger-Lee.

If there was one thing that Stagger-Lee knew he liked, it was gadgetry. The latest issue of Sights & Sounds Illustrated proved that. Infrequently, his lunch pail collided with August's. It was an act that threatened the quiet around them.

"Watch your step!" August criticized. "Anythin' happens to our thermos walkin' these tracks, we'll shrivel like a raisin on the vine out in this-here sun."

August's grievances were in a row awaiting delivery to the hiring supervisor as he watched Stagger-Lee lag behind.

"Today's your second day with me...I gotta-tell ya—" He brooded, trying to feather his complaints. "It was the Theory of Relativity that got you the job."

"Huh?" Stagger-Lee's attention span rivaled that of a newborn.

"The theory of relativity. You came to this country and got a job cause you're related to me."

"That relativity thing's my favorite theory," Stagger-Lee smiled. "What's the problem?"

"Ya'll is too darn slow."

"Slow? Slow, how?"

Not being an insensitive man, August didn't want to risk hurting his feelings. Instead, he attempted his version of verbal tact—that hopefully would preserve his own job.

"Nobody's sayin' ya'lls a bad sort. After eight hours with-ya yesterday, I was constantly wonderin' what's slowin'-down the delay? Ya-falla?"

Stagger-Lee hurried to keep up with the longer legged man who was many years his senior. He swatted aggressive mosquitoes, beating away the flying blood suckers whose numbers had greatly increased since they left the station hours earlier.

August thought that a person had to be a magician to keep that young man's attention. "That-there was an indoor mosquito. It's harmless. Ya'll see the difference once we get way out near the swamp. Dems da mosquitos that's the man eaters."

August continued, "We've got a lot of track to inspect. Regardless of how quiet it gets out here, never let ya'lls guard down. Be on the lookout for the tiniest thang. If you see somethin' and ya'll think it's nothin', it's probably somethin'. Call Central Dispatch. They're skilled at dealin' with everythin'. Even when it's nothin'. But ya-won't know if the somethin' that ya'll thought was nothin', until after it's called in." August assumed the dual role of teacher and hands-on worker. "Am I makin' myself clear?"

How dumb does he think I am? Stagger-Lee considered, sulking. He'll soon change his tune when I quit this lousy job.

The blistering heat made a tempting mirage of everything near and far away. August and Stagger-Lee's skin got darker by the minute. Worst of all, August's aging body wouldn't cooperate the way it once did in the high temperatures.

Gradually, he began to tire, constantly leery that a second heart attack was on its way. He stopped to catch his breath. The strain finally forced him to double-over, panting with hands on his knees. That was part of his problem. The other was that Stagger-Lee was so much younger. Companies always have a youth movement going on to advance their firm's future.

Wearily, they walked with their heads down, eyes fox-trotting, straddling cast iron railroad tracks that rested atop splintery ties. They looked for anything that could lead to problems for the trains that rolled along them.

Stagger-Lee was confused, unable to get an adequate answer as to why they had walked aimlessly for so many miles. Nevertheless, he gave the tracks his best scrutiny.

"Tell me, agin'." He looked at August. "Why do they call it a weed burner?"

"Left unchecked weeds grow thick, tough enough to knock the wheels off the tracks when the train rolls by. The burner cooks away those weeds and undergrowth. The next time ya'll see one roll by, notice the torches on the sides. That's the burnin' part of the weed burner. The torches it carries will turn a man to history."

A northern bound train rolled toward, then away from the men. In doing so it wobbled sections in the track's weak connections.

"That train sure kicked-up a nice breeze." August reached for anything as motivation.

"How'd ya'll get to be so smart?" Stagger-Lee asked with his brand of patronage.

"It was when they made me a supervisor trainee," August boasted. How badly he wanted his retirement horizon to be nearer.

Not so far away, the Blue Train rumbled closer.

*　　　　　*　　　　　*

Usually, the Blue Train traveled during the week at full capacity. It came as more than a casual surprise that it rolled at one third full of the typical occupancy limit.

The conductor, too, found it to be a strange occurrence. He walked the aisle looking for anything out of time, or a passenger in need of something. One additional thing that he took watchful notice of was how exquisitely decked-out each passenger was that day. That enhanced his bitterness that he'd probably always be a worker of low income stature, never able to dress nicely. He maintained his pace, unaware that onboard were the world's top criminal kingpins.

"Everyone around us looks like a somebody," Rikki noticed, whispering to Conchita.

"You're on that same level now, so get used to it."

If she had her true desire, Rikki would've wanted out from the insecurity blanket of Conchita's empire. But through it all, she thought that it was impressive, "I'm honored that you trust me to ride with you." She wanted Conchita to hear. It was impossible for Conchita to absorb Rikki's energetic commitment that was issued under duress. "Don't worry about Slinky. I'll come up with a solution."

That's what Conchita wanted to hear, patting Rikki with assurance.

Many of the passengers appeared disinterested in their immediate surroundings. Instead, they were each taken with their individual concerns, wanting nothing more than to arrive at the destination on time.

When Rikki and Conchita reached the sleeper car, both were pleased with their respite. Then, facing four tired eyes was the smallest sleeping compartment that either woman had ever seen.

"Expecting pigmies?" Conchita speculated, to find the non-existent other door that would lead to a passenger com of usable size.

"These are the days we'll look back on and laugh, because it damn-sure isn't funny now," Rikki mumbled. She sought to comfort Conchita with elastic words of encouragement. "It's only for a few nights." She turned to the conductor with enhanced agitation.

"Correct," the conductor calculated.

Conchita was in desperate need of an attitude adjustment, watching Rikki tip him a few bills.

"I feel inspired to arrive at a faster solution to bring you larger resting accommodations."

With that he exited. Conchita punched the wall.

Rikki infused, "Once we arrive, perhaps a lesson in anger management will be in order."

*   *   *

Outside calm surrounded the train as it rolled down the tracks.

Rikki sauntered the constricted aisle that had equal quantities of sleepover compartments on both sides.

A certain bodyguard was a portly man who approached from the opposite direction. Comfortable passage between them was impossible.

"No one loves a fat man but his baker," he auditioned, patting his bulging stomach. "This is one of the hazards of being on an unguarded train."

Later that evening, the Blue Train inexplicably stopped near where August stood alone. The spirited shrill from its whistle got his attention. He couldn't be sure how long he had been sleeping. Two things were certain: He had fallen asleep shortly after taking a drink from Stagger-Lee's thermos. It was the thermos that Stagger-Lee had insisted August take that drink from. And it coincided with the time when August asked Stagger-Lee if he left the United States on account of him being in some kind of trouble.

He was standing without Stagger-Lee. There was the chance that he had gone the way of so many other first week workers and quit. For reasons of worry, August thought to call Central Dispatch, then chose not to. There was no need. It was too late in the day for the home office to send out a replacement worker.

Rikki had heard the announcement over the PA system that the train had stopped for a short time, but thought nothing of it once the train cranked-up its squeaking wheels and resumed rolling.

"I wonder what price my elixir will fetch." Always conscious of others who might be eavesdropping, Conchita lowered her voice. "The power to make people unseen is powerfully tempting."

Conchita produced a vial of the elixir from her purse, while Rikki looked curiously at the tube of lipstick that she'd managed to carry with her but never used.

"More than once, my chemist tried to explain to me how it changes a person's molecular structure to make them invisible. I still don't understand it. But it works like a charm. The biggest problem is, getting enough diamonds to keep the refining process going. Diamonds don't grow on trees. It takes a bunch of them to make enough of the elixir to keep a person undetectable for only a short period of time."

Circumstances in Rikki's changed life had become circular, constantly revolving to that woman in her dreams who wore that startling, powder-blue dress. She remained confused over what her subconscious was trying to voice; that often made it impossible to grasp the particulars of Conchita's numerous explanations about her business affairs.

Less than an hour after the passengers had finished their meals, each food tray was removed. Some of those seated enabled their overhead lamps to glow, allowing for specialized reading and concentrated study.

The Conductor said, "For your onboard entertainment there will be a movie. It will allow for an easier passage of your travel hours."

All of the lights in the railcar went completely out. There was a machine-like sound of a projection screen lowering from the ceiling to the floor where it locked into place.

An aging, clean shaven, man with a stuffed face came on screen. He was solemn and filled with worry. This couldn't be the movie that was promised, each of those seated thought. Immediately, they focused on him. Something was badly out of kilter. With rising curiosity, they speculated as to what the man of inscrutability was about to say.

"Hello to each of you," the man on screen said with a troubled voice. "My name is Number One."

The mere mention of him being referred to as Number One was enough to alarm the calmest of listeners. Especially after they had already made the inevitable comparison between him and any demonic dictator.

Number One spoke with chilling familiarity, as though he actually looked at each of them shuddering in their seats.

Everyone seated looked amazed, some rose to get a better view of this bearer of suspense filled information.

"Have you seen him before?" Rikki asked.

Conchita's boredom could have been measured with an abacus.

"Fortunately, no," she answered in a huff. "He's obviously some old coot with an unanswered gripe of some sort." She yawned, though she was not really all that sleepy. "Wake me when it's over."

Undetected, Stagger-Lee entered that railroad car. Slowly and silently, he walked the aisle. Then in mid search, he caught a thin dart in the back of his neck. Everyone nearest to him gasped as they watched him loudly gag before falling to the floor. No one moved to help him. Instead, they remained seated—transfixed to the movie screen.

Number One continued. "His demise is a demonstration of my sincerity...By now, you've had the opportunity to look around, possibly speaking amongst yourselves, seeing like members in your crime fraternity here today. To each of you I want to personally extend my utmost thanks for allowing yourselves to be ceremoniously duped by my promise of huge financial benefits if you made reservations to ride this train today."

That was the verbal rusty hook that caught their undivided attention. Though they'd seen men die before, they each jittered that they might be next to depart this life.

"Your being here proves that greed is the sole force that motivates each of you. There's not a shred of human concern among you for the welfare of those who are forced to endure what little remains of their lives because of you. That's easily evidenced by your chosen illegal professions. You all have systematically poisoned the entire world, taking the hopes and aspirations of so many who have fallen into the aftermath, the chasm, that your criminal enterprises have created."

"What da hell's going on?" Conchita snapped out of slumber having heard enough.

Rikki was speechless. It was obvious that the man on screen wasn't there to audition poor acting ability.

Number One went on, "Every half hour, one of you will answer to international demands for justice. For me to acquire that rewarding feeling of retribution means that in the end all of you will die."

The passengers were perplexed, as Number One continued. "Alex Achoa."

From the middle of the car, the street refined Alex Achoa lifted his head above the sports scores that he made a habit to heavily bet on. After all, the Kentucky Derby was coming up. He wasn't about to let it pass without getting a heads-up on who the predicted favorite was.

"At the age of twelve, Mister Achoa began his anti-societal activity, when he began to coordinate the massive sales of marijuana. By the time you had reached your mid twenties, your efforts had blossomed to make you the man to see for teens who were determined to be on the path of that which would lead to their own ruin. I am talking about used to be innocent adolescence who were detoured; to where smoking and using drugs was their forced way to behave. It wasn't until your twenty-sixth birthday that you realized that for every kilo of marijuana you could deliver, that same weight in cocaine would have you on your way to a faster fortune. At last count, you control the growing of coca production plants on such a level that two thirds of the world's cocaine production comes from your skillfully cultivated harvests."

Alex felt praise. At the same time, he knew that this articulation wasn't meant to pay homage to his abilities as a businessman, but to somehow expose him to the authorities—whoever, and wherever, they might be.

"For your efforts, Mister Achoa. You must die."

Suddenly, Alex Achoa grabbed the center of his chest, wincing sharply before keeling over. His rotund bodyguard dove to his side, with gun raised to shoot anyone moving toward the two of them. Finally able to lower his gun, he tried to resuscitate Alex but was unsuccessful. Then he, too, was no more.

A physician seated across from him braved the threat, hastily unbuckled his seatbelt to get to them. After his stethoscope was removed from both men's chests, "They're dead," the doctor announced into the hush of the shaken passengers.

The cabin lights slowly came on to their original brightness.

"I'll figure out who the bastard is. When I do, he'll wish for the police to get to him ahead of me." Conchita's eyes darted, searching for the one person in the car who she deemed responsible. She needed someone who she could unleash her vengeful, homicidal, energy against.

Rikki looked at her watch. It was 10:35.

When Conchita saw no one who didn't look as frightened as she was, her spirit had to be reorganized. "I'm all ears," she buckled to whatever Rikki had to offer. "Get me out of this."

Rikki sorely needed a decisive course of action, but couldn't. The passage of time was on an accelerated pace.

At 11:00 am the lights went out again. The screen lowered, and in those brief few seconds before the passengers dared to consider what would happen next, the projector restarted.

"Manuel Martinez." Number One pointed.

Number One was acknowledged by the tight face man wearing a "Who me?" expression.

"Your transportation network has enabled the cocaine to make its way from Mister Achoa's assembly line to the main streets of every major city in the world. That progression has made you a financial force to be reckoned with—decade after narcotics filled decade."

On the screen were visualizations of people wandering urban streets in search of a narcotics fix. It was a graphic depiction of what the drug producer's world leaves behind.

"For your tireless efforts, I'm afraid that it's time for you to pay the ultimate price for your criminal transgression."

Mr. Martinez produced a small caliber machinegun, springing into the aisle, ready to die while defending himself. He was always prepared for this day to happen. At once, he winced. His head wiggled wildly, seemingly to twist off from the pain. Then he collapsed.

The same doctor quickly examined him, finding equal finality.

Rikki boldly said, "We've got to do something."

The interior lights returned, allowing her to see Conchita. She didn't like what she saw. Seated beside her was an ordinary woman, not the power broker who wouldn't dare to show indecision.

Rikki stood, bending to force her way ahead of nervous others who also stood, and had taken up positions of concern in the aisle.

Visions of Tiny and Sharon faded in and out of her recessed thoughts, but Rikki still couldn't accurately identify them. Then, there was her past policing life—too little by way of recognizable images, to make sense of any of it. That quickly they all were removed from her thoughts.

Rikki rushed from the movie car, scrambling to get to the front of the train. Once there, she pounded on the engineer's door. No sounds came from inside. She turned to the conductor. "I gotta get in there. Where's the key to this door!?"

His answer was, "Due to safety concerns, it's locked from the inside."

At the back of the line, Julius Redmond shouted, "I got something that'll work!"

Everyone frenetically turned to him, willing to believe anything that he had to offer.

Rikki screamed above the others. "Spill it!"

Julius ran to his seat. He reached beneath it, producing a designer briefcase, which he trotted to the front of the train.

"It's lined with steel to protect me from an assassin's gunfire." He bobbed it up and down. "Feel how heavy it is. It'll ram the door open."

Instinctively, Rikki reacted. "Everybody, stand back!"

Julius rocked it back and forth, to gather enough momentum to bang the door. In a final, hefty, swing it slammed against the door, breaking it open.

"Noooo!" sounded resoundingly throughout the swiftly moving rail car.

From her seat, Conchita strained to see.

To everyone's horror the engineer was lifelessly slumped over.

"Who's driving the train?" someone shouted from behind.

They looked at the rising speedometer, sadly convinced that all of them were the living dead.

"Where are we going?" Rikki asked, looking into the hollowed-out face of the conductor who shrugged.

The train heavily rocked as it rolled around a curve. Its speed increased at an alarming rate.

"Back to your seats, everyone," Rikki shouted.

She was taking over. But of what? They were aboard an out of control train that was sure to crash, if something didn't happen to slow it down.

All of them had come to grips with the truth that they were at the mercy of a messenger who periodically announced on screen that their end was near.

They returned to their seats, mostly out of having no place else to go. Chaos hovered. Once seated none of them snapped their seat belts. For that would've had them feeling trapped even more.

With minutes that arrived faster than anyone was ready for, the lights again dimmed. "Oh God," someone said.

The projector began.

"Sandy Bijorska and her trusted assistant, Mister Redmond.

Sandy was quavering in the rear, strangely prepared for whatever he had in store for them.

Within Rikki's thoughts came visions of an extended mountain range. The word Sandy had brought to her confused mind the word Sandies (as in the Sandies Mountains in New Mexico). That repeatedly looped inside her, finally becoming clearer.

Why am I seeing the desert part of the United States?

"Sandy, it is your vast terrorist empire that allows the massive amounts of explosives to be transported from one continent to the next virtually unchallenged. From your secluded ports in Marsais, to the drop-off points throughout the Middle East, you've managed to outwit police for far too long. Your domain of worldwide terror has been perpetuated past my ability to ignore it…The time has to come for you to realize that you cannot evade my vengeance any longer."

Sandy and Julius grabbed their hearts. The reflex had them crashing their heads against each other so hard that his cracked open. His brain fluids oozed out onto the front of her.

The following half hour intervals brought an untimely, yet morally deserved, ending to the lives of other global underworld lords. What remained were four terribly shaken passengers, who counted their minutes to conclusion.

Conchita was pleased to see her competitors leaving the earth one by one ahead of her, only to whimper when thinking about when it would come her time to stop breathing. She clutched more tightly to the vial of elixir.

Against that backdrop, Rikki knew that she was going to be next in line for the executioner's tirade if she didn't think of something fast. In spite of it all, she wasn't completely out of suggestions.

"The projector. Find the projector. That's the solution."

Rikki raced beneath where the projector was, pulling the overhead swing door, springing it open. Frenzied, she disconnected it.

"The man on the tape said people were going to die every half hour." It pained her to add, "So far, he's been true to his word."

She looked at her watch, heart thumping the loudest of those still alive.

"We've got two minutes."

"Advance the DVD to see what's on it," the conductor said.

The man seated nearest to them was the one called Sang. He was the CEO of all heroin leaving Southeast Asia. Suddenly, he went into horrible convulsions by the window and collapsed.

"Obviously," Rikki concluded, "the projector's not killing anyone. It's off, and that man died anyway." Rikki racked her brain for answers that were slow coming. "We've all got something in common that's killing us. Something is linking us together."

Her thinking had become more concentrated, intensified, toward a fast solution. "Think," she commanded the few others.

It was 1:46.

The food, Rikki thought. "What was in the meal?"

"Bluefish, potatoes, vegetables, with a side of fish eggs," the conductor said.

"Caviar," Conchita corrected.

They turned to her glued to her input, feeling that was the root of it all.

They raced to the galley car. Rikki ravaged through the refrigerator, snatching out meal trays, dumping the food on the Formica counter to examine it. She saw the caviar. Without laboratory testing equipment, she could do nothing with her hunch.

She closely inspected the caviar's makeup. The little, deep-blue eggs opened up Rikki's long hidden detective suspicions.

I've seen this scenario somewhere before.

Slowly, it crept into her head that she was once at a police cold case conference. There, a retired cop stood in front of a large group, saying that he had worked a case in which the killer used time released poison that was concealed in food.

"It's in the caviar," Rikki told the others, twisting with the slim chance that there was anyone left who didn't eat it. "Whatever's killing us is doing so at precise thirty minute intervals." Rikki turned to the others. "What did you eat?"

"Everything on the plate," they said in near unison.

She turned to Conchita.

"I've always loved caviar," she told Rikki.

It was 1:49.

"I don't want to die," the conductor mumbled with overflowing tears, then collapsed into the afterlife.

From behind, Stagger-Lee appeared. He hadn't died after all. Unwilling to go down without a fight, Conchita immediately swallowed the elixir.

A violent struggle broke out in the movie car between Stagger-Lee and the invisible Conchita. Around and around they flailed, knocking Rikki's head against the wall, causing her to fall unconscious to the cluttered floor; beside a bland-white stone that had slipped out of Stagger-Lee's pocket. It was a stone that he kept from that night when he delivered the pizza to Heather's home.

When the fighting between Stagger-Lee and Conchita stopped, in front of him was a smoldering mound of burning flesh that was Conchita. In her efforts of self-defense her molecules had overheated and burned her from within.

Rikki's pulse was fading. That was when she saw Heather. "Where are you?"

"Over here," a feminine voice answered.

Rikki's thinking floated towards Heather. "Where have you been?" she asked of her.

"Your father didn't want me around anymore. But I was never far from you...*I'm going away*," Heather told her.

Rikki thought in silent volumes. Mom, don't gooooooooo!

Her dream was interrupted when she saw was Stagger-Lee stepping over various bodies en route to the engineer's seat. Once inside that compartment, he closed the door. A hard jolt bounced the train as it raced along the deserted stretch of tracks, finally coming to a complete stop.

Not long after that, the engineer's door squeaked opened. It was the distinct sharpness of a kitchen knife pressing against his throat that alerted Stagger-Lee that he wasn't the only one onboard who was alive.

"By all means, move," Rikki said, praying that he would, to give her the reason to slice his head off.

Meanwhile, an adjacent track had the background sound of an approaching train.

Stagger-Lee was still, afraid to move.

"Too bad for you I'm the only one onboard who hates caviar."

Suddenly, Stagger-Lee broke free. He ran but a few paces then dove through the window. Out on the tracks he was sprawled, until the approaching weed burner train moved overtop him. His cries were abruptly abbreviated when the torches made charcoal of him.

THE LAST STOP

◆

Home Sweet Home

Sharon stood in Albuquerque's main terminal, watching from in front of countless eager news reporters. She would forevermore be indebted to Erik for rescuing Rikki.

"How'd you know Rikki was on that train?" Sharon asked.

Erik held up the receiver to the satellite navigation that he bought for Rikki last year.

"The transmitter is in her tube of lipstick. I would've been able to locate her sooner, but she was hidden away in the mountains, and the signal wouldn't project from there...Anyway, after she left Vegas, Tony put a tap on your phone to try to locate Rikki. Then, when week after week went by without either of you speaking, he turned to me for the answer. Hence, the lipstick. You broads never go anywhere without your precious lipstick...Luckily for her, I never told Tony about the lipstick."

Sharon muttered, "Tony? But I heard—"

"Things got sticky for him, when Las Vegas Internal Affairs learned that two of their cops, Barnes and a guy named Ernie, were doing hits for the mob. You see, Tony had paid them to silence Rikki."

"Why," she asked.

"He and your honey, Mark, were in on the diamond heists racket together. Mark pulled the jobs, and Tony made sure that no one would ever suspect Mark as being behind them. That was why he fed Rikki the lies about Mark having been killed in the line of duty years ago. Tha allowed Mark to continue doing his business in New Mexico, without anyone ever suspecting that he was still alive…There was also the cash that Rikki found on the skydiver. Tony demanded that she leave the evidence money with him. Instead, he kept it. That was when he circulated the lie that Rikki never gave the money to him in the first place. Anyway, he had the Chief of Vegas police release Rikki, so quickly after they picked her up—after that man was pushed from the window of her hotel. That guy in the Bermuda shorts—who tumbled out of her hotel window, was there to warn Rikki that a contract was out on her through the Vegas PD, and that she had better leave town immediately."

"What's to stop Tony from coming after Rikki now?"

"This morning, Tony learned that he was going to be arrested. Rather than go to jail, he hung himself."

"Heard anything about Mark?"

"After Rikki chased him in that alley, he got word from Tony that she knew what Mark and Tony were up to. So Mark went to Johannesburg looking to ice Rikki."

Sharon and Erik turned to see the airline passengers deplane. Rikki was one of the last to make it to the arrivals area. Sharon ran to her, seeing Rikki holding Sabina tightly in her arms. This time, Olga's limbs were repaired.

"Who's your friend?" Sharon asked.

Rikki pivoted to allow a better view of the child for Sharon.

"Answer her," Rikki said to Sabina, whose face was buried against Rikki. "I'll explain later," Rikki supplemented to Sharon.

The flood of reporters were in hot pursuit. "How'd you recognize Stagger-Lee was the killer?" one of them shouted.

Stagger-Lee fled the country after my mother's disappearance hit the newspapers. After seeing me in the Johannesburg train station, he jumped at the opportunity to do away with me. All along, he thought that I arrived in South Africa pursuing him…When the train continued running, I knew that it had to be someone still alive with train operating skill. The only person in the car who wasn't dead was Stagger-Lee. He used his high-tech skill to create that man on the DVD, to lead everyone to believe that the deaths were the work of a social activist vigilante."

The endless questions from the press continued, finally culminating with Erik personally congratulating Rikki. Promptly, he handed her a check with all of her back salary. Then he presented her with a commendation that granted a promotion to Detective First Grade.

"This is for our new life together," she whispered to Sabina about it all.

Just then Bubba availed himself from the onlookers, firing away at Rikki. Everyone ran, ducking to fall on their stomachs.

"Ahhh!" Sharon wailed, having been hit.

Rikki fell on top of Sabina, cradling her, protecting her.

Erik returned fire. Bullets ricocheted, pinging, until one of them caught Bubba. He fell, rolling across the floor, continuing to shoot back until his pistol jammed. There was flowing blood everywhere as backup police ran into the pandemonium. Finally, Bubba's life petered out when he was struck multiple times from the rampant influx of police. The screaming was slow do die down.

*   *   *

The sun had disappeared far beneath the horizon with an afterglow that gave it a deep amber tint.

In her home, Rikki stood in the living room, watching Sharon, Erik and Sabina sleeping on the couch in front of the TV that played and played. Sabina did so cradling Olga. Surprisingly, Jack was there also. Though he never volunteered what he did with the diamonds, Rikki thought not to press him on it right then. After all, it was her first night home.

Then came the subconscious voices that beckoned Rikki.

Silently, Rikki crept away and walked the stairs to the attic.

There she saw a home-made wooden chest that she had seen Jack constructing countless months earlier to store his assorted surplus items. When she opened it, she saw a lot more.

There were Heather's decayed remains inside a startling, powder-blue, dress. Around her neck were the diamonds that Jack stole from Rikki. They had been professionally drilled, and strung across the front of Heather to make a splendid necklace. Stuffed beside her was a travel bag. Inside it was a wide beam flashlight, and that one way bus ticket. Heather really was going to leave, but Jack was not going to allow that to happen.

Heather had once told Jack how hurt she was when he sold her wedding diamond. He was determined to replace it—to make her look nice with a new one—even in her death.

While still crying, Rikki slowly walked down the stairs, step after thought provoking step, to arrest her father for first degree murder.

The End

978-0-595-40838-2
0-595-40838-9

Printed in the United States
57457LVS00004B/103-126